The KEEPERS

The BOX and the DRAGONFLY

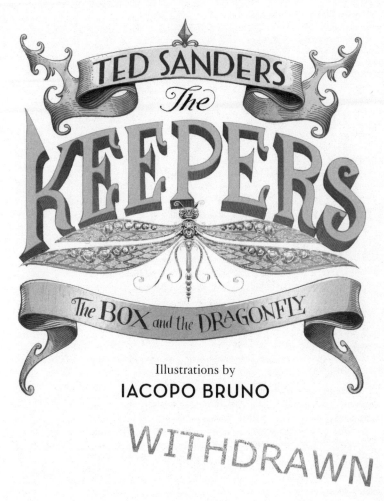

TED SANDERS

The

KEEPERS

The BOX and the DRAGONFLY

Illustrations by
IACOPO BRUNO

WITHDRAWN

HARPER
An Imprint of HarperCollinsPublishers

Library of Congress Cataloging-in-Publication Data

Sanders, Ted, date

The box and the dragonfly / Ted Sanders ; illustrations by Iacopo Bruno. — First edition.

pages   cm. — (The Keepers)

Summary: Horace F. Andrews, armed with a strange wooden box, and Chloe Burke, wearing a mysterious dragonfly pendant, become entangled in a secret and ancient society striving to protect powerful devices from the evil Riven.

ISBN 978-0-06-227582-0 (hardcover) — ISBN 978-0-06-239019-6 (int'l ed.)

[1. Magic—Fiction.   2. Secret societies—Fiction.   3. Amulets—Fiction.   4. Space and time—Fiction.]   I. Bruno, Iacopo, illustrator.   II. Title.

PZ7.S19794Box   2015   2014022228

[Fic]—dc23   CIP

AC

Typography by Carla Weise

15 16 17 18 19   CG/RRDH   10 9 8 7 6 5 4 3 2 1

❖

First Edition

for Jodee,
without whom so much
would not have happened,
including this

The only way of discovering the limits of the possible
is to venture a little way past them into the impossible.
— ARTHUR C. CLARKE

CONTENTS

PART ONE

The Find

CHAPTER ONE

The Sign

WHEN HORACE F. ANDREWS SPOTTED THE HORACE F. Andrews sign through the cloudy windows of the 77 east-bound bus, he blinked. Just a blink, nothing more. He was surprised to see his own name on a sign, of course—and his sizable curiosity was definitely roused—but still, he took the sighting in stride. He had always been a firm believer in coincidences. Given enough time, and enough stuff, it was only natural that the universe would churn out some odd happenings. In fact, the way Horace saw it, a universe in which strange coincidences did *not* occur would be a pretty suspicious place.

The Horace F. Andrews sign was tall and narrow, hanging from the side of a building back in an alleyway off Wexler Street. It featured a long column of faded yellow words on a weather-worn blue background, but it was his name, written large at the bottom, that jumped out at him first, clear and unmistakable:

HORACE F. ANDREWS

The bus rolled on. Just before the sign slipped out of sight, he caught a few of the yellow words in the long list above his name: ARTIFACTS. MISERIES. MYSTERIES.

Sparks of curiosity flared up inside Horace. He blinked—just once—and thought the situation through, tending those sparks like a brand-new fire. What were the odds of his seeing a sign with his exact name on it? Not terrible, he decided. Horace wasn't a very common name, but Andrews definitely was. And it was probably fairly common to have F as a middle initial—certainly better than one chance in twenty-six.

Of course, it was pure chance that he was even here in the first place. The 77 was his usual bus home from school, but this was not its usual route; normally the bus went straight down Belmont Avenue, but construction had forced the bus to detour down Wexler Street instead of driving right by. It was also pure chance that Horace had been looking out the windows at all. Ordinarily, he would have been sitting in the very back row, reading or working on a science problem for Mr.

4

Ludwig's class, building a bubble of concentration against the noise and confusion of the bus. But today the bus was extra crowded, packed with rowdy kids from school in the back and stone-faced adults in the front. Horace had to stand in the middle, at the top of the steps near the rear door, feeling large and awkward and hating his heavy backpack, and wondering just how much he, Horace Andrews, belonged here. All he could do was look out the window and hope the ride would be short.

But then the sign slid by, and a block or two later the bus slowed and jerked to a stop. The rear door opened, and a plump old lady in a purple dress began easing down the steps, clinging to the rail with both hands. Horace looked through the back windows, but the sign was out of sight. Was it for a store? Or maybe someone's office—presumably the office of Horace F. Andrews. The sign had looked very old; maybe the place didn't even exist anymore. But then there were those words—"Artifacts," "Mysteries." And what possible reason could any business have for putting "Miseries" on its sign?

Horace watched the old lady stretch out one chubby leg, reaching for the curb below. The other passengers rustled impatiently. A scrawny red-faced kid Horace recognized from social studies leaned over the stairwell and started chanting at the old lady: *"Go! Go! Go!"*

And then Horace stepped around the woman and jumped out of the bus. He landed heavily on the sidewalk. The old lady squawked at him and yanked her foot back. "'Scuse me," Horace mumbled.

He trotted away, feeling as startled as the old lady looked. He was not ordinarily impulsive, not the kind of person who simply did things without thinking them through ahead of time. But sometimes his inquisitiveness pulled him places he wouldn't ordinarily go. And that sign . . . those words and his name together like that. . . .

The May air was cool but held a hint of thickness that spoke of summer—of freedom, and possibilities. Horace's internal clock, always accurate, told him it was 3:16. This time of day, the 77 eastbound ran every fourteen minutes. He could investigate the sign and then catch the next bus, still getting home before his mother. He hurried on down the sidewalk, searching.

Just as he thought he was drawing nearer to the alleyway, an enormous shape swept across his path, colliding with him hard and knocking the breath from his chest. Horace staggered back, almost tumbling into the gutter.

"Goodness," said a musical voice from high above.

Horace looked up—and up—into the face of the tallest man he'd ever seen. The man was so tall that he hardly looked like a man at all . . . ten feet tall or more. And thin, almost as impossibly thin as he was impossibly tall, with spidery limbs and a torso that seemed too narrow to hold organs. He had hands the size of rakes, with long, skinny fingers. He stank of something chemical and foul. Horace drew back as the man leaned over him.

"Are we all right?" the man asked, not unkindly. Again that singsongy voice. The man—if it even was a man—wore a black suit and dark, round sunglasses. A thick shock of black hair topped his head, out of place on his pale, skeletal body.

Horace tried to catch his breath. "I'm fine," he wheezed. "Sorry."

"Perfectly understandable. I believe you were distracted."

"I'm sorry, really. Just . . . looking for something."

"Ah. Do you know what it is you're looking for?" The man's teeth were slightly bared, as if he were trying to give a friendly grin but didn't know how.

"It's nothing, really," Horace said, faint threads of alarm tingling in his bones.

"Oh, come now. Tell me what you're looking for. You can't know how intrigued I am."

"I'm just looking around. Thanks, though." Horace began backing away.

"Perhaps I can be of some assistance. You *do* need assistance." He said it like a command.

"No, that's okay. I'm okay." Horace skirted wide around the strange man and hustled off, trying to hunker his big frame down beneath his backpack. He was all too aware that the man's eyes were still on him, but when he looked back, he was relieved to find that the thin man was not following. In fact, he had disappeared. Completely. How could someone so large simply drop out of sight? And how could someone be so large in the first place?

But it wasn't just the man who'd disappeared. The sign, too, was nowhere to be found. Horace went almost three full blocks without spotting it. He turned and began to methodically retrace his steps. The Horace F. Andrews sign was nowhere.

Abruptly, a looming shape stepped out of the shadows in front of him. Horace stumbled to a stop. The thin man gazed down at him, still trying that gruesome smile.

"Didn't find what you're looking for?" the man sang sadly.

Panic blooming, Horace tried to catch the eyes of people passing by, hoping to draw their attention. No one even slowed. Several people sat at tables outside a deli nearby, but no one so much as glanced at the thin man. Couldn't they see him? Horace was tall for his age, and he barely came up to the man's waist. Why was no one staring?

"I did, actually," Horace said at last, desperate, with no idea what he was going to say next. But then the words came to him. "That deli right there. My parents are inside, waiting for me."

The man's awful grin cracked open wide. "Of course they are," he said, gazing at the deli. "And I wouldn't think of keeping you from them. But first, a bit of advice." The man bent over, folding like a giant crane. He held a gaunt hand

8

right in front of Horace's face, lifting a single long finger. The smell that came off him was burning and sour and rotten. And the man's finger was *wrong*. It was almost as if . . . did he have an extra knuckle? Horace's own terrified face curved back at him in the man's glasses.

"Watch where you roam, Tinker," the man sneered. "Curiosity is a walk fraught with peril." And with that he shot up, straightening to his full, unreasonable height. He snapped his head to the right, as if hearing some far-off sound, and then he left as swiftly as he had come, stepping out into the street. Six great strides took him across all four busy lanes, and then he effortlessly hurdled the hood of a parked car onto the opposite sidewalk. He sped down Wexler and a moment later vanished around a corner.

Horace stood there for another ten seconds and then, his limbs coming back to life, broke into a run. Whoever— whatever—this man was, Horace wanted to get far away. He made it exactly twenty-seven steps before he was halted in his tracks again. He stood in front of an alleyway, mouth gaping open. He'd passed this alley already and seen nothing—he was sure there had been nothing *to* see—but now here it was, plain as his own hands.

The Horace F. Andrews sign.

Or rather, not exactly.

Horace stared. He forgot all about catching the bus. He even forgot about the thin man. He read the sign from top to bottom again and again.

Oddments
Heirlooms
Fortunes
Misfortunes
Artifacts
Arcana
Curiosities
Miseries
Mysteries
and more at the

HOUSE OF ANSWERS

—⟨ᴑᴠᴑ⟩—

The House of Answers

HOUSE OF ANSWERS. THAT'S WHAT HE HAD SEEN, NOT HORACE F. ANDREWS. Similar-looking words seen from the dirty windows of a bus. "Mistaken identity," Horace said aloud, his words echoing down the alley. The discovery disappointed him at first, but he quickly decided that the sign in reality was more intriguing than the sign he'd imagined. "House of Answers" was a name just begging to be investigated, wasn't it? And Horace—being Horace—definitely had questions.

There were tall buildings on either side of the alley: an electronics store on the right and a Laundromat on the left that looked closed for good. The floors above both obviously held apartments. The alley itself appeared to dead-end at another tall building about fifty feet back.

"I don't see any answers," Horace mumbled. He headed down the alley. It got darker and gloomier the deeper he went, and the sounds of the street faded away. He was just beginning to think he should turn around—he wasn't crazy about how narrow and high the alley was getting—when he was struck with a sense of vertigo. The back wall suddenly, dizzyingly, looked much farther away than it had. Then the alleyway seemed to open up at his feet, and Horace almost pitched down a steep flight of crumbling brick steps that he hadn't seen until he was on top of them. He caught himself, blinking. At the bottom of the staircase, barely visible in the shadows of the three buildings towering overhead, was an arched blue door. On the door was a round sign encircled with yellow lettering, too small to read—but the colors were exactly the same as the House of Answers sign.

"Holy jeez," Horace said.

He glanced around. No one was in sight. Slowly he eased himself down the dilapidated steps. The air grew cool. He reached the small wooden door and read the little round sign.

There were no other signs. No OPEN sign, no PUSH or PULL, no HOURS OF OPERATION. No windows. But this had to be the place. He tugged on the rusty handle. The door held fast.

State your name. "Horace?" he said aloud, feeling foolish.

Nothing happened. "Horace F. Andrews," he tried again. Still nothing.

Horace looked again at the circle of words. "Wait. State your name or . . . name your state?" But that was ridiculous. Why would anyone want him to name his state? The door was here in Chicago, and Chicago was obviously in Illinois. "Illinois," he blurted out anyway, just to see. He tried the door again—nothing, of course. "State your name your state your name your state," Horace whispered, until the words started to make no sense to him whatsoever. And then he remembered the thin man's parting words: *Curiosity is a walk fraught with peril.*

"My state. My state is . . . curious. That's the state I'm in." Horace reached out for the handle again, pulling harder. "Curious and confused and a little bit p—" With a jarring *squawk*, the door flew open. Horace stumbled, his backpack dragging him to the ground.

A rich cloud of smells bloomed out of the opening—dust and wood and cloth and animal—old, thick, damp smells. And another thing, too: a wavering, high river of sound, almost like music. But the passageway was dark and cramped. Horace got to his feet warily. Tunnels were not something he handled well. He had a deep fear of small spaces—claustrophobia, technically, though he didn't like the word. He leaned cautiously in through the doorway.

"Hello?" he called. The strange chattering music seemed to swell briefly. Horace hefted his backpack onto his shoulders

13

and stepped into the passageway.

The door swung closed behind him. His chest went tight as the unforgiving weight of the darkness crushed in from all sides. A panicky voice ribboned up in his thoughts, telling him to go back, to get out, get clear.

But his curiosity wouldn't let him turn back. He swallowed and closed his eyes, and forced himself forward. Ten feet, twenty. He pushed on until he sensed a faint golden glow against his eyelids and, opening them, found himself at the top of another dark stairway. The strange music drifted up from below. Small, busy shadows flickered in a dim amber light. His curiosity doubled, and his heart grew calmer. He descended the stairs, and as the rich sound swelled around him, he realized what it was.

Birdsong.

At the bottom of the stairs, the tunnel widened and the light grew brighter, and he began to catch flitters of movement all around. He realized the walls were filled with birdcages—no, *made of* birdcages, all kinds, wire and wicker, boxes and domes, from tiny cubes to grand bird palaces. Inside them, there were too many tiny darting shapes to count. The walls and ceiling flickered as the birds pattered about, all of them singing, so that the whole mass was in constant motion.

Horace walked through, wonderingly, and emerged from the tunnel of birds into a long and high stone room, hazy and golden. The birdsong faded. The room stretched back into darkness along a line of stone columns that rose high into wooden rafters. The golden haze came from curious

amber lamps affixed to the columns, small stone containers from which drifting swirls of glittering light lazily rose.
A long row of tables ran down the center of the room, and
wooden shelves stretched along the walls. Shelves and tables
both were piled high and crammed with bins and boxes and
containers of all shapes and sizes and colors. The room was
deserted.

Horace slid out from under his backpack and let it drop.
He walked over to a table, his shoes scuffing loudly on the
stones. He eyed the first bin he came to, trying to identify
some of the strange objects it contained. A three-barbed hook
hung over the side—a kind of fishing hook, but this one was
two feet wide, with barbs as long as his hand. Beside it, the
tip of a miniature scarlet pyramid poked into the air, and an
accordion arm with a large spiky wheel on the end dangled
limply. A rabbit head peeked out of the next bin over, motionless; a unicorn horn sprouted between its ears. If this was a
store, it was like none he'd ever seen.

The containers themselves were neatly labeled, but the
labels were bizarre. WHATSITS, one read, and another: WOR-
THY OF CONSIDERATION. Horace read quickly down the bins
he could see.

Lost Bits
Mostly Incomplete
For the Weary
For the Wee
Truculent

Horace had no idea what truculent meant. He resisted peeking inside and kept reading.

Invisible (Defective)
Odd-Shaped
Even-Shaped
Ship-Shaped
Miscellaneous
Foul-Smelling
Unremarkable
Unsellable
Unaffordable
Unbinnable

Horace frowned at that one, a tall, blue metal container. A bin marked UNBINNABLE would have to be empty, wouldn't it? He hooked his finger over the edge of the bin, tugging.

A voice rang out: "Sign in, please."

Horace yanked his hand away. A woman's voice, husky and sharp, coming from deep in the room. Horace squinted, but saw no one. "I . . . I'm sorry?" he called out.

"No need for apologies," the voice said briskly. "Sign in please. At the podium."

Horace looked around the room. Back near the tunnel of birds, he spotted a short wooden podium, atop which lay open a large and elegant-looking guest book. He moved in for a closer look.

The guest book looked new; no one else had signed it yet. It had the usual columns for name and address, but there were a few more columns as well: AGE, REASON FOR VISIT, and finally . . . QUESTION. Horace had no idea what that meant.

Next to the book, there was a long, gleaming white quill, and beside it a green bottle of dark ink. Horace had never before written using a quill, much less an inkwell. He turned to peer once again into the depths of the store, but before he could even open his mouth—

"Sign in please."

The quill was almost as long as Horace's forearm, and surprisingly heavy. Gingerly, he dipped the sharp tip into the dark pool of ink.

Writing with the quill turned out to be more like scratching than writing. The quill rasped harshly across the paper, sending little chills up and down his arm. The ink surprised him, too—not black but a deep, glittering blue. He had to dip the quill repeatedly, but little by little, he filled out the top row:

NAME	ADDRESS
Horace F. Andrews	3318 N. Bromley Street, Chicago, IL 60634

The next two required a little more thought, but he filled them out as well:

17

AGE	REASON FOR VISIT
12.2 years	mistake

He wrote "mistake" because he felt a little silly for having misread the House of Answers sign. But maybe "mistake" sounded a bit rude.

REASON FOR VISIT

mistake first, curiosity second

Now he came to the final column, QUESTION. He considered that, and then wrote:

QUESTION

Where am I?

"Right here, of course," said a voice at his ear.

Horace spun around, dropping the quill. A woman stood there—small, but with stout shoulders and a thick, severe face. She wore an old-fashioned black dress that covered everything but her head and her hands. Her dark brown hair was drawn back tightly into a bun.

The woman bent and picked up the quill, examining it intently. She ran her fingers down it smoothly, straightening the barbs of the feather. She peered at the guest book and let out a long, low hum.

"Horace F. Andrews," she said, not really asking.

"Yes."

She squared up to him and sank her fists into her hips.

Her hazel eyes were as firm as packed dirt. She nodded solemnly. "You are in the right place."

Horace couldn't pull his eyes away from hers. "I . . . I am?"

"Indeed you are, but you won't believe it until tomorrow."

"Tomorrow."

"That's what I said. Tomorrow, when you return."

Horace felt dizzy. "Oh."

She frowned. "Shouldn't you be in school?"

"School's over. I'm out for the day."

"Not a truant, then. What's your best subject?"

"I don't know . . . science, I guess?" Horace said cautiously. Science was absolutely his best subject—and Mr. Ludwig his favorite teacher—but not everybody was impressed by Horace's enthusiasm for it. He didn't mind that being into science made him seem nerdy to some people, but he resented having to defend something that so clearly shouldn't need defending.

"Science," the woman said, her tone unreadable. "How practical." She clapped her hands together. "Very well. Closing time. You'll come back tomorrow." She began moving toward him, her arms spread like she meant to herd him to the exit.

Reluctantly, Horace began to back away. "But I haven't even looked around yet. What time do you close?"

"I tell you we're closing *now*, and you ask what time we close. Maybe you're just asking me what time it is?"

"I know what time it is. You close at three forty-three?"

She glanced at an enormous watch on her wrist and raised an eyebrow. "Goodness!" she said, sounding startled. "Closing is neither here nor there. Tomorrow we'll be open all day, and you'll come back. You'll look around all you like."

"But what is this place? Who are—"

Suddenly the woman lunged forward, grasping Horace's shoulders hard. She leaned closer and sniffed deeply—once, twice, three times. Her frown deepened. She stared at him hard. "You are Horace F. Andrews of Chicago. Twelve years old, here by virtue of accident and intrigue." Her breath was planty, herbal. Horace wondered if she would ever blink. "I am Mrs. Hapsteade, Keeper of the Vora." She poured that earthy gaze into him for another long, heavy moment and then released him. "Now we've been introduced. Are you comforted?"

Horace could not answer. He rubbed his shoulder. He tried not to let his face reveal the sea of uncertainty and frustration and queasy wonder that stormed inside him now. Keeper of the what?

The woman—Mrs. Hapsteade—sighed. "I see. So it is. But your comfort isn't my concern. Here, take this." She took Horace's wrist and dropped something into his hand—a large black marble. It was warm from her touch. "Keep this leestone with you at all times. And if you see the man who smells like brimstone again, walk away at once—but do not run."

Horace's skin went cold. "What did you say?"

"Do not look at the man, nor allow yourself to be seen. Do not listen to the man, nor allow yourself to be heard. Above all, if the man should come to your house, do not allow him to be invited inside. Keep the leestone with you. Return here tomorrow. All will be well. Do you understand these things I've said?"

Brimstone. The thin man. "Who is he?"

"He's a hunter."

"Is he hunting me?"

"In a way. He hunts an object you don't yet possess."

"How can that be? What object?"

"I don't know. You must return tomorrow. No doubt you're frightened and confused, but I don't apologize for that. The leestone will keep you safe. Tell no one. Go now—we are closed."

Horace backed away, gripping the leestone so hard his fingers ached. He gave Mrs. Hapsteade one last look, and then he turned and hurried toward the tunnel of birds, scooping up his backpack on the way. The birds rustled and fussed as he passed, breaking into little flurries of voice. He was almost to the steps leading back to the blue door when Mrs. Hapsteade called out. Her words reached through the birdsong like an outstretched hand, gentle and warm.

"Remember, Horace F. Andrews, fear is the stone we push. May yours be light."

CHAPTER THREE

The Initiate

WHEN HE GOT HOME, HORACE DISCOVERED TO HIS DISMAY that he had lost his house key again. Usually he was a very organized person—compulsively organized—but he was cursed when it came to house keys; this would be the second one this week. Inside the house, Loki the cat pawed at the front window, mewing mutely. Horace waited on the porch for his mom to come home, feeling more helpless than he usually did when he was locked out. What if the thin man had followed him? What if he was watching Horace right now, just waiting for the right moment to . . . to what? Horace pressed his back against the door and fished the leestone out of his pocket. In the sunlight, it now looked more purple than black. How was this strange marble supposed to protect him? Okay, it was not *just* a marble—that was for sure. Horace collected marbles, so he knew something about it. It was extremely large, twice as big as a shooter, and far too light for its size. Weirdly, it still felt as warm as it had when Mrs. Hapsteade first placed it in his hand. He squeezed the leestone, thinking.

When his mother arrived and found him outside the front door, she didn't ask Horace about his key. Instead she said only: "Your locksmithing career isn't working out, I see."

"No, I guess not."

"Well, you're young. There's still time."

They went inside. They were surprised to find Horace's father standing in the hallway by the writing nook, a bowl of cereal in one hand and an upright spoon in the other, like a wand.

"Hey, you," Horace's mother said. "You're home early."

"Slow day," he replied. He pointed the spoon at Horace. "And you're home late. Have you been out on the porch all this time?"

Horace fidgeted. Loki twined himself around his legs. "Not *all* this time."

"Did you lose your house key again?"

"I just can't find it. I'll look for it again. It's not lost. It's somewhere."

His father closed his eyes and tapped the spoon against his forehead. "I agree that it's definitely *somewhere*," he said, still tapping. Horace waited, nervous and impatient. His dad was generally a good guy, but certain things threw him into lecture mode. Horace losing his house key—*repeatedly* losing his house key, as his father liked to repeatedly say—was one of those things. "Here's the deal, Horace," his father said. "Every time we have this conversation—"

"It resurrects every other time we've already had this conversation," Horace finished. His father frowned and sighed. "Those are my exact words. You saying my exact words just proves my point. Do you like having this conversation over and over again?"

Horace shook his head vigorously. "Definitely not."

"Then," his mother said, "I guess you know what to do to avoid it. The key is the key."

Horace glanced back and forth between his parents, nodding. "Gotcha. So . . . can I go?" At a faint nod from his mother, he hurried up to his room.

Horace would worry about the key later. Right now he had research to do. He got on his computer and started looking up words. He checked every spelling of *Vora* he could think of, but found nothing. Another search revealed that there was no such thing as a *leestone*. *Tinker* was a real word; one of its definitions was *a clumsy worker*—but that made no sense. And then Horace looked up the word *arcana*, from the House of Answers sign, a word he'd heard before but didn't really know. The first definition he found was mildly interesting, but not a surprise: *secrets or mysteries*. Another definition was juicier: *special knowledge revealed only to the initiate*. But what was an *initiate*? He looked it up, and faint goosebumps sprouted down his arms. An initiate was *a new member of a secret society or group*. He chewed on that thought all afternoon and evening, even through dinner, feeling antsy and troubled.

After dinner Horace sat at his desk, trying to do his homework. Or sort of trying. Mostly he just rolled the leestone—still warm!—back and forth across his social studies worksheet. Back and forth, back and forth. He'd been mechanically counting each roll, and was now up to eighteen hundred and twenty-three. About a thousand rolls ago, he'd determined that the leestone's color was fading. Black at first, the leestone now was a deep glimmering violet—though hard as he tried, he couldn't actually see the color draining away. He could only see that it had changed, slow as the sun.

When he got to two thousand and one rolls, Horace shoved the leestone back into his pocket. He flopped onto his bed. He tried to concentrate on the spread of glow-in-the-dark stars on his ceiling, picking out the constellations he'd re-created there—weird ones hardly anyone knew about, like Aquila the eagle and Ophiuchus the serpent bearer and Monoceros the unicorn. He had been trying to memorize them by sight, but now he couldn't even remember just where they were in the sky. His mind wouldn't stick to them. Aquila only reminded him of the tunnel of birds, and the sight of Monoceros brought back the stuffed rabbit with the horn and all the other strange sights he'd glimpsed at the House of Answers. Tomorrow, he thought, couldn't come quick enough.

"Hey," came a soft voice from the door. His mother stood in the doorway, rattling the small wooden chess set. "Ready?"

"Oh, right. I forgot."

"Friday night. I never forget." She came to the bed. She held him for a moment with an easy, open look. "Anything wrong? You seemed distracted at dinner."

"Not really. I guess just school stuff? Nothing much."

His mother—unlike his father—always seemed to know when not to push. "Well, let's take our minds off whatever else they've been on. God knows I could use it. And if you're still worried about the key, you've worried long enough. Sometimes things get lost." Smiling, she handed him the box. "The honors, sir."

Maybe chess was the distraction he needed, after all. He opened the box, exposing the green velvet lining and the thirty-two tiny wooden pieces, sixteen black and sixteen white, each piece in its own special compartment, each set a mirror image of the other—very orderly and pleasing to the eye. He poured the pieces out, then flipped the open box over, revealing the chessboard on the back side. Horace loved this chess set; he was fond of clever little boxes. Horace took white, as always. Loki leapt onto the bed and took his usual spot at the corner, his long black tail lashing contentedly. Horace began setting up his pawns.

"Have you thought about going back to chess club?" his mother asked.

"Not really."

"You liked it last fall."

"Alex and Martin were in it last fall." Alex and Martin, twins who had been his best friends since first grade, had moved to Maine just before Christmas. Maine was a long way from Chicago, and chess club was mostly full of freaks without them. Actually, the whole school was. "The year's almost over anyway."

"Will you do me a favor and think about it next year?"

"I'm thinking about it." Horace placed his queen and then said, casually as he could, "Hey, Mom, what's a tinker?"

"A tinker? Oh, someone who likes to fiddle with things. They like to try to build things or fix things, but they're not very serious about it. Like when your dad tries to get the mower to run better. That's tinkering." She put a hand to her mouth and went on in a stage whisper, "Because he doesn't really know what he's doing."

Horace laughed. This was pretty much in line with what he had already read, but it didn't clear anything up. "Is there any other reason why someone would call somebody a tinker?"

She flicked him a look. She fussed with her king. "Did someone call you that?"

Horace shrugged. "I heard some kid at school say it."

"A friend of yours?"

"No."

"Oh. Well, I don't know. People say some strange things, don't they?"

"I guess."

The board was ready. His mother waved across the pieces. "After you."

They began, and soon things grew serious and silent. Horace had never beaten his mother at chess. She was not the type of parent who would ever just let him win, and that was exactly the way Horace liked it. But he was getting closer. What he liked about chess—and his mother said this was an indication of a good chess mind—was that the board and the pieces presented themselves in terms of lines and angles. As he considered his moves, these lines and angles shifted, the possibilities transforming. The effects of each move rippled forward to affect the outcome of the game in measurable, predictable ways, if only you could pay enough attention and think it through. Chess was logical and geometrical, absolute and knowable—unlike everything that had happened to him this afternoon.

They played on. Long minutes passed. One by one, pieces fell. Horace moved his remaining knight into a promising position. But his mother immediately moved a pawn that Horace had been ignoring, and now the entire geometry of play shifted. "Check," she said. Horace examined the board. She was going to checkmate him on the next move, and he couldn't stop her.

"You have me."

"Let's play it out," she said, like always. She said it whether there was any hope for Horace or not.

Horace took his time, determined not to miss anything. His mother toyed with the pile of captured pieces, making a pawn leap onto Loki's head. "So I've been wondering how awesome the thing you got me for Mother's Day is," she said.

"The thing I got you for Mother's Day," Horace repeated, not really listening.

"Mother's Day. This Sunday. You forgot, didn't you?" She sighed dramatically and shook her head sadly at Loki. Loki squinted back, purring.

"Maybe," Horace said slowly. "Or I guess I did, but don't worry. I'll get you something." He turned his attention back to the board. He pushed a rook to protect his king, but they both knew the rook was doomed.

His mother made a little explosion sound as she toppled his rook with her queen, checkmating him. She smiled. "Very nice," she said. "That wasn't your present, was it? Letting me win?"

"Very funny."

"Because I already have a bunch of those. Victories, I mean."

"I'm not laughing."

"Okay, sorry. Look, about the present, I don't really care what you get me."

"You don't?"

She shook her head, seeming to search for words. "No offense, Horace—you know I respect you—but when people are young they're generally terrible at buying presents. Like . . . when you were like six, you bought me that bat. Not a baseball bat." She bared her upper teeth and fluttered her hands like little wings to clarify. "A bat. It was a wooden

29

cutout, wings all spread, and it had this creepy, cartoony face . . . fangs and everything." She shuddered.

"You hate bats."

"Exactly. *You* love them, though. Your favorite animal, at the time."

True. In fact, bats were still his favorite animal, which was kind of strange since he didn't like caves. "But . . . you liked that bat anyway, because it was from me."

"*Like* is a strong word. Put it this way: it's in the attic somewhere—hopefully the only bat in the attic. But the present itself doesn't matter, because it's watching you make the attempt that's so interesting. It's a pleasure seeing you become the person that you are, that you will be. And sometimes that means watching you make careless decisions—like buying a bat for a woman who is mortally terrified of bats."

One of the things Horace liked very much about his mother was that she didn't treat him like a child. Not that she pretended he was an adult—it was just that she was honest about the differences between them. Once, when he'd given up on their weekly chess after losing too many games, she'd sent him a card in the mail. He still had it. Inside, she'd written:

> *If smarts were a race, you would have no hope of having caught up to me yet. Not because you're slow, or because I'm fast, but because I happen to have a huge head start.*

30

It's not fair or unfair; it's just the way it works. One day, you will be where I am now—and beyond.

Please let me know when you're over it. I do miss playing with you.

They'd played again that very night, and she'd beaten him. Badly. They'd been playing ever since. And now Horace found himself seized by a desire to buy his mother the best Mother's Day present ever. He cleared the chessboard and began to pack away the pieces. His mother joined him, the two of them working quietly.

"You like turtles," Horace said after a while.

"I do."

"I guess I need to go shopping tomorrow."

His mother slipped the last pawn into the velvet-lined box and latched it closed. She stood, gazing up at the star-covered ceiling. Loki hopped down and rubbed against her legs. "That's not really the point, Horace." She sighed. "You know what I really want for Mother's Day, right? Far beyond any present? I want to see you continuing to become the person I know you are. Keep thinking. Keep considering. Be smart. Be happy. Be safe."

"I am happy. And safe." The thin man rose up in Horace's mind, along with Mrs. Hapsteade's final words: *Fear is the stone we push.*

"You would tell me if you were in any trouble."

31

Ordinarily he would. But today he didn't even know how to begin. "What kind of trouble?" he asked.

"I don't know. Trouble doesn't always have an easy name, does it?" She dropped her eyes to Horace's and smiled.

"I guess not."

She held his gaze for a moment longer. "I love you."

"Love you too," Horace said automatically.

She left then, Loki slipping out with her. The moment the door closed, Horace let out a long breath. He flopped face forward onto the cool covers of his bed.

The leestone's stubborn heat seemed to pulse slowly into his leg. He swam through images from the day: the House of Answers sign, though in his thoughts it sometimes still read Horace F. Andrews; the tunnel of birds, like a blanket of song; Mrs. Hapsteade grasping his shoulders; the burn of the leestone in his pocket. *Trouble.* He saw the thin man's carnival shape, smelled the thin man's sickly scent, heard the thin man's voice, felt his bizarre fingers taking hold. The man was hunting him for an object he did not yet possess. What did that mean?

Horace fought his fears back as best he could, but he lay on the bed for a long time and lost that battle, over and over. Images of the thin man rose again and again, deep into the night, crooked and looming in his thoughts like grinning scarecrows, like ghouls, like devils.

CHAPTER FOUR

Fellow Passengers

The next morning Horace boarded the 77 westbound. The bus was mostly empty, just a handful of older people up front. Horace headed for the very back row, then realized someone was already sitting there—a girl all but hidden beneath a dark green hoodie. She gave off a distinctly unfriendly vibe. Horace took the seat right behind the rear doors instead, a tingle of something—excitement? fear?—in his chest. He was headed back to the House of Answers.

He'd told his parents he was going shopping for Mother's Day, but Mother's Day was pretty far from the front of his mind now. He could not stop worrying about the thin man. He pondered for the twentieth time that morning what he would do if he encountered the thin man again, especially since Mrs. Hapsteade had really only given him one piece of advice: *avoid him*. Horace had the leestone, of course, whatever good that was supposed to do. He took it out of his pocket—still warm, but it had faded badly overnight. It was completely clear around the edges, all the color shrunken into a jagged purple cloud in the center.

The bus turned the corner onto Wexler Street and immediately wheezed to a stop. Horace looked up and sucked in a gasp of surprise. The thin man was clambering aboard the bus, as if Horace's own thoughts had conjured him. Horace ducked down, peering around the seat.

The thin man looked even more inhuman than last time, like some monstrous insect. He was far too tall to stand up straight on the bus, so he more crawled than walked, bent over between his knees. As he crept down the aisle, his elbows knifed over the heads of the other passengers. They seemed to see him, but clearly not the way Horace was seeing him, because they weren't staring. The thin man spoke to them, his head swiveling on his long neck, his pleasantly lilting voice so out of place coming from that mouth: "Good morning. Lovely day, isn't it? How do you do?" He got polite nods and mumbled greetings in return. His dark glasses were gone. His eyes were black points that flicked from side to side like tiny, darting fish.

Horace dropped completely out of sight, pressing his face against the seat. He squeezed the leestone between his forefinger and thumb and realized he was counting, his brain marking off seconds on its own, as it sometimes did. *Seventeen, eighteen*—how long did it take to walk to the back of the bus?

Thirty-five. Forty. At last Horace sat up slowly and peeked. The thin man, improbably, had folded himself into a seat. He was right in front of the rear doors, his back to Horace, the stairway the only thing separating them. His long-fingered hands were wrapped around his head as though he was deep in thought.

Any moment now, they would pass the House of Answers. If Horace had any chance of getting off the bus unseen, he would have to sneak out behind the thin man and hope that the man didn't turn around. He reached up and yanked the cable to call for a stop. The chime sounded. The bus began to slow. The man was still facing forward. Horace stood, his eyes boring into the back of the thin man's head. The man's hands, thrust into his thick black hair, *did* have too many joints, and his pinkies were crooked, almost like second thumbs. And that bitter burning smell—brimstone? Horace wanted to retch.

Just as he stepped down to reach for the rear doors, the bus lurched to a stop, nearly tumbling Horace into the man. The thin man lifted his head and inhaled sharply. He began to turn, his limbs bending and twisting like a spider's.

The doors opened. Horace leapt from the top step. As he hit the sidewalk, he remembered Mrs. Hapsteade's words: *"Do not run."* But he ran. He sped away from the bus as fast as his too-long legs would let him, cursing his too-shaggy hair that fell across his eyes.

He was just reaching top speed when a voice called out,

clear and loud: "Hey! Here!" Horace slowed. A girl in a green hoodie stood in the doorway of a bookstore, waving at him. The girl from the bus—but that was impossible! No one had gotten off ahead of him. "Here," she said again, gesturing impatiently.

Horace glanced back at the bus. His stomach crumpled. The thin man was unfolding from the rear doors, a savage scowl tearing his long face in two. Horace darted toward the bookstore, hoping desperately the thin man wouldn't see him. The girl heaved the door open and rushed in ahead of him.

The girl was tiny, but she had a confident, feline swagger. She strode deep into the store, Horace at her heels. At the very back, she pushed open a door marked STAFF ONLY. They plowed through a break room, where a plump middle-aged lady watched them pass with wide eyes, apparently too startled to say anything. "Sorry," Horace mumbled. They burst through another door and out into a cramped, shadowed alleyway behind.

The girl spun to face him, throwing her hood back to reveal long black hair. Her eyes bored into him, dark and intense. "Did he see you?"

"I don't know. I don't think so."

"Were there any others? Like him?"

She was a fast talker. It took a moment for the words to sink in. There were others like the thin man? "No, no way," Horace said. It was an almost unthinkable thought.

The girl leaned in, continuing to look him up and down. She was about Horace's own age, but everything about her was fierce. Horace found himself taking a step back. Had he done the right thing, following her here? What did she want from him?

"You see him like I do," the girl said. "The freak. Nobody else sees him like that."

"I definitely don't know what you're talking about," Horace said.

She scoffed. "Of course you do. You were hiding from him on the bus."

"No I wasn't."

"Oh my god, you were. The question is, *Why* were you hiding?"

But Horace couldn't wrap his head around a sensible answer to that question, even if he'd wanted to trust this girl. He was hiding because a strange old lady in a secret curiosity shop had told him to, hiding because he didn't know how a marble—even a mysterious one—was supposed to protect him. And protect him from what? Who was the thin man? What did he want? Horace's fear and his frustration curdled into irritation. He straightened and frowned down at the girl. "Why are *you* hiding?" he fired back.

"No, no—you seem confused. I'm not hiding me, I'm hiding you. I was doing fine. I only led you back here because I want to know what's up with you. I thought I was the only one."

"The only one what?"

She leaned back and squinted her eyes, measuring him. Then she said in an annoyingly patient tone, like she was talking to a child, "Look. You were the one running. There are only two reasons to be running like that: either you're in a hurry to be somewhere, or you're in a hurry to *not* be somewhere. And don't tell me you're late for an important meeting."

An important meeting—maybe. But he wasn't about to mention the House of Answers. "No meeting. I'm not going anywhere."

"Oh, wow. You're a really bad liar. It sort of makes me not trust you."

Horace laughed. "That's like . . . the opposite of—"

"Tell me again why I helped you?"

"I have no idea," Horace said, exasperated. "I didn't even need help." Of course this was not true, not at all. He'd been running blindly, terrified, and he'd followed her back here to apparent safety, to a place he'd never have come on his own.

The girl gave a disappointed sigh, as if reading his mind. "I'm not feeling very appreciated. Is this how you always are?"

That wasn't even a fair question—nothing like this had ever happened to him before.

The girl hitched up her small black backpack and pulled her hood over her head. "I'm going now," she said. "Good luck with all your, um . . . not hiding. Maybe we could call it cowering?" She began to walk away.

Cowering—a mean thing to say, even if she might be right.

He didn't think he liked this girl at all. "Hey, wait," Horace called out. "That man. The thin man." The girl turned and glared at him silently, walking backward now, her eyes deep and simmering. Horace asked, "Who is he? *What* is he? And will he still be out there?"

"He roams. Try not to roam in the same direction."

"What about the bus? You got off first, but I didn't see you. How did you do that?"

Her face softened into clear-eyed innocence. "I definitely don't know what you're talking about," she said, and turned her back on him. Several yards down the alley she stopped, glanced one last time at Horace, and then disappeared through another doorway he couldn't quite make out. Clearly she knew her way around.

Once she was gone, Horace tried to get his bearings—physically and otherwise. He had no idea what to make of the girl. She obviously knew more about the thin man than he did, but she hadn't given him any new information at all. Except to suggest that there were more thin men out there, a thought that made Horace shudder.

He followed the alleyway to his left and was surprised to discover that it opened out onto Wexler Street. Maybe he could still make it to the House of Answers, after all. But if it was true that the thin man roamed, he seemed to do a lot of roaming in this neighborhood. Horace would have to be very careful. After a cautious look up and down the sidewalk, he headed north. Before long, Horace spotted the

Laundromat—and just beyond, and the alley that led to the House of Answers. He quickened his pace, still scanning ahead and behind.

And then just as he was about to round the corner, the thin man stepped out of the alley, directly into his path.

—◦◦◦—

CHAPTER FIVE

Mr. Meister

HORACE FELL BACK, PRESSING HIMSELF AGAINST THE WINDOW of the Laundromat. Remembering what Mrs. Hapsteade had said, he fixed his eyes ahead, not daring to look in the thin man's direction. Horace hoped beyond hope that the thin man hadn't noticed him, that the scrawny green awning above was helping to hide him even now. He gripped the leestone tightly in his pocket, willing the thin man to go away.

"Come out, come out," the thin man sang, his notes cruel and lilting. Goose bumps prickled up and down Horace's body, tugging his skin so hard it hurt. The man gave a long, thoughtful hum, like a greedy man contemplating a table full of delicious food.

And then, almost without thinking, Horace pulled the leestone from his pocket. He stepped out from under the awning and, in the same motion, threw the leestone underhand, hurling it high into the air, far out over the street. Even as it left his hand, Horace thought, *Why am I doing this?* The leestone rose into the sunlight, shimmering violet. It fell into the far lane of the road and shattered, releasing a shrill, almost animal cry that Horace could hear over the sound of the cars. A plume of purple smoke spiraled into the air.

The thin man leapt after the leestone like a predator after prey. Horns blared as traffic jolted to a stop around him, but he paid the cars no mind. He began to circle the remains of the leestone.

Waiting to see no more, Horace darted into the alley. He took the stairs at the end in a single leap, landing hard. He fumbled for the handle of the small blue door, muttering his name. "Horace Andrews, Horace F. Andrews, please let me in. I need to get in. Need, need, need." He tugged once, twice, and the door swung open. He ducked inside, so full of fear already that he scarcely felt the cramped tunnel's chokehold as the door closed firmly behind him. He ran through the passageway and down the stairs, through the thick tunnel of birdsong, bursting into the House of Answers.

The room seemed even more vast and deserted than it had the day before. "Hello?" he called. His voice echoed. He approached the podium. The quill and the ink were still there, and the guest book was open. But the page was blank—his entry from yesterday was nowhere to be seen. "Hello? Mrs. Hapsteade?" No reply.

He slumped to the floor at the foot of the podium, letting

his fear seep slowly out through the cold stone floor beneath him. He'd escaped from the thin man—twice!—to get here, and for what? He was safe, but the place was abandoned. No one knew what had just happened. He still had no answers.

After a long, miserable time, Horace got to his feet. He might as well do what he could on his own. There was something here in this place, something he had to know. He could feel it. But the place was so huge, so overwhelmingly full. He had no idea where to begin.

He lifted the sturdy white quill and dipped it in the ink, unsure what else to do. He started to fill in his name, address, and age, as he had done yesterday, his words once again a beautiful deep blue. He paused briefly to think about the final two columns, and then wrote:

REASON FOR VISIT	QUESTION
seeking answers	WHAT IS HAPPENING?

Horace wandered away from the podium, determined to wait. He wasn't about to risk leaving anyway, not with the thin man outside. He examined the bins he'd glimpsed yesterday. But the bins had been rearranged. Many of them were new.

Odd-Shaped
Ship-Shaped
Shape-Shaped
Implausible

Palpable
Often Lost
Never Found
Tourmindae

That last one was extra mysterious. Horace was just about to reach out for it when, once again, a strange voice—a man's voice this time—stopped him short: "One moment, if you will."

Horace spun around, almost stumbling against some shelves. An old man stood beside the podium, gazing pleasantly at Horace—or at least, his gaze *seemed* pleasant. It was hard to tell. He wore thick glasses with perfectly round lenses, which made his gray eyes appear unnaturally large—especially on the left side, where his eye was magnified to the size of a golf ball. He wore a long red vest covered in pockets—dozens of them, scores of them, all shapes and sizes. The vest, in fact, seemed made entirely of pockets. The man's hair was wild and white, his skin wrinkled and pale.

"One moment, young man." The man had an accent—German, maybe? He pushed his thick glasses into place as he bent over the guest book. "Ah yes, very interesting. Oh, I see. Yes, yes." At last he turned back to Horace and smiled. "Mrs. Hapsteade was right, of course. She is a formidable woman. Terribly efficient. Does wonders with the inventory. Now come, let me have a look at you." He waved Horace over, and Horace obliged, reluctantly. He looked Horace up and down, as though he was shopping for a car, trying to decide whether or not Horace might be a good bargain. Then he stuck out a knobby, gnarled hand. "Allow me to introduce myself—I am Mr. Meister."

Hesitantly, Horace held out his hand. The old man grasped it and gave it a single firm pump. His skin was cold and dry. Horace noticed he wore a multicolored metal ring on his middle finger, a thick band with a neat twist at the top. It was a Möbius strip, Horace realized—a strip with a half twist that meant you could trace a line all the way around the thing, inside and out, and come back to where you started.

"And you are Horace Andrews," Mr. Meister said, and then concern creased his face. "You have had an encounter this morning, I believe."

An encounter. Was that the word? Really, there had been more than one encounter, if you included the girl in the green hoodie. "You could say that," Horace managed. He wondered suddenly how valuable the leestone had been, and if the old man knew he'd destroyed it. And should he tell him about the girl?

"I will want to hear more about it shortly. In the meantime, you say you seek answers. Many answers, it seems. Sometimes we are so full of questions, we cannot choose, yes?"

Horace could only nod.

"Just so. If I may suggest, let us return instead to the question you posed yesterday: 'Where am I?' An excellent question, very sensible. One must always try to stay oriented." He swept one arm theatrically across the room. "This is a warehouse, one of many. But also it is a market, of sorts. It is a museum. A refuge. A subterfuge. For some—like you, I confess—it is a trial."

"A trial? Like a test?"

"Yes."

"Am I passing?"

Mr. Meister laughed in a friendly way. "You passed one test when you first came through the blue door. As for the rest, it is not a matter of passing or failing. Rather, it is a matter of determining facilities, affinities, aptitudes."

Horace felt himself relaxing, his curiosity taking over, even if he didn't really understand what Mr. Meister was saying, exactly. "Yesterday Mrs. Hapsteade said I was in the right place."

"That much is marvelously clear."

"She also said she was the keeper of something. The Vora, I think? Do you know what that means?"

Mr. Meister's bushy eyebrows rose. "I do," he said, and then he turned abruptly and strode deeper into the room. Horace hurried to follow. "Horace, I believe the circumstances demand that we act first and speak second. Therefore, the warehouse is now yours to explore. Perhaps you will encounter what you came here to find. After all—above all—that is the purpose of this place."

"What I came here to find," Horace murmured, still

recalling his conversation with Mrs. Hapsteade. "It's the thing the thin man wants, isn't it?"

Again the eyebrows went up. "Dr. Jericho wants a great many things, none of which we intend to let him have."

"That's his name? Dr. Jericho?"

"It's what he calls himself, yes."

"He's a doctor?"

"Not in the way you might suppose. But you must put him out of your mind for now."

"I'm not sure I can."

"Try. Lose yourself in the warehouse. Search, and perhaps you will find."

"Is this a part of the test?"

"It is a part of the journey—the most important turn you will ever take. But do not fear. You cannot fail this test, Horace." He stopped short, looking at Horace gravely. "Do not touch what you do not want." He put one hand against the wall, took an alarming step forward, and vanished. Horace stared. There was a dark panel set in the stone—it must have been a secret door of some kind. Horace pushed and called out, but only silence came back.

He stood there for a moment, gathering himself. The old man had come and gone like a ghost. *"Perhaps you will encounter what you came here to find."* Great. If only he had the slightest idea what that was.

Horace began to look around, browsing uncertainly through the bins, careful to touch nothing. Most were full of objects that were either utterly foreign or utterly unremarkable. A bin labeled FLAT was full of nothing but blank sheets of paper. Another, labeled SUBTLE, contained just a single object—a delicate arm-length sliver of metal, so thin Horace couldn't see it from the side. A bin marked UTENSILS was full of all kinds of oddities: a corkscrew two feet long and as thin as a finger, a double-headed hammer, a pair of scissors whose blades were sharp on the outside instead of the inside, and something that looked vaguely like an ice-cream scoop—if you wanted scoops of ice cream as big as your head.

Horace worked his way deep into the room. FOR THE FEARFUL held a thick stack of blankets and two ceramic vials twisted together like snakes, one black and one gold. EDIBLES was full of canned corn—at least fifty cans, all identical—while INEDIBLES contained half a dozen rusty gears, a nasty-looking spiked chain, and a golf club. The labels of many boxes were mystifying: PASSKEYS, ASSORTED TAN'KINDI, ONGRELLONDAE. So much meant so little to him, and as he searched he became increasingly sure—and increasingly worried—that the sheer volume of stuff would make it impossible for him to find whatever it was he was supposed to find.

Horace began to move more quickly, working his way toward the far end of the room. For the first time he caught sight of the rear wall, and was astonished—a door stood there that would have been at home in a castle, or a fortress. Ten feet high, wooden timbers reinforced with metal bands, sealed by a crossbar as thick as a leg. "A refuge," Horace muttered, remembering Mr. Meister's words. He wondered how long the old man was going to stay gone.

He continued down the line, now just reading the labels.

Useless
Misplaced
Displaced
Oblong
Unsavory
Tangible

Horace was just starting to think that the labels were becoming less and less sensible when his eyes fell on the label of the next bin down.

Of Scientific Interest

Horace stopped, his interest immediately roused. He leaned over the bin. A small sound nagged at his ears as he did so, a faint, low grind like the sound of a tiny motor winding down. He quickly discovered the source: a small, wobbling ball of clockwork. The size of a plum, the entire object was a seething golden mass of turning gears and whirring springs and tiny obscure mechanisms. Nearly every bit of its surface was in motion, so that it rocked slightly in place.

The OF SCIENTIFIC INTEREST bin turned out to be full of many such wonders. There was a human face—an exquisite mask, thin as paper. Horace understood intuitively that the face belonged to someone, that the face was real, that the woman depicted had been someone's child, sister, mother. There was also a transparent rod, two inches thick and a foot long. Inside the rod was a fish, black as charcoal and nearly as finless as an eel. It was alive. It was almost as long and as wide as the rod itself, and it shimmied slowly, steadily, as though caught in a gentle, unending current. It could not hope to turn around inside the rod; there was not enough room. It could only keep swimming in place, all but motionless. Horace choked back a rising knot of pity. He knew that the fish was unspeakably old.

Perhaps most astonishing of all was a grapefruit-sized globe of the earth, surrounded by a glowing haze within which the globe rotated slowly. Horace watched it for a long time and very nearly did pick it up. It was, he determined at last, real. Horace knew its oceans were filled with actual water; he could see currents, and light bouncing off its surface. Its poles were made of ice that gleamed and felt cool to a fingertip hovering overhead. Its green patches were living, growing plants—microscopic trees?—and the clouds that moved over its surface drifted and swirled. It was—strange to say it—the most unworldly object Horace had ever encountered.

And then Horace spotted a diminutive leather pouch with a buttoned-down flap. The pouch was oval, golden-red in color, a little smaller than Horace's open hand. The surface was inscribed with a twining figure eight—or was it an infinity symbol? Horace tilted his head to one side and then the other, gazing at the pouch, and then, before he even knew what he was doing, he reached out and picked it up.

He opened the flap. He pulled out what was inside—a gleaming oval box. Immediately, the globe and the clockwork ball and the impossible fish—all those marvels—slid from his mind. In many respects, the box was the most ordinary item here: quite small, made of a shimmering striped wood, shades of brown and gold and red. A line of silver snaked across the lid, and on one curving side was a delicate gleaming starburst design. Of all the objects he'd seen so far, only this box could have looked at home on the shelves of an ordinary store. Yet it was the most marvelous thing Horace had ever seen. Next to it, all the other wonders paled like cheap parlor tricks in the presence of real magic.

Horace wrapped his fingers around the box. The world dropped away, and he swooned a little, overwhelmed by the sensation that a question he hadn't asked yet had just been answered.

"This is it," he said, though he had no idea what that meant.

CHAPTER SIX

The Find

THE BOX'S STRIPES SHIFTED LIKE A TIGER'S-EYE STONE. Horace knew the name for this phenomenon—*chatoyance*. He'd done a report on it for Mr. Ludwig in the fall. Although it usually happened in gemstones, it could also be made to happen in certain kinds of wood. But he'd never seen that until now. On the side of the box, a slightly raised black ball was surrounded by a cluster of serpentine rays, twelve long and twelve short, forming a delicate silver star. It, too, glinted in the dim light.

Horace couldn't get the box open at first, until he realized the gentle S shape that ran across the lid was a seam. He pressed his thumb down gently on the center of the silver seam. He heard and felt a tiny *click*. A twist of the thumb, and the lid opened—one half swinging forward while the other swung back, spreading wide like wings. Inside, more of the curious wood, but the bottom was made of a beautiful blue substance, transparent and laced with soft ripples that almost seemed to move.

Horace held up the open box and looked straight through it. Through the blue bottom of the box, the room came truly alive, almost as if it were a living, breathing thing. He stared, exhilarated—*the bristling texture of the rafters, timeworn grooves between the floor stones, floating specks of dust winking in and out of sight.* He turned and panned down the room—*cobwebs shining in the dark corners, straight-edged bins and boxes and crates, labels smudged out of recognition or turned sharp as knives.* Horace noticed that certain patches shifted from clear to hazy and back again. Bright spots looked dimmer, but dark places looked brighter. The whole effect was marvelous, full of clarity and mystery at the same time; full of confusion and depth. It made him feel powerful, somehow, or wise—as though he was seeing the world in a way that no one else could.

"What is this?" he breathed.

Behind him, a polite cough. Mr. Meister stood there, his huge eye roving eagerly across Horace and the box. Horace swung the lid of the box closed. The two halves came together with a satisfying *snick*.

"I will ask for your caution in this moment, my young friend," Mr. Meister said. His voice was as mild as his stare was keen. "The box is a subtle contrivance, and I would like to avoid any mishaps."

Horace slipped the box back into its pouch and pulled it tightly to his chest. For some reason, he was terrified that Mr. Meister would take the box away from him.

But Mr. Meister only smiled. "I gather you would like this to be yours?"

Horace wanted to say the box was the most wonderful and important thing he had ever seen, or would ever see. He wanted to say the box already *was* his. He wanted to say he would not be able to leave this place without it. But he could hardly speak. He pressed the box harder against his chest. He didn't know how he knew, but he knew. Finally he said, "This was made for me."

"Better to say that you were made for it." The old man's face was full of a quivering energy. "Be at ease, Horace. I will not take the box from you. Indeed, let me speak aloud the truth you are already beginning to know: the box is yours now."

"To keep?" Horace asked, his voice squeaking.

"Yes, to keep. This box has been in my possession for twenty years, but it was never mine so deeply as it is already yours."

"You don't want to keep it?"

"Goodness no. I could not even use it if I tried. It belongs to you now, Horace. You know that it does. Need I say it again?"

Horace shook his head, his throat closing. He tried to summon words of gratitude but could not. At the front of the room, the trilling birdsong began to rise again. Horace listened, swaying, feeling buoyant and loose and happy.

"Your place in the world is changing, Horace. You feel this, yes?"

"I'm not sure what I feel. I feel . . . like I'm falling. Like gravity is pulling me somewhere strange." He looked down at the box, lost for words. "I know something is happening to me, but I don't know what."

Mr. Meister nodded, his wide eyes warm and shining. "This is the first stage of the Find."

"The Find? What is that?"

"It is a becoming."

"Becoming what?"

"What you are. But do not overthink it. All you need to know for now is that this connection you feel—this pull toward the box—it is good and right and true. The rest will be revealed in due course."

Horace nodded. He didn't really understand, and he had a habit of overthinking things, but he found that he could not quite summon up his usual curious urgency. The box was in his hands. He felt floaty and untouchable. He watched as Mr. Meister lifted the clockwork ball and the miniature earth from the OF SCIENTIFIC INTEREST bin, making them disappear into his vest. Up front, the birds kept sewing their river of song. "Those birds," Horace said at last. "You sure do have a lot of birds."

"Ah, the birds, yes," said Mr. Meister. "They are a precaution."

"Against Dr. Jericho?"

Mr. Meister's face contracted, becoming hard and serious. "Just so," he said, his voice like a hammer. "Against him, and others of his kind. You saw him this morning, yes? Was he alone?"

The terror of Horace's flight from the thin man had drifted apart, pushed by the easy waters of this new peace. The box was in his hands. Still, he recognized the anxiety on Mr. Meister's face. "Yes. He chased me."

"Chased you?" Mr. Meister said, clearly alarmed. "He was aware of your presence? But were you not carrying the leestone?"

Horace rubbed his thumb across the engraving on the pouch, tracing the infinity symbol. "I was, but . . ." He tried to remember how it had happened, what he had done. "There was a girl, about my age, wearing a green hoodie. She helped me."

"A girl. What was her name?"

"I have no idea. Bossy McSomething."

Mr. Meister didn't laugh. He studied Horace, then began to rummage through his vest pockets. There seemed to be hundreds of them—pockets within pockets, even. The old man pulled out a tiny notebook and a stubby pencil. He began to scribble, muttering. He finished, tucked the notebook away, then dug through his pockets again. He produced a delicate white sphere, roughly leestone sized, but shoved it back with a grunt of impatience. He stalked off, scanning the shelves of bins. Horace followed, still cradling the box. Mr. Meister stopped and stretched high to reach into a wooden bin marked RAVENS' EYES. He pulled out a small dark purple sphere and thrust it into Horace's face. "This was the color of the leestone when it was presented to you, yes?"

"Yes," Horace replied, glad that the leestone hadn't been one of a kind.

"And what color is it now?"

"It *isn't*," he said. "The last I saw, it was almost clear all the way through."

Mr. Meister's face went slack with shock. "A single day," he muttered. Then his gaze grew sharp again. "I believe I am correct in guessing that you no longer possess the leestone."

Horace told him the whole story as best he could. It seemed like a thing that had happened to someone else. When he described the destruction of the leestone, Mr. Meister interrupted, "If I may ask, what prompted you to do this thing?"

"I'm not sure. I guess I thought that if whatever was inside the leestone was let out, all at once, it would distract him. I thought maybe he wouldn't be able to look away."

"And so it was," Mr. Meister said. "Remarkable."

"But I don't know why. I don't know what a leestone is. I don't even know who Dr. Jericho is. Or *what* he is."

"He is the enemy."

"That's no kind of answer," Horace replied.

"On the contrary, Horace, it is the heart of the answer. To

know your enemy is to know where you stand."

"No," Horace said. "No, that's wrong. I think you have to know where you stand before you can know your enemy. And I don't know where I stand." He looked down at the box in his hands. "I only know exactly one thing right now."

Mr. Meister stood in silence for several breaths before speaking. "Well spoken, Horace, my friend. And forgive me for the blindnesses you must endure. But for now you only need to know one thing about Dr. Jericho: stay away from him."

"That's the same advice Mrs. Hapsteade gave me. It didn't turn out too well."

"Fortunately, I have the solution you need." They cut across the aisle and worked their way toward the front, stopping before a wide, shallow bin with a single item in it—a small statue of a turtle with a bird on its back. The bin was marked:

For the Initiate

Initiate. The word sent a tingle across Horace's skin. The statue itself was about six inches high, very lifelike, carved from some dark stone. The turtle's face was lifted to the sky, eyes closed. Atop it, the bird looked alertly off to the side, like it was keeping guard. It had a thick hooked beak and huge taloned feet that gripped the turtle's shell.

"Is that a crow?" Horace asked.

"A raven. A formidable creature, extremely intelligent."

"And how is this going to help me?"

"This is a leestone, Horace. A mighty one. So mighty that I feel confident entrusting you to it."

Horace frowned. "I hope it works better than the last one. I think that one was defective or something."

"Not defective, no. That was a raven's eye—not a particularly powerful kind of leestone, but it was working just fine. Indeed, it was working hard. Had it failed you utterly, Dr. Jericho might have noticed you the moment he boarded the bus. You see, Horace, a leestone is a kind of distraction. Leestones soak up unwanted attention, absorbing and draining the focus of those who would seek you out. Focus, thought, perception—the contents of the leestone absorb all these in the same way a black cloth absorbs light."

Horace considered this. "So that's why destroying the raven's eye distracted Dr. Jericho? I released what was inside, and all his attention was drawn to it."

"Just so."

"You said the raven's eye was working hard. And you were surprised it faded so fast. Did it fade because Dr. Jericho was thinking about me? It was absorbing his thoughts?"

"Correct again. You have a scientist's mind indeed. Like that black cloth in the sun, the raven's eye fades with use. Clearly your first encounter with Dr. Jericho yesterday made an impression on him."

"But if the raven's eye was working, how did he know

59

what bus I was on?"

"I doubt that he did. Understand first that it's the warehouse that draws him to this neighborhood, not you. He and his brethren are always searching for it, though they are unlikely to find it. As for why Dr. Jericho boarded the exact bus you were already on?" Mr. Meister waved a hand through the air. "The raven's eye might have lost some potency, yes. Clearly Dr. Jericho can sense the . . . difference in you, when he gets close enough. But perhaps, Horace, it was not you that drew him onto the bus today at all." His face tightened into a knot of thoughtfulness for a moment, his mind clearly elsewhere. Horace understood at once—the girl in the green hoodie. What could the thin man possibly want with her? Was she different, too?

Mr. Meister stirred, laying a hand on the statue. "But back to the issue at hand. This leestone is many times more powerful than an ordinary raven's eye, and it will not fade. Take it home, keep it there, and all who live under your roof will be protected, wherever they go. Should you encounter Dr. Jericho—on the street, at your school, even outside this very warehouse—he will take no notice of you and may, in fact, even avoid you without realizing that he has done so. Unless, of course . . ." Here he paused and looked pointedly at Horace.

"Unless what?"

"Unless, of course, you were to do something drastic, to draw attention to yourself in some way. Or—especially—if

60

you were to brandish something that was of particular interest to him." His eyes dropped to the box.

And with those words, the peaceful veil Horace had been wrapped in was yanked away. Sparks of anger and fear flared up inside him. Questions blossomed in his head like fireworks. "The thin man . . . Dr. Jericho. He's hunting the box?"

"He will take it from you if he can, yes."

"Why?"

"He collects instruments like the box." He swept his arm across the warehouse. "Just as Mrs. Hapsteade and I do."

"But how did Dr. Jericho even know I would find the box? How did you?"

"I did not know. Nor did he. Even now he does not know you possess the box."

"Why was he after me, then?"

"As I said, he sensed the difference in you." The old man's voice was maddeningly calm.

"What difference?"

"You have an affinity, Horace. An aptitude."

"I don't even know what that means."

"Let us say you have a talent."

"For what?"

"That is for you to discover."

Horace frowned down at the ground, squeezing the box against his belly and clenching his other fist. So many questions, and so few answers—he thought he would burst. He bent and pressed his forehead against the box, soaking in its presence, letting the veil of easy peace begin to fall over him once again. "Okay," he said at last. "Okay. I guess you won't tell me more. Even if I don't understand *why*." He straightened and looked at the leestone again, gazing at the raven's shining eyes. He reached out and rubbed the head of the bird. "Ravens. And a turtle. My mom likes turtles."

Mr. Meister pressed his lips together, as if he were suppressing a smile. "A happy circumstance, with Mother's Day upon us. The leestone would be a most appropriate gift, Horace, in ways you cannot yet begin to fathom. Let me prepare it for you, and you can take it home to your mother. As for the box, it must go with you as well—but perhaps your mother does not need to know about it quite yet, yes? Nor anyone else."

Horace nodded but again could not find the right words. Mr. Meister puttered around and found some cloth to wrap the leestone in. He made no such offer for the glass-bottom box, and that was just as well; Horace had no intention of letting the old man touch it.

Mr. Meister saw Horace all the way to the front door. He reassured Horace that with the leestone in hand, he would see no sign of Dr. Jericho on the way home. When he cracked the front door open, throwing a long slice of bright sun onto the dark entryway, Mr. Meister stepped into the light, closing his eyes and lifting his face.

"We don't get much of this, of late," he said, basking. He gave Horace a last stern look. "Remember, Horace: use the box with caution. Whenever you use the box outside your home, you run the risk of drawing Dr. Jericho's attention, even from a distance—leestone or no."

"Use the box?" Horace asked. "But what does it even do?"

The old man fussed with his Möbius-strip ring. "I cannot tell you that, Horace, for many reasons, reasons that range from the practical to the sacred. You are in the Find. The path before you belongs to you alone, for a while. It may not be an easy path, but eventually something will happen. Clarity will come. Afterward, we will speak more."

"Why won't it be easy? What will happen?"

But Mr. Meister shook his head. "You must experience the Find for yourself, Horace. Be with the box. Once you have come to an understanding, we will meet again, and much will be revealed."

Horace sighed. "So I guess it's good luck to me, then, huh?"

The old man hesitated, then cleared his throat. "The coming days are likely to bring you discomfort, Horace—confusion, anger, even despair. But I believe I can give you two pieces of advice that may help you through the Find." He leaned closer, his left eye keen and searching. "These are not really warnings, but simple facts. Do you understand me?"

"I think so," Horace said, feeling lost.

"First: you should not open the box without reason."

Horace started to ask what qualified as a *reason*, but instead only nodded.

"Second: you cannot keep anything inside the box."

Horace looked down at the box, mystified but unsurprised. Somehow the idea of putting anything inside it had never even occurred to him. "Okay," he said, and looked up at the sliver of sky far overhead. The world around him was shifting fast, to strange new places. "I don't really understand that, or any of this, but . . . it feels right."

"Above all, remember this one firm patch of ground: the box belongs to you."

Horace swallowed. "I guess I should thank you."

"That remains to be seen. Let us not misunderstand the situation: in matters such as this, Mrs. Hapsteade and I do not do favors. We do what is best."

Horace searched the old man's face. "Best how? Best for who? What's this even all about?"

Mr. Meister gazed up at the sun again. "I will never lie to you, Horace Andrews, and so I am inclined not to mislead you now. Your life is about to take a turn that you could never have foreseen, one you cannot undo. Are you prepared for such a turning?"

Horace wanted to say yes, and he wanted to say no. There was so much to take in, so much left unknown, so much still to process into a logical shape. He couldn't promise that he was prepared. Instead he said the simple truth: "I have no idea."

Mr. Meister smiled. "And so with honesty we proceed. And indeed, the choice may already have been made. Who knows when the first turning has been taken?" With these words, he ushered Horace out into the sunlight, closing the door softly behind him.

CHAPTER SEVEN

The Fifth Key

HORACE SPENT THE AFTERNOON LYING ON HIS BED, HOLDING the box and gazing at it, running his finger along the silver seam of the lid. He opened it a few times, looking up at the ceiling and around his room, noting again the strange mix of clarity and cloudiness that the box gave to familiar items.

He hadn't forgotten what Mr. Meister had said about not opening the box without reason, but it was hard to resist. The old man's other piece of advice, though, was easy to follow. Horace put nothing inside the box. The thought seemed ridiculous anyway—somehow he felt that the box was supposed to remain empty.

The pouch that held the box had a strap and a buckle on the back, presumably so it could be fastened to a belt loop and carried around. At first Horace couldn't get why someone would ever want to do that, but when his father called him down for dinner, he suddenly understood. The thought of leaving the box behind, even for the short time dinner would take, was unbearable. And yet he had to keep it hidden. He didn't want anybody asking any questions. What to do? Experimentally, he buckled the pouch to a belt loop at his right hip. It peeked out from under his shirt—but just barely. He dug around in his dresser and found a few oversized shirts. He pulled one on, a hand-me-down from his father. It was a glaring yellow, featuring the logo of a restaurant called the Eleven Spot, someplace Horace had never been. But the hem came down below his hips, covering the box completely. Perfect. Now hidden, the box remained at his side all through dinner, and all through the evening. That night Horace fell asleep early and happily, with the box hidden beneath his pillow.

But the next day, Mother's Day, was miserable.

Horace awoke with the box in his hand and a troubled spiderweb of dream fragments clouding his head. He sat up, half remembering a dream in which the box was an unseen beacon over an endless landscape of green hills, calling out for Horace but never letting itself be found. "What do you want?" Horace said to the box now. "What am I supposed to do?" And through his bones and his flesh Horace felt—or thought he felt—something in return, as if the box were waiting for Horace to understand, to act. But Horace did not understand. He did not know what he was supposed to do. His uncertainty made the base of his skull ache, made his stomach heavy, turned his mood sour and surly. Nonetheless, he kept the box at his side.

After a late breakfast, his mother opened her gifts. His father had gotten her a massive two-volume collection of Sherlock Holmes stories that she'd clearly expected to get, and a moonstone pendant that she clearly hadn't. Horace looked down at his thumbs while they hugged and smooched. Next she unwrapped the raven-and-turtle statue, and when she was done she turned and gave Horace such a frank look of surprise that for a moment Horace thought he'd done something wrong. He'd been so distracted by the box that he'd almost forgotten that the statue wasn't just a statue—but of course his mother didn't know that. She shook her head, her face seeming to flicker on the edge of a question before she broke into a smile. "I love it," she said. "It's perfect."

Horace, meanwhile, was feeling worse and worse. After presents, he excused himself and returned to his room, taking the box from its pouch. Later, when his parents wanted to go down to the lakeshore, Horace told them he felt sick, and this wasn't exactly a lie. The box seemed to burn in his hands, carving out a hollow space in Horace's gut that he had no idea how to fill.

The next several days passed like a fever dream. Horace felt more and more connected to the box, but that connection became more sickly, more tainted, as if Horace was searching for an answer to a question that hadn't been asked. He took the box with him everywhere, keeping it hidden. At school he kept one hand on the box at all times, protecting it from the bumping and jostling in the halls between classes. He worried about the box almost constantly, struggling to pay attention in class. Ordinarily Horace loved school but now he found himself counting the hours until summer—only two weeks away now. It couldn't come soon enough. On Tuesday he realized he'd forgotten to do his project for social studies, a report about Wyoming. On Wednesday he even bombed one of Mr. Ludwig's pop quizzes.

"Troubles?" Mr. Ludwig said, smiling through his bushy beard as Horace slumped to the desk to turn the quiz in. Usually Horace was the first one done; today he was the last.

Horace shook his head. *Just one*, he thought.

And what a trouble it was, a trouble without a name. As the week wore on, Horace took the box out less and less, even in the privacy of his own room. Sometimes he opened the box and looked at his clock through it, noting how sharp and chiseled the numbers always looked. Sometimes he looked at the stars out his window—they too seemed to glow with extra precision. But mostly he kept it closed. He did manage to experiment with it a bit, cautiously.

He found that being separated from the box caused a painful, panicky sensation that became worse the farther he moved away, as if he were tied to the box by a great elastic cord anchored in his bones. He also learned that he was oriented to the box like a compass needle to north. He could point to the dead center of the box, even with his eyes closed, even through walls. But none of this could help him escape the growing sensation that the box was . . . *disappointed* in him. That it regretted having been found by Horace, maybe—a sad and sickening thought. The only good news was that Dr. Jericho was nowhere to be seen. Maybe the leestone was working after all.

After school on Thursday, five days since encountering the box at the House of Answers, Horace arrived home and discovered that, once again, he couldn't find his key. He slouched on the porch, waiting, one hand clasping the box at his side, his thoughts curling around it. At 4:18, his mother came home.

"Lose your key again?"

"No."

"Misplace it? Temporarily?"

"Maybe," Horace said.

She sighed. "Horace, I love you, but you've got to meet us halfway on this stuff, okay?"

"I know, I know."

Inside, Horace immediately closed himself in his room. He tried to force himself through his math homework, needing the distraction. But his brain wouldn't work right. After an hour of struggling, he gave up and got the box out. He lay on the floor, the box on his stomach, watching it roll with each breath he took—radiant and mysterious and maddening. Mr. Meister had warned him that the coming days would be difficult. And how true it was. Horace lay there letting the minutes flow by uncounted, trying to remember everything the old man had told him, wondering if he ought to go back to the House of Answers. But he knew he couldn't. If there were any answers to be found, he had to find them on his own. Mr. Meister had basically said as much.

"But he told me something would *happen*," he said to the box. Horace had always been a watcher, a patient observer. Now, though, just when he had absolutely no idea what he was supposed to be waiting for, he felt anything but patient.

Horace was still lying there at precisely six o'clock, when he heard a voice down in the hallway. Then footsteps on the stairs and a shout—his father, calling for him. "Coming," Horace tried to shout back, his voice croaking, and he rolled awkwardly to his feet. Before he could slip the box beneath his covers, his father gave two quick knocks and walked in.

Horace froze, holding the box tight against his belly.

"I've been calling you," his father said. "What are you doing?" His eyes dropped to the box. "What's that?"

Horace squeezed the box harder, trying to cover it completely. "Nothing."

"It's clearly something."

"It's just a thing."

His father held out a hand. "Can I see it?"

"No," said Horace.

His father's face crinkled in surprise. "What?"

Horace gathered his thoughts. He knew if he stood his ground, his father would probably let it go—but he also wouldn't forget. Better not to draw too much attention to the box. Horace forced his arms to unfold, holding out the box.

His father took hold of it. Immediately, a sharp spell of vertigo slammed Horace hard, as if the room had been violently twisted. Bile rose in his stomach. He stumbled and put a hand to his forehead.

"Where did you get this?" his father asked, oblivious.

There was nothing Horace could reasonably say right now that would not be a lie. "At a store."

"You bought this? Looks expensive." His father turned the box over and over in his hands. Horace swayed. "Is this one of those trick boxes? How do you open it?" He shook the box, listening.

"Don't shake it," Horace said, gritting his teeth and reaching out. "Just please give it here, all right?"

His father plucked at the lid with his thumb. "Seriously, how do you open this thing?"

Before he could stop himself, Horace lunged forward and ripped the box from his father's hands. The moment Horace took hold of it again, a rush of warm relief surged up through his arms, so powerful that he thought he might collapse.

His father, meanwhile, just stood there, his face confused and thundery. "What is going on with you, Horace?"

Horace's heart pounded. He tried to catch his breath, shocked by himself. "I just—you have to be careful with it."

"What have you got in there? Love notes?"

"No, no," Horace said, blushing. "Nothing's in there."

"Then let me see. Why are you being so weird?"

To open up the box in front of his father somehow seemed beyond indecent, but again Horace reasoned it out, convincing himself that less secrecy now meant more secrecy later. Slowly he held out the box, then swung the lid open with an easy twist of his thumb.

His father made a small noise of surprise, leaning over the box to peer inside. His eyes moved from the box to Horace and back again, his brow crinkling. Then he gave a little shake of his head. "There's nothing in here."

"I told you."

His father studied his face for a few moments more, then raised his eyebrows in surrender. "Well, that's just as well." He reached into his pocket and pulled out a shining silver key. "This is the real reason I'm here. Your mother tells me you lost yet another house key. How this sad phenomenon continues to happen, I don't want to know." He paused, as if waiting for an explanation, but Horace said nothing. "This'll be the fifth key we've given you this year, Horace. If you lose it, the next one's going to have to come out of your allowance."

"That's fine," Horace said, hardly listening.

"Does that sound fair?"

"Yes." Charge him for a million keys, but stay away from the box.

"This weekend I want you to come up with a plan for how you're going to keep track of this key. But for now, let's keep it in your box here, since you don't seem to be using it for anything else."

Before Horace could speak or even move, his father placed the key in the box. It scraped softly as he laid it down. Horace stood there, frozen. The box thrummed in his hands. He couldn't breathe.

"Close it up," his father said. "For my own sanity, I need to see it safe inside."

Horace did so, slowly, his face burning. He watched the gleam of the silver key as he slid the lid closed over it. The latch snicked. His hands went tingly and numb.

"What is wrong with you?" his father asked. "You okay?"

"Yes. Nothing's wrong."

His father pointed at the box. "Remember, next key isn't free."

"I got it, I got it." *Leave, just leave now,* he thought.

But his father lingered. Horace turned away. "You know, Horace," his father said, "I don't like having these talks. This isn't the kind of conversation I'd like to be having."

"It's fine," Horace said. He just needed him to go. He needed to get the box open again, take out the key.

"Okay. Well. Dinner in half an hour," his father said, and left. As soon as he was down the stairs, Horace leapt up and closed the door, desperate to get the key out, out, out.

He flicked the box open.

He blinked—once, twice.

The key was gone.

CHAPTER EIGHT

Night Experiments

HORACE TORE HIS ROOM APART.

He searched for the key high and low, under and over, all around where he and his father had been standing. He groped through the carpet inch by inch. He looked in completely impossible places—beneath his mattress, inside his marble chests, in his own pockets. He checked the box itself about a dozen times. No key, anywhere. But then he didn't really expect to find it.

He didn't expect to find it because as he searched, Mr. Meister's words came back to him. Comprehension dawned on Horace so fully and so blindingly that he felt stupid for not having figured it out sooner.

"You cannot keep anything inside the box."

Not a warning.

A simple fact.

At dinner, Horace ate voraciously, feeling hungry for the first time in nearly a week. Afterward he returned to his room and laid the box on his bedside table. He waited, planning. He wanted complete privacy for what had to come next. After good nights and lights out at ten, he spent the next hour watching the ceiling's glowing stars slowly lose their luminescence, fading eventually to black. He heard his parents getting into bed, saw their own light wink out beneath his door. Fifteen minutes later, at 11:03, he got up. He turned on his lamp.

The box gleamed in the lamplight, the twelve-spoked star alight. It seemed like the only true object in the room, alive with potential. There was no doubt that the box had made the key disappear. Horace had acted at last—or rather, his father had; a funny thought—and now the box was ready to talk. This, he understood at last, was the Find.

Horace slid the box open. Inside, the blue bottom glinted. He lifted the box to look through it, as if he would be able to see where the key had gone, even though he knew that was not how it worked. He looked around the dim room— *the crisp mess of the desk; stars on the ceiling sharp and alight; the bedside lamp, strangely dark; the glowing numbers of the clock, reading 11:04 now; everything thick and textured, shifting and keen.* Horace rose to look out the window: *darkness revealed, clouds low and sculpted, trees thick and rustling, the old red canoe beside the toolshed like a half-closed eye, and there!—a quick dart of movement.*

Horace lowered the box and squinted into the night, but

saw nothing. He raised the box once more, and with that extra clarity, saw again—*a stealthy black shape along the side of the canoe, small and swift and sure; a disappearance behind the shed.* He was startled at first but then realized it had to be Loki. Somehow the cat had gotten out. He would be at the back door in the morning, mewing to be let in. "Done being dangerous?" his mother would ask.

Horace closed the box and put his plan into motion. He quietly gathered up a few small items from around the room—an eraser, a couple of expendable marbles, a plastic D&D figurine—and knelt beside his bed. *"You cannot keep anything in the box."* Right. But that didn't mean he couldn't *put* anything in the box. And now that he understood that, it was time to experiment.

He chose the eraser first. It seemed like a harmless thing. He opened the box, eraser in hand, and said softly, "Okay?" But he felt no hesitation from the box—no resistance, no alarm. Just a kind of quiet patience, maybe. He put the eraser inside. Nothing happened. Horace swallowed. It was 11:10. He thought he would wait until 11:11, a suitably memorable time for such a momentous occasion. He watched his clock, unblinking, and as soon as the zero blinked to a one he closed the lid. He felt a faint tingle in his hands, a strange living pulse.

"I felt that," he said. "I felt that before."

He opened the lid. The eraser was gone.

As he sat gazing into the empty box, Horace knew he

should be feeling shock, or wonder, but more than either of these things, he felt regret. He was disappointed in himself for having taken so long to discover what the box could do. Maybe he'd simply been too afraid to let the box speak to him clearly. He'd believed all along that the box had to remain empty—and it turned out to be true! Just not at all in the way he'd imagined.

Horace placed the D&D figurine in the box—an elven archer—and threw in the two marbles for good measure. He held the box over his head, looking up at it. The archer's form and the two marbles were just visible—smeary silhouettes through the glass. Horace slid the lid into place, hoping he'd be able to see what was happening inside, but as soon as it closed, he could see nothing. There was no flash of light or anything—just the tingle, and then: no more archer, no more marbles.

Horace leaned back against his bed, the box beside him. He knew that objects could not be completely destroyed, leaving nothing behind. Plus, it just didn't make sense that the box would work that way—what would be the point? No, the only reasonable hypothesis was that the box was sending these objects somewhere else, a tantalizing thought. "Teleportation," Horace whispered aloud. But if that's what was happening, where were these objects going?

It was time to put the next part of his plan into motion. He crept to his desk, opened a notebook, and began to write in his neatest handwriting.

> My name is Horace Andrews. If you are the finder of
> this message, please contact me immediately.

He thought hard about what to say next. He had never before written a note to be delivered by teleportation. He needed to convince the finders of this message to tell him where they were—to tell him where the box was sending things. He tried to think what sort of message would make him, Horace, respond to a strange note that appeared out of nowhere.

> This note has gotten to you by a power I can't
> control and don't understand. It is a mystery I am
> desperate to solve. I can only solve it with your help.
> Please believe me, I am 100 percent serious. Here is my
> address:
> Horace Andrews
> 3318 N. Bromley Street
> Chicago, IL 60634

He read over what he'd written. He crossed out *can't control* and wrote *haven't mastered*. After the address, he added:

> USA

He considered it one last time, and then added a final line. After all, you just never knew:

79

Horace read the note over about twenty more times and decided it would do. If there was anyone—or anything—on the other side, surely this would get a response. He folded the note it until it was small enough to fit inside the box. On one side he wrote PLEASE READ, and on the other NOT GARBAGE. He put the note inside the box.

Just then, a soft scratch at the door yanked Horace's heart into his throat. It came again, and Horace realized with a sigh of relief—it was only Loki. Horace leaned over and cracked the door. The cat sauntered in out of the shadows, brushing awkwardly against Horace's leg.

"You're just in time," Horace whispered, latching the door. He gripped the box firmly. He closed the lid. He felt that prickly vibration in his fingertips again—the note had been delivered. Now all he had to do was . . .

Horace frowned. Now he had to wait. It was 11:59; the new day was about to begin. How many more days would he have to wait before he got any answers? He realized now that he should have listed his phone number on the note, or his email—not his address. Addresses were too slow. And speaking of addresses, what had he been thinking? *Earth?* Logically speaking, that was a pointless thing to say . . . wasn't it?

Frustrated, he rummaged through some of his stuff. Idly he picked up a blue pencil sharpener and sent it through the box—a tingle, and it was gone. The act was so satisfying—the box was actually *doing* something—that he did it again, this time sending a plastic golden coin. And he kept on going: a broken toy dragster, a dried-out chunk of modeling clay, a probably-dead battery. The top half of a toy dragon head, a poker chip, an entire handful of pushpins. Loki jumped up onto the desk to watch, and Horace kept going absentmindedly, not really sure of the reasons but caught up in the sheer momentum of the act—bit by bit, the mass of his room was shrinking. It was vanishing slowly, like a pool down a drain. Or not even like that, it was just . . . ceasing to be here. In theory, if he could break the whole room down into small-enough pieces, he could send it all through the box, right? The whole house, even, sent away—wherever *away* was. He imagined a fuzzy, tentacled alien cautiously examining an unknown artifact: a toy dragster with a missing wheel. He imagined a boy in a distant room playing with a small plastic elf. He saw his note, untranslatable, encased in glass in some extraterrestrial museum.

Eventually, most of what remained on his desk was too big or too important to send: a calculator, a postcard from Alex and Martin in Maine, a stopwatch that was once his father's, a pair of scissors. Loki, of course. Horace spotted a Super Ball lurking beneath an old workbook, let the cat sniff it, and sent it on through last of all. He pictured it falling out of thin air under a stormy sky, dropping unseen into a broad blue sea.

He opened the box one more time and let Loki look inside. "See?" he said. "Gone. Disappeared into the night like—"

He stopped. "Wait a minute," he said, remembering. Just an hour ago he'd caught a quick glimpse of the cat, disappearing behind the toolshed.

Outside.

After everyone had gone to bed.

Goosebumps swept down Horace's arms as he stared at the cat. "Loki . . . who let you in?"

CHAPTER NINE

Arrivals

HORACE DID NOT SLEEP WELL THAT NIGHT. HE LAY CURLED under his covers, the box on one side and Loki on the other, trying not to imagine how the cat had gotten inside, or—worse—what might've come in with him. He knew it was silly, but it wasn't easy to keep Dr. Jericho from creeping into his thoughts. He tried to tell himself that Mr. Meister's leestone was working just as it was supposed to. Logically speaking, the cat he'd seen in the backyard must not have been Loki after all. Or maybe his mother had slipped down sometime between eleven and midnight and let Loki in.

What other explanation could there be?

The night passed slowly, the minutes creeping by. The carefully plotted constellations on his ceiling gradually faded from sight, but not before they started to take on new shapes in Horace's eyes—leering faces and tall, stooped figures. At some point, however, Horace must have fallen asleep. He woke to his father's voice—and sunshine. He rolled over and felt Loki's fur against his face. The cat stretched and yawned.

"Loki's home," Horace slurred.

"So I see," his father said drily. "Let's go. Time for school."

Horace got up and got ready. He watched Loki sleep as he dressed, trying to shake loose the cobwebs of the night before. But all day at school he was extra muddled, not really waking up until the final bell rang, when he abruptly remembered he didn't have his house key. The key had disappeared to wherever the box sent it. He'd have to tell his parents that he had lost the key again, even though this was the first time it *really and truly* wasn't his fault. He couldn't stand the thought of waiting on the porch for his mother two days in a row, so he hung around on the school steps for a while and caught a later bus that would get him home after his mother arrived. The bus was back on its regular route now, but when it cruised past Wexler Street he found himself staring out the window, still feeling lost.

At home, he made his excuses and went to his room. He put the box on the desk, leaving it in its pouch and laying a workbook over it. He couldn't bear to look at it right now. He examined the stars on his ceiling, remembering the rough night he'd had, and decided then and there to redo them all. He'd take them down, put up new constellations—peaceful ones like Lyra the harp and Circinus the compass. That would take his mind off of everything else for a while.

He got out a bin full of glow-in-the-dark stars and one of his astronomy books. He sat on the floor with scissors and got to work trimming the stars down so they were round, the way stars truly were, making different sizes for the different stars he'd need. Soon he was deeply engrossed. Loki came in to watch, as usual, keeping a respectful but curious distance. And then, just as he was peering at the star chart for Eridanus the river, he caught sight of a glinting movement, a falling shimmer. He flinched as something dropped heavily into the bin of stickers. A shower of stars exploded upward.

Loki leapt to his feet, bristling and wide-eyed. Horace sat frozen, scissors in one hand and stars scattered across his lap, the floor. "Was that you?" he asked Loki, but the cat was an arm's length away.

Horace reached cautiously into the bin. Beneath the white and yellow stars, he spied the glint of something shiny and silver. Horace plucked the silver thing from the pile.

It was the house key.

The key his father had put into the box yesterday evening.

The key that had vanished from the box.

Horace looked stupidly into the air. Where had it come from?

He stood, brushing stars from his lap. He spun in a circle, still holding the key, looking everywhere, but there was nothing to see. They key had come back to him, but he had no idea how, or why.

"Lost?" said a voice at the door. His mother.

Horace closed his fist around the key. "No, I . . . ," he said slowly. "No, not lost." *Found*, he thought to himself. *But how?*

"Listen, I know it's chess night, but Dad and I thought we could all do dinner and a movie. The three of us. And maybe some ice cream afterward?"

"Um, yeah. Sure."

"Great. It's a little after six—"

"Six oh four," Horace said absently, slipping the key into his pants pocket.

"Right. We'll need to leave in forty-five minutes if we want to catch dinner before the movie at nine. And then we'll do chess tomorrow, okay?"

"Chess movie, right," Horace said. He pushed little questing thoughts at the box on his desk, but nothing came back at him—no feeling. Nothing. The box was quiet.

Horace, of course, did not want to go to the movie. He wanted to stay home. The key had returned, and more than anything he wanted—needed—to perform more experiments with the box. But of course he could say none of this.

Forty-five minutes later, as he and his parents headed out the front door, Loki escaped. He shot out like a shadow, squeezing through Horace's awkward attempt to pin him against the doorjamb with his foot.

"Danger time," his mother said mildly, watching him go.

"What I don't understand," Horace's father said, "is where he goes, and how he finds his way back."

Hearing these words, Horace could almost feel the key in his pocket, heavy and foreign and mysterious. "Tell me about it," he said.

LATE THAT NIGHT, Horace sat in the backseat of the car. They were headed home at last after an enormous deep-dish pizza, a movie that was almost one hundred percent boring—almost—and ice cream cones that no one needed. With his left hand, he held tight to the box in its pouch. With his right, he fiddled with the cold, sharp shape of the house key.

All evening, the reappearance of the key had been consuming his thoughts. At first he'd theorized that the key had been sent back to him by someone—or something—on the other end of the box. But logically, that didn't make much sense. Why would the key come back alone? Why hadn't anything else been sent through—the eraser or the archer or a response to his note? Plus, if true, this theory meant that there had to be *two* boxes, didn't it? His, and a second one to send the stuff back. But Horace knew somewhere deep in his heart and his flesh and his bones that there was only one glass-bottom box. No, he was missing something simple. Something just a step away—but a strange step away, a step sideways and back, or a step into the air, or a step into another pair of shoes entirely.

And then they went to the movie. During the movie, there was a scene in which a boy buried a toy truck in his backyard, and then, decades later, this same boy—now an old man—dug it up. It had been lying there undisturbed for years and was now reemerging into that distant future. Horace had barely been watching, but when the old man pulled the truck from the dirt, Horace went as still as wood, staring. Something shifted and settled in his head, and the whole pile of thought he'd been juggling all night collapsed into something simple and clear. "Oh!" he cried out, sitting up straight. His father shushed him.

Now, headed home, Horace felt crystalline and sure, the way he felt when a long, tense stretch of examining the chessboard ended in a moment of clarity and the perfect move. The box was a warm glow at his side, steady and comforting. He tried to give a name to what was coming from it. Not disappointment, not anymore. Instead, power. Presence. Reassurance. When they got home, he said good night to his parents and headed for his room. It was nearly midnight. He turned on his light, eyes already trained on the carpet beside his bed.

Four shapes, still and sharp and clear.

An eraser. Two marbles. An elven archer.

Kneeling, Horace took them into his hands. He'd been convinced that the box was a teleportation device of some kind, that it had been sending the objects somewhere else, but that was all wrong. It wasn't a teleporter.

It was a time machine.

Horace's face broke into a smile so wide it hurt. The box sent things not to a different place, but to a different time—one day into the future, to be exact. It all fit: the key going into the box a little after six o'clock on Thursday, and then falling into the bin of glow-in-the-dark stars twenty-four hours later. It had reappeared exactly where he and his father had been standing the day before, when his father put the key in the box. The marbles and the eraser and the archer had disappeared through the box last night at precisely 11:11, and now here they were, exactly where their journey had begun, having moved not through space, but through *time*. One day into the future. And suddenly Horace understood: the silver emblem on the front of the box wasn't merely a star; it was the sun. Twelve long rays and twelve short, twenty-four total for the hours in a day. Everything made sense. Horace swung toward his desk. It was 11:58, and if all this was true, that meant that any second now, the note—

A quick knock, and then Horace's door cracked open. His father peered in. "You're still awake."

"I'm sleep!" Horace said shrilly. "Sleepy, I mean. Very."

His father cocked his head quizzically, and in the same instant at Horace's desk there came a soft *pop*, very faint, like a plop of ketchup hitting the floor. Horace stared as last night's note, sent just before midnight, materialized out of thin air and tumbled onto the desk. He sucked in a great breath of wonder and alarm, then tried to pretend he was only yawning. *I was right!* he thought.

His father leaned in farther. He hadn't seen the note reappear, but the tightly folded paper was coming undone now, opening slightly. His father spotted it and came inside, picking it up. "'Not garbage,'" he recited. "'Please read.' Sounds important."

"It's just a school thing." Thinking quickly, Horace invented a story about Mr. Ludwig's class, a new project having to do with the SETI program, the Search for Extra-Terrestrial Intelligence.

His father opened the note and read it over. "Looking for aliens," he said.

"Yes."

"Going to pass them a note. Invite them to dinner, maybe."

"Well," Horace told him, feeling flustered, "there's a whole thing involved." It was now precisely midnight. At this time last night, he had just been about to send the blue pencil sharpener through the box. Things were about to get . . . interesting. His father had to go, of course, but instead he just stood there and made a couple more jokes about the note. Horace laughed dimly, trying to sound as sleepy as possible.

At last his father said good night and left. No sooner had he closed the door than there was another *pop*. The pencil sharpener materialized and clattered onto the desk, dropping out of nowhere. Horace let out a giddy sound of relief and ran over, snatching it up.

Horace ran his hand through his hair, tugging at it. "That was close," he whispered. Another soft *pop*, and a golden plastic coin fell, glinting faintly. Horace lunged, almost grabbing it out of the air. "You're here. You're back." He tried not to laugh as objects continued to materialize out of thin air, a new delivery every several seconds. They appeared as if by magic, with just that barely audible pop. No flash of light, no nothing. *Pop . . . pop . . . pop.* Item after item. And through it all, he marveled to think that—in a way—he'd been holding these very same objects in his hand just moments ago. He wondered if they might still be slightly warm from yesterday's touch.

The Super Ball was last. He caught it on a hop.

Horace breathed. Now that it was over, the room felt rudely silent and small. Flat. With the channel to the past closed, it was as if the world had lost a dimension—which in a way, it had. He wrestled with what had just happened. He owned a time machine—a small one, sure, but still. Time travel was the stuff of stories, of science fiction. And in most of those stories, it turned out to be dangerous. Messing around with time could theoretically lead to all sorts of trouble. Lives changed. Histories reversed. Paradoxes. But right at this moment, to be honest, Horace hardly cared. What was happening right now was the most amazing thing that had ever happened to him, danger or no danger.

Horace's brain was now in high gear. Even now, knowing what the box was capable of, he felt like he'd wandered into a huge room full of everything he *didn't* know. He was only twelve, after all, but he had access to a power that shouldn't even exist. And for what purpose? What was he to do? He needed instructions. He needed peace of mind. He needed . . . answers.

At once he thought of Mr. Meister. But no sooner had the thought materialized than he shoved it away. Mr. Meister had wanted him to discover what the box did on his own, and Horace had done that. Maybe the old man would open up now, tell him the rest, but somehow Horace didn't feel ready. He himself wasn't yet satisfied with what he knew. The box was a time machine, yes, but how was that even possible? How could such a machine work? No, if Horace was going to go back to the House of Answers, he was going to go back there with some answers of his own.

He turned on his computer. He set the box down beside the keyboard. He got online, clicked on the search bar, and slowly typed:

is time travel possible?

He glanced at the box. "It's a rhetorical question, I know, because obviously it's possible. But I have to start somewhere."

He hit enter. His screen filled with hits. He leaned forward and began to read.

———✿———

CHAPTER TEN

What the Universe Would Allow

"TIME TRAVEL?" MR. LUDWIG SAID, HIS VOICE SQUEAKING scratchily as he raised it in mock disbelief. "Are you looking to take a trip into the past? Right some wrongs? Maybe take another crack at that quiz you bombed last week?"

Horace shook his head. He barely even remembered taking that quiz. "Future, actually," he said, and was surprised by how serious his voice sounded, how low and loud as it echoed through the empty lab. It was Monday after school. Horace had waited until all the other students had already gone before approaching his teacher's desk.

"Then you're in luck," said Mr. Ludwig. "The future is probably easier than the past."

"That's what I read," said Horace. "The past is already set, but the future is still full of possibilities. Plus, if it's possible to travel into the past, why haven't we seen any visitors from the future?"

"You've already done some research on this, I see."

Over the weekend, Horace had done a lot of searching and reading. And then there was the box itself—in a way, he'd already done some research that Mr. Ludwig would hardly be able to imagine. "Research, yeah. But I still have some questions."

"I'll see if I can help. Tell me what you know."

"Okay," Horace said. "From what I understand, it seems like time travel might sort of be possible, and that speed might be the key."

Mr. Ludwig sat back and fluffed his beard, his eyes twinkling. "Explain."

"Well, first, it's not so much that we can travel *through* time. It's that one person can experience time differently than another person."

Another twinkle. "You mean like how time flies for somebody who's on vacation, but goes slow for somebody who's stuck at school?"

"No, no. Not like that. I mean time can *actually* go slower or faster for different people in different places. Like, clocks and everything."

"Very good. Just testing you. But what did you mean when you said speed is the key?"

"Well, because it turns out—and this is the part I don't really understand—that our experience of time is connected to how fast we're moving. Especially if we're moving really, really fast."

"Close to the speed of light," Mr. Ludwig said.

"Yes. And it's sort of backward, because the faster we go, the slower time passes for us."

"But will it feel slow?"

"No. Even if we're physically moving really, really fast, time will still seem normal to us. Clocks will seem normal. But in reality, time will be passing slowly, relative to everybody else who isn't moving as fast."

"That's right. It's that relative part that's so important: the faster we move, the more slowly time will pass for us— *compared to someone who is not moving as fast.* So, for example, if person A is standing still, and person B is moving really, really fast—like in a spaceship, moving at speeds approaching the speed of light—each of them will think they are experiencing time normally. That is, they won't notice anything strange about themselves, or the passage of time." Mr. Ludwig fluffed his beard again, a sure sign that he was concentrating hard. "But *relative* to each other, time will progress much more slowly for moving person B than it does for stationary person A."

"Right. But why?"

"That I can't explain, man. I mean, I really am unable to. It's Einstein, the theory of relativity. Relative, right? Very heavy stuff—I understand the idea of the theory, but I couldn't really explain how it works. I'm no Einstein. For now, we just have to accept that the faster you move, the more slowly time will pass."

"Okay."

"Now the next question is, how could that concept be used to travel through time?"

Horace considered. He understood the concept, sort of, but it was hard to put into words.

Mr. Ludwig got up and turned to the chalkboard. He drew a dot and labeled it 2015. "Let's try this. Here I am on earth, today. Now let's say thirty years go by." He drew a high, narrow arch, up to the top of the blackboard and back down. At the top of the arch he wrote MR. LUD = 30 YEARS. At the other end of the arch, he made a second dot. "So what year would this be?"

"It'd be 2045."

"Right," Mr. Ludwig said, labeling it.

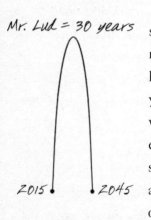

"But now let's say that in 2015, you, Horace, set out on a trip through space, traveling at a really high speed. Much, much faster than me here on earth. And remember that because you're going so fast, time inside your spaceship will be moving much more slowly than it is on earth, even though you won't notice it. Let's say you plan to be gone for one year—one year according to you, and according to the clocks on your spaceship—before you return to earth. Could you draw that on here? And remember that we're just estimating the times, to make a point." He held out the chalk.

Horace stood and took it from him. He considered the

diagram, and then bent and drew a short straight line from the 2015 dot to the 2045 dot. Beneath it he wrote HORACE = 1 YEAR.

"Perfect," Mr. Ludwig said, watching. "And why is that time travel?"

"Because I've taken a shortcut to the future. I'll feel like I've been gone only a year, like it should be 2016—but on earth it'll actually be 2045. I've traveled into the future."

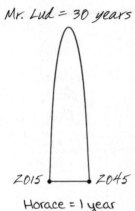

Mr. Lud = 30 years

2015 ● ━━━ ● 2045

Horace = 1 year

"Exactly. To me, though, it'll just seem like you were in outer space for a really long time and hardly aged at all while you were there. Pretty cool, huh?"

Horace thought hard, feeling a deep thrill at the wonder of it all. He already knew that time travel was possible—he'd seen it—yet he couldn't seem to apply any of this to the box. The box had nothing to do with speed. Nothing was actually traveling. Was it?

"I think I understand all this," Horace said. "Sort of. But do you think you could build a device that did all that without traveling fast? That could send things to the future without going fast?"

"Could *I*?" Mr. Ludwig fluffed his beard again. "No, I can't. But is it possible?" He shrugged. "If you're looking for someone to tell you that it's outside the realm of possibility, you've got the wrong guy. I do think it's something the universe would allow, even if we don't yet know exactly what all the rules are."

All the way home, Horace thought hard. Sometimes he felt close to understanding how the box worked—at least in theory—but whenever he got close to grasping the idea whole, it slid away, evaporating. It was like the way dim stars appeared brighter in your peripheral vision, but as soon as you looked directly at them, they faded from sight.

Mr. Ludwig hadn't done much to clear up the mysteries of the box, but he did have Horace asking a new question: What was a trip through the box like? If an object placed inside the box was taking a shortcut to the future, Horace wanted to know just how short that shortcut seemed for the object itself. But how could he find out?

That night, he came up with an experiment that would have made Mr. Ludwig proud. He got out his father's old stopwatch, one that actually had a moving hand. At 8:02, he clicked the stopwatch's green button, starting it up, and then placed it inside the box. He listened to the watch tick as the red hand swept around. As soon as the hand hit the ten-second mark, he snapped the box closed.

At 8:01 the next evening, Horace sat on his bed, his eyes trained on the spot where the watch would arrive. When the stopwatch finally materialized, loud and startling, it dropped gently onto the covers, the red hand still moving. It was just ticking forward to eleven seconds. Apparently, the trip from one day to the next took almost no time at all—less than a second. Horace scooped up the watch, letting it continue to run, marveling. He considered the implications while the watch ticked forward. As the second hand approached the half-minute mark, he put the watch back into the box. "Keep going," he said, and at thirty seconds exactly he snapped the box closed, sending the watch forward yet another day.

Horace was comforted by his discovery that the trip through the box was a short one. Between the time an object disappeared one day and when it reappeared the next, it had to be *somewhere*, didn't it? It was easy to imagine dark voids, airless alien dimensions, spinning vortexes, frozen abysses. The idea that sent objects weren't spending much time at all in . . . wherever they were . . . relieved Horace greatly.

And with that relief, he knew what his next experiment would be.

Horace crept down the stairs and eased the back door open, slipping into the cool, wet night. Ghostly yellow lights blinked and floated across in the lawn, dozens upon dozens. "Perfect," he said. He went out into the dusk, and on his first gentle swipe, caught a lightning bug in his cupped palm.

He brought the firefly back up to his room. He opened the box and gradually maneuvered the bug inside.

"Come on, little bug. This is for science."

The firefly began to motor uselessly around the inside of the box like a car with its blinker on. Horace watched it—a living thing. He had no idea what would happen to it once the lid was closed.

"I'm sorry. In advance. If things go bad."

He closed the box. His hands lit up with the familiar tingle—perhaps a little stronger this time. Horace opened the box again. The lightning bug was gone.

It would be another full day before Horace found out if the bug had survived. Horace felt a little guilty, but he told himself that wherever the bug was now, no time at all was passing.

And then he saw a very faint flash of light inside the box. But no, not inside—farther away. Deeper in, somehow. A blinking light. He held the box high and looked closer. There it was again. *Flash. Flash. Flash.* The lightning bug—was it caught in the glass? Horace brought the box close to his face, so close that instead of looking at the glass, he was looking through it, and through the glass he saw: *nothing but the ceiling of his room, glow-in-the-dark stars, and then—flash.* But it wasn't in the glass or the box; it was out there, in the room. Flying around.

Horace lowered the box, expecting to see the firefly buzzing around the room. It must have escaped somehow. But when he looked, he could see nothing. No lightning bug. He looked again through the box, and his skin began to prickle with excitement—*a flash, over to the left, and then the silhouette of the dark circling bug itself, wings whirring; a few seconds later, another flash.* He turned, following the flight of the bug as it flew around the room, looking through the box as though he were looking through a pair of binoculars. His room, this room. And yet the bug was not here—it was only there, through the box.

"Oh, please," Horace said. "Oh, please please please." He

turned with the box—*the door, closed; the desk, messy; the bed . . .
lying there, a small shape, perfectly round.* Chilled, Horace bent in
for a closer look. The stopwatch. The stopwatch he'd just sent. It
wasn't here, not now, but he could see it through the box.

Horace straightened, eyes fixed through the glass. He slid
his free hand around the back side of the box, where he ought
to be able to see it through the glass. He felt a queasy lurch in
his stomach as his hand passed in front of his face but through
the box he saw nothing, as though his hand didn't exist. And
it didn't. Not where he was looking. Horace spun farther, and
when he got to the bed, he nearly dropped the box, even though
he was half looking for what he saw there—*someone sitting on the
bed, watching; not just someone, no . . . Horace himself, looking large
and serious and staring hard but not quite straight ahead, a piece of
paper in his hands, propped upright on his belly, meant to be read—
five thick-lettered words.*

"Oh, holy creeping cow," breathed Horace—this Horace,
himself, here now.

The sign the other Horace held read:

YES HORACE,
THIS IS TOMORROW

PART TWO

The Girl Who Walked through Walls

CHAPTER ELEVEN

The Weight of Tomorrow

HORACE SAT AT HIS DESK, FROWNING THOUGHTFULLY AT HIS sandwich. There was nothing wrong with it—thin-sliced hard salami on plain bread, Horace's favorite—and he had every reason to believe it was delicious. The box, in fact, had already revealed to him that he would eat it.

And so he thought perhaps he wouldn't.

It had been five days since Horace had discovered what the box allowed him to do, but sometimes he still had to say the words out loud to himself, just to make it seem real: "I can see the future." He'd been seeing the future through the box all along, of course; he just hadn't realized it. That night he'd seen Loki in the backyard, for example, only to discover him inside the house an hour later—he now knew that the Loki he'd seen outside, through the box, was the Loki of the future. And some of the other things he'd seen—the warehouse, his own clock, the stars in the sky—he'd been seeing those things one day in advance, but there'd been no way to know it.

The past few days, he'd been more choosy about what he looked at, and the box had revealed a host of fascinating sights. His own future self, always looking big and clumsy and shaggy headed, just like today. His mother and his father, reading the next day's paper or watching the next day's television. He'd seen tomorrow's windswept trees where today's sat still and calm, seen today's shirt in tomorrow's dirty laundry.

The box was a blazing fire of temptation. From tests at school to the weather to a simple greedy urge to gather knowledge no one else had, a big part of Horace wanted to be glued to the box all the time. But he tried—*tried*—to use it sparingly. Horace strongly believed that this newfound power was not meant to be used carelessly. Mr. Meister had said as much—*"You should not open the box without reason."* The box itself seemed to encourage this kind of caution, something Horace felt instinctively, in the same way you might know you were coming down with a cold before you actually felt sick. Horace was now so in tune with the box that he could no more betray its wishes than he could cut off his own arm. And there was another thing, too, something harder to describe. Horace was beginning to understand that seeing the future meant living a kind of folded life, a life in which the present always wrestled with expectations from the past. He found himself measuring what happened to him against what the box said was *supposed* to happen, and this seemed—there was no other word for it—bad.

Once, the box showed him a dead mouse in tomorrow's laundry room, one of Loki's victims—though *today* the mouse was almost certainly still alive somewhere, unaware of what was about to happen to him. The box showed him a fire truck flashing by out front, and when the fire truck actually did scream by the next day, responding to some unplanned-for and unforeseeable crisis, Horace was struck with a sadness he didn't totally understand. It was distressing to know that something bad was going to happen but to be powerless to stop it.

But above all, Horace had learned one very important thing about the box and its visions of the future.

It could be wrong.

Last Friday before dinner, for instance, he managed to observe nearly a minute of the next evening's meal—pork tenderloins and asparagus, gestures and unheard conversations, the whole scene shifting wildly between blurry and clear. And then on Saturday, halfway through that actual dinner, Loki jumped up onto the table, a moment Horace had seen hazily through the box. Just as Loki landed, Horace—with reflexes only a knowledge of the future could have given him—put a hand in the cat's face. Disaster ensued: scrambling cat, sliding placemats, tipped wineglass, scattered asparagus . . . angry father. None of which the box had revealed. Horace didn't know who or what to blame, or if "blame" was even the right word. The whole episode made him sick to his stomach.

He was learning that there were consequences for looking through the box.

This incident helped him figure out why the box made some things look clear and other things look blurry. The clearer the viewing, the more likely it was to actually happen. Routine or regular events—meals, arrivals and departures, sleep, clocks—were usually very clear, and tended to happen just as the box showed. But if the box was hazy, that meant the future was in doubt and might not come to pass. Highly random events, meanwhile, flickered violently and were impossible to predict, as Horace learned when he tried to watch the lottery drawing on TV.

The scientist in Horace could not always resist testing the box. And it was the scientist in Horace that made him decide not to eat the salami sandwich this particular Sunday afternoon, even though the box had said he would. Never before had he *deliberately* set out to alter a future the box had revealed—the box was wrong sometimes, yes, but he had never *deliberately tried* to make it be wrong.

Horace was doing this partly because of the sign he'd seen himself holding, that first night: YES HORACE, THIS IS TOMOR-ROW. He'd realized the next day that in order to make that future come true, he'd have to actually write the sign and sit on his bed with it at exactly the time he'd seen it the night before. He'd done that, a queasy feeling of déjà vu coming over him as he wrote the sign he'd already read. But ever since, he'd been going over that moment again and again, wondering what would have happened if he had chosen *not* to write the sign.

Horace put down his sandwich without taking a single bite, a direct contradiction of the future he'd already seen. Immediately his vision bent, as though the world was wrinkling around him. A fierce, dense pain stabbed through his head and down into his belly. He rose, staggering, clutching his skull. He felt twisted and out of his body, like he was trapped in a bout of extreme dizziness, or a clinging dream of falling. It scared him. It hurt.

Horace stood, holding his head. He felt for the box, like feeling for the walls of a hallway in the dark. The box was there. It was not alarmed. It simply seemed to want a new future, a different path to replace the eating of the sandwich. So Horace threw the plate into the hallway. It bounced, scattering the sandwich across the carpet. His head took another stabbing lurch, and he swayed to the bed. But the box spoke to him, a steady, supporting hum. Horace lay down on the bed, looking at the stars on his ceiling, naming them one by one. Slowly—very slowly—the real world swam back into focus, began to feel solid again.

He was still lying there an hour later, still gathering himself, when a voice startled him to his feet. His mother's perplexed face peeked in, reading glasses perched high on her forehead. "Horace, why is there a sandwich in the hall?"

He let a few unlikely lies filter through his mind, but just said, "I'm sorry. I had a moment."

"Well, moments happen. But later we clean them up."

"Yes. Sorry. It was recent."

"You okay?"

"I am . . ." Horace felt for the firmness of his presence in this instant, like feeling for the sturdiness of ice underfoot. "I am good," he said. And he was.

His mother glanced back into the hallway. "I'm leaving that. Try to beat the cat to it, okay?" She came in, wandering past his desk. The box lay there, right out in the open. She let her fingers drift just over the top of it as she passed by, nearly touching it, freezing Horace in place. She crossed the room and slid onto the floor beside the bed, banging her head softly against the wall. "Ow," she said.

They sat in silence awhile, and then, before Horace could stop himself, he asked, "Hey, Mom, if you could see into your own future, would you?"

"You mean actually witness it?"

"Yes."

"No," she said immediately. "I wouldn't want to be distracted from my life by a script that tells me how it's supposed to go." She nodded, sure of herself, and Horace thought how neatly she'd described exactly what he'd been feeling. "Why do you ask?"

"Oh . . . we were talking about it in science class. Time travel. The future."

"Horace, let me tell you something about the future. Everything the future is made of is happening right now."

Late that night, Horace was still up. His mother's words had stayed with him, but he wasn't thinking about the future just now. He was thinking more about the past—at any moment, the lightning bug would be arriving from yesterday.

When the firefly had materialized first after its maiden voyage through the box, Horace had expected it to eventually die, to be honest. But it hadn't. And a few hours later, having watched the bug blink across the ceiling of stars like an airplane, Horace had done something impulsive: he got up, recaptured the bug, and sent it back into the box. That was how it had begun. When the bug reappeared the next night, Horace let it fly around a bit, then sent it forward again. And again the next night. And every night since.

Horace wasn't sure how the bug felt about it, but he himself had no plans to stop. Somehow, sending objects through the box—even living objects—seemed like a game, whereas spying on the future felt like a very serious endeavor. Plus Horace reasoned that he was extending the bug's life span. By a lot. According to his research, lightning bugs normally lived for two months. But in the last four days, the bug had actually aged only twelve minutes. The rest of the time, it was traveling, aging very little or not at all. At the rate it was going, Horace calculated, the lightning bug might outlive Horace himself. He looked forward to greeting the bug again every night. He viewed it as an adventurer, a pioneer. He had even come up with a name for it.

At 11:22, a tiny *pop* announced the bug's arrival.

"Greetings, Rip," Horace said softly. He let the bug circle overhead for half a minute, then scooped it up with the box and sent it on. He peeked through the box, catching sight of the bug again in tomorrow's room. He checked it this way each night, a kind of maintenance test for the box. "You are flying," he told the bug. "You will be flying."

He went to the window. Not much was going on in Monday's backyard, although it looked as though it would be windy: *swaying trees, a car sliding by a block over on Glendon, the toolshed sagging and rundown, the red canoe*—and wait! Horace inhaled sharply.

A shadow on the lawn. A running figure. *A small figure, hood up around its face, scurrying across the side lawn, pressing itself against the shed.* Horace looked up quickly, trying to get a better view with his naked eye, forgetting he was looking at tomorrow. He hastily checked the box again. There she was, still standing in the shadows along the shed—the girl from the bus, from the alley behind the bookstore. She was here, sneaking into his backyard in the middle of the night.

Horace felt a surge of anger—Dr. Jericho was interested in this girl. She'd admitted it. What if she ended up leading the thin man here tomorrow night? She had to leave, now. Or not *now*, exactly, but . . . Horace held the box tight, watching the dark shed, waiting for her to move.

He didn't have long to wait. But when the moment came, he was utterly unprepared for what he saw: *the girl turning, not away from the shed, but into it, her shoulder disappearing into the wall itself, as if it were water; now a leg vanishing, and half her torso; her hooded head, swiveling first into the wall and then out again, reappearing briefly for one last look around the yard; now another step, and her body was swallowed, trailing arm and trailing leg vanishing last, gone inside the shed.*

Horace blinked. He blinked again. She could walk through walls.

For a moment he thought maybe this was a new kind of uncertainty the box hadn't shown him before, an illusion. But he knew it wasn't. He could see the future. She could walk through walls. Did she have something like he did, some instrument that gave her this power? Had she been to the House of Answers herself? Of course—this had to be why Dr. Jericho was after her, too.

Horace swung into action. He snuck out of his room and down the stairs. He slid out the back door and into the cool yard. He raised the box toward the shed and immediately jumped at what he saw—*the girl, bursting out of tomorrow's toolshed wall at a run, headed right for him but glancing back at the shed; her lips, moving; anger on her face.*

As she drew closer, Horace saw she had her hand at her throat, and in that hand a bright object burned, looking for all the world as though it was white-hot—was it a cross? No, there was something funny about it. But this was the thing. This had to be what let her walk through walls. The girl ran right past where Horace was standing now and ghosted through the fence on the far side.

Horace set off after her. He was not a stealthy person, by any stretch of the imagination, but he had at his disposal a foolproof method of spying: the box. He could follow this girl tonight, without any risk whatsoever of being seen, and see what she would be up to tomorrow night. If he wanted to, he could follow her home now, just as she had followed him.

But keeping up with the girl proved to be very difficult. Using the box while moving was hard enough—like running while trying to watch the video screen on a phone. He could only catch glimpses of her, checking her progress every few seconds. Even worse, though, the girl cut straight up the center of the block, right across every backyard, which meant fences. Lots of fences. She passed through them as though they weren't there, and it was an incredible sight—the way the chain link fences materialized out of her back as she moved through them, the way she vanished into tall hedges without a rustle, like a phantom. Horace, however, had to hop those fences, fight through those hedges. He had stupidly left his shoes behind, too. When the girl disappeared through a tall wooden fence, Horace groaned; he was winded and his face was scratched, and his feet ached. How to catch someone who could walk through walls?

But that was it. That was the key. She could walk through walls; he could see the future. And because he knew the future, he could outmaneuver her. In a way, he could *outnumber* her. It was now 11:29. He was here now, on Sunday night, and he'd be out here again Monday night, waiting for the girl

114

at the end of the block, where she seemed to be headed.

With that, he secured the box in its pouch and cut across to Glendon Lane, one street over from Bromley. When he hit the sidewalk, he turned and ran north, the same direction the girl was headed. If she kept on as she was, the girl would emerge at the end of the block onto Marie Street, just across from a tiny neighborhood park where Horace used to play when he was little. His bare feet slapped against the concrete, stinging, hoping to beat her there. When he arrived, he pulled out the box again—*the girl, already here, hooded and hurrying down the sidewalk, coming straight for him; her head low; a glance over her shoulder and a quickening step; and there, far behind her, another figure, coming into the glow of the distant streetlight at the far corner.*

"That's me," Horace said aloud. He was both behind her and in front of her, an incredible thought—he had her surrounded. "I've got you."

And then the figure at the far end of Marie Street came more fully into the light, and Horace realized something was wrong. *Not himself, not at all; long limbs, a spider's gait; arms and legs and arms and legs; a crawling, towering mass of a man, smudged and smoking but dark as black—Dr. Jericho.*

Seeing the thin man again was like waking into a nightmare—all the more so because this Dr. Jericho was even more horrible than when he'd last seen him on the bus. Through the box, the man was crisp and clear, but smudged and blurry at the same time, as though he were both certain to be here

115

on this street tomorrow but unpredictable in every other way, and this made him look more monstrous than ever—a bigger, boiling, tentacled version of himself. And he was headed this way, fast. He was chasing the girl. He *would be* chasing the girl.

"Run," Horace said aloud, uselessly, as the girl approached. "Hide." Only ten feet away now, her face showed no fear— just a fierce, chiseled concentration. She wasn't running, but clearly she was aware of the thin man. Around her neck, tucked into the unzipped V of her sweatshirt, the pendant she wore was shining bright and plain to see—a long, thin body and wide double wings, a tail like a sword. Not a cross—a dragonfly. And it was exquisite, beyond beautiful. Horace gaped at it as the girl passed by.

Dr. Jericho pulled closer still, surging forward horribly after the girl. And now the girl turned abruptly and broke into a run, barreling into the road. Horace rushed after her, struggling to keep track of today's world and tomorrow's simultaneously. He risked a glance back with the box as he ran. Twenty yards behind—*Dr. Jericho, spilling into the street, multilimbed and growing bigger, spreading across the road and the sidewalk, a ghastly insect.*

Horace tripped over the opposite curb. He ducked beneath the branches of a tree and came to a halt at the edge of the park. The park was triangular shaped, streets running along each side. It had a few benches and a creaky swing set and a couple of those old wobble horses on thick springs.

There was nowhere to hide—no buildings, no nothing—but the girl had vanished.

Horace, box in hand, watched as the cloud that was Dr. Jericho crept up onto the curb and churned forward between two of the trees at the park's edge—*his long, shifting, multiple faces, swinging from side to side; great hands parting two tall trees like curtains.* Horace backed slowly away, up into the park. Every bone in his body shouted at him to flee, and even the box itself seemed to want to cringe away from the sight of the thin man, but that was illogical. Dr. Jericho wasn't here—he wasn't *now*. Horace had to stay, had to know what would happen to the girl. Maybe then he could help, if something bad happened. He could help change the future. Maybe warn her so that none of this would happen in the first place.

But as Horace watched and hoped, as the horrible thin man who wasn't a man at all drew nearer, his appearance began to change: *blurring lines growing sharp; ghostly limbs solidifying; many shifting faces meeting, becoming one face, a face with button eyes turning in Horace's direction, growing closer; the many-bodied beast becoming one towering man, and that man staring at Horace, approaching.*

What was happening? Could he see Horace through time? Horace held his ground. Dr. Jericho leaned forward, looking Horace straight in the eyes through the impossible barrier of the box's blue glass, and Horace was just beginning to understand what that might mean when Dr. Jericho frowned and narrowed his terrible eyes, cocking his long, thin head, and then: the long, horrid hand, with its four-knuckled fingers, swiping viciously through the air at the box itself.

Horace cried out. He stumbled back, arms pinwheeling. The box tumbled into the sand beneath the wobble horses. Dr. Jericho could not get to here from there, could not reach him from the future, absolutely not—and yet he had tried. He'd known. Horace snatched up the box, brushing it off and inspecting it. The lid had slid closed in the fall. Horace did not even consider opening it again.

Mr. Meister had warned Horace against revealing the box to Dr. Jericho, even with the leestone's protection. Now it was clear that Dr. Jericho could sense the box being used—even from the other side of the glass! Horace's stomach crumpled as he realized that the girl must be in even greater danger. That strange white pendant . . . no doubt Dr. Jericho could sense her using it, too. But if she was still here, hiding somewhere, Horace could save her. He could draw attention away from her to himself. And he ought to be able to do so without fear. Dr. Jericho would be drawn to the box, but he could not harm Horace. Right? Horace closed his eyes. He swallowed. He squeezed the box, feeling its constancy and strength. And then he opened it.

*The thin man, creeping between the trees; but now turning back toward the open box, cocking his head as though trying to pick out a faint sound, swinging his head to look directly at Horace; stepping out across the sidewalk again, moving fast, so fast—*Horace gasped and took a step back, jolted by Dr. Jericho's slashing swiftness. Dr. Jericho surged after the box, and Horace turned and ran, leaving the box open, luring the thin man away from the girl. Horace left the park behind, rounding the corner at full speed. A block up, he slowed to check the box. Clearly the box hadn't been built to be used while running. The thin man was right there—*leaping forward, opening his mouth as wide as a football, a ferocious bite at the air.* Horace almost felt he could hear the man's long teeth gnashing together. Then the view through the box went completely dark, and Horace understood: the box was seeing into the inside of Dr. Jericho's mouth, inside his throat, occupying the same space tonight as Dr. Jericho's horrible body would tomorrow.

Horace turned and ran, block after block, the soles of his feet burning now. At last he stopped, exhausted. It would have to be far enough. He hoped the girl had been able to get away. Horace raised the still-open box, gasping for air, looking back along the way he'd come—*nothing; the dark street, the empty sidewalk.* "Where are you?" Horace murmured. He spun slowly in place. And then—*Dr. Jericho, close enough to touch, huge and glaring, hunkering down on the sidewalk, one ghoulish finger pointing straight into the box, straight into Horace's face.* The man shook his long head, wearing a thin smile like a scar. He spoke, his mouth forming words Horace couldn't hear. The man's lips curled slowly and greedily around two final words, and Horace understood them: *Find . . . you.*

Horace slammed the box closed. He pulled it tight against his gut. He wilted to his knees, there on the empty sidewalk.

He thought he might drown in his own exhaustion. The solitude of the neighborhood at night closed in around him. The burn of his muscles and the sting of his feet and the stitch of his lungs were all that remained of what he'd just done. Horace held them like the last rags of a dream. Dr. Jericho couldn't get to him here, tonight. Of course he couldn't. The truth was, Horace had been alone all night. There was no girl here, no Dr. Jericho. None of what he'd just been through had really even *happened*.

Not yet.

CHAPTER TWELVE

The Girl Who Walked through Walls

THE NEXT NIGHT, AT 11:18, HORACE CREPT DOWNSTAIRS. HE took the toolshed key from the nail by the back door and slipped outside. The night was windy and cool, invigorating him. He felt confident and ready—in the right place at the right time. The box was at his side.

He'd had no school that day—Memorial Day—so he'd slept late and spent most of the afternoon thinking about the night before, wondering what to do next. It was a grand puzzle, just the kind of problem his mind was suited for. He'd decided he could not leave the experiences of the previous night unlived. That was the right word, *unlived*, because he had begun to believe that the future the box revealed was dead—the territory of ghosts. At first, he tried to convince himself that he had already done what he needed to do. He had lured the thin man away from the girl's hiding place.

But was that really true? After all, the girl hadn't hidden yet. The chase hadn't even happened. There was no guarantee that they *would* happen, because the box could be wrong. And unless the events of tonight unfolded exactly as he'd seen, the timing of the whole sequence of events would be off! The box had already been opened at specific moments in time, in the past. Those moments had to align with what would happen tonight, in order to lead Dr. Jericho away from the park. And if they didn't, the girl might not be saved.

But maybe—just maybe—none of it had to happen in the first place. He now knew the girl was coming. He knew when and where. He could intercept her and warn her, or at least scare her off. It'd be the last thing she was expecting.

Quietly, Horace let himself inside the toolshed to wait for the girl. The shed was really a tiny old garage, swaybacked and decrepit, with a gravel floor. Most of its paint had peeled away, and the single window was covered in a curtain-thick layer of grime. When he was younger, Horace used to play in the shed sometimes, but now they only kept lawn stuff in here. It still had a bunch of other junk in it that the previous owners had left behind—shelves full of weird old cans and broken tools, a workbench propped up on homemade sawhorses, a refrigerator door, an ancient and chainless bicycle hanging from a hook like a side of beef.

Horace swiped the cobwebs out of a corner with an old rake. He stood beside the hanging bicycle and waited, squeezing the flat tire and spinning the wheel occasionally. At 11:27, he stilled the bike and went completely quiet. The girl would be here any minute now. But now he had a sudden, troubling thought—if he was deliberately changing the future he saw, would he feel sick again? The way he had with the sandwich? He began to wrestle with that new thought but was interrupted as a shadow sprouted out of the opposite wall. A small leg, and then an arm, materializing through the wooden slats. And now the girl's face, hooded and pale, swinging inside to peer around, disembodied. Horace sat utterly still, amazed to see this in person. The face disappeared, but a moment later the girl backed into the shed completely, silent and magical, as if she were made of the darkness itself.

Horace held his breath. Now that she was here, he had no idea what to do. The girl snuck over to the window and tried to peer out, looking up toward Horace's bedroom. She licked her fingers and tried to rub the grime from the glass. He thought he heard her curse quietly to herself.

Horace stood up, not bothering to be quiet. His feet scuffed against the floor, and his shoulder knocked over the rake. The girl actually jumped into the air like a cat, spinning to face him. The dragonfly around her neck swung in the dark, gleaming. She pressed herself against the wall. Her face was livid with shock.

"Wait," Horace said, feeling stupid. "I knew you would be here. I . . . saw you coming."

The girl glared at him. "How did you—? You saw me. You

saw me just now." She clutched the dragonfly, hiding it in her hand.

Horace laid a hand on the box at his side. "Yes, and I—"

But in a flash, the girl was gone. She turned and bolted through the wall before he could say another word.

Horace stood there for a few seconds, stunned, and then went after her. He sprinted out the door just in time to see the girl disappearing through the fence on the north side of the lawn. He realized this was exactly the future he'd seen last night—she'd run from the shed because of Horace. "The thin man," he called after her, hopefully not loud enough to wake anyone, but loud enough for her to still hear. "He's coming. He's going to find you."

But the girl was gone. So much for changing the future. He'd actually created it, by being here in the shed and scaring her off! The wind tugged at Horace's hair and shook the trees overhead. He thought quickly. He hadn't seen his future self last night through the box, but that didn't mean he wouldn't be there, right? He just had to stay behind yesterday's Horace, out of sight of yesterday's box, so that he'd be sure not to contradict what he'd seen. He counted to twenty, envisioning the chase of the night before, giving his past self—so strange to imagine it!—a head start. Then turned to his right and cut across to Glendon once again, knowing that Dr. Jericho was somewhere off the left, headed toward the park.

Horace ran up Glendon. He reached Marie Street just as the girl was running across into the park. Dr. Jericho sailed behind her, exactly as the box had foretold. The sight of him burned a nugget of fear and disgust into Horace's gut. Dr. Jericho was not the many-headed beast of last night—the box must have made him look that way—but Horace's heart pounded as he crouched down behind a hedge to hide. Unlike last night, tonight Horace could be seen. Seen, and worse. Dr. Jericho stepped off the sidewalk after the girl, drawing closer.

Horace watched the girl. This was the moment he'd lost sight of her last night. She skirted around a thick tree trunk, putting it between herself and the thin man. She paused, glancing around, and then silently stepped inside the tree.

Horace almost cried out. He had passed right by this tree last night, ducked under its branches. Buried alive inside the tomblike trunk of the tree—how could she tolerate it, even for a moment?

Dr. Jericho stepped up between the trees, examining them as if he were picking out a bouquet of flowers. Surely the girl couldn't see him—could she hear? Could she *breathe*? The thin man prowled, bobbing and searching and sniffing. Horace waited, tense as a bowstring. He waited for the moment that had to come, any second now—the moment he himself had caused, simply by being here last night with the open box. The man began rummaging through the forked heart of the very tree that held the girl, testing the limbs, snapping branches. He drew his fingernails down the trunk, splintering furrows into the bark like a bear. It made a sound like a boulder being dragged through gravel.

And then it happened. Dr. Jericho whirled, crouching. In the same motion, he uncoiled and pounced across the grass, a fifteen-foot leap, brutal and alarming, taking a savage swipe at absolutely nothing. But of course it wasn't nothing. It was the box, open in the past, not really here and now but somehow drawing the thin man's attention nonetheless. And as startled as Horace had been by this attack last night, he knew now that he hadn't been nearly frightened enough. He cowered down behind the hedge at the sight of it, even though he was thirty yards away. The blow was vicious and massive, a killing blow. The man let out a rumbling throaty sound, too, almost like a growl—and then he paused, looking lost. He dropped his animal manner, stretching to his full two-legged height and looking calmly around. Horace understood. In the past, the box had been closed at this moment, having fallen from Horace's hands. And then, to Horace's surprise, the thin man spoke, his tinkling voice carrying easily across the street to where Horace hid: "Surely not. Surely, surely not."

After a long, suspicious hesitation, Dr. Jericho turned back toward the tree where the girl was. For a moment, he seemed to look straight across the street at Horace's hiding place. Horace stopped breathing. He pressed himself deeper into the shadows of the hedge. He told himself not to panic, that the leestone was working. The thin man took a long step in his direction, humming tunelessly and cocking his head from side to side. Horace told himself: *Do not run. Do not run.* Any moment now, the box would open again in the past, and

Horace knew that the open box would draw Dr. Jericho like a magnet.

Sure enough, the thin man snarled. "Not possible!" he snapped. He spun and lunged again—away, thank goodness, away—charging across the park, lured by yesterday's Horace, by the open box. Horace stood up, stunned by how fast Dr. Jericho was going. Had Horace actually been running that fast yesterday? He felt a weird flutter of pride.

Within moments, Dr. Jericho had reached Bromley Street and hurtled out of sight around the corner, chasing the call of the box. Horace counted to ten and let out a long, trembling breath. The future he'd seen had come to pass. Or close enough, anyway—the girl had been saved, right?

Or had she? He was in unknown territory now. There was no sign of movement from the tree she'd hidden in. He waited, and was just starting to think that something had gone wrong, when a low branch shook and sank, and the dark figure of the girl dropped lightly to the ground, alighting on all fours. She angled across the park and moved up Glendon at a trot.

Relieved, Horace trailed her, leaving Bromley Street— and the thin man, he hoped—behind. The girl rounded the next corner and Horace followed, keeping his distance. She showed no signs of slowing. He jogged as quietly as he could, keeping to the shadows as much as possible, but the girl never glanced back.

They ran on, heading east for another three blocks, into a part of the neighborhood Horace scarcely knew. His chest burned. He was just beginning to wonder how long he could keep up when the girl slowed to a walk. She jogged up the steps of an apartment building. Horace ducked down behind a low brick wall to watch. The girl reached the door and turned to press her back against it. She looked up and down the street. Then she leaned back casually and disappeared through the door.

Horace sat down atop the wall, considering. Something seemed wrong here. Somehow this girl had discovered where he lived, and he was determined to do the same to her. It would make them even, in a way—he didn't like not knowing things. But was this place really where she lived? If so, how was she managing to keep it secret from Dr. Jericho? Horace himself had followed her here without difficulty, and he was no spy. And after all, she could sneak into any building she liked, pretending it was home.

But she had her ability, and he had his. With the box— and a little luck—he might be able to spot her coming home again tomorrow, if this really was her home, and if her late-night outings were something of a habit. Big ifs. Was it worth the risk of opening the box? He had no idea where Dr. Jericho was now, or from how far away he might be able to sense the box being used.

Horace waited. He wasn't even sure what for. Five minutes passed. Ten. It was now approaching midnight. No new lights came on inside the apartment building. At last, in a rush of impatient suspicion, Horace pulled out the box. He would just take a quick peek.

He opened the lid. He looked up at the apartment building but saw nothing strange. A few different lights on, that was all—and it was raining heavily. He looked for another thirty seconds before realizing just how stupid he was being. What were the odds that the girl would be coming or going exactly now, in twenty-four hours' time? Slim to none. He turned to look up the street, hoping to see something— anything—and he nearly dropped the box. *A hooded figure, swift and small, headed this way.* The girl, here again tomorrow. She approached the steps of the building she'd gone into tonight, but instead of slowing, she passed on by, walking right past Horace's perch.

Horace stood up, watching her walk away—blurred by the rain but still clear. He closed the box. He'd had it open for too long. He glanced up at the apartment building again. Tomorrow night, she wouldn't be entering or exiting this place. Instead, by the looks of it, she was headed back in the general direction of Horace's house. "I was right," Horace murmured to himself. "You don't live here after all."

Horace slipped the box back into its pouch, thinking hard. He asked himself again—what were the odds? He'd had the box open for less than a minute, and the dragonfly girl happened to walk by this exact spot in that exact moment? He wondered if maybe—

Abruptly, a slap of wind brought a stinging, sickly scent to his nose. Brimstone. Heart galloping, Horace dropped into a crouch, hunkering down beside the wall again, listening. The smell grew stronger.

Now he heard footsteps, heavy and slow. Breathing. A long shadow slid across the grass in front of him, and Horace turned, ever so slowly, to look.

Dr. Jericho stood there, not ten feet away. His chest heaved from the effort of running. Horace was exposed, hidden only by the shadow of the wall he was cowering against—the shadow, and the promised protection of the leestone. Horace cursed himself for opening the box.

For fifteen full seconds, the thin man stood there, looking around from his great height. At one point, the man looked down in Horace's direction—Horace could have sworn their eyes met, and his heart stopped—but the man's gaze passed right over him. The leestone was working! A moment later, the man swung sharply away, staring up at the apartment building where the girl had gone to ground. Dr. Jericho stood there for another minute, and then he strode off in the direction he'd come.

Horace stayed put. The leestone had done its job, but he didn't dare draw any more attention to himself now. He was still crouching there when the front door of the apartment opened and the girl stepped out. She glanced over at the street corner where Horace was still hidden in shadow, then took off up the street, in the opposite direction from the one the thin man had just gone.

Horace straightened painfully. He got to his feet and

continued to follow her. It wasn't easy. She was one of those naturally quick people, whereas Horace was decidedly *not* quick.

The girl wove a path east and south. She crossed Diversey Avenue. Often she kept to the shadows—she clearly did not want to be seen—but she did not use the dragonfly.

And then the girl stopped outside a little grocery store. The store was dark; a gate barred the door. Horace stopped and watched from behind a row of newspaper boxes as the girl glanced up and down the street and drew her hood close. She sidled into the thick shadow of the store's dark doorway, and then stepped right through the gate, gone in an instant.

Horace hesitated. There were apartments above the store, but maybe this was just another secret route of hers. Maybe she was escaping out the back even now. Horace cut down an alley and emerged at the rear of the store, between a couple of dingy, greasy-smelling Dumpsters. He crouched behind one of them and waited. Sure enough, two minutes later, the girl emerged through the store's back door. There was a huge cookie hanging from her mouth, and a bag of groceries in one hand. Horace almost gasped in shock. This was how she was using the dragonfly's power—sneaking into stores to steal cookies! The idea infuriated Horace, made him ashamed for her, for the dragonfly itself. His anger surprised him, and as the girl walked past his hiding spot, he very nearly stood up and confronted her. But instead he let her walk on, more determined than ever to find out where she lived.

Turnabout, after all, was fair play.

At last the girl cut into a lawn on a corner, across from a fenced-in train yard. Horace crept along the fence beside the train tracks and then hunkered down behind some tall weeds to watch. The girl walked up the steps of a ramshackle white house—was this her home? A mini trampoline sat in the yard, along with a rusted-out swing set that was missing its swings. The raised front porch had no railings, and the front window was boarded up, making the place look abandoned, but a light shone inside. The girl approached the front door, clearly trying to be quiet. She leaned up against the boarded window, cupping her hands around her face—Horace suspected she was sticking her face through it. Then, gingerly, she opened it and slid inside.

A minute later, a light in one of the upstairs windows went on. A shape moved behind the flat blue curtain there—or not a curtain; it looked more like a sheet. This was where she lived. For real. Horace looked up and down the street, taking stock of the neighborhood, realizing now how different it was from his own. Smaller, dingier houses; hardly any trees. The house across the street from hers had a car parked on the lawn. Two blocks up along the railroad tracks, the homes gave way to warehouses and industrial buildings.

He looked up at her bedroom again and was surprised to see a sliver of light in her window. The girl's face was peeking out from behind the curtain, looking out into the night—looking straight at Horace? Just then, a car alarm burst to life down the street, spooking him. The curtain in the window flicked closed, and Horace stumbled to his feet and took off, heading home as quickly as his worn legs would let him.

When he finally arrived back in his room, utterly exhausted, he closed his eyes as he eased his door shut. He took a guess at the time. "Twelve forty-five," he whispered, and opened his eyes. Sure enough, the clock read 12:45. A long night, no matter how you measured it. The firefly crawled across the ceiling, probably wondering what was going on. Horace stepped up on his bed and swiped it gently down, wobbling with fatigue.

"At least my life's not as weird as yours," he told it, and sent it through the box.

Horace's legs felt like logs as he got undressed. He had just gotten under the covers when there was a knock, and his mother leaned in from the gloom, looking small in her pajamas and her mussed-up hair. "Hey."

Alarm bells went off dimly in his head—did she know, or had she just woken up? "Hey."

"I thought I heard you moving around. Can't sleep?"

"I . . . was thirsty. I was in the kitchen."

She came close. She pointed at Horace's chest. The box was right there, in plain sight. "And there's that box you've been carrying everywhere. Where did you get it, anyway?"

"The same place I got you that turtle-bird statue." He wondered if she would ask him to see the box. To hold it. And would he let her? But instead she took him completely by surprise.

"And do you like what you see when you look through it?" she asked. When he didn't answer—*couldn't* answer—she said, "I've noticed you doing it. I'm just curious."

Obviously he hadn't been as careful with the box as he thought. "Well, there's nothing to see," he said, as if it hardly mattered. "Stuff's just blue."

"Look at me through the box. Don't peek around it. Tell me what you see."

Reluctantly, Horace lifted the box close to his face. He opened it and looked. But of course, she wasn't there. "I see you," he lied. "You're blue." He started to lower the box, but she spoke again.

"And how many fingers am I holding up? Remember, no peeking."

Horace froze. He almost laughed aloud. How funny that the box—which gave him this incredible vision—could also make him blind. She was right here, but he couldn't even see her. "I don't know," he said. "I can't really see." He was so tired, and this conversation was so strange, almost like a dream. "Fourteen," he said at last, and lowered the box to his chest. He frowned at his mother's two fingers. "Oh, man. So close."

She laughed and laughed. "That's very good," she said. "Very funny."

Horace laughed with her, relief flooding him. He sank back into his pillow. "Don't ever put anything in the box," he murmured sleepily.

"I wasn't planning to. But why not?"

"You can't keep anything in it. You keep nothing in it. It's where I keep nothing." His eyes were heavy. Maybe they were already closed.

"I guess you have to put nothing somewhere."

"I do. Imagine if I just put my nothing everywhere. There would be a lot less . . . something."

"You're funny."

"Yes. It's true," Horace said, or thought he did, and he never remembered anything else either of them might have said that night.

CHAPTER THIRTEEN

In the Boys' Bathroom

IN SCIENCE CLASS THE NEXT DAY, TUESDAY, THEY WERE DOING an experiment that involved Bunsen burners. Horace fumbled with his flint lighter, sort of a giant paper clip thing that made sparks, but it kept springing out of his hands, over and over. A couple of other kids were pointing and laughing at him. Horace's lab partner for the day—a dull-witted, painfully skinny girl whose name he couldn't remember—watched him blankly and never once offered to help. At last Mr. Ludwig came over and shut off the gas Horace had been letting leak into the room for the last thirty seconds. He called Horace aside. "Horace, what's the scoop, man?"

"Sorry. I'm a little tired."

"Still having troubles?"

"Let's just say I'm coping with some stuff that people don't usually have to cope with."

"I see. Something at home?"

"No, nothing like that."

"Is it a girl?"

"It is a girl, actually, but not like that. This girl . . . she's just as weird as the other problems I'm having in the first place, which are the reasons she's even around."

"Sounds extremely complicated."

"You have no idea."

"Well, I tell you what. Whatever it is that's distracting you at the moment, it's not very compatible with open flame. So how about you take a nice slow walk to the restroom, get some air, get a drink or something. Okay?"

"Okay. Thanks."

Horace took a hall pass and headed for the bathroom. As usual, it stank, and the floors were damp. He leaned over the last sink, breathing through his mouth and looking at himself in the mirror. He looked pretty mental. He promised his reflection he would sleep all weekend long.

Suddenly a girl's voice sounded, quiet but firm. "Considering a new hairdo?" Horace just about jumped out of his shoes. He spun around and there—hands on her hips, her face like a dagger—stood the girl who walked through walls. She wore a long black skirt. The dragonfly pendant lay gleaming across her collarbone.

The girl came toward him. Horace leaned away, despite being a half foot taller. He laid his hand atop the box through his shirt, bending back until he was practically sitting on the sink. "You *could* use a trim," the girl said.

"What are you doing here? How did you find me?"

"I'm stalking you. Sound familiar?"

"I'm not stalking you."

"Sure. And I haven't been spying on you. If you're not stalking me, why did you follow me all the way home last night?" So he'd been seen. Apparently Horace was even less sneaky than he thought he was. The girl read his expression and said, "Yeah, if I'd wanted to lose you, I would have. No offense, but between the two of us, I'm definitely the stealthy one."

"Then why did you let me follow you?"

"I wanted to see what you were up to. At first I thought you might be with the freak. I thought maybe he'd gotten to you. I watched you waiting outside that apartment building, the first one I snuck into. I saw you get that thing out, whatever it is." She looked him up and down, openly curious. She seemed not at all troubled that they were having this conversation in the boys' restroom. "You were holding up that thing, and a couple of minutes later the freak arrived. I thought maybe you had called him."

"What? No way."

"I know that now. I saw you hide from him, even if I still don't understand how he didn't see you. But he showed up because he sensed you using that thing, right? Just like he senses me when I use the dragonfly." She sighed and crossed her arms. "Look, here's what I'm saying. I can do the impossible, and I think you can too."

And he could. But Horace couldn't bring himself to say it. He just stood there, mouth open, shaking his head as if he were going to deny something—but what was there to deny?

She narrowed her eyes at him. "Are you okay? It seems like you might be bugging out."

"I'm not bugging out."

"Then are you dim? I was thinking you were smart. Are you not smart?"

"I'm smart."

"I was going to come up to your room last night." She said this as though it were the most reasonable thing in the world. "But then you saw me in the shed. You startled me. I haven't been caught in the act like that in a long time." She grasped the dragonfly hanging around her throat and stepped up close to Horace, holding it out. It looked perfectly real, like an actual dragonfly. Its wings even had the same lacy structure. Horace couldn't look away. "See this? This is magic. This is how I do it. I know you understand me." The girl let the dragonfly drop. "And the magic thing you have, it lets you know stuff. It lets you find me when you shouldn't be able to find me." Her face grew even stormier. "People don't find me."

"The box isn't magic, it just—"

"It's a box?" She looked him over again. "Where is it? Don't you have it?"

"I do, actually," Horace said, and before he knew it he had yanked up his shirt a few inches, letting her glimpse the box in its pouch.

Her eyes flicked to it. "And what does it let you do?"

Somehow the fact that she wasn't asking to see the box made him trust her more—but not quite *that* much. "I . . . look through it," he said vaguely.

"You said you saw me coming. Can you see people from far away? Spy on them?"

"Not really."

She looked at him long and hard, clearly concentrating. "Can you see through walls?"

"No."

"Into people's minds?"

"No."

"What then? What does the box show you?"

The words popped out before Horace could stop them. "The future, okay?"

The girl's eyes widened. She took a step back. "For real?" she whispered.

"For real," Horace said, feeling a strange flood of relief that the words were out there. And what was more, she believed him. He could see it in her face.

"Oh my god . . . you can see the future. How far in the future?"

"Only a day. That's how I knew you were coming. I saw you the night before."

"That is . . . phenomenal. Where did you get that thing?"

"Same place you must've gotten yours."

She inhaled sharply and stared at him even more fiercely,

her eyes like a hawk's, but said nothing.

Horace continued. "You know. You have to know. That's where I was going that day you saw me on the bus."

"I *don't* know. Tell me."

Horace considered it. If she truly didn't know about the House of Answers, then where had she gotten the dragonfly? But surely she wasn't pretending—why bother? Horace wasn't sure he should even be having this conversation. Then again, he'd already told her about the box. And suddenly he was realizing, maybe for the first time, just how big the burden of all these secrets had been. "Okay look, it's this weird place. They have all kinds of crazy stuff. There's an old man there, Mr. Meister. And Mrs. Hapsteade."

"I don't know those people."

"They have all these boxes and bins. Full of bizarre things. Awesome things. That's where I found the box." Horace nodded at the dragonfly. "And it must be where you—"

"Wait," she said slowly, her eyes far away. "Were there birds? Singing?"

"Yes! Lots of birds. Hundreds. In cages."

"I remember the birds," she said dreamily. She fiddled with the dragonfly at her throat. Horace noticed that the skin there, all around the base of her neck, was mottled and scarred, like she'd been burned.

"You've been there. I told you."

"I don't know, I don't know. How long have you had the box?"

"Just a few weeks."

"A few weeks!" She mulled it over, then shook her head as if to clear her thoughts. "I'm Chloe."

"Horace."

"I know," she said, but didn't bother explaining how. She looked around the restroom, wrinkling her nose. "Anyway, we should talk. But not here."

"Definitely not here."

"I'm coming over tonight. Don't say no. What time should I be there?"

And then a bizarre, folded-back sense of remembering came over Horace—something like déjà vu, but not quite. He almost laughed aloud. What time? He knew what time. He'd seen her in the box last night, outside the apartment building, headed back in the general direction of Horace's house. And now he knew for sure that that was exactly where she'd be going. "Midnight," he said.

The bathroom door swung open. An older boy walked in. He stopped dead in his tracks when he saw Chloe.

Chloe turned to Horace in a flash. "See you at midnight tonight, then. I'll let myself in—don't freak out." Horace nodded. She spun away and skirted around the frozen boy, slipping through the door—like a normal person, the normal way—leaving Horace there in a daze.

The older kid just stood there for a long moment, gazing at Horace, his mouth open. Then he grinned, nodding. "Nice, dude."

CHAPTER FOURTEEN

The Impossible

AT MIDNIGHT THAT NIGHT, HORACE LAY ON HIS BED WITH HIS clothes on, the box on his belly. Outside, it was pouring. An occasional flash of lightning flared in the window, followed by a rumble of thunder.

"Knock-knock."

Horace bolted upright, nearly letting the box tumble to the floor. Chloe stood in the doorway, looking small but as solid as a pillar of stone. Behind her, his door was wide open onto the dark hallway beyond.

Horace hissed a whisper: "Close the door, close the door," he said, waving her in. He had figured she would just come right through the wall.

Chloe said, "You're supposed to say 'Who's there?'" She pushed the door closed almost noiselessly. Loki slipped in at the last moment, like a shadow between her feet.

Chloe clucked softly down at the cat and came in without a hint of unease. She slouched down to the floor beneath the window, the way his mother always did. She'd changed out of her black skirt and was now wearing shorts and what he thought of as her sneaking outfit—the dark green hoodie. Loki took a station off to the side, sitting up alertly as though he intended to be a part of this. Whatever this was.

Chloe's relaxed manner, so sure of everything, somehow only made Horace more nervous. He watched her out of the corner of his eye, trying to think of something to say.

"I didn't know if you'd make it," he said. "I thought the rain might stop you."

"Nah." Chloe waved the thought away. "I don't get wet much if I don't want to."

Horace had to think before he understood. "The rain goes through you?"

"Well, I go through the rain. Do you have anything to eat?"

"Um, no. Sorry. Not in here. What do you mean, you go through the rain?"

"Stuff can't actually go through me. I go through stuff. Man, I'm starving."

"I don't understand."

"It means hungry."

Horace frowned.

"Okay, sorry, jeez. Here, grab the pillow. Come here." She patted the floor. Horace slid off the bed, pillow in hand.

"Now hold it up like a shield, and I'll go thin." When Horace gave her a quizzical look, she explained. "That's what I call it when I do it. When I get all ghosty. I mean, technically what I become is 'incorporeal.' But that doesn't really roll off the tongue."

"Oh."

"It's weird to do this in front of somebody. To show them, I mean. I keep it secret. I don't even let my sister see."

"But I already know," Horace offered.

"Yeah, but the only reason you know is because you have that." She pointed at the box. "I'm usually really careful not to be seen, but how am I supposed to know if you're watching me through time? Plus it's only because you have it that I'm here at all. Just so we're clear. I'm here because if you're the only octopus in an aquarium, and then one day you spot another octopus, it seems like a conversation should happen."

"You've never met anyone else like us?"

"Maybe? I've seen this one girl. She plays an instrument, a flute. It sounds weird. She plays it, and sometimes she finds me. But I always get away."

Horace wondered what it was about the flute girl that made Chloe want to get away. Or maybe a better question: Why was Chloe here with him now?

Chloe grasped the dragonfly lightly by the tail. "Look, do you want to see this, or not?"

"I do, yeah."

Horace startled as the dragonfly's delicate white wings

began to vibrate silently, so fast they became an almost invisible blur. "You see that?" Chloe asked. Horace nodded, fascinated. Chloe reached out toward the pillow in Horace's hands. Her fingertips passed right into it, as though it wasn't there. Then her palm. Horace looked closely at the seam where her skin met the pillow, but there was nothing to see. They were just . . . joined.

All at once, Chloe lunged forward and her hand popped clean through the pillow, right in Horace's face. She jabbed two fingers toward his eyes. He jumped, and Chloe fell back laughing quietly, her hand sliding back through the pillow and out. Loki glared at them both, unimpressed.

"What did you do that for?"

"Your face, you just—you're so shockable. It's hard to resist." She grinned at him. "But okay, now watch. Throw the pillow at me."

"Why?"

"Just do it." She closed her eyes and stretched out her arms. The dragonfly's wings were still vibrating.

Horace tossed the pillow at her. He expected the pillow to pass right through her, but instead it hit her in the face and fell into her lap.

"See? I can pass through stuff, but stuff can't pass through me. So I'm not like, bulletproof or whatever. But in the rain, if I move fast, it's more me hitting the raindrops than the raindrops hitting me. I don't know. It's weird." Suddenly she seemed awkward, plucking at the pillow in her lap. The

146

dragonfly's wings had gone still. "That was kind of a wussy throw, by the way."

"Yeah, well. I didn't want to hurt you."

Chloe snorted and rolled her eyes. "As if." From her pocket, she produced a ragged roll of wintergreen mints. She popped one into her mouth and offered them to Horace. He shook his head. They were probably stolen. And anyway, he was distracted, trying to imagine how the dragonfly worked. He knew that solid matter was actually mostly empty space, once you got down to the microscopic level of atoms. Maybe the dragonfly made it possible for Chloe to move the molecules of her body between the molecules of other objects? Was that even possible?

"I've been thinking about that box of yours," Chloe said, weirdly mirroring Horace's own thoughts. "It sounds like a headache."

Horace glanced at the box. If it was a headache, it was one he wanted to have. "It's tricky, but . . . I'm figuring it out."

"All right, so show me."

So Horace showed her. He was surprised to find that he wanted to. Chloe was both fascinated and respectful, never moving to touch the box. Instead she had him hold it while she looked through it. To Horace's relief, she saw nothing unusual; just today, slightly smudgy and blue.

"Tell me what *you* see," she said.

Horace warned her, "There won't be much." And there wasn't. "I see my bed. And myself, sleeping. It's dark."

"Am I there?" Her face wrinkled in confusion. "Or . . . here, tomorrow?"

"Why would you be?"

"I don't know. But if I *were* here, you could tell me what I'd be doing. Right?"

He explained to her how lots of the things he saw never ended up happening, and how the box could be clear or fuzzy. He described his failure with the lottery. When Chloe said it sounded like the box was wrong a lot, he frowned. "Not a lot," he said. "And I usually know."

"Prove it," Chloe said.

"Prove it how?"

"Let me test you."

"No, that's stupid."

"Stupid, or scary? Afraid it won't work?"

"No," he said, but he was. He realized he very much wanted to impress this girl.

"Then show me. Be a show-off, Horace. I'm guessing that doesn't come naturally to you, but come on . . . you've got a *time machine.*"

"What kind of test would you even do?"

Chloe looked slyly around the room. After several moments, she said, "I got it. But you can't look." She flapped a hand at him.

Reluctantly Horace turned around. He desperately hoped the box would be clear this time. He listened as Chloe began to rummage through his desk drawer.

After a moment she said, "I feel like I should confess I've been in here before."

"What?" Horace wasn't sure he was hearing correctly.

"I came into your room. One night when you and your folks went out. Sorry . . . it's a habit. I needed to find out who you were after I saw you on the bus that day."

Horace should've been angry—right? But he wasn't. Instead he felt embarrassed, flattered . . . weirdly thrilled. "Did you look through my stuff?"

"Oh, sure. Rummaged through your underwear drawer, read your diary."

She was kidding. Horace didn't even have a diary.

"No, seriously," she said. "I just wanted to find out your name, where you went to school. I was only here a minute or two. It won't happen again." Another rustle, footsteps. "Give me a second. Don't peek." A very faint squeaking sound, and a few moments later: "Okay. You can turn around."

Horace opened his eyes. Chloe knelt beneath the window, one hand pressed flat against the wall. In her other hand she held a black marker.

"What did you do?"

"I wrote a message on your wall."

"Oh, man!" Horace groaned. "With marker? That's permanent—how am I going to get that off? I'm going to get busted for that."

"Look, this is the test. The box should let you see what I wrote, right? Through my hand. Tomorrow the message will still be here, but my hand will be gone. So you should be able to read it with your box right now. Am I right?"

"First you break in, now you write on my wall. This is not cool."

"Oh my god, stop being a baby and just look. Come on, I wrote it small."

Reluctantly, Horace lifted the box—*his bedroom, his nightstand, no Chloe; the wall beneath the window—blank?—or no, a gray patch, fuzzy and blurred, right there.*

"I don't know. It's blurry."

Chloe kept her hand against the wall. "I already wrote it—why would it be blurry?"

"Usually that means the box isn't sure if it'll be there or not. Or maybe you're smudging it or something."

"I'm not smudging it. And it's there. Why can't you see?"

"I told you, it usually works. Usually isn't always. Man, I can't believe you did that."

Chloe furrowed her brow. "Wait a minute—are you going to clean this off?"

"You *wrote* on my *wall.*"

"Right, but you're going to clean it. As soon as I leave, probably."

"Yeah, so my dad doesn't see it."

Chloe nodded at him. "Right, right. But now promise you *won't* try to clean it off."

Understanding slowly dawned on Horace. "Oh, holy cow," he said.

"Promise you won't clean the wall," Chloe said. "Don't just say it. Mean it. Even if you get in trouble."

Horace nodded slowly. She'd shown off her dragonfly, hadn't she? "Okay, I promise."

"Okay, then. Now check."

Horace checked the box again, thinking of a future where he chose not to clean the wall—not for twenty-four hours, at least. He tried to convince himself that he felt good about the choice. In fact, the choice had already been made. And now, through the box: *same wall, no Chloe, dark with the lights out, but there—four tiny scribbles of black.* "I see it," Horace said thickly.

"This. Is so. Wicked."

"I can't read it, though. It's tiny."

"I told you I wrote small."

Horace walked forward on his knees until he was just a foot or two away—*tiny words in four lines, impossibly neat, written in black.*

"'Dear Horace,'" Horace read aloud. "'I hope this doesn't get you in trouble. Your friend, Chloe.'"

Chloe pulled her hand away and drummed her palms against the carpet in excitement. Loki jolted to his feet, then sauntered coolly away. "Yes, yes, yes!" Chloe hissed. She sat back and pointed both index fingers at the box. "That was sweet. That thing is crazy."

Horace was still absorbing what had happened. He looked again at the tiny message. He doubted his parents would notice it.

Chloe said slowly, "Okay, so . . . you couldn't see it at first because you were planning to clean it off right away. Which meant that by this time tomorrow night, it wouldn't be there anymore. Or it would be smudged, at least."

"Yeah," said Horace.

"But then when you told yourself you *wouldn't* clean it off, you could see it."

"Yeah."

"Man, that thing is *crazy*," Chloe said again. "Oh, and I meant what I said." She squinted at the wall. "I did write really small—do you think your parents will even see it?"

"Probably not," Horace admitted. He wondered if she also meant the part about being his friend, but he was afraid to ask. He wasn't sure he wanted to be friends yet with this girl—she broke into places, stole things, snooped through people's stuff. Still, it was a rush, and a relief, to be able to talk about the box with somebody. And as reckless as she was, he had to admit Chloe was unusually brave. Plus she seemed very smart. This test she'd come up with was clever.

"Let's do another one," Chloe said, clapping her hands silently together.

Horace hesitated. "I'd rather not. The box . . . it's like it needs rest, or something. Or like it doesn't want to do that trick too often. I don't know. That probably sounds stupid."

"Hmm," Chloe said. "I don't think it's like that for me. When I first got the dragonfly, I used it all the time—I was thin more often than not. For no reason, even. I've slowed down a lot, but I don't know. It feels wrong not to use it. Like leaving a horse in the stable."

"Well," Horace said, smiling. "There is another thing the box can do. An easier thing, for some reason."

Chloe raised an eyebrow, her own crooked grin spreading slowly across her face. "Is it also awesome?"

Chloe was practically giddy when she learned the box could send objects into the future. They spent several minutes dropping objects inside and closing the lid. Some marbles, a Matchbox car, a yo-yo—which was about the biggest thing the box could take. They sent a few pennies from Chloe's pocket, plus her last wintergreen mint.

"Where do they go?" Chloe wanted to know. "Before they come back, I mean."

"I don't know, they're just . . . traveling, I guess."

"Traveling, right," she echoed dreamily.

As a consolation for not being there tomorrow night when the stuff reemerged, Chloe wanted to send a burp through the box. "So you'll smell it in your sleep," she said. Horace refused. He also refused to let her send a lit match through the box, even though it was a fascinating idea—one he should've thought of himself. When he told her it was too dangerous, she scoffed and said, "Yeah, and looking at your own future is *totally* safe."

Horace looked at little clusters of thin, slashing marks around her throat. "Speaking of danger," he said, gesturing. "Are these—?"

She gave him a quick, one-shouldered shrug. "I get a little sloppy sometimes. Sometimes I'm not paying attention to what's thin and what's not, and the cord or something gets into my skin without me realizing it and if I go solid again while it's still in there . . . yeah."

"So stuff is like . . . trying to occupy the same space as you are." Horace tried to imagine what that must feel like. "Does it hurt?"

"Oh, hell yes. But I go back thin, I make sure it's out. It doesn't hurt the dragonfly, but it leaves a mark on me."

Horace was feeling faintly horrified. It must have shown on his face, because Chloe scoffed at him again. "God, Horace, it's not that big a deal. It happens to me all the time." She rocked forward onto her knees and cocked her left arm, showing Horace a small constellation of irregular scars below her elbow. "Rocks," she explained. "Fell down crossing the train tracks one time and sort of flashed thin and thick again without really meaning to. Got some gravel in my skin for just a second."

"Oh, man."

She threw her other arm up over her shoulder, revealing her triceps and a jagged, purplish stretch of skin that went from her elbow to her armpit. "This was from a curtain. Backed into it, didn't know it was there."

She hiked up the hem of her long shorts, revealing a small, faintly raised patch of thigh that Horace couldn't begin to identify. It was fan-shaped, square on one side but sort of spiny on the other—it looked like a fossilized plant of some kind, embedded in her skin. "Corner of a book. Got distracted. Oh, and these," she went on, putting both shins forward and showing front and back. All around the bottoms of her legs there were dozens of very faint, knife-thin scars. From far away, it looked like the skin was just lighter there, but up close he could see the texture of all the little blemishes. "Weeds," Chloe said. "Just long grass, from the empty lot across the street. We used to play tag out there and I would . . . you know." She grinned sheepishly at Horace. "Cheat. And then I'd go thick while I was running, and if I wasn't careful, the weeds would tear at me."

Horace didn't know what to say. It all sounded awful. "You should be more careful."

She hugged her legs against her chest. "Maybe. I'm much, much better than I used to be. And if I'm *really* in something—if something's overlapped with me deeply—I feel it right away when I start to go solid, and I stop before anything really awful happens."

Horace tried to imagine what Chloe might consider "really awful." He said, "You could, like, break bones and stuff."

"Oh, I have. A long time ago. Actually, I could totally die. But I would have to really not be paying attention for that to happen. Or I would have to run out of breath inside something."

"Run out of breath?"

"I can't do this forever, you know." The dragonfly's wings

155

began to vibrate again, and Chloe began swaying, waving her arms around. She swung them through the floor like it was water. Through the walls, through the nightstand. She leaned over Loki where he lay like a loaf of bread and swept a hand through him, from rump to front. Loki's golden eyes got huge. As her hand emerged from his chest, he sprang up and spun in place, sniffing. He sat down and glared at Chloe. Chloe laughed and hugged herself, her face lit with intensity. "I'm holding it, like you hold your breath. I run out after a while," she said. Then she went quiet, carefully stretching her arms out, free of everything. A moment later, the dragonfly went still too.

Horace thought of her hidden in the trunk of the tree. He tried to keep his voice light as he asked, "So, how long can you . . ."

"Stay thin?" Chloe finished. "Like two minutes, maybe. I've been practicing. Plus if my face is inside, I actually *do* have to hold my breath. But I can hold my breath for a long time."

Two minutes. He'd saved her, then, that night in the park. He'd gotten Dr. Jericho away just in time. But still, two minutes inside the trunk of a tree—for someone with claustrophobic tendencies like Horace, the idea was unbearable. Suddenly a new thought occurred to Horace, both horrible and wonderful.

"So could you, like, go into the earth? I mean like undergr—"

"I can't," Chloe said, cutting him off.

"But why not? You can go through walls and grass and trees. Metal, even—I've seen you. So what's to stop you from going underground?"

Chloe scowled at him. "I said I can't, okay? That doesn't happen."

Horace frowned, annoyed. It didn't make sense that she wouldn't be able to go underground. Matter was matter. But he searched for something new to talk about. "So . . . weird fact about the box. It can't see itself. I never see the future box through the box."

"That's strange."

"And awesome."

"Yeah." Chloe looked down at the dragonfly. "Okay, here's one for me: I can hear the dragonfly. When the wings are going. I . . . hear it in my flesh. It sounds like music. Like a kind of wind that sings. No one else ever hears it."

"That's cool. How about this—did you ever do anything really stupid with the dragonfly?"

"I think most of the things I've done with it are probably stupid," Chloe said, tugging a strand of black hair and crossing her eyes to look at it. "Like, come on—cheating at tag?"

"No, I mean embarrassing. Because you didn't know any better yet. Like, at first I thought the box was just sending stuff someplace else—teleporting it, right? So I wrote a note and sent it through. I thought about it really hard. I said a major scientific discovery was happening, or something. I included my address and I wrote 'Chicago, Illinois, USA, *Earth*.'"

Chloe let out a little titter. "If the note's going *off the planet*, you don't need to put earth on there. You're probably screwed anyway."

"Yeah, I thought of that later. Oh, and my dad found the note. After it came through."

Chloe slapped her hand over her mouth and huffed into it, her eyes wide with delight.

Horace laughed with her, trying to stay quiet. "He goes, 'I don't know whether to praise your creativity or question your sanity.'"

Chloe scooped Horace's pillow from the floor and buried her face in it. They laughed for a long time, Chloe's muffled shrieks leaking out. Horace hoped the pillow didn't stink or anything. At last she lifted her head and fell back against the wall. "Oh man. Oh man," she said. "That is so funny."

"Yeah, well. I figured it out. That's the important thing."

Chloe pointed into the air over Horace's head. "Hey, there's a firefly in here."

Horace turned and craned his neck. "Oh, that's just Rip."

"Rip. You live with a firefly named Rip."

Horace blushed. "Yeah, well, that's not his full name." He stood up and scooped the bug out of the air. "It's twelve forty-five. He just got here."

"What do you mean?"

For an answer, Horace held up the box. Chloe's eyes popped open. "Are you serious?"

"Yeah. I guess—speaking of stupid things. But it was because of him that I even figured out what the box can do. With the viewings, I mean." He knelt and gently deposited the bug inside the box. Loki watched with wide dark eyes, his tail thumping softly into the carpet.

"Is that safe?" Chloe asked, leaning forward to see.

"I've been doing it every night for over a week now. He seems fine." Horace closed the lid. He felt the tingle, then reopened the box so Chloe could see the bug was gone.

"Little bug," she called out. "Little Rip." She sat back and cocked her head at Horace. "Horace, tell me you didn't name a firefly Rip Van Winkle."

"I didn't."

"No, you're cleverer than that. I'm close, though."

"*Really* close," Horace agreed, pleased that she'd called him clever.

She narrowed her eyes and chewed on the corner of her mouth. At last she said, "Horace, do you have a time-traveling lightning bug named Rip Van Twinkle?"

"I do." They caught their laughs in their mouths again, rocking silently in the gloom.

Chloe pinched the bridge of her nose and let her hand fall into her lap with a sigh. "I don't laugh much, usually."

Horace didn't know what to say to that. He fiddled with the lid of the box. "Anyway, it's your turn. Something embarrassing. Something dumb you did with the dragonfly."

"Oh, that." Chloe looked thoughtful for a bit, and then

she rolled her eyes. "Okay, but it's *really* embarrassing."

"I won't laugh."

"I don't care about that. Just . . . don't be gross about it."

"I won't." What did she mean, *gross?*

"Okay, so. When I first started going thin, I had a problem with my clothes." She gave him a sideways glance. "If I stood still, I was fine, but as soon as I moved, my clothes wouldn't move with me, and I'd . . . you know. Be naked."

Horace felt himself blushing again, hugely now, to hear Chloe use the word *naked*. He was grateful for the dim light in the room. "Wow, that's . . . really weird," he said. He tried to be logical about it. "But I guess it makes sense. There's no substance for the clothes to hang on to."

Chloe shrugged. "I guess. And even though things can't pass through me, of course I can pass through things, so as soon as I started walking, I walked right out of my clothes. My clothes would just fall in a pile where they were—shoes still tied, socks still inside them. Like I'd melted, or something." She pointed at him. "I told you it was embarrassing."

"No, it's cool. I mean, it's not *cool*. But it's interesting. The science of it is interesting."

"The science."

"You know what I mean."

"I suppose. Anyway, like you said, I figured it out. I remember practicing, telling my clothes to come with me. I tried to think of them as a part of me, and eventually they just *were*. Now it's automatic." She looked down at the dragonfly.

"I don't know. We just made it so it worked."

We, Horace thought. "Chloe, how long have you had the dragonfly?"

"Awhile. I don't remember how long."

"Did you ever go back to the House of Answers?"

"You mean that place? That's what it's called? I don't know for sure I was ever there."

"But you remember the birds. And you were in the neighborhood that day we met. Plus, where else would you have gotten the dragonfly?"

"I'm not lying to you, Horace. But okay, I'm in that neighborhood a lot because there's something there that . . . calls me. Or pulls at me. I don't know, I just feel drawn there. But I don't know what it is."

"That's the House of Answers," Horace said, leaning forward. "Mr. Meister says it draws the thin man there too."

Chloe's face seemed to fight itself. Her brow kept twitching and her mouth seesawed—firm and determined one moment, lopsided and anxious the next.

"What is it?" Horace asked.

"The tall man. The freak."

"Dr. Jericho."

"That's his name?"

"He's not actually a doctor."

"No kidding," Chloe said, as if that was obvious. "Anyway, that day on the bus wasn't the first time you'd seen him, was it? I think you've probably talked to him, even."

Horace shuddered, remembering his first encounter with Dr. Jericho. "I have. Once. And then he chased me off the bus that day you were there."

Chloe fidgeted, looking uncomfortable. "Yeah, well. Get used to it. He follows me, all the time. Sometimes he's with two others like him. And I've seen other . . . strange things."

"You mean like the girl with the flute?"

"Yes. I saw her talking to the freak once. But mostly it's just him—three or four times a week for the last few months. He's followed me here, even, but I make sure I lose him first. I've had some close calls."

"I know, I—"

"I mean, I'm not afraid. Not for myself."

"Why not?"

She shrugged and looked at him as if he were dumb. "Because I can't be caught. Period. But then there's my dad. And my sister."

"Chloe, you should—"

"The freak was in my house."

Horace tried to stay afloat atop the dread rising inside him. "What did you say?"

"Last night. Late. Talking to my dad. He was asking about me." She swung a sad look at him. "And you."

CHAPTER FIFTEEN

The Vora Speaks

CHLOE AND HORACE STOOD AT THE BLUE DOORWAY TO THE House of Answers. Chloe let out a slow, thoughtful sigh. "Yeah, right," she said dreamily. "This place. This is the place."

"You remember this?"

"Maybe. Like I've been here or I dreamed it, but I can't tell which."

"How come you don't remember more?"

"Nobody's perfect, Horace. But you're forgiven for assuming."

It was Monday, just after noon. The school year had ended for them both that morning, with a mostly pointless half day of school. Since their first long talk they'd been meeting every night, and Chloe had at last agreed to go to the House of Answers. It turned out that when the thin man had showed up at Chloe's house asking questions, she hadn't been able to hear the whole conversation because she'd been hiding as only she could hide. *"In the heart,"* she'd said, which meant nothing to Horace. But Chloe had heard Dr. Jericho ask about her, about the dragonfly, about the boy with the box. It was unclear how Chloe's father had answered Dr. Jericho's questions, but Horace got the impression that something wasn't quite right with him. "My dad does some stupid things sometimes," Chloe had explained. There was a little sister, Madeline, but she'd been at an aunt's house that night. No mention of a mother had been made at all.

Chloe had been downplaying the thin man's visit. When Horace told her about the warnings Mrs. Hapsteade and Mr. Meister had given him, she'd said, "Yeah, but they're like really old, right?" Nonetheless, at least she was here.

"So," she said now, looking at the round sign. "I don't remember this sign, but I guess we state our name and we name our state. That's easy." She gave the door a little bow. "I'm Chloe Oliver. Slightly skeptical."

"Oh—and I'm Horace Andrews," said Horace, marveling at how Chloe made him feel like he was the newcomer here. "I'm, uh . . . expecting."

Chloe doubled over, laughing. "You mean expectant?" she said.

"Oh, right. Expectant," he said, blushing hard. "Expectant."

"That's good, because otherwise you would have a lot of explaining to do."

Chloe tugged the door open and stepped confidently into the tunnel, leading the way. She ambled down the narrow passage as though she were on a tour, trailing her fingers along the walls and looking around. Tiny as she was, her shape blocked the path, making the space seem even more confined. Horace tried to will his feet to move in after her.

Several steps in, she stopped and turned. "You coming?"

"Yeah. Of course." He stepped into the gloom. The door closed behind him. With Chloe blocking the passageway in front, all his nerves began to jangle, his flight instinct kicking in as though he were being pushed beneath waves. He froze, pressing his hands against the walls. Chloe cocked her head at him.

"You're claustrophobic," she said, her voice echoing and slow.

"Small spaces make me nervous, that's all. And you're in the way." His own voice sounded too sharp, too fast.

Chloe pressed herself against the wall, motioning him through. As he squeezed by, she said, "Lots of people are claustrophobic, you know. It's nothing to be ashamed of."

"I'm not ashamed," Horace said, climbing down the steps toward the tunnel of birds.

"Everybody's afraid of something."

"You're not."

"Of course I am. You just haven't witnessed it yet."

Ahead, the birds' song seemed fuller, louder, as thick and buoyant as a river, carrying them forward into the House of Answers. Chloe spun almost giddily as they walked.

"They remember me," Chloe said. "I remember you," she told the birds, giggling. Spinning and giggling was about the last thing he expected from her, but he said nothing. He too was glad to see the birds again. Once through, Horace came to a sudden halt beside the podium. Chloe stopped chattering and went still just behind him.

The place was nearly empty.

The swirling sparkling columns of amber light glowed as steadily as ever, but the tables beneath—once overflowing with loaded bins—were bare. The shelves along the walls had been stripped as well, with just a few tipped-over bins here and there. The inventory was being moved out.

Before Horace had even finished looking around, a shadow detached itself from the darkness along the wall and swooped toward them, swift and rustling. Horace drew back and Chloe gave an angry huff of alarm, but then he saw.

"Mrs. Hapsteade," he breathed.

Mrs. Hapsteade swept up and gave them each the tiniest nod. "Horace Andrews," she said. "Chloe Burke."

"Oliver," Chloe murmured, clearly unsettled.

Mrs. Hapsteade seemed not to hear. She gestured back to the nearest table, where bowls had been set out beside a steaming metal pot. "We'll eat soup now. A hungry mind is a dull mind, especially for Keepers like us." And then she whisked to the table and stood there silently, her back to the children.

Horace and Chloe exchanged looks. Chloe's face was thick with doubt.

"That's Mrs. Hapsteade," Horace whispered. "She's okay."

Mrs. Hapsteade called back to them. "We've met, Horace Andrews, thank you. Come now—soup."

Horace and Chloe approached the table. Mrs. Hapsteade took a seat on one side and directed them impatiently around to the other, where two rickety chairs had been set up. They took their seats as Mrs. Hapsteade ladled thick golden soup from the pot. A planty, earthy smell rose from the soup, but there were no spoons.

Horace asked, "What kind of soup—"

"Ginkgo soup. Made from the leaves, not the nuts."

Horace frowned at the soup, tried to change the subject. "You were waiting for us."

"I don't wait. I prepare."

Chloe scoffed at that, but said nothing.

"Why is the warehouse empty?" Horace asked. "Where are you taking everything?"

"It was time. No warehouse lasts forever. Eat, and then we'll talk." Mrs. Hapsteade ladled a bowl of soup for herself. She solved the mystery of the missing spoons by lifting the bowl to her mouth and sipping carefully. After a moment Horace did the same, Chloe watching his progress from the

167

corner of her eye. The soup was delicious—not at all the way it smelled or looked, but sweet and light and almost crisp. Horace finished his bowl quickly, to his slight embarrassment, and Mrs. Hapsteade filled it up again.

"Don't worry, it's not Turkish delight," Mrs. Hapsteade said to Chloe, a comment that was lost on Horace but evidently meant something to Chloe. Chloe hummed doubtfully but took a sip. Although she looked determined not to like it, it was clear she found it as delicious as Horace did. Horace pretended not to notice as Chloe set into the soup with barely disguised gusto.

Horace wiped his mouth and looked at Mrs. Hapsteade. "A minute ago you said 'Keepers like us.' And the first time I was in here, you told me you were the Keeper of something."

"Yes, I am the Keeper of the Vora."

"But what does that mean? What is the Vora?"

"Funny that you ask, since you've used it. The both of you."

"Both of us? How is that possible?"

"The Vora belongs to me the same way the box belongs to you, Horace, and the dragonfly belongs to Chloe."

Chloe set down her bowl and spoke for the first time. "You're saying this Vora is a magic thing? Like ours?"

Mrs. Hapsteade snorted. "Magic? Magic is a word used by the ignorant to explain things they don't understand." She glared at them, then lifted a sturdy finger, pointing from one to the other. "Don't you be forgetting. If you go around believing in magic, you'll be searching for excuses even when there are none."

Horace wasn't about to believe in magic. But he had a thousand questions, each one leading to a thousand more. "So if these things—"

"Instruments."

"If these *instruments* aren't magic, then what are they?"

"They are devices, like any other. They obey the laws of the universe, even when they seem not to."

"And what are they called?" Horace asked.

"There are many names, depending on the item and the circumstances. Collectively—from the dragonfly to a raven's eye and everything in between—such devices are called Tanu. The box, the sign on our front door, the lights that illuminate this very warehouse—all Tanu. Some of these Tanu will work for anyone—they do not take the bond, and they do not have a Keeper. These devices are known as Tan'kindi."

"Like leestones?" Horace offered.

"Yes. Tan'kindi are fairly common, and you don't have to have any special talent to use them. But there are certain rare Tanu that can only be used by those who possess the proper talents. When such a Tanu takes a Keeper, it becomes Tan'ji." She gestured to each of them in turn. "The box, the dragonfly, the Vora. These are Tan'ji. *We* are Tan'ji."

"Tan'ji," Horace said. He pronounced the word carefully, rhyming it with "on *me*," stressing the second syllable. "What does that mean?"

Mrs. Hapsteade's eyebrows lifted a fraction of an inch. "From the biggest of questions to the smallest," she murmured. "There are no precise words of translation. You might say it means 'the opened gift.' Or 'the taken route.' Or maybe more to the spirit of it, though less accurate wordwise, 'the ridden horse.' Tan'ji is not just the object; it's also the act, the state. It's the entwining of the power and the self. But as I've said, the language doesn't always suit itself to translation."

Chloe was leaning far forward in her chair, listening intently, and as Mrs. Hapsteade spoke she made a little noise of understanding, as though the old woman were speaking aloud something Chloe had long suspected herself.

"And what language is that?" Horace asked.

Mrs. Hapsteade dropped her chin. She plucked briefly at the cuffs of her dress. "A dying one." Her voice was so sad that even Chloe lowered her eyes.

The three of them sat in silence, letting the birdsong rise around them. After a while, Mrs. Hapsteade said, "You came through the Find more quickly than we thought you would, Horace." Chloe looked up curiously.

"Really?" Horace said. "It seemed to take forever."

"I'm sure it did, but it was relatively swift, all things considered. I was a year in the Find myself."

"A year!" Horace could hardly imagine a worse torture.

"What's the Find?" Chloe asked.

"The Find," Mrs. Hapsteade explained, "is what we call the time right after we first encounter our Tan'ji, when we are left to discover our new instrument's powers on our own."

"Yeah, about that," Horace said. "Why—?"

"Too much knowledge spoils the process," Mrs. Hapsteade said briskly. "The bond has to form through discovery rather than instruction. Curiosity rather than expectations. Think of it this way: if you want to know the forest well, don't walk the trail; instead, wander lost until you know your way."

Mrs. Hapsteade glanced at Chloe, then picked up her bowl and drained it in a single long gulp. She nodded approvingly and stood up, gesturing for them to follow. "Come. You'll be interested in what I have to show you."

She strode to the podium where the guest book lay open. She turned and gestured over the podium, her stern face almost aglow. "Here is my Tan'ji—the Vora."

Horace gaped. "The book? That guest book is the Vora?"

"The book? No, no, no." She lifted the book and tossed it aside. It hit the floor with a *whack*. "That's just a book." Mrs. Hapsteade gestured again at the podium. "The Vora."

Horace came closer, Chloe just behind. "The quill," he said. The tall white feather lay atop the podium. He remembered dropping the quill that first day, and how Mrs. Hapsteade had picked it up with such care. "It's the quill— that's the Vora."

Mrs. Hapsteade raised a finger. "One part. The quill is the tongue." She pulled the stopper from the bottle of ink. "The inkwell is the breath. Together, the Vora."

Horace looked at the long white quill with new eyes.

And for the first time, he examined the jar that held the ink: square and dark green, covered with small inscriptions and tiny, almost hieroglyphic images. "I don't understand—the breath and the tongue. They speak to you?"

"The Vora speaks for others. It speaks for the wielder."

"The person writing, you mean?" Chloe asked.

Mrs. Hapsteade dropped her heavy, unflinching gaze onto Chloe. "Of course. The Vora speaks truths even the writer might not know about herself."

"But how can that be?" Horace objected. "When I wrote in the book, I wrote just what I meant to. The quill didn't write anything different, and it didn't make me—"

"You want proof. A demonstration?" Horace thought he detected the faintest twinkle in Mrs. Hapsteade's eye.

"I'm not saying I don't believe you, I just don't understand."

"I don't either," Chloe said.

Mrs. Hapsteade opened a wide drawer on the front of the podium and pulled out another guest book—there looked to be an entire stack in there. She spread it open and plucked up the great white quill. "Who's first?"

Neither Chloe nor Horace reached for the quill. Because Horace had no idea what to expect, he wasn't sure he wanted to go first—and judging by the look on Chloe's face, she wasn't sure she wanted to go at all.

"Worried?" Mrs. Hapsteade said, looking from one to the other. "Fearful? You've both used it before. Think it will bite you now?"

Chloe shifted uneasily. "You keep saying that, but I don't remember—"

"'Name: Chloe Burke,'" Mrs. Hapsteade said, as though reciting. "'Address: Chicago. Age: five. Reason for visit: none given. Question: Who is asking?'"

"Chloe was here when she was *five*?" Horace asked, incredulous.

Chloe looked just as stunned, staring at Mrs. Hapsteade. "You're saying I wrote that? When I was here?"

"You are Chloe Burke, correct?" said Mrs. Hapsteade.

"My name's not Burke anymore. That was my mom's name."

"Nonetheless, plainly I refer to you. You needed some help—you were too short to reach the podium, and you didn't understand how the Vora worked, at first. I assisted. But you wrote. You did very well, for such a small child. And your response to 'Question' . . . 'Who is asking?' Very funny. I was amused." Mrs. Hapsteade looked anything but amused.

Horace turned to Chloe. "Wait, so you've had the dragonfly for *seven years*?"

Chloe had her hand at her throat, worrying her pendant. "I guess so, Horace. I told you it was a while."

Horace reeled this new information in. When she'd told him about her clothes falling off the first time she used the dragonfly, he'd envisioned a Chloe just like the Chloe of today. But she'd been just *five*. A sudden warmth flooded through him, pooling toward Chloe as if she had gravity. He thought about her rundown house and her boarded-up windows, and he pictured her bedroom, spare and gray and dark with sheets for curtains. For a long, dizzy moment, he fought off an urge to reach out and take Chloe's hand.

Mrs. Hapsteade broke into Horace's thoughts, holding the quill forward again. "And now, who will try?"

"I will." Horace took the quill and stepped up to the podium. He dipped it into the ink and brought the tip over the paper, hovering. "What should I write?"

"Anything. It doesn't matter."

Horace thought for a moment and then touched the pen to paper. Deep blue ink flowed from the tip as he wrote.

Chloe and the dragonfly

"Yes," said Mrs. Hapsteade, reading over his shoulder. "Yes, just like I remembered it. Maybe more so." She glanced at the box at Horace's side.

"But what does that mean? What does it do?"

"So much impatience. Let Chloe have her turn, and we'll see."

When Chloe saw what Horace had written she shot him a look of annoyed disbelief, much to his embarrassment.

Chloe dipped the pen into the ink and began to write without hesitation. As soon as the pen started to move, though, she stopped and let out a little cry: "Oh!" Horace leaned in as Chloe continued to write.

You are not reading this.

Horace's brain was wrapping itself around what Chloe had written, but then he realized—Chloe's words were red. Deep bloodred. Above them, his own words still gleamed in bright, shining blue.

"Wait a minute, there must be—" he began.

"It's the same ink," Mrs. Hapsteade interjected. "This is what the Vora does."

"I don't understand," he said.

"I do," said Chloe. "The color of the ink . . . it changes depending on the writer. And the color means something to you, doesn't it?"

"The color just for starters, yes. I see much more."

"This is how you find out about us. How you know what we can do."

"Yes."

"Horace's box doesn't work for me. Probably the dragonfly doesn't work for him. And you can tell that just by looking at what we wrote."

"Exactly. The Vora reveals what aptitude, if any, the writer has for wielding an instrument. For becoming Tan'ji. The color and intensity of the ink reveal your strengths, your tendencies toward certain kinds of instruments. And there are other, more subtle signs to read there, too."

Chloe laid the quill across the open book. "This is how you recruit us."

Horace was startled by the word. Mrs. Hapsteade's expression didn't change, but she said, "We don't recruit."

"And who exactly is *we?*"

"We provide. We assist."

"Out of the goodness of your own—"

"Out of necessity." Mrs. Hapsteade reached across and restoppered the ink, twisting the plug down tight. Then with a swift clean jerk she tore loose the page they had written on, folding it neatly into her front pocket.

"What necessity?" Chloe demanded. "And why are you taking that?"

"You misunderstand. We want you to be safe. We want your Tan'ji to be safe."

"From what?"

"Is that a question you really need to ask? You stink of brimstone, just like Horace did when we first met. You've had your encounters with Dr. Jericho too, haven't you?"

Chloe shifted uneasily. "So? That's my business, not yours."

"You're angry because all you can do is run and hide. Wouldn't you like to do more?"

Chloe's jaw dropped, her face lit with fury. Horace stepped in. "What do you mean more?" he asked. "What do you want us to do?"

Mrs. Hapsteade shrugged. "We want you to fight."

CHAPTER SIXTEEN

The Rescue

"YOU WANT US TO BE SAFE, BUT YOU WANT US TO FIGHT," Horace said.

"We want you to join us. We are the resistance. We fight to defend our Tan'ji—and the other instruments in our possession—from our enemies."

"Dr. Jericho."

"The Riven. It's time you knew the name. The Riven are everywhere; Dr. Jericho is only one of many. The Riven want to possess and control all the Tanu, including our Tan'ji."

Horace swallowed. "But if we defeat Dr. Jericho, we'll be safe once and for all, right? Our Tan'ji would be safe from the Riven?"

"No," Chloe said abruptly.

"Chloe is right. If you defeat one soldier—even a captain—have you won the battle? And what of the war?"

Battle. War. Horace laid his hand on the box, unsure what part he could possibly have to play in such things. "And how are we supposed to fight?"

"With your Tan'ji, of course. And with the other Tanu in our possession. Don't misunderstand me. Not everyone who fights actually does battle. There are many, many Tanu in the world. Some are more . . . martial than others, but whatever their purpose, all Tanu can help us in our fight against the Riven."

"But who are the Riven, exactly?" Horace insisted. "*What* are they?"

"Mr. Meister will tell you more. For now, know that your Tan'ji are in constant danger. But you mustn't simply hide them away. The Tanu are our best def—"

Mrs. Hapsteade cut herself off, her head whipping around toward the entrance. Back through the tunnel of birds, sunlight and shadows flickered complexly on the floor. The front door was open—someone was there. The birdsong swelled suddenly, becoming shrill and urgent, escalating until it was painfully, piercingly loud. Horace clapped his hands over his ears. The shadows in the tunnel began to dance more wildly, not just shadows but shapes, or one great shape, coming closer, pounding loud and blotting out the sun, and Mrs. Hapsteade turned to the two of them. Horace could read but not hear the word that formed on her lips.

Run!

They ran, Mrs. Hapsteade out in front, streaking ahead.

She led them deeper into the room, deeper into the darkness. Horace's footsteps hammered in his bones. He glanced back, knowing what he would see—Dr. Jericho, catching them here together at last.

But it was not Dr. Jericho.

The shape that poured from the mouth of the tunnel now was not a man. It was a shadow chiseled from stone, from many stones, a shifting mass like a living black wave. Slowly it rose into a looming tower, countless thousands of sliding black rocks moving as one. It gathered itself until it nearly touched the high ceiling. Though it had no eyes, it crashed forward after them. It was as if the earth itself had come to life, come to bury them all. And it was gaining on them.

The massive door at the far end of the room appeared out of the gloom ahead, the door that Horace had wondered at when he first saw it—ten feet high and built to hold off an army. If they could get to it in time.

Except they weren't going to make it. The grinding mass was too close behind them. Mrs. Hapsteade stopped and turned. She reached into her collar and pulled out a round white pendant on a chain, tearing it free just as Horace and Chloe caught up to her.

"Get behind me," she said, her usually strong voice thin beneath the approaching thunder. She held the small round object in her hand—a raven's eye? No, clearly some other kind of Tanu, somewhat larger and milky white.

Mrs. Hapsteade raised the white sphere high into the

air and crushed it in her fist, shattering it. A vast, deep note thrummed, like a harp string as thick as a tree being plucked. The sound, pure force, knocked Chloe from her feet, threw Horace against the door. Horace caught the scent of flowers. All around them a clear, shining dome appeared, its curving face coming between them and the black avalanche roaring down.

The stone beast crashed against the dome. It shook and groaned, but the shield held. The beast rose up and boiled and churned over every inch of the curved surface, but it could not get in.

Mrs. Hapsteade whirled to the door and hefted the wooden crossbar from its braces. The door creaked open, pulling in a stream of cold air. "Hurry," she said. "The dumin—the shield—won't last for long. We must get away."

Chloe ignored her, instead climbing to her feet and stepping close to Mrs. Hapsteade's shield. Through the dumin, the boiling black mass still struggled to get at them. It was a swarm of almond-sized black chunks, as smooth and shiny as beetles, but they weren't creatures at all. Horace saw they were some kind of chiseled shape, all identical, yet they worked together with a kind of intelligence he couldn't begin to understand.

Chloe spoke for them both. "What is this thing? Why is it after us?"

"It is a golem. It is not to be trifled with."

"A golem?" Horace said. "I thought that was just a legend, a story."

"Sometimes legend and fact cross paths. Come. We must go." Mrs. Hapsteade looked back through the dome, almost seeming to peer through the black mass of the golem. Her face was creased and pained.

And then Horace realized. "The Vora," he said.

Chloe looked puzzled, but then her expression slid from shocked to angry as she understood.

They'd left the Vora behind.

Mrs. Hapsteade dragged the massive door open, revealing a wide, dark passageway. "Come," she said. "It's time."

"You're just going to leave it?" said Chloe.

Mrs. Hapsteade turned away. "I have no choice."

"But it's your Tan'ji. You can't abandon it."

A stab of unmistakable anguish flickered across Mrs. Hapsteade's face. "It's already lost."

Chloe shook her head. "No, it isn't. I can get it back."

"Don't be ridiculous. You do not know the golem. You cannot get it back."

"Of course I can." Chloe laid her hand on the shimmering surface of the dumin, testing it. "I can do more than just run and hide."

"There's no way—" Mrs. Hapsteade began, but the dragonfly's wings were already thrumming. A grimace of effort and delight washed over Chloe's face as she pushed her hand through the dumin. As it emerged slowly into the seething black mass outside, Chloe winced.

She turned to Mrs. Hapsteade. "Tell me I'll be able to get

back in through this shield. It's so . . . *there*."

Mrs. Hapsteade shook her head, staring at Chloe's hand, her eyes wide with shock. "You should not be able to do what you already are."

Chloe pulled her hand back inside, squeezing it. Horace flinched as something sharp and bloodred—jagged and fish sized, shaped like a blade—darted hungrily through the black swarm where Chloe's hand had been. "I'll have to be fast," Chloe said, "but I can do it."

"Wait," Horace said, reaching for the box. "Let me check."

"I don't need you to check."

"I'm doing it anyway." Horace opened the box. He pointed it toward the dumin: *darkness out in tomorrow's room, stillness; no dumin; no golem; the place in shambles; shelves torn down; tables crushed and tossed; farther on into the room, one of the stone columns ripped apart, turned to rubble and dust.* He snapped the box closed. "That thing is strong, Chloe."

Mrs. Hapsteade watched them with burning eyes. "Strong is not the word. Please, we must—"

"Let it be strong," Chloe told them. "Let it waste all its strength on me."

Horace felt almost sick with worry. And then an idea occurred to him. "Chloe, do you have any mints?"

Chloe considered him, still squeezing her hand. "I do."

"You'll get the Vora. You'll give me a mint when you come back, and I'll leave it here as a sign that you made it. Do you understand?"

She nodded slowly. "I do."

"This is a fool's proof," Mrs. Hapsteade said. "It means nothing. We have to go."

"If I don't see the mint," said Horace, "you don't do this."

Chloe shrugged. It was the best he would get. Horace fell to one knee, scanning the floor. He quickly found what he was looking for—a half-inch crack between two of the floor stones. He focused on it, telling himself that if Chloe made it back safe again, he would take a mint from her and drop it into this crack. Then he opened the box.

The stone floor, gouged and scratched; loose rubble and crushed stone all around, nothing to see, but then—a glint of white between the debris, just there. "I see it," he said, then realized he wished he hadn't. Nothing would stop Chloe from trying this now. He gazed at the mint, waiting for it to fade, to shift, but it didn't. If anything, it sparkled.

"It's here. You'll make it." He tried to make himself believe the words.

"This is madness," Mrs. Hapsteade said. "The box doesn't make guarantees."

"You said we should do more," Chloe said. "So let us do it."

Mrs. Hapsteade shook her head. "You trust the box with your life?"

"I trust Horace." Chloe smiled at Horace, dazzling. The dragonfly began to hum again. "Besides, I was going to do it anyway." And with that she was gone.

The golem whipped into a fury as Chloe emerged into the room, swirling around her like a tornado. But Chloe, clever Chloe, led the beast into one of the massive stone columns in the center of the room, where it had to break apart momentarily while Chloe passed clean through. He caught a glimpse of her on the far side, running full out, just before the column shattered.

Mrs. Hapsteade's face was unreadable. "This will be remembered."

The golem vanished into the darkness of the long room, and Chloe with it. Horace realized he was counting: *seventeen, eighteen, nineteen.* He found his voice. "How much longer will the dumin hold?"

"She must hurry," said Mrs. Hapsteade.

Twenty-six, twenty-seven, twenty-eight. The golem barreled back into sight—not a tornado now but a fist, a churning knot, coming closer. Chloe had to be at the center of that knot, running blind as the stony coils of the golem tore through her. *Thirty-five, thirty-six . . .*

The golem slammed against the dumin with the force of a truck. A moment later, Chloe sliced through the shining wall, crying out, stumbling to her knees before Mrs. Hapsteade. The golem fumed and thundered, trying to get at them all. The ground trembled. The dumin held.

Chloe choked and coughed, looking as though she might vomit. Her arms were peppered with a dozen little wounds—black, purple, red. The quill and ink bottle spilled from her hands.

"Hold on," she croaked. "Hold on." Horace watched, horrified, as one of the black shapes wormed its way out of the skin of her forearm and clattered to the floor, motionless. Chloe reared back, one hand on her chest, gagging. Another stone emerged, this time from the little hollow at the base of her throat. It fell loose, and the dragonfly went still. Mrs. Hapsteade crushed the two black stones beneath her heel, one after the other. They made a ghastly gritty sound and left a powdery stain on the floor. Mrs. Hapsteade bent and picked up the quill and bottle, slipping them into a pocket in her dress. Her eyes shone as she gazed down at Chloe.

"Felt them in me," Chloe gasped. "Don't know how they got in there." She looked back at the golem, pressing a hand against her side. "And there was something else in there. I felt it, like a knife or something. So fast, and sharp."

"We'll speak more of what you've done here, Keeper," said Mrs. Hapsteade. "For now it must be enough to say—" Her voice broke, and she clutched her dress. "It must be enough to say that no words will do."

Mrs. Hapsteade helped Chloe to her feet. Once she was standing, Chloe pulled a roll of mints from her pocket. She thumbed one loose into Horace's waiting hand. She nodded.

Horace knelt, searching for the crack he'd found earlier. He spotted it and dropped the mint into it, like a coin into a slot. As he stood again, he found Mrs. Hapsteade's eyes on him. "What would happen if you didn't do this? If you didn't follow the future revealed by the box?"

Horace was surprised to be asked. He shrugged. "It would hurt."

Mrs. Hapsteade nodded. "Good." She stepped into the open doorway, her hand under Chloe's arm. Horace peered past her into the dark. Behind them, it sounded as though the golem had begun to tear apart the very walls around the dumin.

Mrs. Hapsteade reached into her collar and pulled out another chain, this one long and black. How many necklaces were hiding under that collar? A slender black crystal hung from the chain, mounted in a silver setting that curled open like the petals of a flower. The crystal glowed, emitting a strange blue-black light. "Just through here is an unpleasantness," Mrs. Hapsteade said, nodding into the dark. "Unavoidable, I'm afraid. I won't ask whether you're ready."

"We *are* ready," Chloe replied. She stepped away from Mrs. Hapsteade, straightening.

"That's unlikely, but it hardly matters. Hold on to yourselves as best you can." Mrs. Hapsteade closed and barred the great door behind them. The eerie light from the long black crystal around her neck lit the passageway dimly. Once their eyes adjusted, they discovered the dumin's back end, here in the tunnel. Apparently the shield wasn't just a wall, but a complete sphere. As Horace struggled to imagine how it worked, though, the dumin flickered out of sight with a faint crackle. An instant later, the door shook seismically beneath the golem's weight. Dust and grit showered them.

"We need to hurry," Horace said. "It's going to get through."

"The golem won't come through the door." Mrs. Hapsteade glided into the tunnel, apparently untroubled. Horace and Chloe followed the circle of black light that spread out from her necklace. Much to Horace's relief, the tunnel was large—as broad and as high as the House of Answers itself, and pleasantly cool.

"Why won't the golem come through the door?" he asked.

"Can't you feel it?" Mrs. Hapsteade replied.

"All I can feel is that it's cold in here," Chloe said.

"As a matter of fact, it isn't," Mrs. Hapsteade said, and led them on. Despite her words, the air grew noticeably colder. The beast's pounding eventually faded, and Mrs. Hapsteade turned and pointed a stern warning finger at them both, lingering for a long moment on Chloe. "You must not reach for your instruments. Understand?"

They nodded. In a few steps more, their scuffling footsteps became hollow and clanging as they stepped out onto ridged metal plates of some kind. Before Horace could wonder what the surface was, a heavy, numbing chill struck him like a blow. It was a cold so pure and so sharp that it sank into him like a fist of icy knives, a pain beyond nerves. Horace could no longer feel himself, could not sense the floor beneath his feet, could not taste the air he presumably still breathed.

And he could not feel the box.

CHAPTER SEVENTEEN

In the Tunnels

HORACE CRIED OUT. THE BOX, A CONSTANT PRESENCE IN HIS mind for so long now, had vanished, stolen away by this cruel cold. He groped for the pouch at his side, slapping blindly, but his fingers were numb and could tell him nothing. He dimly registered Chloe's scolding voice, off to the left somewhere, an angry note of panic.

"Do not struggle," came Mrs. Hapsteade's voice, thick and deep and slow. They might have been miles apart. "Only walk."

"The box. It's gone," Horace called out, or tried to, his words seeming to freeze and drop to the ground.

"It's not gone. The box is with you."

"No, no, it's gone," Horace pleaded. "It's not . . . here." By *here* he meant in his head, in him. He searched for Chloe and Mrs. Hapsteade, saw a sliver of light, and movement within it—they were drifting, fractured shapes, slow and distant.

"This is the Nevren. Don't fear it. The bond is temporarily cut, but it'll return. Keep moving and you will return."

But Horace wanted to stop. He did not want to hear Mrs. Hapsteade's voice. He did not care about the Nevren. He could not even feel that he was moving forward, so why should he bother? The box was gone. What else mattered? There was only emptiness and hopelessness.

But now Chloe's voice pierced through his fog, thin and far but as keen as a needle. "Keep moving, Horace," it said, and then he heard or did not hear it go on: *You're almost through.*

"There is no through."

"Don't be stupid. I'm through. Here, let me—"

Another voice cut through the stillness. *"No. He must come on his own, if he will come."* Mrs. Hapsteade. But who was Mrs. Hapsteade again?

"I think you are ghosts," Horace said. "I'm a ghost. Stop talking to me."

"None of us are ghosts. You're almost there. Just keep moving, and you'll be free in no time."

Horace shook his head, if he had a head. "No, no," he said. "There is no time. No such thing as time."

"Yes, you saw tomorrow already—another time. The box showed you."

Ruined pillars of stone. A gleaming white crescent. The box. "That isn't real," Horace slurred, and maybe he went on talking or maybe he didn't. . . . "None of that is real. The box isn't real."

The voice returned. Why wouldn't it leave him alone? *"The box is real. It's here. I have the box, Horace. Here, I have it."*

Horace lifted his head, saw sliding silhouettes. *The box?* "You have the box?"

"Yes. I have it. Come take it from me."

The voice had the box. That was wrong. Why had she taken it from him? The box was his. "The box is mine."

"Come and get it."

Horace told himself he would do that. He told himself to move. He wanted to get the box away from the voice—from Chloe. Mrs. Hapsteade. The golem. The Nevren. And now a burning began to fill him, an unbearable warmth, and he could feel himself again—but only as a vessel of tingling agony, as though his entire body had fallen numb and was now rousing to life all at once.

And there, miraculously, was the box. It was *here*, its presence sweeping through him like an embrace. He laid a hand on it and staggered, nearly falling to the ground. He opened his eyes, shocked to realize they were closed.

Chloe stood before him, inches away, with a look of such relief that he thought she might embrace him. The golem's marks burned on her arms, her throat—how brave she was. Horace drank in the box, reveling in how near it was, how much of himself it was, how whole he felt. And how warm Chloe was too, and pretty, and maybe he would say that to her, maybe she was waiting to hear it. Everything was good, so good.

Chloe searched his eyes. Horace swayed. She opened her mouth. "Dude, what the *hell*."

"It's not his fault," Mrs. Hapsteade said. "It shouldn't have been like that for someone so new."

Horace rode the warmth back into himself. It felt so good he could not understand what Mrs. Hapsteade was saying. He looked back along the passageway behind, but there was nothing to see. Just the metal plates covering the floor.

"Shouldn't have been like what?" Chloe asked. "What do you mean?"

"Horace was almost dispossessed."

"Dispossessed?" Chloe's voice was sharp, full of fangs.

"When the bond is severed for too long, we can sink into despair. We can become orphans, our instruments lost to us. Some Keepers have been swallowed whole by the emptiness of the Nevren, their minds gone forever, never to return even to what they were before the Find. A few don't make it at all."

Chloe rounded on Mrs. Hapsteade, furious. "You stopped me from going back for him, when you knew that could happen? What is wrong with you?"

Sludgy still, Horace wasn't sure he was understanding. Mrs. Hapsteade had stopped Chloe from helping him?

"He needed to prove that he could make it on his own. He shouldn't be carried."

"Like I carried the Vora? Maybe you think I shouldn't have done that either?"

"Don't play on my gratitude, Chloe Burke," Mrs. Hapsteade replied, her voice as flat as a blade.

"Don't call me that," Chloe spat.

"The box is different. The Keeper of the box—"

"The Keeper of the box was almost *dispossessed*, thanks to you. If that had been me in there, would you have left me, too?"

With a speed that dizzied Horace, Mrs. Hapsteade's arm shot out. She grasped the dragonfly and held it up in front of Chloe's eyes. Chloe became a statue, outrage stamped on her face. Horace heard himself gasp.

"This," Mrs. Hapsteade hissed, shaking the dragonfly, "is the ripple of a bird in flight." She threw out her other hand, pointing to the box. "And that is a hurricane. You astonished me today, Chloe, and maybe you think you are the most powerful Keeper standing in this passageway. But let me be clear: the tricks you and your trinket can perform are nothing compared to what the Keeper of the Fel'Daera needs to show me now." She spun away, dress twirling, and stalked off down the passage, taking the black glow with her. Too stunned to move, Horace and Chloe stood there until they were nearly in darkness. Silence mounted around them.

At last Chloe spoke. "So apparently you're a hurricane now."

Horace said nothing. He slid two fingers into the pouch and laid them along the side of the box. The box had a name—a wondrous thing.

"The Keeper of the whatsit?" said Chloe, looking down at the box. "The Fel'Daera?"

"I guess," Horace said, but he let the name play over and over in his mind. *The Fel'Daera.* A beautiful name. The right name. He felt the box swell beneath the thought.

In the distance, the black glow had come to a halt. "She's waiting for us," Chloe said. "What does she want with us, anyway? What does she expect us to do?"

"I don't know. She said I had something to prove." And with a little curl of excitement and dread, Horace wondered if Mrs. Hapsteade might not be right—maybe he did have something to prove. He was no match for Dr. Jericho or the golem, not in the way that Chloe had just proven she was, but the power the Fel'Daera granted him was so mysterious and huge. It was one thing to walk through walls. It was another thing entirely to see through time itself.

Chloe's eyes searched his face—concerned at first, and then going bright with mischief. "Okay, okay. I see the grandiose thoughts rolling around in there. But don't let her get you all freaked. She also said the dragonfly was a trinket. Do I seem like a trinket owner?"

Horace laughed. "Not really."

She stepped close to him. "Here." She held out a hand toward him, pointer finger extended. "Feel. Go ahead." Horace lifted the tip of his finger slowly to hers, and just as they were about to touch, the dragonfly stirred in the dark. His finger slipped into the tip of Chloe's, their flesh overlapping by just a fraction of an inch. In that fraction, a massive pulsing energy coursed, an ocean of new sensation, unfiltered and unnamed. Horace breathed, and she breathed with him. He could feel her heartbeat, thought he could feel even the tiny work of the cells that comprised her, the creeping growth of her bone, and beneath it all the sweet clarion song of the dragonfly itself, as much a part of her as anything else.

"Does that feel like a trinket to you?" Chloe said low.

"Definitely not," Horace said, his own voice hoarse.

She dropped her hand, breaking the connection and leaving him dazed. "So let's go show her."

They turned and went after Mrs. Hapsteade. The floor became crunchy, wet gravel. When they reached her, Mrs. Hapsteade surprised Horace by turning to Chloe and making a tiny bow. The glowing black pendant swung. Faint shadows bobbed and weaved around them. "My apologies, Keeper. There's no cause great enough to excuse the handling of another's Tan'ji without permission. I'm embarrassed." Chloe didn't respond, but Mrs. Hapsteade didn't seem to expect her to. Instead, she turned to Horace. "And my apologies to you, Keeper. I failed to act when I should have. It's not my place to ask that you prove anything to me. That task belongs to others."

Horace did not need to look at Chloe to know that she was as surprised by these formal apologies as he was. "It's okay," he murmured.

But Chloe was not so forgiving. "Why should he have to

prove anything to *anyone?*" she insisted.

"The Fel'Daera is dangerous. As dangerous as any weapon. Time is not a trivial matter, you know. It's not a simple force to be tweaked, like gravity or the push and pull of atoms. Time is the very fabric of our existence, our identities. More than any other element of the universe, it connects us all."

"But Horace is the Keeper of the box. He knows—"

"Maybe he does know best. I hope so. But not everyone agrees that the Fel'Daera should be offered up to new Keepers in the first place. Certainly it was never meant for deeds like the one I just witnessed."

Horace, listening mutely, perked up. "Then what was it meant for?"

Mrs. Hapsteade ignored him. "We must go see Mr. Meister. He'll need to hear what has happened. Will you walk with me, Keepers? It's not far." After a moment of awkward hesitation in which Horace wondered what "not far" meant to Mrs. Hapsteade, the three of them set out.

They entered a new tunnel, broader and higher yet, a wide arched passage running perpendicular to the first. Overhead, bits of sunlight streamed through irregular patches in the ceiling, odd rectangles and circles. Noises filtered through as well, rumbles and roars over a hissing river of sound—traffic. The patches of sun were sewer grates and drains in the street above. The ordinary world was still there, just above them.

They walked, footsteps crunching. More than once Horace thought he heard the squeak of a rat. A faint cool breeze and the windows of light above helped keep his head clear. Plus the tunnel, at the moment, was big enough to drive a bus through. He hoped it would stay that way.

"I'm wondering about the Nevren," Chloe said. "About why it's there."

"It protects us," Mrs. Hapsteade replied briskly. "Inside the Nevren, Tanu can't function, because they can't feed on the energies that allow them to be what they are. The golem, for instance—if it attempted to pass into the Nevren, it would crumble to pieces."

Horace couldn't help himself. "Wait . . . the golem is a Tanu?"

"Of course. Did you think that it was alive?"

Chloe shook her head. "It passed through me. I felt it. It's not alive."

"That's right. The golem is a device, like all Tanu. And like all Tanu—or almost all, anyway—it can't function in the Nevren."

"Does the golem have a Keeper, then?" Horace asked. "Were the Riven there, too?"

"The golem has no Keeper, not like you think. The golem is a very powerful Tan'kindi. It does not take the bond like a true Tan'ji, but it does require a controller—someone to hold the leash, if you like." Mrs. Hapsteade glanced back the way they had come, eyebrows high. "Yes, the Riven were there.

But they can't follow us any better than the golem can."

"Why not?"

"For the same reason we ourselves struggle through the Nevren. Understand that the Riven are highly dependent on their Tanu, in ways big and small. And most of the Riven have their own Tan'ji—sometimes more than one. The Riven bond very tightly with their instruments, to the point where one cannot be separated from the other. The bond is so tight that they can't suffer the Nevren nearly as well as we can. The moment the bond is severed, and their Tanu cease to function, they are incapacitated. Dispossession comes quickly." She looked heavily at Horace. "But the Nevren can be dangerous for us, too. I should've prepared you better, Horace. Stupid of me not to be more cautious."

"So, this Nevren thing," Chloe asked. "It's a Tanu too?"

"The Nevren's not a thing at all. It's an area of influence. A field."

"Like a magnetic field?" said Horace.

"Yes, much like that."

"And what creates that field?"

"The Nevren exists wherever we need safety. To reach any of our most intimate sanctuaries, you first have to pass through the Nevren."

Horace noticed that wasn't exactly an answer, but he didn't push her. "So there's more than one Nevren. But the House of Answers—we didn't pass through one when we came through the front door, or we would have felt it, right?"

"The front door has other safeguards. They aren't perfect, as you saw today when the golem came through, but I still don't know how the Riven found—" Mrs. Hapsteade stopped abruptly. She gestured for them to do the same, tipping her head as if she were listening. Her chest rose and fell, making the ghostly pool of black light around them pulse slightly. After a moment she spoke, her voice thick and low. "Wait here. Don't move." She slid forward down the tunnel.

Horace realized the passageway had become darker, and a lot narrower, grimy stone walls eight feet apart. He'd been too distracted to notice. Now it grew darker still as Mrs. Hapsteade pulled away swiftly, taking the black light with her. Ten feet, twenty feet, forty. Far away, and with the light in front of her, she looked like a paper doll. Then the light snuffed out, dropping them into total darkness.

"You okay?" Chloe said immediately.

Horace closed his eyes, concentrating on the faint, cool breeze. "What happened?"

"Don't know." Chloe shuffled impatiently. She called out. "Hello? Seriously?"

"We can't get out of here without her."

"Don't be dramatic. Of course we can."

A sharp rustling sound. The black light sprang back to life. Mrs. Hapsteade was returning. But there was someone at her side now, someone tall and lean and dark—not Mr. Meister. "It's all right," Mrs. Hapsteade called ahead to them. "A friend is here. There's been a change of plans."

Mrs. Hapsteade and the new arrival spoke to each other in low tones. Horace couldn't make out what they were saying. There was a strange extra beat to the sound of their approach, and as they drew nearer, Horace realized the stranger was walking with a cane. It dug crisply into the gritty floor with each step.

"Who meets people in the sewers?" Chloe mumbled.

The stranger stopped before them and stood ramrod straight, gazing vacantly over their heads. He was a tall black kid, high school age, maybe. He had short-cropped hair and wore dark clothes—long sleeves, long pants. There was something extremely proper about him, calm and reserved.

"No formalities," Mrs. Hapsteade said sharply, as though they'd been about to launch into handshakes and how-do-you-dos. "Horace, Chloe, Gabriel. I feel safe in saying we can all be trusted."

The tall boy—Gabriel—bent over his walking stick and made a small, elegant bow. The cane itself gleamed, dark but with a silver foot. Horace couldn't see details in the eerie light—and he couldn't say how he knew it—but it was obvious that the cane was Tan'ji.

"Gabriel will escort you safely home," Mrs. Hapsteade said briskly.

"But Mr. Meister—" Horace began.

"Certainly he must speak with you, but not today."

"What's going on?"

Mrs. Hapsteade brushed the question off. "Can you meet

again tomorrow—for the afternoon?"

Tomorrow was the first full day of summer vacation. Horace's parents would be at work. "I guess," he said. Chloe shrugged as though the question hardly mattered.

"Wait for me at the corner where you catch your usual bus to school, Horace. Twelve o'clock. You'll be home by four." Horace nodded, not bothering to ask how she knew where his bus stop was. "As for tonight, Chloe must stay with you, Horace. She'll be safest there."

"How am I supposed to arrange that?" Chloe protested, though from what Horace had seen, she could come and go as she pleased. He was more worried about where she'd sleep.

"Let's not invent problems until we have none," Mrs. Hapsteade said. She turned as if to go, then looked sharply up at Gabriel. "Remember, don't let the girl use the passkey."

Chloe let out a huff of indignation. "The what?"

Mrs. Hapsteade ignored her. "Keepers," she said with a nod, and then she spun and hurried back in the direction of the House of Answers.

"What was that all about?" Chloe said.

"The Kesh'kiri are in the tunnels," Gabriel replied.

The word, vicious and sharp, sent a chill through Horace. "Who?"

"Sorry—the Riven."

"Why did you call them that?"

"That's what they call themselves. Come. Mrs. Hapsteade and Mr. Meister will deal with them, but we must

200

go." He strode off in the opposite direction, cane swinging, leaving Horace and Chloe hurrying after him. As they drew swiftly farther from Mrs. Hapsteade, the darkness closed its fist around them. Gabriel seemed not to care. Horace found himself hardly able to breathe.

Chloe spoke from the gloom. "Do you always walk in the dark like this?"

Gabriel laughed. "I've been known to. Just stay behind me and follow the sound of my footsteps."

They walked on—unfamiliar, exhausting work in the dark. Horace closed his eyes to prevent them from straining uselessly at nothing. He kept tripping and veering into the walls, so he took to holding his arms out at his sides. He stumbled again and again. He wondered if the others were having the same difficulties, if they were as worried as he was that the Riven were down there with them somewhere.

"So, the Riven," Horace said. "They made it through the Nevren?"

"No," Gabriel replied. "They found another way."

"What happens if they catch us?" Horace asked.

"They will not catch us."

"But what if they did?"

Chloe piped up. "They'll try to take our Tan'ji. But good luck with that."

"They would not simply take your instruments," Gabriel corrected. "They would take you."

"Why?" said Horace.

"Without you, your Tan'ji would probably be useless to them. In order to actually wield the powers of your instruments, they would have to find another Keeper with the same talents as you—the same aptitudes and affinities. And the more formidable the instrument, the fewer people there are that have the ability to use it."

"So what they really want is for us to join them," Horace said.

"Yes. They want your power."

"I can't imagine anyone wanting to join them."

"Do you even know who they are?" Gabriel asked. "Do you know their cause?"

"No," Chloe said, "but it sounds like you do."

Gabriel went silent for several seconds. "All I mean to say is, many falter when faced with the choice the Riven offer: join their cause, or have your instrument taken from you by force."

Horace went cold. He tried to imagine what that would be like—would it be like the Nevren? Or would he be able to sense the Fel'Daera still, even though he no longer possessed it? He wasn't sure which was the worse fate.

"Many falter when faced with the choice, you say," Chloe said to Gabriel casually. "Would you falter?"

"Never," Gabriel said, dropping the word with an immediate and unmistakable firmness. "But it seems you've been told very little. Save your questions for Mr. Meister."

Just then, a brutal *crack!* slapped through the tunnel from far behind. Horace jumped. A few seconds later, a blast of wind slapped past them.

"The Riven," Horace muttered.

"No, that was a good thing," Gabriel said. "But we must keep moving."

The passageway dipped sharply, leading them through a shallow puddle of foul-smelling water. On the far side, they had to clamber up a low, slick wall. The air grew ever more damp.

Chloe cleared her throat. "So, Gabriel—this stick of yours. What does it do?"

"Something useful. Let us hope it doesn't come to that."

"Sounds scary. My theory is it's a lightsaber."

"There's no such thing as a lightsaber."

"That's not a very convincing argument. I've come face-to-face with a lot of no-such-things lately. Earlier, I ate ginkgo-leaf soup."

"It's decidedly *not* a lightsaber."

"Well, I'm going to go on believing that it is until I find out otherwise."

Gabriel's footsteps ground to a halt, and for a moment Horace thought he was going to scold Chloe. But instead he said calmly, "Stop. Quiet."

They stopped. Horace listened hard but heard nothing except the sound of their own hushed breathing and the constant *rumble-hiss* of the tunnels.

"Riven," Gabriel said. "Hunters." And now, from far

behind, Horace heard a new sound rising, a complex beat rattling toward them. Footsteps. Coming fast. Horace felt Gabriel's strong hand on his shoulder. "Only two. I'll take care of them. Keep moving, quickly. Ahead there's another wall to climb. Wait for me at the top of the ledge. Do not use your instruments."

"I can help," Chloe said.

"You cannot," said Gabriel, already turning back. "Go with Horace. Get to the top of the wall." He began to race away, his strides light and long.

Horace felt his way onward through the dark as fast as he dared, Chloe beside him. He listened to the footsteps behind—Gabriel's soft ones receding and the heavier ones coming ever closer. Hunters, whatever that meant. Horace and Chloe reached the wall, as high as his shoulders. He heaved himself over the top with some difficulty, grunting, while Chloe seemed to scamper up as easily as a cat.

From far behind now, Horace heard talking, echoing and indistinct—first Gabriel's serene voice and then another one, thin and sinister. Dr. Jericho? Then Gabriel clearly said, "Come and find me, then," but abruptly his voice was cut off. A massive silence swallowed the passageway below, as if the tunnel had been sealed with a giant earplug.

"What was that?" Chloe whispered.

"I don't know."

They waited. Ten seconds. Twenty. And then as suddenly as it had come, the silence broke, torn away by a thunderous roar. For a moment Horace was sure it was the golem, but then he realized—it was water. A rushing torrent, filling the tunnel below so quickly Horace could feel the air pressure increase, making his ears pop. This was why Gabriel told them to climb the wall; the passageway below was flooding. But where was he?

The thundering water grew closer. Now footsteps again, slapping hard through the wet, and Gabriel's voice: "Make way." And then he was beside them, having vaulted up onto the ledge with apparent ease. The front wave of water slammed into the wall below a moment later, spraying Horace's legs. Slowly the thunder of the rising flood began to subside.

"We're safe," Gabriel said. "They won't be following us now, and refuge is just ahead."

"Was it Dr. Jericho?" Horace asked.

"No. Friends of his."

"What did you do?" said Chloe.

"Where there are sewers, there is water. We were lucky they caught up to us here, where I could reach the floodgates."

"That's not what I meant. I meant before that—the silence. You did something with your instrument, didn't you?"

"Yes," Gabriel said simply. "I had need." He turned away, leaving them to follow.

Two hundred yards on, he stopped again. "Close your eyes." A painful screeching and grinding bit into them, and the darkness was split by a blinding slice of light overhead. Horace threw his arm over his eyes. The light grew. The ceiling was being pulled apart. But no: a pair of doors was opening above them. Fresh air poured in, crisp and welcome. Daylight. Blue sky. The pale green branches of a tree—a ginkgo.

Gabriel clambered slowly up a steep set of crude stone steps. Chloe and Horace followed, emerging through a pair of doors in the ground, like old cellar doors, into a small brick courtyard, completely enclosed by a stone wall perhaps fifteen feet high. The entire space was no bigger than Horace's own living room. With the encircling wall looming overhead, it felt like being in a zoo enclosure. There were a few benches here, and an assortment of thin shrubs along the wall. Horace noticed a ring of oddly shaped stones, about ten feet across, laid into the brickwork floor. In the center was a flat stone in the shape of a bird. Its wings were spread. It was so black it shone. A raven, he was sure—a leestone. The sight of it comforted him.

"What is this place?"

"A cloister," Gabriel replied, lowering the cellar doors back into place. "A safe haven."

Seeing him now in the sunlight for the first time, Horace's mouth fell open. The older boy's eyes were milky white with threads of blue, all the more startling against his dark skin. His gaze was distant and unfocused, not quite looking at them even though his head was cocked alertly in their direction.

"Crap, you're blind," Chloe blurted out.

Gabriel laughed, broad and loud. "As a bat," he replied.

Horace didn't bother protesting that bats in fact could see

just fine. But maybe after all it *was* accurate to say that Gabriel was as blind as a bat, since he seemed to get around all right. It was the walking stick, of course. Horace took a good look at it now—a dark wooden shaft and an engraved silver handle. The ornate silver tip was pointed sharply. Horace tried to imagine how it worked—echolocation, maybe?

Chloe, meanwhile, was waving at Gabriel, her face thick with doubt for some reason. She pretended to throw something at him. No reaction from Gabriel. Did she think he was faking it?

"You're wondering if I can see you," Gabriel said. "I can't. I can hear Chloe waving her arms around like a monkey, but I don't need to be Tan'ji to do that."

He sidestepped a frowning Chloe and crossed the courtyard, moving easily, using the cane more like an ordinary walking stick than a blind person's cane. "Every cloister has more than one way in or out. Some are just a little harder to find than others." He felt along the wall, quickly locating a white, kite-shaped rock about the size of an eggplant. It was set flawlessly into the stonework, out of place but not so conspicuous that it drew attention to itself. He pressed his thumb and two fingers against the stone. They disappeared beneath the surface, the same way Chloe's hand had disappeared into the pillow.

"What?" Chloe said.

"This is a passkey," Gabriel said. Keeping his fingers buried inside the white stone, he stepped forward and vanished through the wall as though it weren't there. Horace gasped, and Chloe actually *tsk*ed. She looked thunderous, apparently angry that the passkey seemed to grant the same power as the dragonfly. A moment later, Gabriel reappeared. He stood clear and pulled his fingers out of the stone. "Chloe, it would be best if you did not—"

"I heard what the lady said." The dragonfly's wings were already a blur. She gave the passkey an irritated huff through her nose and swept through the wall beside it.

"Now you," Gabriel said, his ghostly gaze floating just over Horace's head. "Push your fingers into the stone. Inside you will feel a small cube—the tumbler. Keep your fingertips pressed against the tumbler while you move through the wall. Don't let the contact slip, even for an instant. Once you're through, pull your fingers out through the other side of the stone, being absolutely sure they emerge last. I don't think I have to tell you what will happen if you lose contact with the passkey."

Horace, of course, did not need to be told. He thought of all of Chloe's scars. He stepped up and pushed his fingers against the stone. It felt a little like dipping his fingers into very thin water, slightly cool. Beneath the surface, he found a small, hard shape and gripped it firmly with his fingertips. He stepped forward, and the tumbler rotated with him. The wall passed through him like a tingling curtain. On the far side he found Chloe, watching skeptically. She stood at the bottom of a short stairwell outside a tall building. The sounds of the city were all around them, rude and loud. Horace eased his fingers out of the kite-shaped stone. Overhead, the high wall of the cloister rose up into the branches of the ginkgo behind it, but other than that there was no sign of the little hidden courtyard that lay just beyond.

"Wicked," he said.

Chloe rolled her eyes. "Please," she said.

In the next instant Gabriel joined them, spinning nimbly through and pulling his fingers from the stone like a dancer. He moved slowly up the stairs—his blindness apparent now, making him slow and cautious up the steps. He used his cane to find his way.

Out on the sidewalk, Gabriel led them to an already waiting taxicab, idling at the curb. Gabriel herded the two of them inside, closing the door behind them. He nodded to the driver—a heavily bundled, lumpy figure that Horace couldn't identify as man or woman.

Horace rolled down the window. "I don't think we have money for a cab," he said. He felt the driver's eyes on him in the mirror.

"It's fortunate, then, that this isn't that kind of cab," said Gabriel. "We will meet again soon, I hope." He gave a small bow. "Keepers," he said, and with that he stepped back, and the cab swung into traffic.

CHAPTER EIGHTEEN

The House Guest

Horace stood in his driveway for a long swirling moment, his head full of all he'd seen and heard and done. He was disoriented, wrestling now with the simple act of walking into his own home. It seemed like one of the most bizarre things he could be asked to do. After leaving the cloister, the cab driver had dropped them a block from Horace's house—wordlessly and without taking any money—the fare meter on the cab had read 0.00 the entire trip.

Chloe had been surly during the cab ride. She was pouting, Horace guessed, because of the passkey. It did what the dragonfly could do. Now she stood scowling in his driveway.

"That thing. That passkey," she said, as if he'd been reading her mind. "What was it like?"

"I don't know. Weird. Kind of cold. It wasn't the same as the dragonfly."

"How would you know?"

Horace shrugged. "How would you?"

She narrowed her eyes at him, then nodded. She rocked back on her heels and rubbed her wrists together, looking at his house. "So. This is where you live, huh?"

"You're hilarious," said Horace.

He took her inside. This was the first time she'd used the front door. Somehow it made things different for Horace, more grown-up; he wondered if she felt that way too. They found his mother in the kitchen, up to her wrists in dough, working on a turkey potpie. Horace introduced Chloe, saying he'd run into her at the park, that they'd remembered each other from the districtwide chess festival back in April—a story Horace had worked out on the cab drive home.

If his mother was skeptical, or even surprised, she didn't show it. Horace had already decided he couldn't ask his parents if Chloe could stay the night. His mom was cool, but probably not that cool. Or even if she was, his dad wasn't. Meanwhile, Chloe was the only girl Horace had ever had over at all. He barely knew what to do or say, or where to go.

To his surprise, however, Chloe turned out to be a parent charmer. She shook his mother's hand, despite the flour and dough bits, and asked if she could help with dinner. His mom said no, but looked happy just to be asked. Chloe complimented their home, mentioning a painting in the hallway that Horace had never given a thought to before. Then the two of them started raving about some other artist they really liked, and so on, and when Horace tuned back in, they had somehow gotten around to making jokes about the filthiness of Horace's hands and the general disarray of his hair—as though the implausible cleanliness of girls gave them the right. Horace hardly said a word. Before long, Chloe got an invitation to dinner.

Chloe called her father—or pretended to; it was hard to tell—and then led the way up to Horace's room. Horace wasn't sure this would be allowed, but Chloe took it so much for granted and his mother seemed so unconcerned that he felt stupid for having to follow Chloe's lead.

They waited for dinner. Chloe didn't seem inclined to talk about the day's events, so Horace didn't bring it up. They got out his marbles, and he taught her how to play. He beat her soundly, without really trying, but she kept at it. They weren't playing for keepsies, obviously. He beat her seven times in a row, but she never suggested they do something else.

"It's because your hands are so small," Horace pointed out. "It's harder to hold the shooters right."

"There are people with smaller hands than me. I don't hear them failing at marbles."

They came downstairs later to check on dinner and encountered Horace's father in the kitchen, peeling a corner of crust off the turkey potpie. His father turned and caught sight of Chloe, the crust halfway to his mouth.

"Who are you?" he asked, ignoring Horace altogether.

"I'm Chloe."

"Are you the girlfriend?"

Horace thought he might die, but Chloe hardly blinked. "We prefer not to label things."

"That's very progressive."

"We just believe it's wrong to fence things in."

"So it's a free-range relationship."

"Horace *said* you were funny."

"Oh, yeah? He did?"

"Repeatedly. It's all he talks about."

Horace's father put the crust into his mouth and chewed slowly, looking thoughtfully at Chloe. "I like you," he said at last.

By the end of dinner, it was clear that Chloe would be welcome to visit whenever she wanted. She chattered happily all through the meal, answering every question Horace's parents asked and more, a flood of talk that Horace suspected was at least fifty percent lies: her parents were divorced, her father was a structural engineer, she had a younger sister, she went to Thomas Paine Middle School and hoped to be an engineer herself one day or maybe a writer, she was a Libra by birth but not by temperament—not that she believed in that anyway—her favorite food was whatever was on her plate, her favorite color was not so much any one color but a tone, she couldn't sing or dance, was a terrific swimmer, loved cats but had no respect for dogs, didn't watch much TV but read voraciously, liked Hawthorne but hated Poe, belonged to the chess club, the fencing club, the academic bowl team, and thought her school's dress code was not nearly strict enough. Horace was pretty sure this last one was a joke. She turned to his father and said, "Think about it, Mr. Andrews—if Horace were a girl, how short would you want his skirts to be?"

His father chewed and swallowed, took a drink of water. "You make an excellent, if disturbing, point."

After dinner, Chloe pretended to leave for home. Horace's parents made a fuss over her. They were determined to give Chloe a ride, which she kept politely declining, saying it wasn't far and the sun was still up, until at last Horace caught his father's eye and mouthed at him: *Embarrassing!* His father, to Horace's everlasting surprise, relented at once, telling his mother he was sure Chloe would be fine. Perhaps if she would do them the favor of calling when she got home. Chloe agreed at once and was out the door, waving and throwing thank-yous. She winked at Horace as she went.

The plan was for Chloe to get back in the house secretly and hide in the attic. But by eleven thirty, Horace was beginning to worry. When she did show up, a few minutes later, it was dramatic and heart-stopping—she dropped clean out of the ceiling, landing in a quiet crouch.

"Gotcha!" she whispered, raising her fingers like claws.

Horace clutched his chest. "What is wrong with you?"

"The usual. Sorry it's so late. Your parents stayed up talking for a long time."

"You were spying on them?"

"Not on purpose. Just being safe. But I think they like me."

"So all that stuff you said at dinner . . . did you make that up?"

Chloe plucked at his blanket. "Some of it."

"Your parents are divorced?"

"No." She frowned. "Actually, I don't know."

Horace let that simmer, then changed the subject, unsure if she wanted to talk about it or not. "Do you really play chess?"

"No. I mean, I have. But my dad and I mostly used to play go."

"What's go?"

"It's a Japanese game. It's like chess. Sort of. It's like . . . if chess was a garden."

"Huh." Horace couldn't make any sense of that. "It sounds cool."

"It's okay."

"Chloe, I thought you were awesome today. What you did, at the House of Answers." It was a relief to finally be able to talk about it openly, but he blushed; he hadn't meant to say those exact words.

"You'd have done the same. Anybody would have, if they'd been the one with the dragonfly."

"I wouldn't have, though. I know for a fact I wouldn't have. No way."

"Well, whatever. I guess one of us doesn't know you very well." Chloe got up and began to circle the room. She fiddled with some of the stuff in his desk, pushing the buttons on his chess clock and rattling a box of marbles. The dragonfly glinted in the dark. She walked into and back out of his closet without opening the door. She leaned out through the wall of the house—apparently to take a look around.

"It's not like I wasn't scared," Chloe said, coming back and standing at the foot of the bed. "At the House of Answers. That dumin—I've never been through anything so . . . so *present* before. And the golem. It was all through me, hurting me."

Suddenly Horace recalled that first night she'd been in his room. "Before, you said stuff couldn't move through you. You told me that. I threw the pillow at you."

"Yeah, well." Chloe dropped her head, pressing her chin briefly against the dragonfly's back. "Turns out I was wrong about that," she said.

"How could you be wrong? You've been Tan'ji for most of your life."

"I think I might be getting . . . better? But even so, some of it got stuck in me. You saw. And there was one piece of it—hot, and sharp, faster than the rest."

"I saw it," said Horace. "It was red and jagged, like a crystal. It was swimming in there, like it was alive."

"It wasn't, but it hunted me somehow," Chloe said. "It hurt me." She began to lift up her shirt along her right side. Horace stopped breathing. She revealed a stretch of pale skin, two bony ribs, and at last a cruel, bubbling wound, red and raised.

"Oh my god, are you all right?"

"I'm okay. It just feels like I got smacked with a belt." She

216

touched the wound gingerly, wincing. "A belt of electricity. Or like on fire. Or both." She let her shirt fall. "Anyway, things are happening. Have you ever had a bigger day . . . Keeper?"

"I think . . . no."

"We've stumbled into a war."

"Yeah," Horace said. "And we don't even really know what the sides are yet."

"I'm pretty sure the Riven are the bad guys."

"Agreed."

"Because more than anything, I know that having the dragonfly is *right*. And therefore anyone who wants to take it from me is *wrong*."

Horace felt himself reaching out a warm arm of thought toward the Fel'Daera. "That's like the best thing you ever said, Chloe."

"Pssh," she scoffed. "Today, maybe. So anyway, what do you think the Riven are?"

"I've thought about that. They're either aliens or some humanlike thing, right?"

"Very logical. But they don't look very human."

"Compared to every other living thing, they do. And I don't really believe in aliens."

"That's random."

Horace shrugged. "I mean, I *do*, I just don't believe they're here on earth. Or at least, I never did before."

"Well, whatever they are, we agree that the Riven don't have our best interests at heart, right? But here's the thing—that doesn't mean Mrs. Hapsteade and Gabriel and the rest are automatically the good guys."

Horace started to object to that but found that he couldn't. "I guess that's true," he said. Tomorrow they would meet with Mr. Meister. They would hear what he had to say. And then . . . what?

Chloe sighed. "I guess I've been waiting a long time for things to happen. And now they are, and it's not anything I expected, but in a way I think it sort of is. I think I was ready for anything. Even this."

Horace didn't know what to say to that. He felt so unready for everything, so unprepared for what had happened that day. But he couldn't put it into words. After a minute he said simply, "*We're* the good guys."

"Right on," Chloe said. And a few moments later, when she climbed onto the bed and lay down on top of the covers, her feet at Horace's head and vice versa—not so close that they were touching but not so far that he couldn't smell her sweat, smell the tunnel damp in her socks—it felt good, comforting, not at all awkward. Horace felt as right with the world as he could ever remember being—the box at his side, this astonishing new friend, the shared knowledge of this craziest of days.

They lay there, mostly not talking. When Rip Van Twinkle arrived—earlier now than the week before, because Horace hadn't sent him the day after Chloe's first visit—Chloe rose and caught him silently. They put him in the box, where he sat not moving, as if waiting. At last Horace closed the lid and Chloe said softly, "See you on the flip side." They lay back down again afterward and floated through a quiet hour. Horace wondered if Chloe was thinking about tomorrow as much as he was, if she was at all frightened. He wondered how a person got to be so brave, so fierce, so sure. He'd already checked through the box, a dozen times at least, to see if he would arrive safely at home tomorrow night. He'd seen himself, and so he wasn't really worried. He'd even caught a glimpse of Chloe. Still, he felt very much on the brink of something big, something unknowable, and he wished he had a better sense of what it was. Things were happening, all right.

"Anyway," Chloe said into the silence, as though they had been talking. "I think I need to sleep now." She clambered to her feet and began to bounce gently on Horace's bed. "Watch this," Chloe said, and the dragonfly began to blur again. She threw her arms over her head and bounced high—once, twice. Her hands went into the ceiling, as though she were leaping up into a cloud. Somehow she grabbed hold up there and hung. She dangled for a moment, handless and giggling. "I wasn't sure I'd be able to do this," she told Horace, and then she swung herself up into the ceiling, up into the attic, disappearing from sight like a ghost.

A moment later, her head and shoulders reappeared, looking down at Horace. Her raven hair hung around her face and the dragonfly swung low, wings whirring, like it was flying up to greet her. "Those damn passkeys," she said. "I bet they can't let you do *that*."

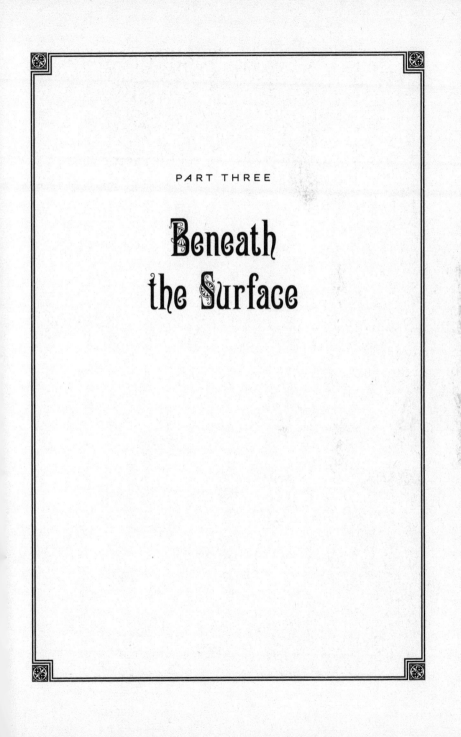

PART THREE

Beneath
the Surface

CHAPTER NINETEEN

The Great Burrow

"KEEPERS," MRS. HAPSTEADE SAID WITH A NOD. IN HER usual black dress, she looked out of place at Horace's bus stop, like a confused traveler. But as it turned out, they weren't getting on any bus. Mrs. Hapsteade herded them into a waiting cab instead. The driver was the one from the day before, squat and round and once again mysteriously wrapped from head to toe—hands, nose, mouth, hair, all covered. They could see nothing of his—or her—face, except two bright blue eyes that checked the mirror now and again. A small cloth bag hung from the mirror, blue and faded and bulging. The fare on the cab's meter still read 0.00, but under extras it clearly said HAP. Horace refrained from asking any of the hundred questions that billowed in his head.

They drove in silence, headed toward the lake. They swung south on Lake Shore Drive, toward downtown. They passed the Hancock Center—Horace's favorite skyscraper—and crossed the river. They took a right by a sign that said BREAKWATER ACCESS and traveled several strange blocks underground, through a kind of tunnel. They emerged and crossed Michigan Avenue, but after that Horace completely lost track of where they were. He liked going downtown, but also found it messy and confusing, kind of overwhelming. The buildings rose out of sight overhead, blotting out the sky and trapping the noise of the city. The cab took a few more turns and at last pulled up in front of an old stone building three stories tall. It looked like a library, or maybe a museum, with a double staircase that led up to an absolutely massive green door between two pairs of huge stone pillars.

"We are here," Mrs. Hapsteade said. "Thank you, Beck." The driver nodded, peering shyly at them in the mirror.

They got out and followed Mrs. Hapsteade up the steps. Above the door, garlands of flowers were carved into the stone, and a curving inscription read:

THE MAZZOLENI ACADEMY

"A school?" Chloe asked.

"To begin with, yes," said Mrs. Hapsteade. "This is the way to Mr. Meister."

"Mr. Meister is a teacher?"

"He would say no, but he doesn't care for titles. He's not a teacher in the way you might be imagining. He is the chief taxonomer, though he doesn't much care for that title either."

Horace knew that a taxonomer identified things, put them into categories—like putting animals into a certain species or genus. But somehow he didn't think Mr. Meister classified animals.

Mrs. Hapsteade opened the great green doors. Inside, the Mazzoleni Academy looked like any ordinary school. They passed an office where a fat lady glanced out through a round window and exchanged a knowing nod with Mrs. Hapsteade. Beyond, lockers lined the front hall, and the walls above were decorated with student projects. Horace realized school was actually still in session—he could hear children's voices. They passed a classroom door and glimpsed a teacher through the glass, standing in front of a class of little kids.

The teacher held a sword.

"What do they teach here?"

"What do you mean?" replied Mrs. Hapsteade. "It's a school."

"In that classroom, the teacher had a sword."

"Don't excite yourself. The academy is a boarding school, so the students live here in the building, but otherwise it's no different than most other schools. Mr. Franklin teaches history, nothing more. It's an ordinary school, in most respects. Ordinary children attend classes here."

"But *we're* here," Horace pointed out. "You're here. Mr. Meister is here. That doesn't add up to ordinary."

"No, I suppose it doesn't," Mrs. Hapsteade agreed. "But

he is not exactly *here*." They passed several more classrooms. A bulletin board displayed all the usual flyers: a notice for a band concert, a poster about recycling, the week's cafeteria menu. They walked by a small recess in the wall, covered in glass. Behind the glass was a black statue of a great raven, leaping from a gnarled branch, stretching its wings upward to catch the air. Yes, an ordinary school—in most respects.

They walked on. Mrs. Hapsteade led them through a door marked STAFF ONLY and down a narrow staircase beyond. At the bottom, they filed along a cramped, grimy hallway until Mrs. Hapsteade stopped in front an old-fashioned accordion gate. She unlocked the gate with a crude black key pulled from the collar of her dress and pushed it noisily back. "Going down," she said. Horace's stomach crumpled as he realized that the space beyond wasn't another hallway, but a tiny elevator. Horace hated elevators. And this was the tiniest, sketchiest elevator he'd ever seen.

Mrs. Hapsteade stepped inside. "Well?" she said, her eyes on Horace.

"Are there stairs?" he asked, his voice cracking just a little.

"Where we're going is too secret for stairs."

"It's a sanctuary, then," Chloe said. "Down below the school. Will we have to pass through the Nevren again?"

The Nevren. Of course it would be here, probably worse than the one behind the House of Answers. The dread bubbling in Horace's gut rolled to a boil.

"Once we're below, yes," said Mrs. Hapsteade. "But Horace won't have to do it alone. None of us will. Come. The elevator ride will be brief—twenty seconds."

That didn't sound brief, but Horace eased into the elevator, one hand gripping the box. Eyes closed, he flinched as the gate slammed shut. Mrs. Hapsteade inserted her key into another hole and turned it once to the left, once to the right. The elevator lurched into motion, trembling and rattling. Horace wondered how old it was, and whether anyone would even know to come looking for them. *Eight, nine, ten* . . . The elevator trembled and rattled as it descended. *Fourteen, fifteen, sixteen* . . . And suddenly the elevator shuddered to a stop. Horace squeezed his eyes closed until they hurt, sure the elevator was stuck, sure they were trapped here—but then the gate clattered back, and Mrs. Hapsteade spoke.

"Now we continue. Below us is the entryway to the Warren, our greatest refuge here in the city."

More stairs leading down. How deep were they going? Horace counted seventy-nine steps before they stepped out into the mouth of a large, domed cavern. The far side was lost in darkness. The cool air smelled vaguely of animal and water. Immediately to their left and right, three other archways like the one they'd just come through opened into the great chamber. Directly ahead, a loose brick pathway led onward into the gloom, cutting across a gleaming black floor.

Horace stepped forward. He accidentally kicked a little grit, spraying it across the black floor. Several feet ahead, clouds of tiny ripples broke out, a sprinkle of splashes. And then he understood—this was no floor. The cavern ahead was filled with water, as black as night, smooth as glass. The brick walkway was a bridge across an underground lake.

A silent shadow cut through the air out over the water, swooping low. Now another, and another, swift and flickering. A soft splash and a rustle from somewhere out in the blackness.

Chloe saw them too. "Bats?"

"Owls," Mrs. Hapsteade replied.

Horace eased out onto the brick walkway. He was disappointed that there were no bats, but owls were pretty fascinating, too. His footsteps echoed loudly around the cavern. Before he'd gone more than a few yards, though, a sharp, biting cold caught him by the wrists and ankles, pressed hard against his chest.

"The Nevren," Horace murmured. He stepped back and reached for the box. "It's here."

"Powerfully so," said Mrs. Hapsteade. "This is Vithra's Eye. We must pass through it."

Horace looked at Chloe. "I can do this. I can do it if you follow me." Mrs. Hapsteade said nothing, but Chloe nodded. Horace began to walk forward into the cold.

"Best to be brave while hope remains, Horace Andrews," Mrs. Hapsteade said, "but there's no hope along that path."

Horace stopped. "What do you mean? This is the only way."

"For the uninvited, yes." Mrs. Hapsteade reached back and undid one of the chains around her neck. She revealed the long black crystal from yesterday, shining still, lighting her face like a ghost's. She let the chain hang to its full length, the black stone dangling nearly to the floor. "This is a jithandra. This is the only way across. Observe," she said, and walked to the edge of the quiet lake. She dipped the jithandra briefly into the water, then lifted it out again. There was an immense crackling, as though a sheet of paper the size of a city block was being crumpled. The black water gathered itself around the ripple where the crystal had touched, lifting and turning lighter and then beginning to grow outward in a jagged circle. It was solidifying. In an instant, a patch the size of a manhole cover had bloomed—gray and shining and slightly translucent—where before there was only black water.

"Our path starts here," Mrs. Hapsteade said.

"Is it ice?" Horace asked.

"Not exactly, no. It isn't cold, or slick, but it is liquid made solid."

"How long will it last?"

"Keep watching," she said. Horace watched, his inner clock already ticking. After several moments, the patch suddenly dissolved with a soft hiss, turning back to water again. Eleven seconds. The patch had lasted only eleven seconds. "Slightly longer than long enough," Mrs. Hapsteade said. "Come." She reached out to Chloe. Chloe raised an eyebrow and frowned at the offered hand. Mrs. Hapsteade's expression did not change, but she turned to Horace instead. Horace took her hand, too nervous to be very embarrassed. It was firm and dry, neither hot nor cold. He was still getting used to the feel of it when he sensed Chloe taking hold of the back of his shirt. He looked over at her. She looked right past him but gave his shirt a quick tug.

"Don't let go," Mrs. Hapsteade told them.

"Are we going around the Nevren?"

"So many questions. No, we must pass through the Nevren here, but we'll skirt the edge, avoiding the worst of it."

"What if I fall?" Chloe asked.

"You do not want to fall into this lake," Mrs. Hapsteade said.

"Why?" Chloe asked. "What would happen?"

"First, you would get wet." The way she said "first" discouraged asking what came second.

Mrs. Hapsteade dipped the crystal into the water again. The gray patch began to form again noisily, and she led them out onto it. The stuff felt like wood underfoot, firm and organic. Mrs. Hapsteade kept moving, letting the jithandra dangle into the open water ahead, and where it fell the water came together, extending the path. They headed left along the wall, moving slowly around the curving edge of the great chamber, staying as far away from the dark center as possible. "This will be a longer trip through the Nevren than before," Mrs. Hapsteade said over the soft roar of the water rearranging itself. "Keep moving. Stay to the path. You know what's coming. Do not let go."

The cold was already over Horace, but as braced as he was for what would happen, still it felt like a punch to the gut when he lost touch with the box. He let out a whuff of air. A moment later, he felt Chloe's hand on his shirt bunch into a fist. Another step, though, and even that faded. *Keep moving,* Horace told himself. *Only walk. The box is here.* He made his mind tell his legs to keep moving, though he had no idea if they were listening. It was like treading water in a pool filled with air.

"*Halfway,*" said a voice, but the word was meaningless. Halfway to nothing was nowhere. The only thing that was anything was the stupid, busy talk of his mind, nagging at some futile chore, but he kept that thread alive because it was all there was. *I am not,* Horace told himself, but he wasn't listening. *I am not. I am not.*

And then at last they were through. The presence of the box blossomed again, bringing a burn to Horace's eyes. He heard a soft gasp behind him, knew it was Chloe, knew she could feel the dragonfly once more. They walked on in silence, shuffling along the strange wet path, nearly to the opposite shore now. A small shadow flashed across Horace's field of vision, bulky and swift and soundless. An owl.

They stepped onto solid ground. Horace glanced back. He guessed they'd come at least the length of a football field. Directly behind them, the path they'd taken—the solid-water trail made by the black crystal—was dissolving as swiftly as it had formed, returning to water. And that other path—the brick walkway that cut across the middle of the water.

Chloe was looking back at it too. "That bridge, then. It leads through the center of the Nevren? It's harder to pass there?"

"Yes, much harder. The Nevren works on everyone who has the bond, friend or foe, and I know of no Tan'ji who could pass straight through the heart of Vithra's Eye. No one who's tried has returned whole."

"What about Mr. Meister?" Horace asked.

"Mr. Meister least of all." Mrs. Hapsteade put the jithandra back around her neck. She turned away from the water and began walking. "But perhaps you would like to ask him yourselves. We're nearly there."

Ahead, a perfectly round tunnel—big enough for a train—led onward and downward, running for a hundred feet or so before it opened up again.

Before them lay what looked like some sort of underground forest. The cavern was two stories high, with the same stone floor and a brownish-blue ceiling. There were more of the glowing amber lights here, but these were much larger, with great spiraling gouts of twinkling illumination rising and spreading from them. And then, stranger still: the place was filled with dozens of massive, round stone columns that rose from floor to ceiling, as wide as they were high. They were not simply support columns, though—they were hollow inside, and had open doorways, windows. Horace tried to make sense of what he was seeing.

Chloe stepped forward. "It's a town." And it did look like one, made up of little houses, chiseled from the trunks of gigantic stone trees.

"Once, perhaps," Mrs. Hapsteade said. "A place of refuge, anyway. These buildings are called dobas. This chamber is the Great Burrow, the topmost level of the Warren."

"Do you live here?" Chloe asked.

Horace frowned at the question. Somehow it was strange to think of Mrs. Hapsteade living anywhere.

"From time to time."

"And what about Mr. Meister?"

"He does keep a doba here. We're going there now."

She led them forward through the columns. Their footsteps—Mrs. Hapsteade's sharp and brisk, Horace's shuffling, Chloe's light—echoed through the huge, quiet space. It really was like a forest, lit faintly in gold by the rising shimmer of the great amber lights. The columns were irregularly spaced, not in any kind of pattern. As they passed deeper into the Great Burrow, the air became crisper, fresher.

Most of the dobas were empty, or looked like they were being used for storage, but a few had furniture—couches, tables, chairs. Horace saw a rumpled bed in one that had clearly been recently used. They passed by another and were startled to see a figure standing at the window. It was a boy, about their age, with glasses and a ponytail and extremely pale skin. He watched them with a flat, measuring gaze. He wore a T-shirt with a picture of a reclining sea otter, paws folded serenely across its chest. Beneath that it said GODLY OTTER. He and Mrs. Hapsteade exchanged a silent nod.

"Who was that?" Chloe asked, after they passed.

"Brian," Mrs. Hapsteade said, but it was clear she meant to say no more.

At last they came to a doba larger than the others. This one was perhaps fifty feet across, filling half the passageway. Mrs. Hapsteade led them straight inside through a reckless clutter of crates and boxes. Horace recognized some of the bins' labels—MISPLACED, DISPLACED, UNSAVORY, DESPERATELY UNNEEDED, UNBINNABLE. Horace broke into a smile, remembering. "These are from the House of Answers. The warehouse."

"Indeed," Mrs. Hapsteade replied, weaving through the crates toward another curving wall deep inside. "We got them out just in time, as it turned out." Horace realized there was sort of a room within a room here. The boxes from the House of Answers occupied the outer ring. An open door led into the inner circle, which was made of wood. A shadowy red light poured out from inside.

"One moment," Mrs. Hapsteade said, and she disappeared through the open door. Voices spilled out. They heard Mr. Meister's laugh. Mrs. Hapsteade reappeared and nodded, gesturing inside. "I'll wait outside. I'm not meant for this conversation."

They passed through, Horace somewhat cautiously and Chloe with her usual sureness. Mrs. Hapsteade closed the door behind them.

Mr. Meister's office, if it could be called an office, was a riot of red—bloodred, apple red. It was twenty feet across and completely round. A workbench ran around half of the room, while a wooden couch curved around the rest, piled high with pillows. The red wall rose high overhead, ending in a smooth red dome. A glowing white crystal hung from the peak.

Beneath the dome—and this was what made the place remarkable—every last inch of the red wall was covered with a dazzling assortment of compartments, no two quite the same: cubbies and drawers and holes and tiny gates and panes of glass. Even the inside of the thick door turned out to be a bizarre assortment of compartments, in every conceivable shape and size. The doorknob itself was tucked away in a round pocket of its own. It looked almost as if some crazed colony of cliff-dwelling birds had come in and built a head-spinning assortment of fantastic nests in the walls. And Horace let out a little "Oh!" of surprise—some of the holes actually did have birds in them. Small, black, bright-eyed birds, hopping and peeking. One fluttered across the room, darting into a hole shaped like an eye.

Most of the compartments did not contain birds, however. They held Tanu. Horace had no doubt that was what they were—dozens upon dozens of them, tubes and boxes and figures and crescents and sticks and rolls of paper and stacks of cubes and chunks of glass and slabs of stone. Horace could almost feel the energy collected here in these objects, like he was standing in a power station. The collection at the House of Answers had nothing on this.

In the middle of it all, Mr. Meister sat behind a cluttered, crescent-shaped desk, watching them take it in. His many-pocketed red vest gleamed. His gray eyes swam hugely behind his glasses, like he was looking at them through the wall of a fish tank. His left eye loomed.

Chloe scratched her nose, squinting. "Hoard much?"

Mr. Meister laughed. "Not nearly enough, I sometimes think."

"These are Tanu," Horace said. "You collected all these? Where did they come from?"

"Where *didn't* they come from?"

Mr. Meister's desk was covered with Tanu as well. There was a raven statue—a leestone, obviously. Another bird sculpture, an owl with a single, glittering yellow eye, was smaller but far creepier. There was an object the size of a small chest but bound like a book, with pages as thick as fingers. A gold compass with no markings, just a blank white face, featured a red needle that pointed directly at Mr. Meister. Horace also caught sight of two more objects he recognized—the smooth mask of a woman's face and the miraculous tiny earth, spinning and alive. Horace desperately wanted to know what everything did.

"Do you use all these?" Chloe asked the old man.

"Certainly not. Many of them I am unable to use; they are instruments still in search of Keepers. But even if I could use them all, it would be most unwise to do so."

Horace perked up, pulling his attention away from the miniature earth. "Why?"

Mr. Meister seemed to measure his words. "Tanu stake a claim on their users. And not just our Tan'ji. Even the merest Tan'kindi takes a small toll—ravens' eyes, dumindars, pass-keys." He glanced around the room. "What lies within these walls would be far too much for any one person to wield, even with the most extensive precautions."

Horace thought of Mrs. Hapsteade's seemingly endless supply of necklaces, all those Tanu she used. How much of a toll had they taken on her?

"I remember you," Chloe told the old man abruptly. She said it like a challenge.

"Do you now?" said Mr. Meister. "I'm flattered. It's been some time since last we spoke."

"You told me the dragonfly would help me. That it would keep me safe."

"And has it?"

"I don't know," said Chloe. "It keeps me safe from the dangers it brings. Would you call that helping?"

Mr. Meister's eyes squinted with pleasure. "My dear, you astonish me. But under the circumstances, yes, I would call that helping. Understand, please: you would be in danger even if the dragonfly were not in your possession. The words you wrote with the Vora tell us as much." He cocked his head, peering closely at the dragonfly and then back at her face. "You passed through the dumin. You were within the body of the golem."

Chloe shrugged.

"Have you any idea of the difficulty of these feats?"

"Now that I've done them I do."

Mr. Meister nodded, beaming. "As ever, the Vora speaks truly," he murmured. "And you, Horace, you have come through the Find with haste. You have opened yourself to the many possibilities of the box."

"Yeah, I suppose."

"Just so. I suspected it would be swift, but you have exceeded my expectations. Sit, please, sit."

Chloe and Horace sank into the big red couch, into the sea of pillows, which smelled vaguely musty. Horace fussed with the pillows, trying to get comfortable; Chloe perched on one and folded her legs beneath herself like a cat.

The old man continued. "I already know how I wish this conversation to end. Therefore I leave it up to you to decide how it will begin." He watched them, his face full of anticipation.

After a moment Horace said, "Mrs. Hapsteade told us you were chief taxonomer."

"Oh, my." Mr. Meister shook his head. His glasses glinted rosily. "Well. I am the doer of what I do. And I did these things long before anyone thought to attach a title to them."

"You catalog the Tanu. You give them names."

"Never give. Rather, I unearth them when I can. These are not natural beasts; they are creations. And I study them. I am an historian, a researcher, a collector, an appraiser, a curator, a steward. And yes, a taxonomer. I am not the chief of anything, but I suppose I am what you would call an expert." He squeezed the fingers of one hand with the other. "Indeed, if you will allow me the immodesty these times demand, I am perhaps *the* expert."

"Does that mean you'll answer my questions now?" Horace asked.

Mr. Meister spread his hands. "I will answer what I am able. I promised as much, did I not? You have come through the Find and discovered the power of your Tan'ji. I am now free to share what I know. With you as well, Chloe. Understand first, though, that there are limits to what I know."

"There are limits to what *we* know," Horace said.

"Let us enlighten each other, then. I will answer your questions, and then perhaps you will answer one of mine. Certainly there is no path that would not benefit from a little enlightenment, yes?"

"Yes," said Horace.

The old man settled forward in his chair. "Very well. We proceed. Now—who will go first?"

CHAPTER TWENTY

The Box and the Dragonfly

"THE FEL'DAERA. THE BOX OF PROMISES," MR. MEISTER said to Horace, pressing his glasses tight against the bridge of his nose. "Unique even among the rare."

Horace looked down at the box gleaming in his lap. "The Box of Promises? Why is it called that?"

"A rough translation. But also a bit of a joke—the Box of Promises makes no promises."

"What's that supposed to mean?"

"You have already learned what the box allows you to do." Mr. Meister straightened a single knobby finger. "First, you can send objects forward, into the future." He uncurled another finger. "Second, you can open the box and observe the future directly. Yes?"

"Yes."

"And when you observe the future, do your visions always come true?"

"Sometimes the box is wrong about the future, if that's what you're saying."

"I would not say *wrong*. Better to say that sometimes events do not follow the path suggested by the Fel'Daera."

"That's right, they don't. Is that a problem?"

Mr. Meister shrugged innocently. "Is it?"

Horace considered. "Sometimes the future I see in the box is fuzzy, blurry—those things are less likely to happen the way I saw them. But sometimes even when it's really clear, the box turns out to be wrong. Or at least, I can make it be wrong."

"You mean you can change later events so that they do not match what the box revealed."

"Yeah." Horace rearranged his pillows, frowning. "But it feels . . . bad." He told Mr. Meister about the sandwich he'd chosen not to eat.

Mr. Meister listened intently to the sandwich story, then dug into a pocket and pulled out his little notebook. He wrote a few words hastily and tucked it away. He sat silent for a few moments, brow furrowed with concentration, and then spoke cautiously. "Do you know why the Box of Promises makes no promises, Horace? Why we can never be one hundred percent sure of the future it reveals?"

Horace thought it over. He thought back again to the day he chose not to eat the sandwich, and the nagging urge that had made him try the experiment in the first place. If the box was never "wrong," then it meant no one had a choice about anything—the future was already set. But the future *wasn't* set. It could be changed. "Because of free will," Horace said. "If the box was never wrong, that would mean we had to do whatever the box revealed. We would have no free will."

"Excellent. If the box shows you eating a sandwich in the future, do you then have to eat that sandwich? Or let me put it into different terms. If the box shows you stepping into the path of an oncoming train, do you then need to do so?"

"Of course not."

"Of course not. As you have already discovered, you are always free to make whatever choices you like, no matter what the box has revealed. Choose to eat the sandwich, or do not. Choose to step in front of the train, or do not. But consider this possibility: perhaps, long before that future arrives, *the truly important choice has already been made*." He said this slowly, stressing each beat with a gesture like he was throwing darts.

"What choice?"

"You know the answer to that. Think, my friend. The future always depends upon a sequence of prior events—one event leads to another, and another, and so on. But when we are talking about the future you witness through the box, of course, one of those prior events is . . ."

"Looking through the box in the first place," Horace finished.

"Just so. Looking through the box is an extremely important event, because choosing to observe the future has a dramatic effect on how the future turns out. Let us consider the name again—the Box of Promises. Do you know what it means, to promise?"

"To promise? I guess to . . . say you will do something."

"An adequate description. But the root of the word, quite literally, means—"

Chloe, listening silently so far, suddenly piped up. "To send forward."

"Quite right," said Mr. Meister. "Wonderful. To *send forward*. The Fel'Daera is, of course, able to send objects forward through time. But what you must understand is that even when you merely look through the box, you are also sending something forward. Do you have any idea what that something might be?"

"I'm not sure," Horace said slowly. "But I guess . . . my awareness? My observation?"

"Very good. And this is what you must understand, Horace: until the moment you observe it, the future could be anything. In fact, it is *everything*—every possibility. But the moment you look into the Fel'Daera, that changes."

"You're saying when I look into the box . . . I . . . make the future what it is?"

Mr. Meister lifted a contrary finger. "Not quite. You create a future you believe in."

Chloe stirred again. "The marker," she murmured at Horace. "The message I wrote on your wall."

"Right," Horace said, concentrating furiously, remembering how Chloe's blurry message had become clearer once

Horace convinced himself not to clean it off. His belief had changed the future. The realization made him feel heavy all of a sudden, burdened by the weight of the power the box gave him. "A future I believe in. But what if I believe . . . I don't know . . . that everyone will die?" His voice cracked a little.

"Don't be absurd," Mr. Meister said. "Your visions are like ripples of the true future—which has yet to be formed—but they are sensible. They are likely. You are a practical-minded individual, Horace. You must be, in order to be the Keeper of the Fel'Daera. The future the box reveals is a logical extension of the moment in which you look through the box. It is not a flight of fancy."

Horace frowned down at the box. He thought of the fire truck he'd seen through the box, racing past his house on the way to some emergency. "But if I'm responsible . . . ," he began, and then lost the words. He sank deeper into his seat, feeling Chloe's eyes on him.

Mr. Meister leaned forward. His voice became velvet and low, gentle as a leaf. "Do not misunderstand me, Horace. You do not actually determine the future. You do not control it. No one person could be granted such power. You have a talent, to be sure—you are the Keeper of the Fel'Daera, and you can glimpse what no one else can—but you are still just a boy."

Horace tipped his head back, blinking back the sudden water in his eyes and looking up at the curving red vault of compartments above him. "No, I'm not," he said after a moment.

The strength of his own voice surprised him. "The box, what it can do . . . I'm not just a boy. Not anymore."

Horace waited for the old man to argue with him, but Mr. Meister just sat there, his face dark and drawn with concern.

"He's right," Chloe said. "And I'm not just a girl. Don't ask us to pretend we are."

The old man went on saying nothing.

"Look," Horace said at last, "I don't need to be told what I am, or what I'm not. But I wish you'd tell me, if you know: who decides what I see when I look into the box?"

"I have said too much already."

"Tell me," Horace insisted. "Who decides?"

"No one decides," Mr. Meister said, his voice thick now.

"You said I see a future I believe in."

"Belief is not a decision. Nor is it absolute knowledge. That's why the box is so often blurry."

"Why did I feel sick when I didn't eat the sandwich? Was it because I was going against a future I had believed in?"

"You're missing the point. It's not that you must choose to do—or not do—whatever actions you see in the box. Instead, the seeing and the doing are a *single act*."

"That doesn't really answer my question."

"Once you've opened the box, you are beholden to whatever future you see. You still have free will, yes, but with that free will you *already* chose to open the box and observe the future. Therefore you should try not to take actions that would deliberately change that future."

"In other words, I should eat the sandwich."

"Yes!" Mr. Meister roared, throwing his hands up.

Chloe sat up, her eyes flashing. "And should he step in front of the train, too?"

Silence fell as Mr. Meister hesitated. He hesitated for ten long seconds. Fifteen. At last he spoke, quiet again, choosing his words carefully. "As I told you on the very first day, Horace, you must not open the box without reason." He stared at Horace hard.

Suddenly Horace understood. Not without *a* reason—*without reason.* "I have to be logical," he said.

"Yes. Remember that you are altering a chain of events. Before you choose to look through the box, recognize the path you are on. Recognize your motivations for looking through the box. Consider those around you who may have a part to play in the events to come. If you keep your head and your heart clear, and think logically about the consequences of the current moment, I believe that the Fel'Daera will speak to you truly." He shrugged. He reached out and ran a bony fingertip across the brow of the delicate ivory mask in front of him. "What you choose to do after that is . . . as always . . . a matter of your own free will."

Horace filled himself with breath and let it out. Beside him, Chloe was shrewd and alive, alert like an animal. "Okay," Horace said. "It's funny—it all sounds like something my mom said to me: everything the future is made of is happening right now."

"Mothers often know best," Mr. Meister said. "I could not have said it better myself. Now, is there anything else?"

"No—or actually, yes. Why does Mrs. Hapsteade hate the box?"

Mr. Meister sighed. "She does not hate it. She fears it. And let us admit that there is reason to be afraid. But whereas she would let her caution steer us away from the Fel'Daera entirely, I believe that a healthy respect for the box's powers can lead its Keeper to a greater understanding, and a greater mastery. Mastery you are still acquiring. Does this make sense?"

"I think so. But even if I get more . . . mastery . . . what good could the box possibly be in a fight? If you expect us to go up against the Riven, I just don't know what good the box would be, no matter how much mastery I have."

Mr. Meister shook his head, feigning sadness. "So much logic, so little imagination. Let us consider this scenario: I am about to put myself in danger; I can choose either to have ten companions at my side or knowledge of the future— knowledge of the events that are about to unfold." He raised his eyebrows and spread his hands. "I will choose knowledge every time. And that is just a part of what the box has to offer."

Chloe glanced over at Horace. "No pressure, though."

"Seriously," Horace said.

Mr. Meister sighed again. "Do not worry about purpose. Surely you have enough desire to master the box without such outside concerns. And do not worry about Mrs. Hapsteade, either. She understands that we do what we must." He straightened and slapped his thighs. "Very good. We have dug deeper than I thought we would, and come close to the limits of what I can tell you. Any other questions?"

"Definitely not. Not yet. I just need to . . . think."

"As you should. More than any other instrument, the Fel'Daera requires it of you." The old man settled back into his chair. He fiddled with his glasses. "And now Chloe," he said, turning his attention toward her. "Not just an ordinary girl."

Chloe gazed back at him. "Are we going to pretend to trust each other now?"

Mr. Meister chuckled so kindly that Horace almost forgot the dark silence of a few moments earlier. "Does the thought frighten you?"

"Not particularly."

"Then let us embrace trust. Come. The dragonfly. An exquisite piece, one of the most beautiful Tanu. What is it you wish to learn?"

"I don't really know."

"Perhaps you want the science of it?"

"No," said Chloe firmly, at the same moment as Horace said, "Definitely."

Mr. Meister raised his bushy eyebrows.

"I don't want to know how it works," Chloe said. "Everything you just told Horace—I don't need to hear that kind of stuff. And I mean, what if knowing how it works makes it not work anymore?"

Mr. Meister's gaze was as steady as a cat's, his left eye appearing to bulge crazily behind the thick lens of his glasses. "But tell me, how could such a thing happen?"

Chloe frowned. The dragonfly's wings were vibrating ever so slightly. "The dragonfly works because I need it to, not because I . . . push a button or engage a gear or contemplate the universe or something. There's no on switch; it's just . . . on when I need it."

Mr. Meister laughed softly. "Like right this moment, for instance?"

The dragonfly's wings went still. "What I mean is, I don't want to overthink it. I don't want to know how it works." She trailed off for a moment, searching for the words. She held up the dragonfly. "This *belongs* to me. When I go thin, I am—*we are*—just doing the natural thing."

Horace felt his fingers tighten around the Box of Promises in his lap. Although he understood what Chloe was talking about, still the dragonfly and the box were machines. Amazing, mysterious machines, yes, but it was not a matter of being natural; it was a matter of understanding the function of the machine.

Chloe abruptly broke into a torrent of talk. "It's like when you get really, really good at a video game, because you play it all the time, and then you're teaching a new person to play and they're like, 'Hey, how do I do this, what button does that?' And you *can't say*. Your fingers know, but your conscious brain doesn't know, because it can't be bothered to keep track of stuff like that anymore, because you've gotten so good at it—so natural. Well, it's like that. And I don't want to all of a sudden be thinking about what buttons I'm pressing, you know?"

"My young friend," Mr. Meister said, "I have absolutely no frame of reference for what you're talking about, but I know precisely what you mean." He beamed at Chloe. Chloe stared back at him thoughtfully, clearly still trying to figure the old man out.

Horace looked back and forth between them, realizing that no explanation for how the dragonfly worked was forthcoming. "Well, I think I can guess how it works. Solid matter is mostly empty space anyway, when you get down to particles—"

"Hush," Mr. Meister interrupted harshly, his hand cutting through the air. "You are not the Keeper of this Tan'ji. If Chloe does not wish to hear the inconsequential ramblings of an old man—or a young one—who has no claim whatsoever on this instrument, so be it." He turned to Chloe, his face softening. "As for you, young lady, please accept my apologies. Young Mr. Andrews and I . . . we perhaps got carried away with our talk of science and other apparent sensibilities." He sat up and slapped his hands against his knees. "So tell me then, Chloe, is there anything you *do* wish to know about your dragonfly?"

Chloe scowled. "Tell me it's not just a glorified

whatchamacallit. A *passkey*." She spat out the word like a curse.

Mr. Meister laughed. "First, understand that passkeys are fairly common, as Tanu go. They are mere Tan'kindi—anyone may use them. Most passkeys bond to an object or location, but a rare few passkeys bond to a Keeper instead—they can become Tan'ji. Some of these rare Tan'ji are known by name, but the records are sparse and vague. The oldest passkeys are among the oldest of all Tanu."

"How old?" Chloe asked.

"Old," said Mr. Meister, drawing the word out long and low. "I sought for a long time to identify the Tan'ji you now possess—long before you came for the claiming, seven years ago—but I could not. I confess I assumed it was a Tan'ji of only middling importance. And then, yesterday, Mrs. Hapsteade told me of your exploits at the warehouse." He shook his head in disbelief. "Clearly you do not appreciate it, but what you did was astonishing. Perhaps unprecedented. Though you could not know it, the dumin is meant to keep out everything and everyone, including—indeed, *in particular*—those who wield the power of a passkey. You should not have been able to pass through the dumin. And yet you did. And then to walk into the golem itself, to carry the Vora through the golem and back into the dumin again! Astonishing."

If Chloe was embarrassed by any of this, she didn't show it. "So it's not a passkey."

"No, though it is related. You might say that it is the queen of passkeys."

Horace couldn't help himself. "And so what's the king?"

Chloe shook her head, her eyes fixed on Mr. Meister. "There is no king."

"Just so."

"And does it have a name?"

Mr. Meister smiled. "In all these years, have you never given it a name?"

"No. Why would I? That would be like . . . naming my hand."

"Well said." Mr. Meister looked at his own hand and hummed. "Yes indeed. However, I must tell you that although with the Fel'Daera there can be no doubt of its true name, I am less certain when it comes to your dragonfly. If I could be allowed to examine it more closely, I could be sure."

"Tell me what you think the name is, and I'll tell you if you're right."

Mr. Meister's glasses nearly slid off his nose. "Very well. I suspect it is the Alvalaithen. The Earthwing."

Wonder blossomed on Chloe's face. She bent over the dragonfly like it was a pet. Her eyes shone and her lips moved—mouthing the name to herself, Horace knew. He mouthed it once too, just to feel it. No one had to ask if the name was right. *The Alvalaithen.*

"Why do they call it the Earthwing?" Horace asked.

For an answer, the old man posed a question of his own to Chloe. "Tell me, Keeper, have you ever taken the dragonfly underground? Beneath the surface of the earth?"

Horace looked over at Chloe. He'd asked her this same question once, and she'd been weird about it.

"No," she said tersely.

"And yet you could," pressed Mr. Meister.

Chloe crossed her arms. "That's not how it works. What do you know about it?"

Mr. Meister studied her silently. Horace said, "Does that mean it's not the Alvalaithen? You said you weren't sure."

"It means nothing. But there are many Tanu that do what the dragonfly can do, roughly speaking. I wonder, Keeper," Mr. Meister said to Chloe. "May I examine the dragonfly? It has been long since I saw it last, and if it is indeed the Alvalaithen . . . let us just say, given that I failed to discover its true identity before, I would very much like to examine it again. Such opportunities do not come around very often."

Chloe's hand went to the dragonfly. "Will you have to touch it?"

"That would be easiest, yes. But I will be most delicate. And I assure you I have a great deal of experience in such matters."

"For a minute, then," Chloe said after a long, silent deliberation.

"My gratitude." Mr. Meister began polishing his glasses with a small square cloth pulled from one of his vest pockets. "Forgive me," he said. "My eyes are not what they could be. And indeed, without these glasses of mine I would be unable to perform my duties at all." Horace studied the fastidious care the old man took with his glasses—folding the cloth to a point and wiping each lens with tiny, cautious circles. Every so often he brought them up to his face and scrutinized them closely. Sudden realization dawned over Horace. How could he not have seen it before?

"Your glasses," he said. "They're Tan'ji."

Mr. Meister glanced at him in surprise, his eyes tiny but bright. "Indeed they are," he said. "Your eyes are getting keener." Done polishing, he tucked the cloth back into his vest and put the glasses back on, looping the curved arms behind his ears with a practiced flick. He reached out a hand to Chloe. "I ask your permission one more time, Keeper," he said formally. "May I intrude upon what is yours?"

Chloe lifted the dragonfly by the tail. A quick shimmer of the wings, and it was free. Leaning forward, she laid it in Mr. Meister's palm. It looked much smaller there. A little wave of distaste shimmered across Chloe's face as she let go.

Mr. Meister bowed his head. "Thank you, Keeper." He brought the dragonfly close to his face, peering at it with his enormous left eye. "Ah, yes," he said. "Quite right. Remarkable." He twisted his hand, looking at the dragonfly from all angles. Chloe watched him intently, bristling faintly but bearing it.

"What do your glasses do, anyway? If you don't mind me asking," Horace said, partly to distract her.

"Hmm? Oh . . . the glasses are ordinary, for the most part. However, this lens in particular," said Mr. Meister, lifting a finger to the thick round lens over his left eye, "is an oraculum. A common enough kind of Tanu, as such things go, but like the dragonfly here, a cut above the ordinary."

"What does an oraculum do?"

"Many things. Some allow the user to see long distances, or see things that are very small—though of course ordinary human devices will do the same. Some grant the power to see through darkness, through flesh, through lies. Through walls."

"Through time?" Horace asked.

"Very clever, but no—no oraculum can do what the Fel'Daera does."

"But yours lets you see through the Tanu," Chloe said. "You can see what they do."

Mr. Meister nodded, still peering closely at the dragonfly. "I can see patterns in their energies, the same way a carpenter sees patterns—sees potential—in the grain of a piece of wood. Function, condition, origin, strength, beauty. These things are made known to me through this lens, and through the knowledge gained from a lifetime of study."

"And you can see us too, can't you?" Horace asked, watching the old man look at Chloe. "That's how you knew I would be able to use the box."

"In part. As has been explained to you, it was the Vora that first revealed the general nature of your talents. That is its purpose—indeed, the purpose of the entire warehouse. Those who have the aptitude are drawn to the warehouse—by a sight, a sound, a sensation."

"Horace F. Andrews," Horace murmured to himself, remembering back to the first day he'd seen that sign.

Mr. Meister continued as if he had not heard. "Once inside, visitors use the Vora. The ink of the Vora reveals much, if you know what to look for. Mrs. Hapsteade sees much more in the ink than I, of course, but I had strong suspicions about you when I saw your entry in the guestbook, Horace. And once I got a look at you in person with the oraculum, yes—I knew. Almost knew. And I had to know, because the box— well . . . let us say there is only one Fel'Daera." Just then Mr. Meister startled and gave a little cry. The dragonfly's wings swept into motion, and it fell clean through his hand. In the same moment Chloe darted forward and snagged it out of the air, drawing it to her chest.

Mr. Meister stared and muttered something beneath his breath that Horace couldn't quite catch. It sounded like *"By the loom . . ."*

Chloe sat back and threw them both a sly, challenging look. She shrugged at Mr. Meister. "You seemed like you were done," she explained.

CHAPTER TWENTY—ONE

The Wardens

MR. MEISTER WIPED THE SURPRISE FROM HIS FACE. "QUITE done." He gestured at the dragonfly. "You needn't feel so sour about passkeys, my dear. They are no more like the dragonfly than a puddle is like the sea. The dragonfly's power is subtle, but unmistakable now that I know to look for it. If this is not the Alvalaithen, it is its equal. And the Alvalaithen has no equal."

Chloe seemed not to be listening to him as she sank back into the couch, fussing instead with the dragonfly and the cord, but Horace was sure she was soaking up every word.

Mr. Meister gave a satisfied sigh. "The Fel'Daera. The Alvalaithen. Two talented young Keepers. If I may say—if you will not allow it to go to your heads—you possess potential the likes of which I have not seen for many years, and your powers, I feel sure, will only continue to grow. Your Tan'ji are instruments . . . well . . . of legend."

Horace and Chloe shared an embarrassed look—or at least, Horace felt embarrassed; as usual, Chloe looked more surly than shy.

Mr. Meister leaned forward. "But now that I have given you your answers, you will return the favor. One question only. *Will you join us?*"

"Join your fight, you mean," Chloe said. "That's what Mrs. Hapsteade said you wanted."

"Indeed we do. But understand that our fight is your fight too. We simply want you with us."

Chloe bent forward. "Who exactly is *us?*"

"We are the Wardens."

"Wardens," said Chloe. "Like guardians."

"Yes. Mrs. Hapsteade, Gabriel, myself, and many others— all Wardens. It is my fervent hope that you will be one too."

"Mrs. Hapsteade said you were the resistance," said Horace.

"Indeed. The Wardens are defenders. As Mrs. Hapsteade no doubt explained, we protect that which our enemies would call their own." He looked pointedly up at the busy walls, indicating the Tanu all around them. "The Riven would do anything just to possess the instruments in this room alone— and there are other rooms, other strongholds. Some of the most powerful instruments remain in the protection of the Wardens. The Riven seek to control every last one—especially Tan'ji—but we stand in their way."

"So basically," Chloe said, "you sit around here and guard the stuff you've hoarded."

"Hardly. The Riven have their own collections of Tanu, and we take from them just as they attempt to take from us. But there are signs that our long conflict is nearing an end."

"But if the Riven have their own Tan'ji, why do they want ours?"

"They believe they are the rightful owners of all Tanu. And they consider it a blasphemy that ordinary humans like us would call ourselves Tan'ji."

Horace pressed on. "Ordinary humans? So the Riven—what are they, exactly? Are they human?"

Mr. Meister sat back. "I do not know," he said plainly.

This frank admission of ignorance caught Horace by surprise. "Okay then . . . but why do they think they're the rightful owners of the Tanu?"

Mr. Meister hesitated. "The long answer is not for today. The short answer would perhaps mislead you."

"Try us," Chloe said. "The short answer. Who are they?"

"The short answer." A sigh. Another measuring look at the two of them. "They are the Makers." A slow shrug, and then a sweeping gesture at the room around them, all the compartments and shelves full of mysterious devices. "They are the Makers of the Tanu."

Silence fell. Horace's thoughts raged forward. Hand on the box, he sipped at its presence in his mind, testing. Chloe twisted the dragonfly rapidly between two fingers, spinning it back and forth, the wing tips tapping her skin. It had never once occurred to Horace to wonder who made the box, but the idea that the likes of Dr. Jericho could have had anything to do with something so beautiful and so . . . *alive* . . . as the Fel'Daera—or the Alvalaithen, for that matter—was beyond incomprehensible. It was revolting.

"I confess I misled you, just a trifle," Mr. Meister said. "The Riven today—what Dr. Jericho and his kind have become—are not to be confused with those who forged the Box of Promises or the Earthwing. Or the Laithe of Teneves, for example." He pointed to the spinning globe on his desk, shaking his white head. "Such feats are beyond them now. Nonetheless, it is true that the Riven are descendants of the Makers."

"This is—" Horace began. He glanced over at Chloe, who looked both furious and confused at the same time. "I think we need to hear more. The long story."

"Truly, that is not my tale to tell. And I only know what has been passed on to me, or what I have been able to glean from a few timeworn manuscripts. But very well; let me encapsulate what I can." Mr. Meister sighed again, dropping his chin to his chest. When he spoke again, it was in low, somber tones. "The Makers—the Altari, they called themselves then—once lived quietly among us, not quite hidden. They had the ability to create the Tanu, and this they did for the betterment of their own lives, for the sake of curiosity, for aesthetic reasons, for the pursuit of power. They alone had the ability to become Tan'ji. The histories are unclear, but gradually discord grew between the Altari and ordinary humans, and the Altari went peaceably into hiding. Even then, though, there were those among the Altari who were friendly. They gave us gifts of their own making, simple things . . . Tan'kindi. In fact, that's the origin of the word they still use for us today—"

"Tinkers," Horace said, comprehension dawning.

"Yes. They mean it as an insult now, where once it was a term of affection. Centuries after the Altari went into hiding, though, it was discovered that some ordinary humans had the aptitude to become Tan'ji. They possessed the talent, much to the surprise of the Makers. Some of the Altari welcomed this development, but many others revolted violently against the idea. They wanted to keep the Tan'ji for themselves, believing that only they had the right of ownership, and that we were inferior creatures unfit to take the bond.

"A kind of civil war broke out among the Altari. Those who opposed the friendship with ordinary humans broke away, calling themselves the Kesh'kiri—the Riven. They remained in darkness but began to interfere with human affairs, hunting down the human Keepers and their instruments, and struggling bitterly against the other Altari, who meant us no harm."

Horace stirred, fascinated. "Those Keepers—were they the first Wardens, then?"

"In a manner of speaking."

261

"And what about the rest of the Altari? Are they still around?"

"Some remain. Most have become more deeply secret than ever, refusing to meddle as the Riven do. The Riven, meanwhile, have declined in skill and power, but they will never stop fighting until the Tanu are under their control, one way or another. Some among them only want to escape the lot that was given to them, to crawl up from their nests and hide no more. Others seek nothing less than the subjugation of all humankind, hoping to rule over us all. But every last Riven wants to see the long diligence of the Wardens come to naught. They hate that we possess the powers that we do, that we continue to hold fast. They will do whatever they can to put things, as they see it, back to rights. Their time is short, however. Their desperation grows. And therefore I ask again: will you join our fight?"

Horace took it all in, breathless. What was this tale he had wandered into? He looked at the others. Mr. Meister, shrewd and expectant. Chloe, intense and fuming, perhaps at the thought of anyone considering her to be unworthy of the dragonfly. Neither of them looked the least bit frightened or uncertain. Horace wondered what his own face looked like.

"As I feared," Mr. Meister said after a time. "I've taken you beneath the surface, shown you the bulk of the iceberg. It is too much."

"No, no, it's just . . . ," Horace began, but trailed off.

"You feel small, perhaps. You have come into the tail end

of a story as big as the ages."

Chloe scoffed, but that was exactly how Horace was feeling—small. And he still had so many questions. "The tail end of the story," he said. "And you said their time is short. Why?"

But Mr. Meister shook his head firmly. "I will say no more. You must decide. Will you join our fight, or won't you?"

Horace glanced at Chloe. She just sat there, still saying nothing. "Well," Horace said, "I think maybe we've already been fighting—in our own little way."

Mr. Meister's eyebrows slowly lifted. "Indeed? How so?"

"Chloe . . . ," Horace said, but she stayed as still as stone.

"I know about Horace's encounter on the bus," said Mr. Meister, watching the two of them closely. "And the golem and your escape in the sewers, of course. Have there been any other recent confrontations with the Riven?" The old man turned to Chloe, his bushy eyebrows still arched high and his left eye shining. But Chloe only shook her head.

"Mr. Meister," Horace began, "Dr. Jericho was—"

"Following us," Chloe cut in suddenly. "He's trying to find out where we live."

"He follows Chloe," Horace corrected. "He—"

"He tries," Chloe said, firing a furious glance at him. "He can't keep up with me."

Mr. Meister drilled his gaze so hard into Chloe that Horace felt pushed back into his seat just being near her. Chloe, however, took his piercing scrutiny without a blink. The little black birds twittered overhead.

"Perhaps you do not realize how dangerous Dr. Jericho is," Mr. Meister said. "You've heard the tale, but still there is much you do not know. Among the Riven, his kind is called the Mordin. They are hunters, much taller than ordinary Riven, and more fearsome than most. Their senses are attuned to the Tanu, and to the humans who use them—particularly to Tan'ji. Mordin are single-minded, obsessive. They have one purpose: to seek out and acquire Tan'ji, by whatever means necessary."

"That's interesting," Chloe said dryly.

Mr. Meister grimaced and turned to Horace. "Tell me."

Horace cleared his throat. "I've seen Dr. Jericho. He hasn't seen me since that day on the bus, though. Or at least . . ."

Mr. Meister craned forward. "Yes?"

Horace hesitated again. But whatever Chloe's reasons were for not telling Mr. Meister about Dr. Jericho, this story had to be told. "I was following Chloe one night, using the box. And Dr. Jericho, he was following her too. This was all in the future, of course." Chloe had her chin in the air, eyes on the ceiling. Her lips were stone. "But Dr. Jericho looked strange through the box—more like a monster."

"A side effect of his disguise."

"Disguise?"

"The Riven use Tanu to weave illusions around themselves. No doubt you have noticed that the Dr. Jericho you see is not what other people seem to see—though it is still a disguise."

"Some disguise," Chloe muttered.

"Make no mistake. We see Dr. Jericho as we do only because he allows it. The Mordin are an arrogant bunch. Granted, we who have the talent are much harder to trick than those who do not, but Dr. Jericho could fool us, briefly, if he really tried." He held out both hands to Horace. "But the Fel'Daera casts the Riven's disguises in a . . . shall we say . . . very noticeable light. Their disguises are changeable, shifting. The box, when viewing the future, interprets this variability as an extravagance of form."

"It was extravagant, all right." Horace shuddered, remembering the sight. "But also, Dr. Jericho, he . . . knew the box was there. He could sense it. Through time, I mean."

"That is not possible."

"Well, okay, but it happened. He came after the box. I used it to lure him away from Chloe's hiding place. He knew I was there, on the other side. He even tried to speak to me through the box."

Mr. Meister's sharp stare darted again to Chloe, who was still contemplating the ceiling. Her mouth had fallen open slightly, though. Horace had never told her this story. "You were hiding from him."

"I hide from a lot of people. Creatures. Whatever. I'm not in any danger."

"We are all in danger. Earlier you said he was following you—is he alone when he appears?"

"Usually."

"But not always. How often do you see him?"

Chloe shrugged. "Once every couple of weeks, I guess."

She'd told Horace the thin man was following her far more often, but even with the lie, Mr. Meister choked back a gasp. "This should not be. What of your leestone?"

"Like the statue in Horace's house? I never had one of those."

"No, yours was different—the keel of a raven. I gave it to you myself. No new Keeper leaves a warehouse without a leestone."

Chloe scoffed. "You gave it to me when I was five? That was forever ago. And anyway, what's a keel?"

Mr. Meister put his fingers to his forehead, murmuring, his thoughts clearly elsewhere as he said, "A bone. The breastbone of a bird." He looked up again. "This would be a flatter bone, almost like the fin of a shark. It was engraved with markings. Gruesome, but you were fascinated. Careless of me to assume after seven years . . . but now I understand."

"Look, things are . . . things have been . . ." Chloe squeezed her eyes shut and worked her jaw. She sighed. "My dad, sometimes he pawns our stuff. To get money."

"I see." Mr. Meister thought some more and then said, "I think I am correct in assuming it was you, Chloe, whom Horace saw on the bus that day. The girl in the green hoodie, as I recall. Are you aware that it must have been your presence that pulled Dr. Jericho on board, putting you both in danger? That very likely it was only the cloud of the raven's eye in

Horace's pocket that kept the Mordin from noticing you?"

"It doesn't matter. The freak can't catch me. And I helped Horace escape."

"It's very curious that Dr. Jericho was even aware of Horace, considering Horace had the raven's eye. Did you use your Tan'ji on that bus? To slip out the back unnoticed, perhaps?"

Chloe had no answer for that one, which of course was all the answer there was. She clenched her jaw and looked away.

Mr. Meister rolled on mercilessly. "And no doubt you've also realized that it must have been you who led the Riven to the warehouse yesterday."

"What?" Horace cried, unable to hold back any longer.

"I would never do that," said Chloe.

"Perhaps not intentionally. But I have no doubt it was your trail they followed to our door."

"How was I supposed to know?"

"I do not care. I am not interested in dwelling on the past. But now that you do know, would you like to reconsider your answers to the questions I've asked you?"

Reluctantly, almost poutily, she said, "I see the freak more than every couple of weeks. It's more like every other day."

Mr. Meister's eyes widened. "And does he know where you live?"

"Probably," Chloe said, then sighed. "Yes."

"Your father. You live with him."

"Him and my sister."

"Yes, of course. Madeline. How has your father been behaving? Has he been normal?"

"Normal for him."

"Which is?"

"Drunk. Unemployed. Asleep half the time, gone the rest." Her eyes flashed angrily. "Seems like you maybe ought to know all this already. Seems like you ought to keep better tabs on your Keepers."

"Much of this we do know. We know of your mother."

Chloe shot to her feet, quivering. Mr. Meister went on smoothly. "Have you noticed anything strange in your father's possession? Something new? Something with which he is reluctant to part?"

Chloe's eyes carved across the old man's face. "A Tanu, you mean." Mr. Meister nodded. "What kind of a thing?"

"Something small. A token, perhaps, or a figurine. Probably black, probably made of stone, or glass."

Chloe dropped back into her seat. "No, nothing like that. Where would he get something like that, anyway?"

"We speak now of the malkund, gifts of the Riven. These are Tanu meant to compromise the holder, to make them more susceptible to outside influences. A malkund may exhaust you, distract you, sadden you. It may increase your natural weaknesses—your fears, your obsessions. It may make you suspicious of those you have heretofore trusted, make you more likely to listen to those you would not ordinarily trust."

"My dad trusts everybody."

"When the malkund takes possession, it is extremely troublesome to deal with."

"It's lucky there isn't one, then."

Mr. Meister sank into a silence so deep and so long that Horace began to wonder if he had fallen asleep. He held his head in one hand, a single finger across his lips, face lowered. After a couple of minutes, a bird fluttered down from above and alighted in his white hair. It hopped there cheekily—twice, three times—and darted away again with a rustle.

At last, after four minutes, the old man stirred. "All that I hear troubles me a great deal," he said. Then he stood up abruptly. "It is time for you to go. I have much to look into. In the meantime, do not use your Tan'ji unless absolutely necessary, for fear of drawing the Riven's scrutiny. If you see Dr. Jericho again, steer well clear of him, and do not draw attention to yourselves." He dug into a pocket and pulled out a raven's eye, handing it to Chloe. "Take this with you. And be sure you sleep beneath Horace's roof each night, no matter what it takes. As long as you do, you will have the protection of his leestone."

Chloe shoved the raven's eye into her pocket without a glance. She looked at Mr. Meister hard for a few seconds. "That's it?"

"For now, yes."

"So we just . . . what? Go home with our Tan'ji and take up knitting?"

"Think on what I have told you. Consider my invitation. I

hope you will decide to join us—not just for our sake, but for your own." But then he spread his hands, making a gesture of acquiescence. "I will not pretend we do not need your help. There are now only a half dozen Wardens in the city, counting Mrs. Hapsteade and myself. Gabriel is a third—you've met him. We are all Tan'ji, of course, some of us powerful indeed—though I will confess none of us possesses an instrument quite like the Fel'Daera, or the Alvalaithen."

"That's it?" Chloe said. "Six of you?"

"There are other Wardens in other places, but I would put our total numbers at less than two hundred."

"And how many of them are kids?" asked Horace.

Mr. Meister shrugged. "As you say, we have been recruiting. The Find comes most easily to the young. But there are Wardens even older than myself. Much older."

Horace had a hard time imagining such a thing. But their numbers—only six Wardens in the city! How many Riven were there? He had a feeling it was a lot more than six.

"Now you know why we seek out new Keepers. I admit it is a frustration—I have a great many Tanu of considerable power in my possession, but they are unclaimed. Once there were many of us, but we have dwindled. In stature. In numbers. In will. Some were taken. Some dispossessed. Fused, faded, killed, cleaved. Turned." He fell silent. Overhead, a bird rustled sleepily. "But as the tide goes out, so too it must come in. The unclaimed Tan'ji are finding their Keepers. Chloe, you have come into your own. You, Horace, have bonded to the Fel'Daera. And there are others who will be making their way to us soon. Still we search." He sighed. "All of them young, yes. It seems that will be the way of things here at the end."

Horace took it all in, feeling again the mysterious weight of this old story into which he himself had so recently wandered. What must Mr. Meister's life have been? And how tiny a thing was Horace compared to everything else Mr. Meister must have seen and done in all his years?

Mr. Meister shook himself. "Forgive me. I wax sentimental. It is time now for you to go. We will meet again soon."

"And how soon is soon?" Chloe asked.

Mr. Meister thought for a moment, then turned to Horace. "There is a shed behind your house, I believe. Rarely used, by the looks of it."

"Yes, the toolshed."

"Can you meet me there tomorrow night? Around midnight? I hope to have an answer to some of my questions by then. We will have more to discuss."

"Sure. Okay," said Horace. Chloe nodded.

"Very good. Look for me tomorrow." He began to herd them toward the door. "In the meantime—" He laid a hand on each of their shoulders and fixed them with a final steely gaze. "Fear is the stone; may yours be light."

CHAPTER TWENTY-TWO

Confessions

BECK DROVE THEM HOME. THEY WERE HEADED TO CHLOE'S house first, so she could get clothes and make arrangements for Madeline. As they drove, Chloe rolled the leestone mindlessly between her cupped palms, peeking at it now and again, and once or twice pressing it to her cheek.

"Why didn't you tell him?" Horace asked her, after several silent blocks.

"About what?"

"You know what." Horace wasn't sure how much Beck understood—or actually, whether Beck could even talk.

"I can handle it. I'm used to dealing with things on my own."

"I don't think that's smart."

"I never said I was smart." She tilted her head at him. "So you lured Dr. Jericho away that night, huh? When I was hiding inside the tree?" Her brow wrinkled. "Or no—the night before."

"The night before, yeah."

"You didn't really know me yet."

Horace shrugged. "It didn't matter. You needed help."

"No, I mean you didn't know me well enough to know I didn't need help." She pressed the leestone against her cheek again. Horace turned away, irritated. It wasn't like he'd been bragging about what he'd done, throwing it in her face.

They dropped into silence. Horace thought they were nearly to Chloe's house now; the neighborhood seemed familiar. Chloe leaned forward and spoke to Beck.

"Actually, I don't need to go home. Can you take me to my aunt Lou's instead? It's close by." Beck regarded her in the mirror for a moment. "My sister is there," Chloe explained, and after another little pause, Beck nodded.

Chloe started to give Beck directions, but Beck just reached up and tapped a sticker on the dashboard that read:

ANY ADDRESS ANYWHERE

"Oh, sorry," Chloe said, and she rattled off a street and number. As they swung around the next corner, Chloe leaned into Horace. "Are we supposed to take that literally?"

After a couple of blocks, they pulled up in front of a squat blue house with four little girls playing outside. Chloe got out and one of them, a girl of seven or eight with copper-colored hair, came running. They hugged, and then Madeline pointed at the cab, a question on her face. Chloe turned, and Horace saw the words form on her lips—*my friend Horace.* Horace offered up an awkward wave. Madeline just stared.

An enormous woman with short hair came out of the house. More hugs, more talking, more pointing at Horace. Another embrace. They went inside briefly, and two minutes later Chloe reemerged, carrying an overnight bag. As she headed back to the cab, Madeline wrapped herself around her leg. Chloe staggered down the sidewalk, making the most of it, dragging the leg and Madeline with it. Horace could hear the laughter—Madeline's high squeal and Chloe's laugh, too, rich and childlike, a laugh he hadn't heard from her before. They made it all the way to the cab, and then Chloe heaved Madeline to her feet with a groan. He could hear their talk now, round and muffled. Madeline's face bent into a pout. "Tomorrow," Chloe said. "Promise."

Chloe pried herself away from her sister and opened the car door. Madeline's sad, suspicious eyes locked onto Horace.

"Horace, Madeline," Chloe said. "Madeline, this is Horace. Say hi."

"Hey, Madeline," Horace offered, and gave another wave.

Madeline pointed abruptly to the pouch at Horace's side. "What's that?"

"It's just a box," he said, putting his hand on it.

"No it's not," Madeline shot back.

"It's a special box," Chloe explained. "Like the dragonfly.

Special and private. Okay?"

Madeline nodded, eyes wide. Horace could see he'd gone up a notch in her mind. Now came yet another hug, and promises that Chloe would return in the morning. As the cab pulled away, Madeline ran alongside briefly, bare feet slapping on the sidewalk, waving frantically. Her eyes were bright and eager, but Horace saw something else in them, too—something that pleaded and pulled. Chloe waved back until she dropped out of sight, then sank into the seat with a faraway look of concern on her face. Before they'd gone a block she said, almost to herself, "She's scared. Too smart not to be."

Horace cleared his throat. "I thought she didn't know about the dragonfly."

"Oh, yeah. She knows it exists, of course. I don't think she knows what it does."

"You don't think?"

"I told you I don't go thin in front of her—not since she was really little—but I don't know. She's smart. She might remember things." A wry smile slid onto her face. "I used to play a pretty awesome game of peekaboo."

A noise erupted from the front seat, gruff and startling, like a heavy fist pounding into a punching bag. Beck's shapeless shoulders heaved with the sound. The driver was laughing: *"Hurhh, hurrhh, hurhh."* In the mirror, blue eyes squinted back at them. Chloe began to laugh too.

"What was that place?" Horace asked. "Who was that lady?"

"Oh, that's Aunt Lou. Not really an aunt, but whatever. She watches Madeline a lot. And me too, when I was younger."

"So Madeline's staying there. You *do* think there's danger, like Mr. Meister said."

"God, Horace." Chloe leaned her head against the glass.

"That was some story he told us. I feel kind of . . . small after hearing all that."

"Yeah, some story."

"So are you going to join them? The Wardens?"

"Are you?"

"I guess it depends on what you do."

She turned toward him. "Why?"

"Well, if I go off and join the Wardens, who's going to stick around to rescue you?"

"Very funny. Look, I get that they want our help protecting the Tanu. I'm just not sure yet that I want theirs."

Five minutes later, Beck dropped them off a few houses down from Horace's house. He could see his mother was already home from work. Chloe refused to come in, not wanting his parents to see her and invite her to dinner.

"They'll invite me even if they don't want me," she said. "They're polite."

"So come to dinner. They love you."

"Nah. I'm really not in the mood to deal with parents right now. I just need to think for a while."

"You sure?"

"Sure," Chloe said, already backing away. "I'll sneak up

to the attic. See you tonight." She slipped between two neighbors' houses and disappeared.

Inside, Horace's mother said nothing about his lateness. Horace probably would not have cared even if he had gotten in trouble. The sudden absence of Chloe was muddling his mood. Later, during dinner, he had to stop himself from looking at the ceiling every thirty seconds, imagining Chloe up there alone. At bedtime, he left his desk lamp on, pointed at the wall, and waited impatiently in the near-dark for her. Time crept by like clouds. Where was she? At last, at 10:18, there came a soft knocking, and she stepped through his closet door.

"Howdy," she said.

"Hey," Horace whispered. "We have to be quiet, okay? My parents are still up."

"I know. I'll use my inside voice."

The sight and sound of her was like a cure, like a fog thinning. Chloe moved around the room like a cat without a care, wandering to his desk and digging aimlessly. She found a bottle of bubbles, sat on the foot of the bed, and blew a barrage of bubbles into the air. As they drifted down around her, she went thin, holding out her arms and letting the bubbles sink unpopped through her flesh.

"How was dinner?" she asked.

"Strangely normal. I brought you a couple of rolls."

"Thanks, but I'm not really hungry. I snacked." Chloe pushed her finger into the center of a small, tight bubble, wearing it like a fat ring. "Did you get in trouble for coming home late?"

"No. My mom didn't even ask. My dad would've, but he wasn't home yet."

"Well, it could be worse. My dad . . . he never asks where I've been anymore. He might not see me for a whole day but never miss me. I haven't even been grounded in years, and some of the stuff I do? Seriously."

"My dad grounds me for stupid stuff sometimes," said Horace. "That would be weird now, wouldn't it? Getting grounded? Here we are with our 'instruments of legend,' and I can't even watch TV."

Chloe snorted. "Yeah. You can see the future . . . but in that future, there will be no dessert." Horace laughed, but Chloe went on: "Actually, my dad grounds me all the time. I just never listen. He never remembers. Last time he grounded me, he called me by my mom's name. He didn't even say what it was for." She dipped the bubble blower into the bottle, brought it to her lips. She coaxed out a bubble as big as a grapefruit. It wobbled over her, glinting. "Watch this." The dragonfly's wings flitted into motion. She leaned forward and let the bubble drop down into her black hair, on into her scalp, her skull. When it was halfway inside her head, the dragonfly's wings slowed to a halt. Chloe's face squinched into a comic pucker and one hand shot open, fingers straight and electric. "Bubble brain," she squeaked, eyebrows arched.

Horace frowned. "Is that good for you?"

"Oh, Horace," Chloe said, blinking and pinching the bridge of her nose. "You're so Horace." She capped the bubble bottle and flopped back on the bed. "So are you going to do it?"

"Do what?"

"You know." She punched her small fists into the air. "Fight. Join the Wardens."

"I'm the one who asked *you* that. You're the one that's being weird about it."

"I'm not being weird. I'm adjusting."

"Adjusting to what?"

"Well, think about it—for you, this whole thing is new. But for me, it's like I've had this private thing for years, and now all these strangers want me to do a little dance." She did a goofy little shimmy on the bed, her face deadly serious.

Horace had to smile. "I hadn't thought about that."

"And the old folks. Mr. Meister and Mrs. Crabhead. Do you really trust them? That story he told us about the Makers—that seemed . . . heavy. All that stuff about the Riven taking over the world."

"You don't believe that?"

"I just think there are things they don't tell us."

"There are things we don't tell them, either."

Chloe shrugged, as if to suggest she wasn't sure about that—a ridiculous idea. "But do you *trust* them?" she said.

And did he? Mrs. Hapsteade's abrupt manner and her obvious misgivings about the box. Mr. Meister's unmistakable

279

shroud of secrecy, even as answers poured from him. It was hard to say how honest they were, how trustworthy. But if it weren't for them, Horace would never have found the box. And if it weren't for them, he might already have lost it by now. "Yeah, I think I trust them. Or how about this? I absolutely trust that they don't want our instruments to fall into the hands of the Riven. For now, that's enough for me." He watched Chloe mull this over, and then he said, "More than them, though, I trust you."

"You do?"

"Of course. If you're in, I'm in."

"And what if I'm not?"

"Then I don't know. But anyway, we'll see Mr. Meister again soon."

Chloe laughed softly. "Sooner or later a moon elevator," she said.

"What? What does that mean?"

"Something my dad used to say. After my mom left." Here she paused, as if making room for Horace to ask about that, but he wasn't sure how to begin. After a moment she continued. "He meant it like, good things will happen eventually if you just have patience. But for me it means kind of the opposite now—it means you shouldn't sit around waiting for rescue."

Horace thought that one over for a while. He said, "I guess it depends on where you are. If you're on earth, it might be cool if a moon elevator appeared one day."

"Right. But if you're stuck on the moon, waiting for an elevator would be a stupid thing to do. And I've been feeling sort of stuck on the moon lately. Far and alone. Like Rip." She pointed straight overhead, where the lightning bug was crawling through the ceiling's field of stars.

Far and alone. Horace watched as the bug took off and began drifting around the room like a sagging zeppelin. Horace had forgotten to send him through the night. He wondered how big a burden the light he hauled was. It looked so heavy, dragging the bug down. And yet it must be everything to the bug, right? Why else bother?

"So, your mom," Horace said softly. "Can I ask you why she left?"

Chloe sat up and leaned against the wall, her face turning to stone. "Apparently you can." She popped a mint into her mouth, chomping. She wrapped her arms around her knees. For a while, the room was silent except for the sound of the mint being ground into powder between her teeth.

"I'm sorry," Chloe said. "I'm feeling . . . antsy. I don't handle antsy well."

"Why are you antsy?"

"All this stuff about trust. Not telling people things."

"Yeah?"

She hesitated for a moment. "And also what I said earlier. About not needing your help?" She let the words hang there, her face still stern but her eyes pleading. She shrugged an apology.

"Chloe, what's going on?"

"I need you to come with me."

"Come with you where?"

"To my house. Like . . . now. There's something I have to do. Something I can't do without you." Dread crept slowly over Horace. If Chloe was being this hesitant, something was seriously wrong. "I have to tell you two things," she said. "Try not to flip."

"I don't flip."

"Well, we'll see. Here goes. One: I did have that bone thing Mr. Meister was talking about. The leestone. Only I never knew what it was. But I had it for years and then it disappeared, a few months back. Around the time the freak started showing up."

Horace opened his mouth to protest—he couldn't help it—but then closed it again. He nodded instead. "Okay."

"Two." Chloe squared herself. "That other thing he talked about. The malkund. I think my dad has one."

Horace had to bite his tongue again. So many lies she'd told to Mr. Meister, so many things she'd kept hidden. "Okay," he said slowly. "What is it, exactly?"

"I don't know, some little black stone. A figurine, I think. He's always rubbing it between his fingers. He always has it. It makes a sound, sometimes."

"What kind of sound?"

"Like a chirp, maybe? I don't know. I think it does. But the whole thing is really weird, and it seems exactly like what

Mr. Meister was talking about. And my dad's been different. He's actually been drinking less, but he's worse, somehow. Farther away. He's not as unpredictable, but it's only because he's . . . deader. And he always has that thing, for the last few months."

"Since you lost the bone?"

"I didn't *lose* it—somebody took it. But yes, maybe that long. It's all sort of recent—the bone, the black stone, Dr. Jericho always after me."

Horace felt his worry rising. If all she was saying was true, Chloe's house was a very dangerous place for them to be. "So what do you want us to do?"

"We take the malkund. We take it and destroy it."

"How? And what if we can't? Mr. Meister said it was hard to destroy, right?"

"*Extremely difficult*, he said. I know. So I thought maybe, if we can't destroy it, we could—if you're willing—send it through the box."

"Are you—" Horace began, and then lowered his voice. "Are you insane?"

"I know, but I've been thinking. This thing has my dad under some kind of spell. Or not a spell, okay, but it has a power over him. If we send it through the box, though, it'll just be—"

"Gone," Horace finished.

"Yes. Better than destroyed."

"But it'll come back."

"Yes, and I'll have to deal with it. But for twenty-four hours, it'll be nowhere. It'll be traveling. Maybe that will break the connection, or something. My dad, he—" Her voice cracked ever so slightly, and she looked so fragile and lost as she searched for the right words that after a moment Horace leaned toward her, putting out his hand. But then the wings of the dragonfly flickered, and Horace snatched his hand back.

"Don't," Chloe said.

"I'm not."

"You were. And please don't look at me like that, all . . . protecty, or whatever." All the vulnerability was gone from her voice now, pushing a stab of embarrassment and a strange, sick kind of sadness through Horace.

"I'm not being protecty, I'm being . . . friendy."

Chloe's throat worked up and down cruelly. She swallowed hard and took a deep breath. "Then be my friend," she said.

CHAPTER TWENTY–THREE

The Malkund

Twenty minutes later, at 11:14, the two of them mounted the back steps of Chloe's house. They entered a tilting screened-in porch that seemed like it was about to fall off the house. Chloe flipped a switch and lit a dim, bare bulb overhead. A broken porch swing lay beside the back door like the skeleton of some dead animal, bleached and collapsing. There was a bike tire, too—flat—plus a couple of cinder blocks and a small white wastebasket with a board over the top. "Don't say anything about my house," Chloe said. "I don't want you to laugh or whatever."

"Why would I laugh?"

"Just . . . don't, okay?"

"Okay."

If things were in disarray outside, the inside was a wreck. They passed through a cluttered, narrow hall into the front room, and here there were papers everywhere, and clothes, and all kinds of everything. There was so much debris that paths had been made through it from door to door. The only furnishings were a single ratty-looking recliner and a couple of wooden kitchen chairs—one of which held an ancient TV—and a kind of coffee table propped up by milk crates. This table, like the rest, was buried beneath a drift of paper and clothes and garbage. Horace spotted a half dozen empty liquor bottles in the mix.

And there was a smell, a nagging stink that Horace couldn't put a name to. Through another door, he could see a cramped, grimy kitchen. The tops of more empty bottles peeked out of the sink.

Chloe led him swiftly across the front room through another doorway. Horace passed a chest-high piece of furniture covered in papers and realized it was a piano. The keys were exposed, and in one place there was a pile of big black crumbs—crumbs, or worse. Horace's face scrunched up in disgust, involuntarily. He quickly tried to smooth it away. To the right, stairs led up to the second floor, where a dingy yellow light shone from a water-stained fixture on the ceiling. To the left, the darkness of another room yawned. A faint, grating snore trickled out through the door.

Chloe put a finger over her lips. She crept nimbly up the steps, keeping her feet close to the right-hand wall. Horace came behind her, following her as precisely as he could. The boards creaked under him, making him feel huge, but the snoring continued.

Chloe led the way into her bedroom. Not nearly so messy here. In fact, the place was far neater than Horace's own room. The only real mess was an astounding heap of books in one corner—stack after stack, some waist-high, piled like a rocky desert landscape. Library books all. Horace got the feeling she didn't plan to return them anytime soon.

Her bed was a mattress lying on the floor. She had a milk crate for a bedside table. The only piece of real furniture was a pale blue dresser. Atop it Horace spied two photographs. One was a recent picture of Chloe and Madeline in front of the Navy Pier Ferris wheel. The other was older, showing both girls laughing in the lap of a large, bearded, smiling man—their father?

The walls were bare, except for one. Around the closet door in the rear wall, someone had painted what looked like an ornate gateway. It was rough and a bit lopsided, but beautiful—iron brown for the most part, but full of winding lattices and curlicues and little colored decorations, flowers and animals and symbols. It was a foot wide on all sides, reaching almost to the ceiling above. Horace came closer and marveled.

"Did you do this?" he asked.

"Oh, no. That's Madeline."

Horace felt his eyebrows float up. "Madeline did this?"

"I know, she's talented. You should see her room."

"It's cool that your dad lets her draw on the walls."

"Oh, yeah, Horace," she sniped. "He's a real art connoisseur. And a devoted homemaker." Horace looked away, embarrassed. As his gaze drifted around the little room, he spotted a shoebox inside the milk crate Chloe used for a nightstand. It was full of food—candy bars, granola bars, a box of graham crackers. Rolls and rolls of wintergreen mints. All stolen, no doubt, but that stealing—here in this stark room with sheets for a curtain, and with the snore coming from the dark, smelly room downstairs—that stealing didn't seem quite so bad.

"So I was thinking," Horace said. "Will it be safe, sending the malkund? It's a Tanu, right? I never sent a Tanu through the box before."

Chloe bit her lip. "We could test it."

"With what?"

"The raven's eye Mr. Meister gave me."

"What? No, Chloe, don't be stupid. You need to keep that. It's helping to protect you."

Chloe sighed and reached into her pocket. "Maybe I'm too stupid to know how this thing is supposed to work, but I get the feeling it's not going to protect me much longer." She pulled out the raven's eye and held it forward for Horace to see.

Horace gasped. The little leestone had faded drastically. The purple cloud inside was the size of a pea, after just seven hours or so. "Chloe, oh my god. That's bad." He searched her face, but it was wooden. "It took almost a whole day for the raven's eye I had to fade this much, and Mr. Meister kind of freaked."

Chloe's eyes flared. "Okay, so it's about to be worthless,

right? So let's send it. If you're willing to try . . . Keeper." She held out the leestone.

"Okay. Okay." Horace took the stone, surprised as ever by the strange warmth. He thought he could almost see the purple cloud shrinking.

He took out the box. Better not to drag this out. He stood over the bed, the box in one hand and the raven's eye in the other. "I'm nervous," he said.

"It's not going to blow up or anything. Mr. Meister would have warned you. It's an instrument of legend, and all that, right?"

"Right." Horace opened the box and put the raven's eye quickly inside. He felt nothing unusual. Before he could doubt himself any more, he slid the lid closed. The tingle thrummed through his fingers—stronger than usual, maybe, but to his relief it was otherwise utterly normal. When he opened the lid, he spotted the raven's eye lying there on tomorrow's bed, sharp and clear, the tiny nugget of color at the center still visible. Apparently it hadn't faded while traveling.

"It worked," he said, snapping the box closed again.

"Yes," Chloe hissed. "So let's do it. Can you do it?"

"I can do it. And then we have to go."

Chloe nodded. She outlined the plan. She would go into her father's room and take the malkund from him. "He sleeps with it in his hand," she explained. Horace would wait on the back porch, and she would bring it out to him. They would try to destroy the malkund, but if they couldn't, they would send it through the box.

They inched down the stairs. Snores still drifted from the gloomy room at the bottom. Chloe stepped just inside the doorway and stood there—letting her eyes adjust to the darkness, Horace realized. She glanced back at him and nodded.

Returning to the back porch was a blessing; fresh air came through the screens, cool and clean. Horace held the box at the ready but kept the lid closed. He resisted the urge to see what would be going on here at this time tomorrow night, worried that they were already using the box too much. He waited nervously, realized he was scanning the backyard for the sight of anything strange.

Murmured words drifted down the narrow hallway from the front room. Chloe. Long seconds passed—*twenty-two, twenty-three*—and at last she appeared, scurrying. She had her hands tightly cupped together around something, as if it might escape. "Coming, coming!" she hissed at Horace. She burst out of the hall and onto the porch. With a shout, she let the malkund fall. "God, it bit me!"

The malkund fell with a clatter, bouncing across the floor and coming to a stop. It was no bigger than a fingertip, shining and black. Horace squatted to examine it. It was shaped like a bug, with a round black head and chunky, folded hind legs—a roughly carved cricket. And it stank. It smelled like Dr. Jericho.

"No, no, crush it!" Chloe lunged forward to step on it.

The malkund leapt into the air, chirping. Horace fell back

onto his butt, slamming his head against a post. The malkund sprang into the wreckage of the porch swing, trying to burrow between the slats as Chloe stomped at it. "It wants to get back to him!" she cried.

The malkund leapt again, coming down between Horace's outstretched feet. Horace backpedaled away. His foot caught a cinder block. The block toppled slowly, then hammered down onto the malkund with a dull crack.

Horace and Chloe gaped at each other.

"I didn't know they were alive," Horace said.

Chloe clutched at her shirt with both hands, wiping them. She frowned down into one palm. "Not alive. Just another kind of Tanu. But it bit me. I could hardly get it out of his hand, and then it bit me or something. It was chirping, too, trying to wake him."

Horace leaned forward cautiously and tipped up the cinder block. Beneath it, the malkund lay still. One of its tiny back legs had snapped off, and it was badly scratched, but it seemed otherwise undamaged. "Do you think it's—" Horace began, and then the malkund twitched violently. Chloe yelped and Horace fell back again, taking the cinder block with him. It scraped his calf as it fell, scoring cornrows of blood across his flesh. The malkund leapt away, wounded but still fast. It skittered around the porch like popcorn popping.

A crash snapped Horace's head around. A man with a great bushy beard and broad muscular shoulders was staggering down the hallway, shirtless and huge. He'd knocked over a lamp and a stack of newspapers and was stumbling toward them, mumbling angrily, his words slurring together into a growl. His red-rimmed eyes locked on to Horace. Chloe's father, but this was not the same kind man as in the photograph upstairs. "Kids," he rumbled. "Gimme, dammit—gimme!" He took another lurching step and fell against the wall. He held one hand downturned, fingers like claws, snapping at the air. He was halfway down the hall now.

"Keep it away from him!" Chloe cried. She took a long step and kicked at the malkund, hitting it square on. It sailed across the porch, cartwheeling crazily, and bounced out of the still-open door. "Get it, Horace, get it!"

Horace sprinted after the malkund, leaping down the back steps. It twitched and hopped across the concrete walk at the foot of the stairs, blundering back toward the house. He stomped at it. It sprang around, trying to escape. At last he got it, felt it snap beneath his heel. When he lifted his foot, he saw the other leg had broken in half. Still the thing squirmed and skittered, dancing around in twitchy circles. It bounced into the dark grass.

"Send it! Send it now!" Chloe called. Her father loomed in the doorway behind her.

Horace dropped to one knee, opening the box, dipping it into the malkund's path. The malkund tumbled blindly into the box, chirping shrilly. Up on the porch, Chloe's dad roared and stumbled out of the hallway. "Chloe?" he bellowed. Chloe stood in front of him, arms raised—so tiny in front of the towering, raging form of her father.

Horace closed the box. The malkund's cries cut off mid-chirp. A long, strong tingle streamed into his hands. At the same moment, Chloe's father collapsed, going down like a tree. Chloe sidestepped him as he fell and then dropped immediately to his side, peering into his face.

Horace searched around on the pavement with eyes and hand until he found the malkund's leg. It was sickening to the touch, somehow stony and fleshlike at once. He took it back inside, his own legs weak, his head pounding.

"It worked," Chloe said, still crouched next to her father. "We did it."

"We barely did it. Is he all right?" Her father was an enormous man, but he looked harmless now—almost sad—crumpled and motionless. Horace noticed that the little finger of one hand was stunted, the last joint amputated.

"He's breathing," said Chloe. "I think he's okay. What time is it?"

He knew why she was asking. The malkund would return. "Eleven twenty-eight," he said, squinting out into the yard. "Did you see where?"

"I saw close enough."

"We need to get out of here."

"You're bleeding," Chloe said. Sure enough, blood was running down his leg from the scrape on his calf, soaking into his sock. The sight of it brought the pain alive in his mind, raw and stinging. His head hurt now, too, where he had cracked it.

He felt for the spot gingerly, found a knot.

"Yeah, well, I'm not graceful," he said, embarrassed that both of his injuries were lame and self-inflicted. "But we need to go."

"I know. You'll have to help me drag him in. But first get that leg that broke off, and send it through. Just to be safe."

"I snapped another one off, too. Part of it," he said, holding it up.

Chloe shuddered. "Send them both."

Horace located the malkund's other leg beside the cinder block. "Do you think this is normal? Do you think they all move like that?"

Chloe watched him as he dropped the reeking bits into the box and sent them, holding the box low over the floor so the pieces wouldn't scatter when they fell through tomorrow. She shook her head and brushed a slash of dirt from her father's cheek. "There is no normal."

CHAPTER TWENTY-FOUR

Good Intentions

THEY MADE THE TRIP BACK TO HORACE'S IN NEAR SILENCE. The whole while, Horace nervously lamented the absence of the raven's eye. An almost-spent leestone was better than no leestone at all, wasn't it? He took comfort by reminding himself that Chloe had spent the previous night under his roof, and that the raven-and-turtle statue had to be offering her some protection right now. But when Chloe, halfway home, wanted to stop and slip into a closed-up coffee shop to "grab some doughnuts," Horace just stared at her intently for so long that finally she said, "Okay, okay. Never mind. I guess you do flip."

By 11:53, they were back in Horace's bedroom. Chloe took her overnight bag to the attic and changed into pajama bottoms and an enormous T-shirt that read BREAD AND JAM. They settled on Horace's bed. On the far wall, Rip Van Twinkle crawled through the acutely angled light of Horace's desk lamp, casting a trundling shadow many times his own size.

"You okay?" Chloe asked Horace.

"Yeah. You?"

"I'm fine. Are you mad?"

Horace started to say yes but realized he wasn't mad. "Shouldn't I be?" he said.

"Probably. But I see that you're not. I don't know how you do that."

Footsteps sounded outside Horace's door. Before he could even tell Chloe to hide, the dragonfly stirred and she dropped clean through the bed, disappearing from sight. The bed rebounded from her suddenly absent weight, and the bottle of bubbles from earlier rolled onto the floor. He was still staring when his door opened and his mother leaned in.

"You still up?" she said. "I thought I heard you talking."

"What? No, I wasn't. But yes, I am still up."

Horace's mother came in with a smile. "You seem to be having a lot of late nights recently." Her foot kicked the bottle of bubbles. She gave a little laugh and picked it up, taking her usual seat beneath the window. She began sending streams of bubbles into the air. Loki came in and sat, cocking his head and gazing at them.

A flight of bubbles bustled up and drifted slowly down. "Have you seen Chloe lately?"

"No, why would I?" Horace said nervously.

"I don't know. She's a friend, right?"

"Yeah, I guess so."

"She seems like a friend." His mother sat forward and blew a string of bubbles toward Loki's face. The cat blinked and flinched, trying to bite them, seeming to forget he had paws. "I like her. She's very . . . capable."

Right above his mother's head were the tiny black words Chloe had written on the wall that first night. Horace pictured her pushing pieces of the golem from her flesh, hiding inside the tree while Dr. Jericho tore at the bark, running with the malkund in her hand. "That's an understatement," he said, and then wished the words back as soon as they were out. Chloe was under the bed right now—or at least he thought she was. He wasn't quite sure where she'd gone. But he had no doubt she was listening.

"What's this?" his mother said. She leaned over and picked up Horace's bloody sock. "Were you mauled?"

"Oh, that. No, I'm fine. I just scraped my leg."

"Can I see?"

Horace sighed and pulled his leg out from under the covers. The scrape was laced now with scabs like beads of drying glue. His mother peered at it. "How did that happen?"

"Long story," he said. "There was a chain of events."

"There always is. Were you a participant in this particular chain, or just a victim?"

"A participant, yeah," he said. "But my intentions were good."

"Well," she said. "Participation. Good intentions. That's a

297

recipe for a life well lived."

A few minutes later, she said good night and left, closing the door behind her. Horace's heart nearly stopped as Chloe's upper half instantly emerged from the foot of the bed, the dragonfly a blur. She stood half buried in the bed as casually as if she were standing in hip-deep water. "So your mom thinks I'm capable, huh?" she said.

"Oh my god, you have got to stop that," Horace whispered. "It is freaking me out."

Chloe shrugged and then jumped high, clearing the bed and folding her legs up beneath her in midair. The dragonfly stopped whirring, and she landed atop the covers. The bed squeaked alarmingly. "That was interesting," she said, lying back down again. "Things have been interesting lately. I feel like I'm getting even more . . . capable. With the dragonfly, I mean."

"That's a scary thought."

Chloe didn't respond to that, but several seconds later she sighed. "I decided I'm going to tell the old folks the truth. Tomorrow night."

"Really? About all of it?"

"Yes."

"Promise?"

The dragonfly stirred again. Her face as stern as stone, Chloe sunk a finger inside her chest. One swipe. Two. "Cross my heart," she said.

The gesture took Horace's breath away for a moment,

made him suddenly conscious of his own heart beating in his chest. He cleared his throat. "Did the malkund change your mind?"

"Partly. But also just . . . being here." She glanced at Horace's door.

"What do you mean?"

"I don't know. Everything just got me thinking. You asked me why my mom left."

"I'm sorry, I—"

"No. I wanted you to ask. There's not much to tell, though. One day she was just gone. I haven't seen her since I was five or six." Chloe shook her head, scowling. "But don't say you're sorry. I'm not sorry. Hell, my dad's not even sorry—he has this crazy idea that my mom leaving was some kind of noble thing. Like we didn't deserve her or she had some higher calling or something, I don't know . . ." Her voice trailed away. "And now all of this. My dad's had a hard time since my mom left, but not like lately. Not like you saw tonight." She threw Horace an apologetic glance. "I'm embarrassed you saw my house. I know it's a disaster."

Horace shrugged. "It's not so bad."

"It is. And then my dad today, god—you must have freaked when you saw him. But he's not so bad, somewhere in there. He wouldn't want to see me get hurt. I know that. He's still my dad, and home is still home, you know?" She went briefly cross-eyed as Rip, flying now, dipped down in front of her face and then floated away. "That door in my room, the one with the gate Madeline drew—that goes into a little hall-way between our bedrooms. Or more like a closet, maybe, but not really, because there's a bench, and a little arched window up high, and the sun comes through in the afternoon. We go in there and we talk and we play, and no one's ever really gone in there but us, and it's about as far from anything bad as you can be."

Horace tried to picture it. "Is that the heart? You said something before about the heart."

"No. The heart's different. Madeline can't go in the heart. No one can." She flashed him a surly glance, discouraging him from asking more.

"But anyway this little hallway that connects our rooms—we call it Go-Between. Like it's a country. For Madeline it's kind of a magic place. That's why she drew those gates. She leaves me notes: 'Meet me in Go-Between.'" Chloe smiled and sighed. "I don't know if it's true what Mr. Meister told us about the Riven, and if all I was worried about was keeping my own Tan'ji safe, I might never go back to the Warren again. I can take care of myself. But that's not all I'm worried about. I'm worried that I could lose something like Go-Between. Madeline's notes. My aunt Lou. My dad—what's left of him. And if I'm worried about losing what I have, you ought to be worried too, with all you could lose. I was listening to you and your mom."

Of course she had been listening. What had she heard? "Oh, yeah?" he said.

"Yeah, and your mom is kind of awesome. Even your dad is. And maybe with the way everything is for you here, it's hard to imagine it being so different, and I mean . . . look, you saw my dad. You saw how that thing made him. But I don't know if it's occurred to you yet to imagine your mom like that."

The picture rose up in his mind, hitting him hard: his mom, a lurching shell of herself, no longer a parent but . . . what? Something empty and cruel, something that maybe no longer cared about Horace.

"And I think that all of this"—Chloe lifted her arms and spread them wide—"and your mom and your dad and Madeline and Go-Between, and the way my dad used to be sometimes, that's the point, isn't it?"

"The point of what?"

She rolled forward onto her knees. She held out the dragonfly. "Of this." She leaned and laid her hand right beside the Fel'Daera on his nightstand, her fingers as close as they could be without touching it. "Of this." She shook her head and sort of shrugged, and gestured back and forth between Horace and herself. "This."

She was right, of course. Everything she was saying was right. But Horace wondered who she was really talking to—Horace, or herself. "Are you trying to convince me to join the Wardens? I already told you—I'm in if you're in."

"I'm in, then."

"So we're in."

"Fine," Chloe said. "But you have to let me be me some-times, okay?"

"Fine," Horace said. As if anyone could stop her. "And maybe sometimes you ought to let you be *me*."

Chloe laughed. "I'm not exactly sure what that means, but it's probably a good idea. What did your mom say? Good intentions? Participation? I think between the two of us, we have those covered."

They sank into quiet again. They lay down, head to foot and foot to head. They watched the lightning bug toil. Horace listened to Chloe's breathing, tried to attune himself to its rhythm. A few minutes later, when Chloe got up and cupped her hands gently around Rip Van Twinkle, Horace said noth-ing. She took the bug to the window. Horace watched, amazed, as she reached right through the glass, the firefly still cupped in her hands. She leaned forward and let him go. The little insect drifted away into the night, blinking.

And then Chloe froze. Her eyes went wide. "Horace," she said.

"What?"

"There's a note on the window."

Horace scrambled to his feet beside her. A small square of paper was clinging to the glass. On the outside.

Chloe bent her wrist awkwardly and plucked the paper free. Horace peered down into the grass fifteen feet below, wondering how the note had gotten there. Chloe brought it inside and held it between them so they both could read:

Under no circumstances should Chloe go back to her home. Await our arrival tomorrow at midnight.

—H. Meister

"They already know about the malkund," Horace said at once.

Chloe gazed at the note, her face alive. "No. They're just being cautious."

"I don't think so. I think they know, and they want us to wait for them. Maybe they want to help us with it."

"It doesn't matter," Chloe said. "They'll be here too late. I have to be there exactly when the malkund arrives."

"What? No, no, you can't go back."

Chloe seemed to hesitate, for the briefest instant, but then she said, "I can. I'm going to."

Horace read the note again—"under no circumstances." He shook the paper at her. "Why are you ignoring this? Ten minutes ago you were all rah for the team."

"God, don't say that. I'm going to puke. Look, I said I'll join the fight, but in the meantime this particular fight can't wait. It's nothing personal."

"You don't even know what you're going to do with the malkund."

Chloe looked over at the window again. "Yeah," she said thoughtfully. Then she rounded on him, frowning. "Look, Horace, you're lucky I haven't left already. If the Wardens came here to warn me about not going home, that means

303

something's wrong. You think I really want to be hiding out here? I'm trying to be patient. I'm trying to be reasonable. But reason tells me I have to be there tomorrow when the malkund reappears. If I'm not, it'll just take my dad under all over again."

"I'm going with you, then."

"No. I'm safer alone. They can't catch me." She held up the dragonfly.

"You don't know that."

"I kind of do. I'll come back, I promise. I'll be back in time for the meeting at midnight tomorrow." She waved a hand at the Fel'Daera. "Go on down there and check."

"You can't—" Horace began, and then stopped. It was 12:04. He looked over at the box. "Seriously?"

"Yeah," Chloe said, clearly warming to the idea. "Let's go check and see. You'll see me there tomorrow night, safe and sound."

Horace took the box in hand, and they eased down the stairs and out to the toolshed. Chloe, as usual, was nearly noiseless, even on the gravel driveway. It was deeply dark inside the toolshed. But with the Fel'Daera, Horace didn't need a light. He began to open the box, then stopped. "Wait . . . if I do see you here tomorrow night, maybe that'll mean you never left at all. Maybe you'll decide to listen to the note."

There was silence in the dark for several long seconds. Finally Chloe, her voice thick with skepticism, said, "Have we met?"

304

Horace sighed. "Is there anything I could see in the box that would stop you from going home tomorrow?"

"Nothing comes to mind. Maybe a newspaper headline that said EVERYONE EXPLODED BECAUSE CHLOE WENT HOME. Maybe not even that. But go ahead and check."

Horace lowered the box. "No. Not unless you promise. If I don't see you here tomorrow night, you don't go. You said we were in this together."

"And I said you had to let me be me."

"I am. But if you're so sure you'll be safe, what's the harm in promising?"

Silence, and then a sigh. "Fine. Promise."

Horace remembered his trick with the mint, back at the House of Answers. How Chloe had said she was going to take on the golem anyway. Would this be like that? "Cross your heart," he insisted.

Another pause. Then at last a rustle, and her arm swung across her chest. "Cross my heart." Horace could hardly make her out in the dark, and the dragonfly was just a faint gleam, so he couldn't tell whether she'd actually done it or not. "Happy now, Mr. Logical?" Chloe said.

Frowning, Horace laid his fingers on the lid of the box. She wanted Mr. Logical? Fine. That was just how Mr. Meister had told him to be. He tried to recall what else the old man had said about using the Fel'Daera. He had to believe; he remembered that much. The problem was, he really only believed one thing about this entire situation: promises or no promises, and no matter what he saw right now, Chloe would still leave.

Horace opened the box, trying to convince himself that Chloe would be safe. And through the blue glass he saw— *tomorrow's toolshed, shadowless and still; the hanging bicycle, the refrigerator door.* His heart sank a little; he could see just fine, but he could tell the shed would be dark. And he saw no one. He spun, still feeling that queasy chill as he passed over today's Chloe and watched her seem to turn invisible in the box. He spun all the way around, searching.

No one. No Chloe—but also no Horace, no Wardens.

"You're not here," he said, closing the box. "No one is."

"No one? What does that mean?"

"Maybe you're in trouble. Maybe we went out looking for you."

"Or maybe it was a short meeting."

But it was only 12:08. "You think Mr. Meister would come out here just for an eight-minute meeting?"

"Probably not," Chloe admitted. "But I'm not staying here tomorrow just because the box showed you nothing. Wait, though—wouldn't you leave a sign? Tomorrow night, you'll know you already looked through the box. Why not just leave yourself a message?"

A message. Of course. The way he'd left a message for himself on that day of discovery, so long ago: *yes, Horace, this is tomorrow.* Horace opened the box again, trying to believe in a future in which everything was okay. One where Chloe returned safe from destroying the malkund. One where the Wardens had come for them—surely that's where he and Chloe would be this time tomorrow, with the Wardens. He believed it. He opened the box. . . .

The toolshed, still empty; but a flicker of motion—the hanging bicycle swinging slightly, its rear wheel spinning slowly to a stop. "Someone was here," Horace said, wondering why he hadn't seen that before. He turned, but still saw no one. Then he looked down at the gravel at his feet—*something different, stones out of place, lines in the floor.* He sidestepped, still staring, and slowly letters came into focus, a foot high, scratched into the gritty ground.

DEAR HORACE,
I AM SAFE.
YOUR FRIEND,
CHLOE

Horace breathed out a sigh of relief and read the message out loud.

"Hey, it's from me," Chloe said. "How about that?"

"Yeah . . . weird." Horace tried to shake off a mild case of déjà vu, remembering the night Chloe had written on his wall. *Dear Horace . . . Your friend, Chloe.*

"I told you," Chloe said. "I'm safe. *Now* are you happy?"

"Yes." Horace looked again, concentrating hard on the message, focusing all his thought on it. The words remained clear and sharp. *I am safe.* He closed the box, trying to ignore the little seed of unease that squirmed inside him now. Something here didn't quite make sense, but he couldn't put his finger on it. "Promise you'll be careful tomorrow, Chloe."

"Are you still worried?"

"Not worried. Just . . . unsure."

"You should trust yourself. Trust the box. The box says I'm going to be safe." She turned for the door. "Come on, let's go back in."

"Yeah," Horace said, and followed after her. But trusting the box wasn't the problem. He did trust it. He believed in the future the box had just shown him. What worried him was the path between this moment and that one. What worried him was tomorrow.

CHAPTER TWENTY—FIVE

The Message Sender

HORACE WOKE INTO A FLAT LATE-MORNING LIGHT. CHLOE stood beside the bed, peering down at him, her hair rumpled and wispy. "Jeez," she said, "you'd think with all that beauty sleep your hair wouldn't be such a wreck."

Horace pointed at her groggily. "You should see your pretty hair, sleeper."

She smiled and rolled her eyes. "You can stay in bed if you want. I have to go."

"Wait." Horace sat up, trying to clear his head. It was nearly noon. His parents must have gone to work without waking him. "You've got like twelve hours before the malkund comes back. Why are you going now?"

"I'm not going home yet. First I'm going to Aunt Lou's, to see Madeline."

"That wasn't part of our deal."

"It wasn't *not* part, either. Relax. I won't go home until late. And I'll be back here before midnight." She turned and headed for the door.

"What will you do with the malkund?" he called after her.

"That's a surprise," she said, and then she was gone.

Twelve hours. Twelve torturous hours to wait and see what would happen. Horace lay there for a while, thinking about the events of the day before, and then he went out to the shed. For just a moment as he was opening the door, he thought he would see Chloe's message there already—and wouldn't that be a bad joke on him? If Chloe had left the message *before* going home, instead of after she came back? But no. The floor of the toolshed was still undisturbed. Horace decided he would risk the box, just one more time. He thought hard about the message he'd seen, and the future it pointed to. He opened the box. The words were there, just as before: *Dear Horace, I am safe. Your friend, Chloe.* That was a relief, but he strained his eyes trying to determine whether it was still as clear as it had been last night. He still could not escape the sensation that there was something strange about this message. Was it possible it wasn't from Chloe after all? Theoretically, the message could have been left by anyone— maybe even Dr. Jericho. But no, as far as Horace knew, Dr. Jericho didn't even know Horace's name, let alone where he lived.

Of course, the Mordin *did* know where Chloe lived. As the afternoon deepened into evening, Horace began to regret letting Chloe go, his head buzzing with worry. He wasn't sure he believed that she wouldn't go home until later tonight—surely she was dying to check on her dad. And then at dinnertime, a terrible thought occurred to Horace—was it possible that the Riven were aware that the malkund had disappeared? Maybe Dr. Jericho already knew what he and Chloe had done. If so, Chloe was in terrible danger.

After bedtime, Horace lay in the dark, juggling his anxiety, trying to sit tight and continue believing in the future he'd seen. At long last, 11:28 rolled around. A mile away, he knew, the malkund was reappearing. He had no idea what Chloe planned to do with it. A surprise, she said, but he couldn't imagine what that might mean. He tried not to imagine a different kind of surprise—Dr. Jericho lying in wait for her. He calmed himself by reasoning that Chloe would surely get away. She always got away . . . right?

By 11:37, he could stand it no more. He went outside and checked the toolshed, hoping beyond hope, but the toolshed floor was undisturbed. The message still had not been written. His viewing had happened at 12:08 last night, which meant only a half hour remained during which the message could have been left. "*Will* be left," he murmured firmly to himself, and then he settled in to wait for Chloe, and for the Wardens, too. The air was cool enough to make him wish he'd worn a sweatshirt. He stood at the door to the toolshed, peeking in and out. He kicked at the gravel on the floor. A half hour. Plenty of time for Chloe to arrive. He figured it would take her a few minutes—maybe five—to do whatever she was going to do with the malkund. Another few minutes to check on her dad. Fifteen or twenty minutes to walk back to Horace's house. That would put her here at 11:55, tops.

But 11:55 came and went. Then midnight. At last, at 12:05, his confidence clinging by a thread, Horace heard footsteps in the driveway, brisk and swift. He hurried out of the shed, heart pounding. Mrs. Hapsteade strode toward him out of the darkness, wearing her usual black dress. She was alone.

"Where's Chloe?" Horace said heedlessly.

The woman stopped in her tracks. "What do you mean? She's not here?"

"She should've been back by now—I was hoping she'd be with you. She . . . went home."

Mrs. Hapsteade's eyes flared. "What? But we warned her. We warned you both. Riven have been lurking around her house since late last night. Mordin. A full hunting pack of three."

The unease Horace had been feeling all day suddenly blossomed into panic. He tried to stomp it down. "No, that can't be. She's safe. Where is Mr. Mei—"

"How do you know Chloe is safe?" Mrs. Hapsteade insisted.

"She left me a message. Here inside the shed. She's *going to* leave me a message." He scanned the yard as if Chloe would appear at that exact moment. "I saw it in the Fel'Daera last night. She said she was safe."

Mrs. Hapsteade inhaled sharply, her eyes lighting briefly on the box. "A fool's proof," she muttered. She stood up straight and lowered her chin grimly. "Show me."

Horace led her inside. He shut the toolshed door behind them and pulled the string on the overhead light. "The message was here," Horace said as the bulb swung above them. "Right on the floor, scratched in the dirt."

"And when did you see it? When exactly?"

"Last night at twelve-oh-eight," Horace said automatically.

Mrs. Hapsteade checked her watch, but Horace didn't need her to tell him. It was 12:06.

"And did you see anyone here?" she asked.

"No. The shed was empty." He pointed. "But I saw the tire of that bicycle spinning, like someone had just been here."

"Leave the message," Mrs. Hapsteade said. "Quickly."

Horace just stood there, stunned. "What?"

"Leave the message you saw, Keeper."

"No, no . . . the message was from Chloe."

"Clearly it wasn't. She's not here and she's not coming. What you saw was a lie. And now you know who told that lie."

"That's not possible," Horace said, trying to fight off the words even as he was realizing they were true. There was no other logical option—the message he'd seen the night before wouldn't come from Chloe after all. It would come from Horace himself. The sudden weight of this knowledge crushed him, made him dizzy. "No, no, no. I don't like this."

"There's very little to like about the Fel'Daera at moments

313

like this," Mrs. Hapsteade replied. "But we're in its grasp now, whether we like it or not. The message has to be left. Now."

Horace remembered Mr. Meister, his talk of free will—how he'd said Horace should try not to fight whatever future the box had revealed. He remembered the uneaten sandwich, and the sickness that had fallen over him afterward. Numbly, Horace moved into action. He rummaged around on a shelf until he found the wooden handle of a hatchet, the blade broken off. He grabbed it and crouched on the floor. He dug into the dirt with the splintered tip of the handle, beginning to carve out the big letters he'd seen. *Dear Horace*, he wrote. *Safe. Your friend.* Each new line he scratched out was like a slow, angry stab of guilt. His fault, all his fault. At last he finished the final word—*Chloe*—and he stood up, tossing the hatchet handle away.

This was the message he'd seen. It looked exactly the same. There could be no doubt now—he'd been the message sender all along. Horace backed away, still not wanting to believe it. He bumped against the hanging bicycle and set its rear wheel spinning. He stared as the spokes flashed beneath the light. "Me again," he said. "My fault."

"Come now," Mrs. Hapsteade said, and she shut off the light. "Beck is waiting, just up the street. We have to hurry."

It was 12:08.

They left the toolshed behind. They piled into the backseat of the cab. Mrs. Hapsteade said, "The girl's house, quickly," and they were away from the curb almost before

314

the words even left her.

They sped through the darkness, streetlight washing over them. Mrs. Hapsteade said nothing. As the cab swung through the streets, Beck's shapeless bulk barely shifted, thickly wrapped arms spinning the wheel effortlessly. After a block or two, Horace realized Beck was humming faintly, almost inaudibly, and gradually he understood that the driver was humming in concert with the roaring engine of the car, mimicking its rises and falls. In the mirror, Beck's eyes shone brightly, sharp as a bird's.

Horace, meanwhile, felt wretched. He threw his head back against the seat and tried to piece together what had happened—trying to figure out what he'd done wrong. He'd seen a future that allowed Chloe to leave, and in doing so had put her in harm's way. But how?

He turned to Mrs. Hapsteade. "You said there were Mordin watching Chloe's house."

"Yes. They arrived last night. One of the Wardens followed them there."

Horace's misery grew deeper, something he didn't know was possible. "Do you know what time they showed up?"

"A little before midnight. They came in a hurry, but we don't know why."

He should have known. How stupid of him—how stupid of them both. "I know why."

And then he told Mrs. Hapsteade about the malkund. She listened in silence, gazing down into her lap. Quickly as he could, Horace described trying to destroy the malkund, sending it through the box, Chloe's mysterious plan to deal with it when it rematerialized. When Horace had finished, Mrs. Hapsteade took a deep breath and asked just a single question—a single question out of all the questions she could or should have asked him.

"If the two of you choose not to place your trust in us, Keeper, where else will it stand?"

It was a question Horace couldn't answer.

They saw the fire from two blocks away. A surly glow over the horizon, amber and shifting. And when they got closer, the glint of red and blue lights too, swinging in the night beside the train tracks at Chloe's corner. A line of somber silhouettes, a paper-doll chain of spectators, and beyond them rivers of flame, ribboning into the night sky. Chloe's house was all but gone, wrapped in the grasp of a monstrous, many-fingered blaze.

Horace was out of the cab and running. He vaguely heard Mrs. Hapsteade calling his name. He could smell the smoke, thick in the air—not clean like a campfire but a crowded, chemical stink. He could hear men shouting through the roar of the fire. He pushed through the line of gawkers into the street. A fireman stopped him, speaking words Horace couldn't understand. The heat of the fire pressed against Horace like a wall. Flames poured from the windows of the house, feathered up through a ragged hole in the roof. Two firemen were dousing the flames with thick beams of water, but they weren't going to save the house. Horace turned to the watching crowd.

"What happened?" he said to no one in particular. "Where is she?"

"Place just went up," a man said. "Happened fast. Didn't see them bringing anyone out."

Along the street and in the front yards, floodlights illuminated a flurry of activity, two gleaming fire trucks, and an ambulance. The ambulance doors were closed. Its lights were dark.

"The ambulance. Who's in the ambulance? Is she dead?"

A tall, gaunt woman in a nightgown stepped down from the curb in front of Horace. "No one's in the ambulance, dear. The firemen can't get into the house." She glanced back into the crowd, as though she were speaking for them all. "We're hoping no one was home."

The smoke and heat and the smell of the fire stung Horace's eyes and nose, making them run. Horace pushed past the woman and back through the crowd. He spotted Mrs. Hapsteade and headed toward her. He heard a fat man in plaid shorts say, "Don't know why they need the ambulance. Too late for anybody inside there now."

Horace shot the man a furious look and turned to Mrs. Hapsteade. "We have to go back."

"Back where?"

"You know where. This didn't have to happen."

The fat man frowned down at Horace, his face twisting

in confusion. Mrs. Hapsteade put a heavy hand on Horace's shoulder and steered him toward the back of the crowd.

"We can go back," Horace insisted. "We can go back and change the message I saw. We can make this not happen."

Mrs. Hapsteade shook her head. "That's not possible, Horace. It has already happened."

"But if we change it to say Chloe's not safe. If we say there was a fire."

"You're being foolish," Mrs. Hapsteade replied, pushing him on. "You're not thinking clearly."

"You're the one being a fool!" The words startled him even as they came out, but he wasn't about to wish them back.

Mrs. Hapsteade yanked him to a stop. She grasped his shoulders and shook him once, hard. "This isn't some image seen in glass, Keeper! This isn't an illusion! This is real. This is happening. It has *already* happened. Wake up to your present, Horace Andrews."

Horace wanted to yank himself free but wasn't sure he could. She was so strong. And of course she was right. The fire had already happened. It couldn't be undone. Horace couldn't change the past. He turned to look again at the smoke spiraling up out of the reach of the lights.

Mrs. Hapsteade let go of him. One of her hands reached up and found his head. She stroked his hair, a startling gesture. He pulled away, but her voice went soft. "It's done, Horace. It's done. But let's not fear the worst. We don't yet know everything about the events of tonight. Have hope for your friend."

His friend. Brave Chloe. She should never have been here. "I did this."

For a moment, he thought she wouldn't reply. But then she said, "No. They did this."

"We have to find her. Maybe they took her. Or she had to have escaped, right? Maybe she's alive."

"Maybe she was never here in the first place. Regardless, all we can do is wait. Let's be patient, and try not to draw attention to ourselves." Then she leaned back and looked into the sky, as if searching for stars. But there were no stars—the glow of the fire drowned them.

Horace watched the fire despairingly, still reeling from the discovery that he had been the one to leave the message. To tell the lie. It had all gone wrong somewhere, but he didn't know where. After a few moments, he turned to Mrs. Hapsteade and was shocked to find her whispering animatedly with a girl. The girl looked to be about fifteen—tall, with brown hair and wide eyes. And there was another figure behind her, he saw now, dark and still—Gabriel! Where had they come from? He heard Mrs. Hapsteade say, "Find him. We will meet him in the Great Burrow." The girl nodded. She glanced at Horace curiously and backed away, melting into the darkness. Gabriel gave one of his formal little bows and slipped away with her.

"Who was that?" Horace asked.

"A friend, obviously," Mrs. Hapsteade said meaningfully—a Warden, of course. "Hurry, come with me." She turned, marching back down the block.

Horace fell reluctantly in behind her. "Wait. Are we leaving?"

Mrs. Hapsteade grasped his wrist hard and pulled him onward. The cab sat waiting. Beck had gotten out and now stood watching them, somehow managing to look urgent. Mrs. Hapsteade hurried to the cab and pulled open the back door, Horace at her side.

A small figure was huddled in the back seat, a dark ball. The skin was gray and dusty, clothes charred and burned in patches. The hair was ragged and filled with debris, blacker than ever, the tips singed and frayed. White eyes stared straight ahead, seeming not to see. The figure leaned back, mouth curling into a painful O, pink tongue flashing through a frightening, wracking fit of coughs. A shuddering breath, and then the figure bent back into a tiny ball, turning to look at them. A white cross-shaped pendant swung loose from the figure's neck, dangling and impossibly bright.

"Get me away from this place," Chloe said.

CHAPTER TWENTY–SIX

Water and Fire

As the cab raced through the dark streets, Chloe kept asking for water. Beck handed back a bottle of water, and she upended it into herself. Dragonfly whirring, she poured the water in through her forehead and let it spill down through her throat and chest and out all over the seat. "More," she said, but there was no more.

At last they pulled up in front of the Mazzoleni Academy, and again Mrs. Hapsteade led them underground, across the dark waters of Vithra's Eye. Chloe took the middle, clinging to Mrs. Hapsteade's dress through the Nevren while Horace brought up the rear. For Horace, the urgency made the Nevren seem shorter, more tolerable—halfway across, he forgot why they were there, but then his concern for Chloe roared back, pulling him through. Body-wrenching coughs broke out of Chloe every few seconds, and she held her arms out at her sides, as though she could not stand to have any part of herself touch any other part.

Mr. Meister was waiting for them on the far side of Vithra's Eye. Two small owls took turns swooping in low above his head. The old man looked a bit like an owl himself, round glasses shining in the gloom.

"She needs water," Mrs. Hapsteade told him as they approached.

"She escaped from the fire. But what of the Alvalaithen?" Mr. Meister peered at Chloe. "Safe, I see. And you, Keeper. Are you harmed?"

"My house is gone. It burned down around me," Chloe said. "I need water. A bath."

"Come," Mr. Meister said. He and Mrs. Hapsteade swept into the Great Burrow, heads coming together as they moved, voices low and solemn. Twice Mr. Meister glanced back at Horace and Chloe, a look of angry surprise on his face.

When they arrived at his doba, Mr. Meister led them inside. He plucked a small blue-green cube made of interlaced panels out of a compartment above the door and handed it to Mrs. Hapsteade. "Take her to Ingrid's doba and let her wash herself clean," he said. "Afterward, I will speak to her."

Mrs. Hapsteade herded Chloe out and away. Mr. Meister leaned back against his desk, bony hands folded in his lap, regarding Horace calmly. Above them in the round red room, the little black birds were silent, probably asleep.

Horace stood there, feeling drained and untethered, a

foreign body in a foreign place. Suddenly words burst out of him before he could stop them. "It was my fault."

"Is that so," the old man said evenly, not really asking. "Mrs. Hapsteade says that the Fel'Daera revealed a message. A message that turned out to be incorrect."

"Yes. I thought it was from Chloe, saying she was safe, but . . ." Horace trailed off miserably.

"But it was a lie. A fiction."

"Yes."

"Can you tell me what prompted you to look through the Fel'Daera in the first place?"

"Chloe was planning to go back home. I wanted to see if she would come back safely. I made her promise that if I saw a future that showed she wouldn't return, she wouldn't go in the first place."

Mr. Meister made a low, thoughtful rumble. His great left eye roved across the box at Horace's side. "Did you believe she would keep this promise?"

"I . . ." Horace began. But no, he hadn't believed her. "She was very determined to go home."

"Because of the malkund."

Horace took a deep breath. He looked out the door in the direction Chloe and Mrs. Hapsteade had gone. "Yes."

"I mentioned the malkund specifically when you were here last." The old man spoke quickly, not raising his voice at all, but throwing the words at Horace nonetheless. "I asked you about it."

"I didn't know about it then. Chloe told me later. She convinced me to go with her to take care of it."

"And you thought this plan was best? Instead of waiting a single day, when you might have enlisted our help?"

"I thought—"

"And where is the malkund now?" Mr. Meister pressed on softly. "What was Chloe planning to do with it?"

"I don't know."

"You allowed her to return home, despite having no knowledge of what she intended? Despite our warning?"

Horace threw his hands up. "I get it, okay? I get it. I screwed up. I looked through the box, and I saw the future wrong—"

Mr. Meister leaned forward and clasped Horace's shoulder. Horace flinched a little, but the old man gave him a suddenly tender look. "No, you did not see wrong. You saw truly."

Horace studied Mr. Meister's face, his thin but encouraging smile. "I guess I did. Technically."

"Just so. Technically, as you say, the future came to pass just as you saw it. But not as you *understood* it."

"So I misinterpreted what I saw. That's just as bad."

"Interpretation was not the issue."

"Then what was? What went wrong?"

"Remember, Horace, that the circumstances in which you open the box have a direct impact on what the box reveals. At the moment you opened the Fel'Daera last night, you believed deep down that Chloe would leave, no matter what you saw. And because of this belief, you helped set in motion a chain of events that *ensured* that she would leave. You saw—you created!—a message indicating she would be safe, a message that fulfilled both Chloe's needs and your own in that moment. Once the message was seen, Chloe was free to return to her family without breaking her promise to you, while at the same time you could take comfort in the idea that she would come to no harm."

Horace took this all in, comprehension dawning. He had tried to use reason when opening the box, but he now understood that he had reasoned himself into a corner. "So it *was* my fault."

"It is unwise to seek fault where the Fel'Daera is concerned."

"What should I have done differently, then?"

"You should have trusted in yourself. You should have trusted in your friendship with Chloe. You should have measured the circumstances in which you found yourselves. And then . . ."

"Yes?"

"You should never have opened the box in the first place."

Horace looked up into the towering red room, hardly able to bear to have Mr. Meister look at him now. But the old man continued, still soft: "You did not need the box to tell you it was dangerous for Chloe to return home. The danger was clear, yes?"

"Yes."

"You had our express warning, did you not?"

"Yes."

"Need I say more?"

Horace shook his head, then turned at the sound of footsteps coming closer. Mrs. Hapsteade was returning.

Mr. Meister seemed to hear them too, glancing at the door. "Mrs. Hapsteade did the right thing tonight, despite her dislike of the Fel'Daera. She recognized the future you'd seen for what it truly was, and ensured that that future came to pass. Should you ever encounter such a moment again, I hope you will remember. But even more, I hope . . ."

"That I'll never encounter a moment like that in the first place," Horace said.

"Just so."

Mrs. Hapsteade appeared in the door. "She's resting. She is ready."

The three of them went back up the path and entered a doba a hundred yards on. This one was equipped like a little apartment, with a table and chairs, one of them an old green recliner. There was a bookcase, heavy with books. Ingrid's doba, Mr. Meister had said, whoever that was—another Warden?

A huge old metal washbasin stood here too, full of water, water all around it on the floor. Chloe had gotten her bath. Washed herself clean—inside and out, Horace guessed. The blue-green cube from earlier sat on the table, somehow balancing impossibly on one corner. It looked wet.

"Does that thing make water, then?" Horace asked.

"Certainly not," said Mrs. Hapsteade.

Chloe was nowhere in sight, but Horace heard hollow coughing overhead. He followed Mr. Meister up a ladder on the back wall, the metal rungs cold and slick in his palms. Mrs. Hapsteade called up after Mr. Meister: "Twenty minutes, Henry, and not a bit more. She must rest."

Henry, Horace thought. So that's what the H stood for.

Upstairs, Chloe lay under the sheets of a small white bed, looking extra tiny. Two candles had been lit, their flames wobbling on a shelf beside her. Chloe's green hoodie, black and charred and ruined, hung from the bedpost. Beneath it lay her shoes, laces burned to stubs.

"Keeper," Mr. Meister said, bowing slightly.

Chloe looked blurrily at them both. She nodded. "Keepers."

"How are you?" Horace asked.

"I'm okay." She fingered the sheets thoughtfully. "I'm wondering whose doba this is. Ingrid, you said. That's a pretty name." Abruptly her voice and gaze went sharp. "Where is Madeline?"

"Still at your aunt's," Mr. Meister replied. "She is safe." Chloe didn't ask about her father, a fact that struck Horace as ominous. What had happened to him?

Mr. Meister took a seat in the lone chair, leaving Horace to stand awkwardly off to the side. "Can you tell me of the events of tonight? Are you able?"

Chloe sighed, sagging. "I am. But you won't want to hear it."

"Rarely do I take the luxury of separating my wants from my needs."

Chloe shrugged. "All right, then. What do you want to know?"

Mr. Meister leaned forward. The candlelight glinted star-like through the oraculum, sending sparks across his eyes. "Begin with the malkund."

If Chloe was surprised that he knew about the malkund already, she didn't show it. "I took care of it," she said calmly.

"Did you. May I ask how?"

"I melded it."

"Melded."

"I guess that's the word, I . . ." She looked at Horace, seeming to really see him for the first time. "I got the idea last night, when I was moving Rip through your window, Horace. I wondered what would happen if I let go of him, right when he was in the middle of the glass."

Horace tried to picture it—two pieces of matter, suddenly trying to occupy the same space at the same time. It certainly wouldn't go well for Rip, and probably not the glass, either. Amazed and vaguely horrified, Horace said, "Wait . . . you're saying you put the pieces of the malkund inside something else?"

"Yes. In the metal beam of a boxcar in the train yard. I

went thin, put the pieces inside the sturdiest part of the beam, and then just left them there. I tried to see if I could get them out again, but I couldn't. They were fused together. Melded."

Horace looked over at Mr. Meister. The old man looked genuinely shocked, gaping at Chloe with open mouth.

Chloe went on. "Oh, and I'm guessing the boxcar has left the city by now, too. Do you think that'll take care of the malkund?"

Mr. Meister closed his mouth. "In fact, I do. You were . . . very lucky." Horace could tell that although the old man was trying to look stern, Chloe's deed had made an impression on him. For a moment his eyes were lit with an almost frightening intensity. But then he shook himself, recovering. "And what happened after the malkund?" he asked, his voice mild and polite. "You returned home?"

"Yes. I'd been at Aunt Lou's all day, had dinner with Madeline. I went back to my house a little after eleven, to check on my dad and wait for the malkund. But my dad wasn't there. When the pieces of malkund came through, I took them to the train yard like I said, and then came back to the house. I thought maybe the malkund might . . . call to my dad when it reappeared. Or whatever. I thought maybe he'd come back. But he didn't." She frowned. "It made me nervous. I thought maybe the Riven knew what we'd done—with the malkund, I mean."

"They did," Horace said.

"Indeed," said Mr. Meister grimly. "The gifts of the

Riven cannot simply be taken by force without alerting the giver. Had the two of you sought my help with the malkund, things might have turned out differently tonight."

"Maybe," Chloe said. Mr. Meister stiffened slightly, but didn't respond. "Anyway I was nervous, being back in the house, with my dad still missing. Something seemed wrong. I knew I had to get back to Horace's. And then I remembered that Horace had sent the raven's eye through the day before, so I went upstairs to get it, and that's when the Riven came in." Her eyes got thoughtful, remembering. "There were three of them, I think. I heard Dr. Jericho for sure."

"Yes, three," Mr. Meister said. "Mordin often hunt in packs of three."

"One of them started to come upstairs. The raven's eye was lying on my bed. There was still a little color left in it. I grabbed it, and I hid in the heart."

"In the heart," Horace said. "What is that?"

"Oh," she said, waving a hand. She gave a sniffling laugh and another huge racking cough. "It's an old chimney that was completely walled off. Only I can get in. I used to hide there when I was a kid. I hid there from Dr. Jericho the first time he was in the house, too—I guess I told you." Mr. Meister lifted his head and raised his eyebrow but did not speak. "It's totally boxed in, but a little bit of light comes in from above. I discovered it when I was little, going thin. And when I was little . . . did you ever play under the table when you were a kid?"

330

"Definitely not," Horace said.

"Right, of course not. Well, you'd hate it in the heart, Horace. But when I was little, it was cozy. Safe. A place just for me."

"Please," Mr. Meister cut in, "what happened then?"

"Dr. Jericho came into my room. I'd used the dragonfly to get into the heart, of course, just for a second, but he must have felt it. So I sat in there and held on to the raven's eye. I heard the Mordin walking around, searching for me. They were talking. They were saying things—" She pushed her hands across her face, sagging. "Some of it I couldn't understand. They were speaking their own language. It sounded like . . . knives being sharpened. I just stayed where I was. And after a while they went downstairs, and I heard more talking, more noises. And then a little bit later I started to feel heat. I didn't understand at first, but then it got hotter. Much hotter. And a sound was growing, too, all around, becoming a roar—fire. So I leaned out and stuck my head through to see, and that was stupid—" She looked up at Horace, her face creased with worry and hurt. She glanced at the candles. "What you maybe don't know is that I can still feel certain things when I'm thin. Temperature, especially. It doesn't actually affect me, can't touch me—but I can still feel it. It feels the same as it would have. Worse, actually, I think."

"I don't understand," Horace said.

Mr. Meister rubbed his chin. "She means that while she is incorporeal, fire will not burn her, physically. Nonetheless, she will feel all the pain of being burned. Her body would escape unharmed, but the mind—"

"Don't," Chloe said. "Don't say it like that. You're right, it's all in my mind—"

"I did not say the pain was not real."

"—and if I was really brave I could've ignored it—"

"Chloe, your bravery is not in question. When you rescued the Vora from the golem—"

"Oh, the golem, the golem. I wish people would shut up about the golem. I only did that because I didn't know any better. I didn't even know I wasn't supposed to be able to go through that shield thing, the dumin. But tonight, I did know. When I was—" Chloe cut herself off. She threw back the sheets and swung her legs over the edge of the high bed, where they dangled like a toddler's. She was wearing a long nightgown, white and old-fashioned, a couple of sizes too big for her. She pressed the heels of her hands briefly into her eyes and then let her head sag farther, her fingers burrowing into her singed and ragged hair. Her words fell like stones into her lap. "I peeked out of the heart. When my head came through the wall, it came out into fire. A cloud of fire. Nothing to see but flames. The flames were in my eyes. Actually inside them. In my mouth, my throat, my skull. In my veins. I screamed. I screamed so loud."

She stopped talking. Her back heaved and several short, cruel barks left her—coughing or crying, Horace couldn't tell. Mr. Meister said nothing. Horace watched the candles sway,

332

tried to imagine the sensation of flames filling his eyes.

"But still," Chloe said after a minute, "there was no fire in the heart. I waited. I thought someone would come and put the fire out. I figured I would be able to stay thin long enough, often enough, so that I wouldn't get burned."

Mr. Meister cleared his throat. "And yet you could have escaped, yes? A quick leap through the wall, through the flames in an instant? Surely you could have done so."

"I thought about it. There were no flames in the heart, not then, but it was starting to get hot. Terribly hot. But I stayed."

Mr. Meister leaned back in his chair and folded his fingers across his lips. "Why?"

Horace couldn't take it any longer. "They were trying to flush her out, right?" he said. "The fire wasn't an accident. Dr. Jericho was still there, waiting for her."

"That's right," said Chloe.

Mr. Meister shrugged. He continued on with the same softly pushing voice he'd used on Horace. "Let them flush you out, then. How could the Mordin possibly hope to capture you?"

Chloe threw a sharp glance at him, her eyes like a wary animal's. "I don't know," she said. "I thought they might have a way."

Mr. Meister said, "It is possible that they *think* they do. Perhaps Dr. Jericho believes he could trap you with a dumin. But you know better."

"Why are you giving her such a hard time?" Horace demanded.

Mr. Meister held up a flat hand. "Let her answer."

"Look, I just hid," Chloe said. "I waited. I did what I do best." She coughed and hacked up a wad of spit as dark as syrup. It plopped onto the carpet. "I let the house burn up around me. I went thin as often as I could, stayed thin as long as I could—"

"And how long is that?" interrupted Mr. Meister. "How long can you . . . stay thin?"

"Almost three minutes." Horace perked up his ears at that. She was getting better. Mr. Meister took the little notebook out of a vest pocket and scribbled in it as Chloe went on. "But I had to keep doing it, over and over again. I got tired. So it got to be much less than that. And the air was . . . bad. It hurt to inhale. But there was a draft up the chimney, and most of the smoke was getting carried up and away, and there was just enough air to breathe. I knew Dr. Jericho was out there, and I knew I could outlast him. I knew people would come. Fire trucks, and a crowd. I guess I thought they might scare Dr. Jericho off. So I kept waiting, but then I started to feel the house shifting around me—the floor kind of gave way a little bit, and one of the chimney walls started to buckle. I knew the house was going to come down, so I went thin one last time and I just . . . leapt out of the heart and let myself fall through the floor. Down into the fire."

She paused, and Horace could see her trying to capture

words in her mouth, as though the things she had to say now were tastes that resembled nothing else. "I remember sparks flying up through my closed eyes. And then I was down in the rubble below, and it was hell. So, so hot. A heat you can't even . . . I was on my hands and knees, trying to stay under the smoke where I could see, and even though I knew I wasn't being burned I felt glued to the floor. Melted. I was crying and my tears were falling, and they turned to steam. Everything was so loud. I kept holding my breath and I crawled, thinking no one would be able to see me in there anyway—if the Riven were still around, I mean. And there were sirens. I crawled through the ruins, but I couldn't even tell where I was. . . ." She gave in to another cruel battery of coughs, her feet curling. She let out a raspy sigh.

Horace was so caught up in the story, imagining what it would be like to be immersed in fire, that he jumped a little when Mr. Meister spoke. "But still you did not leave."

"No."

"You said you heard the Mordin speaking, before the fire. You could not understand everything they said."

"That's right."

"But some of it you did understand." Chloe just glared at him, and the old man went on. "They spoke to you of your father, didn't they?"

Chloe flopped back onto the bed and rolled to face the wall. Horace was bewildered. "What's happening?" he said.

Mr. Meister straightened his glasses. "While I do not

think that the Mordin could manage to capture Chloe, physically, that does not mean that she could not be brought under their influence."

"But how?"

"The Riven have taken Chloe's father. He is their hostage. And one does not take a hostage unless one wishes to negotiate."

Of course. The Riven wanted the Alvalaithen, but more than the instrument they wanted the entire package—Keeper and instrument both. Because Chloe was all but impossible to capture, and because the dragonfly could never be taken from her, the Riven were trying another strategy. Kidnapping. Blackmail. Coercion. And Chloe—fierce, brave Chloe—had been bearing the full weight of that threat while her house burned down around her. Horace ached just imagining it.

Chloe stirred, rolling onto her back. "Dr. Jericho called out to me while I was hiding in the heart," she said. Her hands were balled into fists. "He told me they had my father. He mocked me. He told me there were certain favors they wanted me to do for them—just a few—and that if I complied, I could see my father again."

"I see. And did you consider their offer?" Mr. Meister said, as casually as if he were asking if she'd like more tea. The question took Horace's breath away.

Silence hung in the air for several seconds. At last Chloe said, "That's why I didn't leave the fire. I couldn't say yes to them. But I was . . . afraid to say no. I imagined my father might be there. So I just hid. I figured maybe they weren't even sure I was still there."

"I understand," Mr. Meister said, and then he slipped a little steel into his voice. *"But that still does not answer my question."*

Chloe sat up, her voice growing sharper too. "You want to know if I considered it? Yes. He's my father. In fact, maybe I'm still considering it."

Horace stepped forward. "You don't mean that." He turned to Mr. Meister. "She's upset. Anyone would be. Look at what she did—she didn't give in. She stayed all through that fire, knowing the Riven had her dad."

Mr. Meister ignored him. "And what if it had been your sister?" he asked Chloe. "What then?"

Chloe's eyes narrowed. "You said she was safe."

"We keep watch over her. Your aunt's house is protected. She is safe. But again . . . what if she were not?"

"You *keep watch*? But you don't actually even care about her. You're only watching her because you're protecting an investment. You're afraid they'll take Madeline to get to the dragonfly."

Mr. Meister shook his white head. "We want everyone safe. And your sister—"

"When I showed up here tonight, you asked about the dragonfly first. Then me."

Horace didn't remember if that was true or not, but a fleeting look of embarrassment on Mr. Meister's face told him that it was. "A habit of my profession," the old man said.

"And what is that profession, exactly?" Chloe asked. "Not a protector—you're a treasure hunter."

"Your well-being is—"

"You wouldn't be the least concerned with my well-being if it weren't for this," Chloe said, yanking the dragonfly up out of the nightgown. "Admit it . . . if it came down to a choice of what to save, you would choose this over me. And you would choose the box over Horace, too."

Mr. Meister stood, his long shadow looming across the ceiling. Horace took a step back, his hand reaching involuntarily to cover the box. "Just so," Mr. Meister said, carving the words with teeth that flashed in the candlelight. "That is the way it must be. Have you forgotten risking your own life to save the Vora? Might you not give your life now to spare the Alvalaithen? We are the Wardens. We do not put ourselves first."

"That's painfully obvious."

"Is it?" Mr. Meister thundered. "Is it as obvious as the lack of concern you've shown for your own family all along? You elected to lie about the malkund. You elected to lie about Dr. Jericho being in your home once before. Is this how you would protect your father? Your sister?"

Horace's heart was pounding. Mr. Meister wasn't wrong—so many lies Chloe had told, so much she had withheld. He felt torn and unsteady, angry at Mr. Meister but angry at Chloe too, with a ribbon of fear running through it all. Suddenly he realized Mrs. Hapsteade was standing at the top of the ladder, watching Mr. Meister.

Mr. Meister rolled on, unaware of her presence. "Perhaps the two of you think you are beyond me—you and your Tan'ji. That your powers could prevent the worst from happening, even after the enemy had appeared in your own halls—and in mine! Perhaps you think your instruments alone are enough."

"Henry," Mrs. Hapsteade said.

The old man took no notice of her, continuing to fume at Horace and Chloe. "You are the Keeper of the Fel'Daera. And you are the Keeper of the Alvalaithen. You are worthy of esteem. But do not forget that there have been many Keepers of the box and the dragonfly—perhaps dozens. Some held the reins for a lifetime. Some for just a few hours. And most are now forgotten. You are the Keepers of your instruments—for now. Perhaps you have noticed my respect for the fact that the box and the dragonfly are Tan'ji. And perhaps you have mistaken this respect for subservience, or childish awe. Perhaps you believe your instruments give you a power over me. If so, I wish to correct that misunderstanding now."

"*Henrik!*" Mrs. Hapsteade snapped, stepping forward.

But Horace hardly heard her. Other Keepers of the Fel'Daera—of course, there had to have been others. The very thought filled him with a startling rage that burned away every other emotion, a queasy and jealous blaze. The box was his. It would always be his. He caught Chloe's eye and knew that the same shocked outrage he saw on her face was mirrored on his own.

"Henrik," said Mrs. Hapsteade yet again. "A word, please."

Mr. Meister swung his head around, seeming to see her for the first time. She gestured down the ladder, and after a moment, after another brooding look at Horace and Chloe, he climbed nimbly down.

Mrs. Hapsteade gave them both a little bow. "We'll come back shortly, Keepers. I hope you'll forgive us our occasional tempers." She followed Mr. Meister below.

Once the Wardens' footsteps had faded away, it grew so silent in the room that Horace swore he could hear the candles burning. He and Chloe went on glaring at nothing, and when at last Chloe spoke, Horace actually jumped.

"I'm feeling mean," she said.

"Me too."

"Maybe because . . . because we deserved that."

This was about the last thing he expected her to say, but he only nodded. "A little bit, maybe."

"Me more than you."

"Probably."

"But I'm not wrong about him. All he cares about is our instruments."

"No, you're not wrong." And she wasn't, not completely. But did it matter? The box had been hovering in the back of Horace's brain, brought to life by the argument. It was his. It belonged to no one else. Not now. Not ever, if he could help it. He wondered how far he would go to keep the box from being taken, or destroyed. When he tried to imagine a hardship he would not endure in order to save the Fel'Daera, he had a hard time thinking of one. The thought terrified him, made him wonder if he was imagining hard enough. "I guess the question is, do we really care if that's all he cares about?"

Chloe sighed. "Probably not. I'm mad at everything right now. I had a pretty rough day—my house burned down. My dad is missing."

Horace had no idea what to say to someone whose home had just been destroyed, whose father had been kidnapped. Chloe held out her arms and looked down at them. Horace wondered what new scars she'd gotten this night. "You never finished your story," he said. "How you got out of the house and hid. How did no one see you?"

Chloe opened her mouth as if to speak, but then let it hang. Her brow crinkled and she blinked once, long and hard. "I can't really . . . ," she began, then started again. "Something happened. I think I don't want to talk about it."

"No more secrets, Chloe. What happened?"

"I said I don't want to talk about it. I don't want to talk about it and I don't want it to happen again. I made it into the train yard, and I saw you from there." Her face softened. "You looked worried. You looked mad. I appreciated that."

"I *was* worried." And he was still worried. What had happened to her in that house? Why wouldn't she talk about it?

The ladder rattled slightly. Mrs. Hapsteade's dark head

appeared. A moment later, Mr. Meister followed her up into the tiny room. To Horace's surprise, Mr. Meister crossed and sat on the bed beside Chloe. Chloe scooted over to make room.

"I am sorry about your father," he said warmly, bowing his head. "For your own sake, and for his."

Chloe opened her mouth. She glanced at Horace and said, "Thank you. But it's not your fault."

"I am aware of that. Nonetheless, I am sorry."

"I am too," Mrs. Hapsteade said. "I know what it is like. Many of us have . . . lost people close to us."

Lost, Horace thought. Chloe looked away, her jaw working and her eyes blinking fast.

"Yes," said Mr. Meister. "And because of that, and with your help, I believe we can attempt something we have never been able to do before. Something to set right what has gone wrong."

"What?" Horace asked.

"We are going to attempt to rescue Chloe's father."

"Rescue him," Chloe said, whipping her head around. "You know where he is, then?"

"Not precisely, but the Riven will have taken him to one of their nests. A secret place, underground, much like this one." Horace shuddered at the thought. He felt sure that a Riven nest was a much less pleasant place than the Warren.

"It'll be difficult," Mrs. Hapsteade said, her usually steady voice laced with a thread of something new—worry, or fear.

"Riven nests are treacherous places—hard to find, dangerous to enter, all but impossible to leave. Only one of us has been deep inside a nest and returned."

"I can do it," Chloe said.

"Perhaps you can, with help," said Mr. Meister. "And indeed, we would have no hope of rescuing your father without the two of you, and your Tan'ji. But let me be plain, Chloe—I am willing to let the rescue attempt go forward partly because I do not want the Riven to have any claim over you. Over the Alvalaithen. I make no pretenses about this. Do we understand each other?"

"Yes."

"Good. I asked you both already if you would join the Wardens—"

"Do you even still want us?" Horace asked. "After what happened?"

"You are strong-willed," Mrs. Hapsteade said. "The both of you."

Horace wasn't sure how true that was, at least where he himself was concerned, but he said, "You say that like it's a bad thing."

Mr. Meister smiled thinly. "Far from it, though as you saw tonight it does have its costs. I will say it a final time, gently: what the two of you did is unacceptable. If you are to join us, you must never keep such things from us again. The Mordin. The malkund. This week the two of you veered down a path you should never have taken, but upon that path you did . . .

remarkable things. Foolish things, perhaps even disastrous, but remarkable. And at any rate, we Wardens by necessity are . . . let us say we are a fierce bunch. I expect the same from you. Indeed, I am more comforted by the existence of such obstinacy in you than I would be by its absence."

"In other words," Chloe said, peering up at him, "we're just the kind of hell-raisers you're looking for."

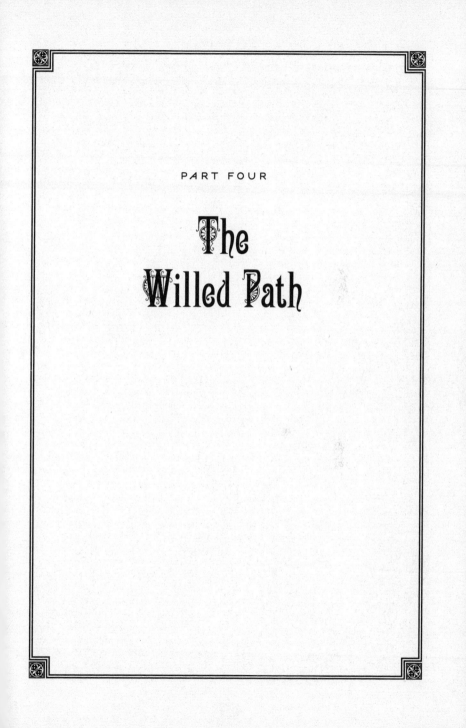

PART FOUR

The
Willed Path

CHAPTER TWENTY-SEVEN

By the Clock

"YOU SEEM DISTRACTED," SAID HORACE'S MOTHER, THE faintest trace of worry on her brow.

"Just tired." Horace threw all his attention at the chessboard, but clarity still wouldn't come. Black and tan figures, standing in a field. He saw how those figures could move, but he could not imagine what the new board would look like, could not hold the consequences in his head. At last he cut his bishop boldly across the board. Loki, curled beside them on the bed, watched with languid interest.

Almost immediately Horace saw that he'd made a mistake—he'd opened up a line between his mother's queen and his rook. His mother must've seen it right off, but she was taking her time, pretending not to notice.

"Oh, just do it," Horace said. "Don't fake it."

His mother sighed and swept the queen into his territory,

knocking the rook aside. "It hardly seems fair. Your head's just not here. It's like boxing an armless man." She sat back and laid a hand on Loki's head, pulling a purr out of him. "Are you worried about Chloe?"

"Not really." And he wasn't. Not exactly.

It was Friday, two days after the fire. Horace was expecting to hear from the Wardens any day now, letting him know that the plan to rescue Chloe's father was about to get under way. He felt strangely patient, waiting, but he hadn't spoken to Chloe since Wednesday night and he was sure Chloe didn't feel quite so calm. He hoped the Wardens knew what they were doing.

Much to his own regret, Horace had told his mother what had happened to Chloe's house. Not the whole story, of course, but the basics. She hadn't asked many questions, but answering them meant inventing lies. It wore him down.

"She's all right then?" his mother asked. "Where is she staying—with her aunt?"

"No, she's—" Horace stopped himself, uncertain how to carve out a line between truth and caution. But he could not see the harm in mentioning the academy. "There's this school downtown. Like a private school. She's staying there right now."

"Who arranged that?"

"Mr. Meister, I guess," he blurted without thinking. Horace stared at the chessboard, trying to keep his face flat, but his heart pounded hard. Why had he said that?

"Who is Mr. Meister?" his mother asked, her voice as light as air.

"Oh, he's just this old dude." Horace scowled to himself. That wasn't going to do it.

His mother broke into laughter. Loki bolted from the bed, scattering the chess pieces.

"What's so funny?"

"Oh, I don't know," she said. "I'm sorry. It just struck me funny. *Old dude.*"

Horace didn't see what was so funny about that. Mr. Meister *was* an old dude. "Anyway. He's a friend of the family, I guess."

"I see," his mother said, back to her calm and thoughtful self. "Well, if there's anything we can do, she just needs to ask."

"You barely even know her," Horace pointed out.

"The last time I checked, intimacy is not a prerequisite for compassion." She began gathering the scattered chess pieces. "Besides, Horace, *you* know her. If she needed your help, wouldn't you offer it?"

"Of course, but she's my friend."

She shrugged. "And you're my son," she said, with such an easy air of finality that Horace had no answer. She began to reset the wrecked board. "Come on. One more game."

"I can't."

"Please? I'm asking nicely. So nicely. We haven't played in three weeks."

"Why would you even want to play again? You called me armless."

"That was a metaphor. Don't take it personally."

"Too late," Horace said, shaking his head. "Okay . . . how about one game of blitz?"

"Seriously? You're on."

Blitz chess was extremely fast chess, and Horace was generally terrible at it. You played it with the chess clock, with each player given five minutes to make their moves—five minutes *total*, for the entire game. If you ran out of time, you lost. Usually it was far too much pressure for Horace, for whom planning his moves was like moving earth—it took time to dig. But for some reason, that pressure sounded suddenly good to him: it left no room for the mind to wander.

His mother brought the chess clock back to the bed and began fussing with the timers. A chess clock had two clock-faces and two buttons, one for each player. You made your move while your clock was running, and then you hit your button. The button stopped your clock and started the other player's. Then, when their move was over, they hit their button, restarting your clock, and so on. When one player ran out of time, a little flag dropped, indicating defeat.

"How about a handicap?" his mother asked. "I'll take five minutes, and you can take eight."

"You know I won't take that." Horace did not take handicaps.

"And you know I won't give it to you. Just making sure

you're still in there somewhere."

"Oh, I'm in there," Horace said. Quiet laughter bubbled up between them.

They began to play. At first the moves came fast—not much to think about yet, so you made your move and hit the button as quickly as you could. Eight moves in, though, as pieces started to fall, Horace began to get cautious. Before long, he had barely ninety seconds left on his clock. His mother, meanwhile, had a full minute more.

And then suddenly his mother gave him an unbelievable gift. He saw it the moment she slapped her side of the clock.

Her queen was open.

Horace hooked his knight around and toppled the queen, hoping it wasn't a trap. He slapped the clock.

Very clearly, his mother said, "Oh, holy crap." Horace's heart raced forward. She bent in, her brow furrowing. It took her thirty-two seconds to make her next move—an eternity, considering she now only had little more than a hundred seconds.

Horace played on fearlessly, taking the shortest turns possible—four seconds, six seconds, two. It became easy, natural. He could see lines of influence on the board shifting, the potential threat of the pieces, the convergence of those avenues of attack, the pockets of safety. Meanwhile, his mother took longer turns—eleven seconds, eight seconds, fifteen. His mother moved her king, slapped the clock, and Horace saw immediately that his mother's king could be cornered and checkmated in two moves. He was going to win. He moved the piece and slapped the clock, heart beating wildly.

His mother looked at the board and then at Horace. "Oh my god. You beat me."

Horace tried to roll the thought around in his brain—it felt weird, foreign, like a seed stuck in his teeth. His mother's clock was still running. Horace watched as the minute hand reached the very top and his mother's flag fell, indicating that she was out of time. Then he smiled. "Yeah, I did."

His mother looked at him quizzically. "Do you know why?"

Horace wasn't sure he could describe how he felt. "I was . . . aware. Like connected."

"Yes, you were in there. And you were confident. Feeling the rightness of your moves, not second-guessing."

"I *was* feeling it. And I was seeing it." Horace let his eyes run hungrily over the board. A wild burp of a laugh popped out of him. He swallowed it, keeping his face—which felt like it was about to burst—low and hidden. His mother gave her own smile and then began putting the little pieces back into their green velvet slots.

"Don't get used to this," she said.

"Winning?"

"Me losing and not demanding a rematch."

Horace grinned. "Next time."

"Next time. I love you."

"Love you."

It wasn't even nine yet, but Horace felt happily exhausted. After the door closed behind his mother, he slid beneath the covers. He grabbed the chess clock and pressed the button on his mother's side, starting his own clock. He counted. At last his flag fell, swinging. Thirteen seconds. Not long at all. Thirteen seconds, the difference between winning and losing.

His door popped open. His father leaned into the room.

"I heard you won."

"It was only blitz chess."

"But you beat her."

Again a grin he couldn't stop slid onto Horace's face. "Yeah."

His father made a fist and raised it high. He bowed his head to Horace. He made the peace sign. He held the pose and backed his way wordlessly out of the room. Horace grinned in spite of himself.

When at last Horace flipped off the light and let himself sink toward sleep, it came quickly, rising up around pleasant thoughts of chess pieces positioning themselves alongside clockfaces and Chloe and the Box of Promises, and other things, too—the darkness of Vithra's Eye, full of swooping owls; the warmth of Beck's cab and the smell of ginkgo soup and the gleam of the oraculum and the dark shine of red ink. Everything folded, spinning, but interconnected and positioned just so, or so, or so.

Horace jolted awake to darkness and a sharp *tak-tak-tak!* His hand squeezed around the reassuring presence of the box. His clock read 11:07. The sound came again, knocking. His window.

Horace rolled groggily out of bed. A flicker of movement outside the window, and the glass rattled again.

Outside the window—his *second-floor* window—was a girl, brown haired and calm. She wore a black turtleneck, which made her face look like it was hovering there, disembodied. But that face was familiar—thin and long, with wide brown eyes. The girl he'd seen with Mrs. Hapsteade the night of the fire. The girl knocked again and impatiently gestured for him to open the window. Her hands flashed in the dark.

Horace slid the window open. The girl spoke, her face blankly innocent but her voice full of mirth. "Oh, I'm so sorry—did I wake you?"

CHAPTER TWENTY-EIGHT

Neptune

"I'M KIDDING, OF COURSE," THE GIRL SAID WHEN HORACE didn't respond. The fact that the girl was floating outside his window rendered him speechless. "I know I woke you. I ought to know; I've been out here forever trying."

"I'm . . . sorry?"

"Is that a question?" Her eyes flickered to the Fel'Daera. "Anyway, Keeper, you need to come with me."

"Come where?"

"The Warren, of course. Mr. Meister sent me. Beck is waiting."

Horace pressed his forehead against the screen. "You're flying," he said stupidly.

"That's a common misconception. Let's go. The cab is out front, down the block." She sank soundlessly from sight.

Horace got his shoes on in darkness, wondering even as

he did so whether he was being careless. Maybe he couldn't trust this girl. He'd seen her talking to Mrs. Hapsteade, yes, but so much was unknown. Before he left, he scribbled a quick note for his parents:

> If I'm missing, go to the Mazolini Academy (sp?), downtown. Ask for Mr. Meister or Mrs. Hapstead. Tell them I went with the flying girl, Friday 11:10 p.m.

Probably there was no reason to leave a note, but the box afforded him a unique opportunity, just in case: he could send the note one day forward. Very likely he'd be back long before his parents even knew he was gone, and he could retrieve and destroy the note himself when it came through. But just in case anything went wrong, the note would be found eventually.

Outside, the cab idled smoothly, several houses down. Horace found the not-flying girl waiting for him in the back-seat. Now he noticed that she wore a long cape, thick and black. Her legs were curled beneath her. Horace climbed in, and the cab pulled away.

"You're very trusting," the girl said. "I thought it would be harder to get you out of the house."

"I left a note, just in case."

"A note. That's quaint. For future reference, you'll gener-ally want to see a token of some kind." She pulled at a chain beneath her collar and drew out a long crystal that Horace recognized immediately, set in a curling silver flower. This one was darkly purple.

"Hey, it's a . . ."

"Jithandra."

"Jithandra. Are you one of the Wardens, then?"

"What else would I be?"

"I guess I don't know. I don't know how all this works. You're the first Warden I've met beside Mr. Meister and Mrs. Hapsteade. And Gabriel, I guess."

"Don't get too excited. I don't sign autographs."

"I don't want an autograph, I just meant—"

"That was a joke," the girl said. "I do sign autographs."

"Oh . . . okay." Horace nodded uncertainly and fixed his eyes on the back of Beck's seat.

"That was another joke. I'm Neptune, by the way."

"Neptune. Like the planet?"

"Planet? What planet?" When Horace didn't respond, she said, "A joke again. You're not very good at this. I'm familiar with Neptune—the planet, I mean. And the person, too—that's me, of course." She said all this in the same lilting voice, but not a trace of humor showed on her face. She went on staring unblinkingly at Horace with her great, guileless eyes.

"Oh," said Horace.

The girl cleared her throat. She shifted and folded her hands into her lap, taking on a faint air of formality. "Well, I at least won't pretend I'm not curious. I wonder, Keeper, may I see it?"

"See what?"

"The Fel'Daera, of course. Here's mine. It's not much to look at, but I think it's lovely." She held out her hand. In her palm was a pyramid-shaped jet-black stone, almost like a spike or tooth. Three sides of it were flat, but the smallest side—the base—was slightly curved.

"It's a spherical triangle," Horace said, recognizing the shape. The single curved face was a section of a sphere. The whole thing was like a wedge taken out of a perfectly round ball.

Neptune made a happy noise of surprise. "That's right. Mr. Meister said you were a science guy."

"I guess I am," Horace said, strangely pleased that the old man had been talking about him. "So your Tan'ji . . . what is it?"

"It's called a tourminda. Not unique—not like the Fel'Daera—but rare enough. It's been in my family for a long time."

"And it lets you . . . what? Not fly, you said."

"Well, not like Superman, of course. That would be silly. It lets me alter my gravity. I can make myself entirely weightless, if I want to."

"So you can float, but you can't move forward in the air. No propulsion."

"Right again. I can't make myself go forward in the air, unless I push off of something solid. So I can leap really far, but I can't just stop in midair and change directions. And I can hover, of course—you saw that. Also I'm extremely sensitive to gravity in general—everything has it, you know. Cars. Buildings. People. Situations."

"Right," said Horace, feeling more awake now and suddenly interested in this blank-faced girl. "So could you, like, jump into outer space?"

"That would kill me," she trilled, one eyebrow twitching.

"I know, but I mean . . . theoretically."

"Theoretically, no. The atmosphere slows me down."

"Right, right—too much air resistance. So how far can you jump?"

"If I get a good wind behind me, pretty far."

"How far is pretty far?"

"Once I jumped to Saugatuck."

"Saugatuck? Where's that?"

"Michigan."

Horace thought his eyes would fall out of his head. "You jumped across the lake? You jumped . . . across Lake Michigan?"

"It's not completely honest to call it jumping. Winds blew me most of the way. I could have gone farther, but after all that water, I had to come down when I got back over land. There were a few minutes, out over the water, where I just stalled. The winds died and I just hung there. Of course I was frightened," she said, her eyes getting even wider for a moment. "I never tried it again. Nothing against Michigan."

Horace looked to Beck. "Is this for real?" he said, half to

the driver and half to Neptune. Beck just glanced at the mirror, giving away nothing.

"What a funny thing for the Keeper of the Fel'Daera to ask, of all people," Neptune said. "Of course gravity's very weak, all things considered."

"I know that. Even a tiny magnet is stronger than gravity."

"Exactly. But time, on the other hand—time's everything, isn't it?"

Horace had no answer for that. He pressed the box against his hip.

"May I see it, Keeper? Of course I'm not a fangirl or anything, but I am curious, like anyone. And I won't touch."

Horace hesitated, then pulled the box from the pouch. She leaned over it, letting off a series of long, expressive hums. After several seconds, she straightened and bowed her head slightly. "Thank you for showing, Keeper."

Awkwardly Horace returned the bow and tucked the box away again.

"It's funny, you know," Neptune said after a few minutes. "The Fel'Daera—it's not as big as I thought it would be."

Horace scowled. "What are you talking about? It's just right."

"I only meant it's rather exquisitely small, don't you think? But of course you do."

They drove on. Horace simmered about the box for a bit, but his curiosity would not let him remain silent for long. He began asking Neptune more about what she'd done with the tourminda. It quickly became clear that she hadn't done much that Horace would have done. Top of the Willis Tower? No. Ferris wheel? No. The Diamond Building? No.

Neptune shook her head at him. "Our Tan'ji don't make us superheroes, you know. We're not supposed to flit around the city being awesome." Her lecturing tone grated on Horace. Or was she kidding again?

"But you're wearing a *cape*."

"It's a cloak. And it's purely for practical reasons."

Up ahead, Horace could see the Hancock Center looming larger as they approached downtown, the top floor glowing like a crown, the great antenna masts towering above. How could you not want to go up there, if you could? He spent a few dreamy moments imagining it. "Anyway," he said, "I don't flit around the city."

"Your friend does, though. The dragonfly girl—Chloe."

"What do you know about it?"

"I've seen her. That's my job. And I met her yesterday . . . but I don't think she likes me very much." Horace was sure that was true; Neptune wasn't really Chloe's style. "Do you think it's because I'm so much taller? Probably she's intimidated."

Horace scoffed. "Yeah, right. That'll be the day."

"You really aren't very good at taking jokes," Neptune remarked, looking sad.

"Oh," Horace said. "Sorry." He didn't bother telling her that maybe she was just bad at telling them. They rode the

363

rest of the way in silence. When they pulled up at the Mazzoleni Academy, Neptune slid out wordlessly. "See you, Beck," Horace said. Beck squinted into the mirror and flashed him a chubby thumbs-up.

Neptune went up the steep staircase three steps at a time. Horace suspected she might be using the tourminda to make the climb easier. The moment they got to the top, Mrs. Hapsteade swept briskly out to greet them, holding open the front door and bowing her head. "Keepers."

Inside, Chloe waited for them. A warm wave of relief overtook Horace. She was wearing a brand-new hoodie—red—and a pair of jeans a bit too big for her. But of course her clothes had been lost in the fire. There was something else different about her, and with the hood up around her face it took Horace a moment to realize: her long hair was gone.

Chloe narrowed her eyes at him. "Yes, Horace, I had to cut my hair." She threw her hood back and spun sarcastically. Her black hair was shorter than Horace's, exposing her slender neck. Her ears—kind of big, as it turned out—stuck out like mouse ears. Horace couldn't decide if it was adorable or ridiculous. "Happy?" Chloe said, and yanked her hood back up.

"I think it looks good."

"Oh my god. Don't be creepy."

"What? I'm trying to be nice."

"It's not nice to lie. I've been mutilated."

"What do you want me to say?"

"Something true. Something helpful. You're usually so helpful."

"Okay, well . . . it'll grow back. And in the meantime, you can keep your hood up."

She spread her arms and smiled. "See? That's all you had to say."

They stood there grinning at each other. The dragonfly flickered into motion for just an instant, and she jabbed a fingertip at him. He nodded.

"This is touching," Neptune sang sarcastically. "It's touching me. It's touching me in the face." She began poking herself in the cheek, the forehead, the eye.

Mrs. Hapsteade sighed and began herding them down the hall. "Come, Mr. Meister is waiting to see you. Though I can't for the life of me imagine why he would want to."

The tiny elevator felt even more crowded with Neptune present. Chloe kept up a steady stream of surly chatter all the way down. Apparently it was Aunt Lou who had cut her hair. "She told me she always wanted to see what I looked like with short hair. I said, 'Yeah, me too, that's why I set myself on fire.'"

They crossed the Nevren in Vithra's Eye with both Mrs. Hapsteade and Neptune in the lead, dangling their crystals side by side. Horace followed behind, with Chloe once again clinging to his shirt. Horace couldn't say he was getting used to the Nevren, not exactly, but entering the emptiness was easier knowing that it had ended before, and would end again.

Mrs. Hapsteade led them through the Great Burrow and right on past Mr. Meister's doba. At the very back of the Burrow, two final dobas stood like sentries beside a towering gap in the wall. A cool breeze spilled over them. They passed through, into a yawning shaft that stretched out of sight above and below. Mr. Meister stood at the edge, talking to two others: Gabriel and the boy in glasses Horace had glimpsed once before—Brian, that was his name. As Horace's group approached, the three looked up and Brian slipped away, over the edge of the precipice. When Horace came close, he saw a zigzagging flight of stairs cut from a sheer wall of bedrock, leading downward. The boy was just disappearing around a bend below. Horace peeked over the edge, grateful that he was claustrophobic and not afraid of heights. Apparently the Warren was even bigger than Horace had realized.

"Keepers," Mr. Meister said, gesturing them closer. "Or I suppose I should say Wardens. By now I believe you have all met, yes?"

Gabriel nodded, his own milky eyes as bright as clouds. His gaze seemed to lock onto Horace, making him uncomfortable.

"Tonight is the night," Mr. Meister continued. "We search for the nest, and with luck we rescue Chloe's father. Gabriel, Neptune, Horace, Chloe—this task requires you all. A formidable quartet. So formidable, in fact, that perhaps you will manage to accomplish even more than the recovery of Chloe's father."

Mrs. Hapsteade cleared her throat but said nothing. "Accomplish even more"—what did that mean?

"A formidable quartet," Chloe repeated, eyeing Gabriel and Neptune. "So what can these two do?"

"Goodness, have you not been properly introduced to their powers?"

"I know Neptune can . . . float," said Horace. "And I know Gabriel's staff helps him see. But that's it."

"You do not know nearly enough, then," Mr. Meister said. He looked at Gabriel and Neptune and gave them a firm nod. "Show them."

CHAPTER TWENTY-NINE

The Staff and the Crucible

NEPTUNE STEPPED FORWARD AND BOWED LIGHTLY.

"Is it the cape?" Chloe said. "Because that cape has some explaining to do."

"It's a cloak," Neptune said. She held out her Tan'ji for Chloe to see. "But no—this is my Tan'ji, the Devlin tourminda. And here's what it does." She made a tight fist around it. Her big eyes took on a faint inward shine. Her hair seemed to get staticky, began to lift away from itself. She pushed off from the ground, rising steadily like a balloon, her cloak dangling. Chloe inhaled sharply.

"The tourminda lets me alter my gravity," Neptune said. She dropped to the floor and then, without warning, darted quickly toward the edge of the cliff. She took four long steps and leapt out over the abyss. She sailed far out into the dark. With her cloak trailing, she looked comically like a superhero.

She spun gracefully to hit the far wall feetfirst, her knees bending deeply, and then launched herself back again—a leap of fifty yards, each way. As she came back to the ledge, she caught the corners of her cloak and cupped it like a parachute, slowing herself in the air—practical, Horace had to admit. She dropped with alarming speed, but then alighted between Horace and Chloe as if she was stepping out of a car.

"Whoa," Horace said.

"Hmph," said Chloe.

"One advantage of the tourminda is it doesn't draw much attention," Neptune went on. "Even a Mordin won't feel me using it unless I'm right above his head. Oh . . . and I'm very sensitive to gravity, of course. I can sense the gravity of objects around me, depending on their mass and distance. I can sense people from maybe a hundred feet away. Average-sized people, of course," she added, looking down at Chloe.

Horace wanted to be sure he understood. "So you can sense us around you right now. Behind you, even. You could see us in the dark."

"Of course. Though not nearly so well as some." She smiled faintly and glanced over at Gabriel, whose expression did not change.

"Can you make yourself fatter?" Chloe asked.

Neptune's smile faded. "More massive, you mean."

"Sure, whatever."

"Why would I want to?"

"Why *wouldn't* you? You could crush a coconut with your

369

foot, for one thing."

Horace swallowed a laugh, but Neptune's wide eyes just got wider and more innocent. "I suppose some people might find that fun. But no, I can't change my mass. I can only decrease the effects of gravity on me."

"Well, if you did get fat—the usual way, I mean—it wouldn't even matter, would it?"

Gabriel cleared his throat and lifted his head high, and somehow that little gesture drew the attention of the entire group. "I believe it's my turn now?"

"Yes, Keeper," said Mr. Meister gratefully. "Please."

"They won't like it."

Horace eyed Gabriel's long, silver-tipped cane with a squirming curiosity. Mrs. Hapsteade said, "No one ever likes the Staff of Obro, until it saves them."

Gabriel stepped forward, laying the staff across both hands, holding it out ceremonially and bowing. "The Staff of Obro," he said. The handle was in the shape of some snaking, scaled body, dragonlike, while the foot was made of four separate talons, curving outward and drawn together into a point at the tips. The shaft was a gleaming, charcoal gray. Gabriel let them look, then placed the tip of the staff on the floor again, where it rested like the delicately perched foot of a savage beast. He leaned heavily on the staff with both hands, his face lowered. "I will not try to describe what has to be shown."

Horace waited, feeling nervous. He glanced at Chloe, but

she was glaring at Gabriel. And then Horace saw. Something dark was seeping out from between the claws of the staff's foot—thin gray tendrils. It was like smoke, but denser, almost liquid. The tendrils seemed to twist and flicker in and out of sight. They crept along the floor, spreading.

"Very pretty," Neptune remarked lightly. "Showing off, or afraid the newlings can't take it?"

Chloe shot daggers at Neptune. She lifted her chin. "Do it," she said to Gabriel.

Gabriel cocked his head. "What the lady wants," he said, and then the gray stuff seemed to spring upward, all at once, and there was a roar, and the world disappeared.

Horace shouted, but his cry was wrapped up, made slow and round, like words under water. The world had gone away—not into black, but into a deep, deep gray so utterly flat and complete that not only could Horace not see, he could barely summon up the idea of sight. He could not see his own hands, his own nose. Horace found himself crouching to the ground so that he would not simply topple over. No shadow, no depth, no movement, no light. No light but no dark.

He heard voices in the nothing, one calm and steady—Mr. Meister?—and another, sharp, angry. Chloe. Their words were shapeless, directionless. Horace kept his own mouth shut and breathed shallowly through his nose, but he could smell nothing. He tried to look down at himself but could not even be sure which way down was. He latched on to the only thing he could—the steady stream of presence pouring from the Fel'Daera. He held on hard.

A voice rang out in the fog, this one deep and clear, full of confidence. Horace lifted his head, marveling at the power of it. Gabriel. "Don't be afraid. Don't move. It won't hurt you. This is what I can do." His voice seemed to come from everywhere at once. Horace found himself wanting to do as the voice asked. "You are blind so that I might see—I admit it. But listen. Listen to my sight." And then the voice began to describe what it saw.

"Chloe Oliver—you've thrown your hood back. Your eyes are open and your face is angry. You're making fists. The wings of the Alvalaithen are moving, *so* fast. That's incredible—you feel . . . oh, now they've stopped. You're raising your hand. You—" And now the voice hitched, made a low laugh. "You're flipping me off. That's lovely. Now you're putting your hands in your pockets. You're not moving. You have a roll of candy in the front right pocket of your jeans—mints, I think. There are seven left." A jolt of surprise lit through Horace— he could see that? But *see* wasn't the right word, obviously, not the right word at all. Horace wasn't sure there was a word for what Gabriel did now.

Gabriel's voice grew low and soft, thoughtful. "You've closed your eyes. You have a tiny wound in the center of your right palm. You have a big healing gash along your ribs—a cut or a burn, I can't tell. And . . . oh, God, you're just—" Now the voice paused for a moment, then came back slow, almost tender. "You're covered in scars."

The room fell utterly silent, became almost as empty as the Nevren. And then the voice started up again, started describing how Horace was hunkered down on the floor, how he was cradling the box to his throat. "You have a cat at home that sheds. The tag has been cut out of the collar of your shirt. You have a flat wad of paper in your back pocket that's been through the wash. In your left front pocket, you have forty cents—a quarter, dime, and nickel. They are from the years 1996, 1973, and 2010, in that order. A scrape on your left calf is almost healed. Your shoelaces are double knotted. You've been squeezing your eyes shut so tight it must hurt, but now they're loosening. Your hair is terribly mussed, like someone just rolled you out of bed. Chloe is looking at you." A brief pause, and then: "Also, you should know I can do this." And then a light but unmistakable pressure enveloped Horace's face, both cheeks, gently pressing his flesh from both sides at once.

Horace jerked back and cried out. He heard another angry yelp that had to be Chloe. A moment later, a violent flicker filled his sight, like a blanket being yanked away. Another tearing roar. The universe returned. Horace could see again, hear again, heard low sighs of relief blossoming around the room, saw Chloe's eyes on him, bright and deep and full of fire. Her hood was indeed thrown back, chin held high. Horace rose from his crouch and turned to Gabriel. They all turned to him. But it was Chloe who spoke first, quivering with anger.

"You should be ashamed."

"I don't make apologies. The Staff of Obro does what it does. But know that I use its power only when I must."

Neptune chimed in. "That's true. He almost never uses it, even though—I mean, think what a temptation it would be."

Gabriel shook his head. "It's not a temptation. It's a gift to be used sparingly."

Horace felt a kind of sudden and sickening admiration for this young man—to be blind, and given a power of sight far beyond the keenest human eyes, but to only be able to use that power at the expense of everyone else. To become powerful only when your companions were made powerless. Horace thought Neptune had it right: what a temptation.

"And it lets you see a little even without the cloud, doesn't it?" Horace asked. "That's how you get around so well."

"Humour, not cloud," Gabriel corrected. "Obro's humour. And yes, there's a constant faint presence, low to the ground. Just enough to let me sense obstacles at my feet. Even now it's there, so thin it can't be seen."

Horace lifted one foot and then the other but saw nothing. Gabriel let out a low laugh. "It won't harm you, Keeper."

"And what about sound? Voices?" Horace asked.

"In the humour, I control who hears what. It takes a substantial effort, but I could deafen you all, or I could allow you to hear one another as clearly as you heard me just now. My choice."

Chloe scoffed. "Your choice, of course. Don't bother

putting forth the effort. And how far can you spread the humour? Could you fill this room? Blind the whole city, maybe? Grope everyone in it?"

"I couldn't come close to filling the Great Burrow, no, much less the city. I can spread the humour maybe eighty or ninety feet, from end to end. But I haven't yet learned to control the humour well. I can't adjust the density, though I've been told"—his head tipped in the direction of Mr. Meister—"I should be able to do so, eventually."

"And everyone and everything else within that space will be made senseless."

"Yes."

"Not everyone," said Neptune suddenly. And of course— even in the humour she'd be able to sense the world around her using the tourminda.

"Well, I guess you're quite the pair, then," Chloe said.

A quizzical look flashed across Gabriel's face. "At any rate, Keeper, you needn't worry that I'll use the staff without reason. And I will always give warning."

"I don't need warnings. I need you to never use that thing in my presence again."

"I won't promise that."

"Then you'll stay away from me."

"Stop. Enough." Mr. Meister stepped into the circle, turning to Chloe. "I'm afraid that will not be possible, Keeper."

"I'm afraid it will," Chloe said.

"You still wish to find your father, don't you?"

Chloe crossed her arms, her eyes dark and wary.

"We cannot rescue your father without Gabriel's help."

"Why not?"

Mr. Meister raised an eyebrow. "Follow me." He led them to his doba. Inside, they all took seats—all except Mrs. Hapsteade, who stood at the door looking worried. Mr. Meister reached up to a large compartment on the wall behind his desk and pulled out a bulky box—more of a chest, really. Nearly buckling under the weight, he tottered to his desk and set it down with a thud. He threw back the lid.

The object he pulled from the chest was a foot and a half high, a crude bowl the color of dirty steel, though it could never have held liquid—it was sculpted from jagged, curving strips that spiraled from the base and bent toward each other at the top. The more Horace looked at it, the more it looked like a huge and gnarled dead hand, cupped into a gesture of grasping. It seemed like it should have toppled over under its own chaotic weight, but it was as sturdy as a stone. Horace hated the sight of it.

"Behold the crucible," said Mr. Meister, laying a hand on the object. "Each nest—and there may be dozens in the city—is kept hidden by an instrument like this one. The crucible keeps the nest secret and protects the Riven who dwell there."

Horace was intrigued, despite his dismay. "So it's a leestone."

"A crucible works somewhat like a leestone, except that it

asks for allegiance. Crucibles are old and dangerous Tanu—they are Tan'ji, in fact. Each crucible has a Keeper, who roams the nest, bearing the crucible. The crucible emits a powerful attractive force. Other residents of the nest, enthralled, willingly devote themselves to the crucible. With that devotion they earn a kind of sanctuary, but they are chained to the crucible—figuratively speaking, of course."

"So the Riven are under the control of these crucibles, then," Horace said.

"The Riven do not think of it that way. And the crucible does not enslave the willing. Nor does it control minds or give orders. You might say the crucible itself defines the nest. When wielded by a Keeper and followed by its devotees, the crucible is merely a physical manifestation of a bond, a pact of secrecy, a kind of fraternity."

Chloe stirred. "It doesn't enslave the willing, you said. But what if you're not willing? What if you're a prisoner?"

Mr. Meister said, "In the presence of the crucible, the undevoted will be lost."

Chloe's face grew cloudy, but Mrs. Hapsteade suddenly spoke. "The crucible won't harm your father, Chloe, but he won't be himself in the presence of the crucible. He will forget who he is, forget his purpose. He'll be helpless until he surrenders. If he surrenders, he'll regain himself, but he will be beholden to the crucible."

"My father wouldn't . . . ," Chloe began, but then she trailed off miserably.

Horace fidgeted in his seat, remembering the little black cricket they'd taken from Chloe's father. "This reminds me of the malkund."

"Very good. Malkunds are forged in the presence of a crucible. In fact, they are tied to a specific crucible at a specific nest. And because we can assume it was Dr. Jericho who gave the malkund to Chloe's father, we can also assume that Mr. Oliver will be found in whatever nest the Mordin is currently calling home. Very likely you will find him close to the crucible, transfixed."

"But," Chloe said, "if the crucible is like the malkund, how are we supposed to rescue my dad from it? Even if we can get him out of the nest—away from the crucible—will he be okay?"

Mr. Meister glanced at Mrs. Hapsteade. He shrugged. "In time, perhaps. Certainly we hope so."

"But you don't *know* so."

Mr. Meister gave a frustrated sigh. "No. Indeed, we know little of what transpires inside a nest at all. Few Wardens have ever been inside one. Certainly it will be thick with Riven—Mordin, the Keeper of the crucible, and others." He gestured at the gnarled sphere. "In an ideal world, you would find the crucible tonight and destroy it, but we do not even know if that is possible. We do not know how to snuff out the light of the crucible."

"The light," Horace murmured. "What do you mean?"

"A working crucible emits a powerful flame or light, the

manifestation of its power. The exact mechanism is unclear, but it's this burning light that—for lack of a better word— bewitches you. The sight, the sound, even the smell perhaps. It emits a strong odor. You've smelled it yourself, on Dr. Jericho."

The scent came to life in Horace's nose. "Sulfur."

"Brimstone," said Neptune.

"Yes," said Mr. Meister. "When lit, the crucible is dangerous indeed—both foul and irresistible. But once the light is extinguished . . ." He poked the crucible, making it rock. "It becomes nothing. An ugly decoration. The Riven who have devoted themselves to it would scatter, homeless and exposed. And anyone else who also happened to be under its thrall would be set free."

"Like my dad," Chloe said.

"Yes. As I said, if you could find a way to destroy the crucible, that would be most impressive." Mr. Meister shrugged again, as if it hardly mattered. "But I do not see how. We are not even sure if the source of the crucible's light truly is a flame. Gabriel is the only one among us who has ever encountered a lit crucible."

All eyes turned to Gabriel. He nodded as though he could feel their gazes. "Yes, and I could not actually lay my senses on the source itself. It had a presence, but it was . . . untouchable."

Chloe threw her hands up. "So if it's untouchable, how do we destroy it?"

"As I said, very likely you do not," Mr. Meister said. "Perhaps it is best to put the notion out of your mind and concentrate instead on simply getting your father away."

But then an idea came to Horace. "No, no. We can meld it," he said. He turned to Chloe. "*You* can meld it."

Chloe studied his face, and then the crucible. "It's awfully big. I've never made anything that big go thin."

"I'm sorry," Neptune asked. "Meld?"

Horace explained how Chloe could make one thing become incorporeal, and then put it inside another. The other Wardens watched him keenly. Mr. Meister's great left eye seemed as sharp as a hawk's. Chloe, meanwhile, kept her head down, as if she was afraid she was going to be asked to demonstrate like the others had. "Chloe can meld the crucible into the floor, or the wall," Horace said. "Surely that would destroy it."

Gabriel cleared his throat. "An intriguing idea," he said, "but unless Chloe can do this to objects much larger than herself—*much* larger—it will not work."

"Why not?" Horace asked, not liking the way Gabriel emphasized *much*.

"The crucible and its Keeper are . . . joined. I could not feel where one ended and the other began. I don't believe Chloe could separate a lit crucible from its living Keeper."

But Horace pressed on. "You don't know what Chloe is capable—"

"Enough," Mr. Meister said, cutting him off. "It is one

thing to dream up a plan. It is quite another to see it through. Let us stay within our limits. All I ask is that you find the nest. Get Chloe's father out."

Horace sank into silence, frustrated. *"Stay within our limits."* The very phrase almost made him want to hunt down and destroy the crucible himself. He was sure Chloe would press the issue, but she didn't. Instead she reached into her pocket and pulled out a mint, popped it into her mouth, began crushing it loudly and deliberately. "So we sneak into the nest," she said. "We find my dad. Maybe I destroy the crucible, or maybe I don't. Either way, we get my dad out. And we do all this under cover of the wonder staff."

Mr. Meister nodded. "The humour of Obro will protect you from the pull of the crucible, yes. And the Alvalaithen, of course, will protect you from almost every other danger."

"But what if I don't want him to come?" she said, pointing at Gabriel. "What if I only want Horace?"

Mrs. Hapsteade spoke, her voice low but full of steel. "Horace would be defenseless. You and Gabriel are the only ones who have a hope of getting safely in and out of the nest."

"Then let me go alone."

Mr. Meister gave two firm shakes of the head. "We cannot do that. Only with Gabriel's help do you have a chance of resisting the crucible."

"I wonder if that's true."

Mrs. Hapsteade's eyes flashed. "Go ahead and wonder. Add your wondering to the pile of everything we freely admit we don't know. Compound our uncertainties, multiply the risks. Ask yourself if that's the best way to help your father now."

Chloe went on chewing, her jaw jutting stubbornly.

Gabriel spoke, his strange gaze sweeping over them. "I know my Tan'ji can make me seem fearsome—"

"I'm not afraid of you," Chloe said.

"That is a lie. Everyone is afraid of me." He said this with such simplicity, with neither pride nor self-pity, that it could not be taken for anything but the plain truth. Even Neptune just gave him those sad, wide eyes. Again Horace felt an unwanted surge of sympathy for the boy. Chloe, mint gone, licked her teeth and worked her lips. She turned her icy stare to the crucible, sitting there like a carcass.

"Okay," she said at last. "Okay then. But that staff of yours—I tell you when."

Mrs. Hapsteade started to speak, but Gabriel only nodded at Chloe. "You may tell me when. But if I see that you are losing yourself to the crucible, I will intervene."

Another long pause, then a curt nod from Chloe.

"Very good," said Mr. Meister. "We are in agreement." He leaned back and laid his eyes on Horace. "But now you may be asking yourself, Keeper, what role you have to play in all this, if you will not be entering the nest."

"The thought had crossed my mind."

"A very important role indeed. Without you, we stand very little chance of locating the nest in the first place."

"Wait," Chloe said, "you don't even know where the nest is?"

"Nests are highly secret, all but impossible for an outsider to locate. Neptune's abilities have proven useful in tracking the Riven, but finding the nest is another matter entirely. Just as the Riven disguise themselves, so too is the nest disguised."

"That's why you need the Fel'Daera," Horace said, remembering the night at the park and the many-headed Dr. Jericho. "I can see what others can't."

"Yes. But there is another reason we will have need of the Fel'Daera tonight." Mr. Meister glanced at Mrs. Hapsteade, and Horace thought she gave him the faintest of nods.

"And what reason is that?" Horace asked slowly.

The old man looked almost guilty as he spoke. "We need it for bait."

CHAPTER THIRTY

Both Sides of the Glass

AN HOUR LATER, HORACE STOOD IN THE BURNED WRECKAGE of Chloe's house, feeling like a fool. It was 1:27. For the last seventeen minutes he'd been holding the box open, raising it every ten seconds or so, scanning the scene. It was Mr. Meister's idea that Dr. Jericho would sense the open box from the future and would come looking for the source, allowing Horace to follow him back to the nest through time. But the whole idea was starting to look like a fail. There had been nothing to see: the dark yard, the rubble of Chloe's ruined home, the neighbor's house looking naked with Chloe's house gone. No Dr. Jericho. No Riven. No anyone.

Except Horace wasn't really alone, of course. There was always the chance that while he tried to lure Dr. Jericho in the future, the Mordin might also be drawn here in the present. And therefore the other Wardens stood guard. Somewhere overhead in the cloudy night sky, Neptune hovered unseen. Gabriel stood in the shadows of the buckthorn trees along the property line, staff at the ready. Across the street, Chloe kept watch from atop a freight car in the train yard. But Horace was beginning to think the plan was a waste of time. He wasn't sure Dr. Jericho would be able to sense the box from the house—he didn't even know how far away Dr. Jericho was, although it stood to reason that the nest might be somewhere near Chloe's house.

Horace waited. Through his shirt, he fussed with the strange new pendant that now hung from his neck, a gift from the Wardens. It was a jithandra, one of the crystals all the Wardens wore. He and Chloe had each received one before leaving the Warren. Horace's jithandra was dark now, but if he were to pull it out, it would glow a brilliant cobalt blue. Chloe's, meanwhile, was bloodred.

The colors, of course, were the same colors as the ink when they'd written with the Vora, back at the House of Answers. Mr. Meister hadn't explained that, but he did explain that although a jithandra wasn't truly Tan'ji, it would work only for its owner and no one else. It was, in effect, their entry key into the Warren. In time, the old man promised, Horace and Chloe would learn to use theirs to cross the waters of Vithra's Eye, just as they'd seen Mrs. Hapsteade do.

And the jithandras weren't the only gifts they'd received. Mr. Meister had spoken to them each in turn, talking in low, private tones. He spoke quietly to Gabriel at length—almost seeming to try and convince him of something—and then reached up and clasped the tall boy's shoulder. He gave Chloe a ghostly white sphere on a chain—one of those little balls that created a dumin when crushed. He made her put it around her neck. He then bent close and they exchanged a few words that Horace couldn't hear. The talk ended, predictably, with a fierce scowl from Chloe.

Finally Mr. Meister had come to Horace and surprised him by leading him away from the group. "I wonder, Keeper, if you could tell me the time. Your most precise estimate."

"Twelve forty-one," Horace said reflexively.

Mr. Meister peeked into his own hand. "Very good. It is always so with the Keeper of the Fel'Daera. But now tell me this: twelve forty-one . . . and how many seconds?"

Horace knew from experience that his inner clock wasn't that accurate. He made the safest guess he could. "I don't know. Thirty?"

Mr. Meister opened his hand to reveal a small gold pocket watch, trim and handsome. It was indeed 12:41. But the second hand—which swept smoothly, rather than moving in ticks—was just approaching the twenty-second mark. "Close, but not close enough," the old man said, and surprised Horace again by slipping the watch into Horace's hand. "Sometimes a plan may succeed or fail because of the difference of a few seconds. This is just a regular watch, not truly suitable for the Keeper of the Fel'Daera—there is only one such device that I know of—yet this watch is very fine in its own right. Take it. Use it. Sometimes we must know the moment precisely, yes?"

"Thank you," Horace said.

"When you elect to use the Fel'Daera tonight, Horace, first remember what you have learned. Use your intuition as well as your logic. Before opening the box, feel for the moment. Feel where you are and why you are there. Feel for your companions. Feel their fears and motivations as strongly as you feel your own."

"I will."

"The box may show you things you do not wish to see. Think hard before you choose to fight the course of action it seems to suggest. If you worry that your free will has been stolen from you, just remember: you already walk the willed path. There are choices you have already made, turnings you have already taken."

Horace drank in Mr. Meister's words. "Who knows when the first turning has been taken?" he murmured.

"Not I," Mr. Meister said, smiling.

And now, nearly an hour later, as Horace stood in Chloe's house gazing into the open box and remembering Mr. Meister's words, he repeated them to himself: "The willed path."

The sudden soft crunch of footsteps announced that someone was there. He swung around, tensing, but it was only Chloe, hood around her face, hands deep in pockets, picking her way through the wreckage. "Nothing, huh?"

"No, not yet."

"I was getting bored. I thought you might be too."

"I'm tired. Tired of standing."

"Yeah," Chloe said, looking around. "This is the first time I've been back here, you know."

Horace hadn't thought about that. "I'm sorry," he said, not knowing what else to say.

"Well, at least this place is still good for something. I hope." She spun in a circle. "Here's where the stairs were. That means we're in the hall." She pointed at a toilet, cracked and blackened. "Bathroom, obviously. The kitchen. This would've been my dad's room here, then. The stump of bricks over there, that's what's left of the heart, I guess. And Go-Between, that's gone for good. It all is." She kicked a heat-blistered stub of wall, sending it tumbling. "My dad, he was always going to fix this place up. And he might've, too. I think he was getting better before . . . all this."

Horace couldn't find anything to say to that. He wondered if it were true. He watched Chloe kicking around, stopping now and again to examine something in the rubble. Then she sighed, tilting her head back and looking into the sky. "You think Neptune can keep that up forever?"

"I think maybe she can. She told me she made it across Lake Michigan once—that must've taken hours."

Chloe grunted, unimpressed. "Yeah, but I bet she had to take the bus home."

"Huh," Horace said, thinking that one over. He scanned the area quickly with the box—still nothing—and then pointed it toward the sky. Tomorrow night would be clear, it seemed. Almost directly overhead, he could see all six stars in the constellation Lyra. It reminded him of the day the house key had rematerialized and fallen into the bin of stars—the day he'd discovered what the box could do. From his house he could usually only see one: Vega, a very bright star.

Horace said, "I saw Mr. Meister gave you one of those dumin things."

"Yeah," Chloe said, looking down at herself. "A dumindar, he called it. I have so many damn things around my neck I feel like one of those jewelry store mannequin heads. Oh, and also, apparently I'm not supposed to be overly brave tonight."

"What do you mean?" Horace said.

"That's what Mr. Meister told me. He gave me the dumindar and told me not to be so brave that I risked not coming back."

"And what did you say?"

"I told him it didn't sound like he understood what bravery *was*. And then he said, 'I understand that when it comes to courage, the lost are no match for the living.'"

"I don't know what that means."

"I do. But he's wrong. It's not that the living are more brave; it's that they have no choice."

"But you do have a choice."

"No, Horace, I don't." She spread her arms, indicating the burned ruins around her. "And you wouldn't either."

"Maybe not, but . . . I don't have Madeline. If my parents

were lost, and I ran into trouble while looking for them, I wouldn't be leaving anyone else behind. Nobody who was counting on me, anyway. Maybe that's what Mr. Meister meant."

Chloe's face was hidden in the shadows of her hood. "God you're fun, Horace."

"I'm not saying don't do it, I'm just saying . . . come back."

She stabbed a toe at the ashes, talking down at them. "Why does everyone think I'm not planning on coming back?" She leaned and called loudly past Horace, toward the scraggly trees off in the darkness. "How about you, Gabriel? Are you planning to come back? Has anyone asked you that?"

Horace grimaced and glanced back at the trees, but there was no reply. "The reason people ask you that, Chloe, is because you're the one that takes all the risks."

"I'm the one that can afford the risks." She threw a thumb at herself, at the Alvalaithen.

"Maybe, but you can't do everything."

"Obviously not. I couldn't stop my dad from being taken."

"That's not what I meant."

"I can't destroy the crucible."

"But maybe you can," said a voice. Horace snapped the box closed, startled. Gabriel was coming toward them, walking across the lawn.

"What do you know about it?" said Chloe.

"I've been thinking about what Horace said earlier. About melding." Gabriel stopped at the edge of the house.

He crouched down and picked up a charred piece of wood the size of a wine bottle. "If I understand correctly, Chloe, there are limits to what you can—how did you put it? Make thin? But if the crucible is too large, maybe we need to think about it the other way around." He threw the hunk of wood to Chloe. She caught it awkwardly with two hands.

"A stick," she said drily.

"Just an example. You meld it inside the source of the crucible's light. Whatever that source is, it's small—smaller than my forearm. You heard Mr. Meister: You don't have to physically destroy the crucible to sabotage the nest, to scatter the Riven there and set your dad free. You just have to extinguish the light."

Horace wondered when, exactly, Gabriel had come up with this idea. He wished he had thought of it himself—he *should* have thought of it. "He's right," Horace said.

"And destroying the crucible will destroy the nest for good," said Chloe.

"Effectively, yes," Gabriel replied. "The crucible *is* the nest."

"Dr. Jericho would take it personally."

"Very."

Chloe looked thoughtfully down at the hunk of wood for a moment or two, turning it. Then she tossed it aside. "I guess we'll see what happens," she said. "But I'm getting my dad out of there, one way or another."

Gabriel prodded the ground thoughtfully with his staff.

Chloe rubbed her hands together, wiping ash from her palms. A strange kind of conviction swept over Horace, watching the two of them: if anyone could destroy the crucible and get Chloe's father out of the nest, it was these two. The thought came with a little pang of envy, but he swallowed it before it could thicken. Nobody was getting rescued unless they found the nest first—and that was Horace's job. "Speaking of see what happens . . . ," he said.

He clasped the box between his hands, recalling Mr. Meister's words: *"Feel for the moment. Feel where you are and why you are there. Feel for your companions."* After the toolshed, Horace was careful not to convince himself that their plan would succeed without a doubt. But he could certainly believe that it might. He and the other young Wardens had the power to rescue Chloe's father, and perhaps to do even more. He believed it.

Horace opened the lid. Immediately, so close he could have touched it—*a standing shadow, just a foot away.* Horace cried out, nearly dropping the box.

"What is it?" Chloe hissed, her voice like a whip. "Is he here?"

"Hang on." Horace took a step back and righted the box, looking into tomorrow. This was it. This was the moment. A figure, standing motionless in tomorrow's burned-down house, hands in pockets. But not Dr. Jericho.

It was Chloe.

"No, no," Horace said. "What are you doing here?" This

was not the plan. And yet there she was—*tomorrow's Chloe, clear and unmistakable, hood thrown back, standing in the ashes alone, not moving or speaking . . . waiting?* "Oh, god," Horace said, wishing there were some way to take this moment back, to unsee what he had seen. "What did I do?"

"Horace?" Chloe in the here and now, leaning toward him, her face wrinkled with worry. Chloe here now, Chloe here then. But why? And if she was here tomorrow, that meant . . .

Horace slammed the box closed. He ran, kicking up clouds of ash, Chloe and Gabriel at his heels.

Chloe was here in the house, tomorrow. And Horace was trying to lure Dr. Jericho into that very spot at that very moment.

He had to get the box away, to lead Dr. Jericho away. Horace barreled across the road and fought through the gap in the train-yard fence, Chloe slipping through behind him. He heaved himself onto the back of a boxcar. He checked the box again. And there across the road—*Chloe, small and stubborn and . . . not alone; a monstrous figure in a ghastly dark suit, pausing at the edge of the ruined house, many-limbed and many-headed, gazing at Chloe, sniffing at the air, faces peering all around, predatory.*

Horace was too late.

Future Chloe was looking right at Dr. Jericho. It seemed like she'd been *waiting* for him. Horace couldn't understand. He could only watch as the thin man strode over the ashes toward Chloe and hunkered down before her—*his lips moving, teeth shining in the dark; a long finger reaching out for Chloe's throat, taking what hung there briefly into his palm.*

"What is it?" Chloe said, nearly in his ear.

"You're there. And so is Dr. Jericho. He's right in front of you. You aren't even running. What are you doing?"

Gabriel said, "You're saying Chloe will be here tomorrow night? With Dr. Jericho?"

Now Dr. Jericho bolting upright, many heads turning in Horace's direction, becoming one snarling face—

Horace snapped the box closed. "He's sensing the box. I have to be careful." It was 1:36. He described the scene to Chloe and Gabriel.

"What about the Alvalaithen?" Chloe fingered the dragonfly, furrowing her brow.

"I don't know. I'm thinking. I'm trying to think." He put his mind to it, taking hold of everything he knew, trying to understand where he himself and Chloe—and Neptune and Gabriel—now stood along the paths they were on. He cracked the box open: *Chloe, still there. Dr. Jericho, monstrous and spidery, writhing, and*—Horace's stomach turned to lead. Two other shapes were moving in from behind now, not quite so tall as Dr. Jericho but the same—*Mordin, surrounding Chloe, bending over her like dark, sinister trees.* The sight of them was sickening and heavy. "There are more now. Three of them."

"A hunting pack," said a voice above them. Neptune landed lightly on top the freight car.

"Are you sure of what you're seeing?" Gabriel asked. "The

Fel'Daera makes promises, but promises can be broken."

Horace thought back to Mr. Meister again, about trusting in the box. "I'm sure. I mean . . . whatever path Chloe is on now, it brings her back here, tomorrow."

Gabriel nodded. "We must follow them, then. Just as we planned."

Horace slid the box open again. Across the street, the little gathering was already on the move: *four figures, three gaunt and shifting and horrible, one tiny and resolute; moving across the backyard, separating now into pairs, the tallest figure sticking close alongside the smallest; now a long, snaking arm reaching down to Chloe, and a tiny hand reaching up*—Horace slammed the box shut in revulsion.

Chloe and Dr. Jericho were holding hands.

"What is it, Horace?" Chloe asked. "What do you see?"

"Nothing. They're leaving . . . you're . . . leaving with them." He pointed the way. He couldn't tell her what he was seeing. Why would she be here? Why would she not be fighting, escaping? He felt frozen. For a moment he imagined the worst—that Chloe was giving in, going with them willingly to save her father. But no—that was impossible. He shook the thought away.

Chloe stepped up as if she'd read his mind, throwing her hood back. "Maybe *I'm* the bait. You don't know. None of us know what's about to happen, what will work and what won't. Not even you."

"It's my job to know."

"It is your job to find the nest," Gabriel said. "Neptune cannot do it alone."

Neptune stood. "So let's go already." She took three powerful, lunging strides, hurling herself into the air. She sailed over the street in the direction Horace had indicated, disappearing into the dark night.

"Come on," Chloe said. "We'll figure it out on the way."

Horace nodded. They set off. He stayed half a block behind the Mordin, using the box as infrequently as he dared. Chloe and Gabriel followed silently. Meanwhile—both inside and outside the box—Horace caught an occasional glimpse of Neptune sailing overhead, or clinging to some improbable perch. When Horace commented on the fact that Neptune would be following the Mordin again tomorrow night, Gabriel said, "Neptune is always watching."

As it turned out, following the Mordin was far easier than anyone had anticipated. The Mordin took such a straight path that Horace barely had to use the box. Once or twice Dr. Jericho looked back in Horace's direction, but he never slowed. At one point, the Mordin turned and took a walkway over the train tracks, and Horace caught a glimpse of tomorrow's Neptune simply walking far behind them, not bothering to stay aloft. Several blocks on, they passed through a rundown little business district and entered a dingy, treeless area lined with old brick buildings and alleyways. They passed a scrap yard, aglow with dirty yellow lights. Just beyond it was an abandoned drive-in restaurant.

Horace checked the box again: *all three Mordin, angling across the street with Chloe in tow, headed for a large brick building, tall and dark and deep, like a little castle, or a church; the building flickered like a flame.*

"Wait, wait," Horace said, lowering the box. He saw the building now, today, nestled between the scrap yard and the abandoned restaurant, but he hadn't noticed it at first. And through the box—*Chloe and the Mordin, walking along the side of the little fluttering castle, down into a darkened stairwell; now the crack of a door, a sliver of deep darkness.* They disappeared inside.

"They're gone," Horace said, pointing. "They went into that brick building there. That must be the nest."

"Which building?" Chloe said.

Horace pointed again, leaning into her. "Right there. Between the scrap yard and the restaurant." Neptune dropped out of the sky onto the street, cloak billowing. She could not seem to understand what Horace was talking about either.

"The crucible conceals itself and hides the nest," Gabriel said. "Describe the place, Horace. Help them see it." Horace described it: the strange, boxy canopy out front; three arched windows above; a rounded and ornate roofline; windowless brick walls down the sides. As he spoke, first Chloe and then Neptune let out astonished breaths, seeing it at last.

"This is the crucible at work," said Gabriel. "But the Fel'Daera was able to see otherwise, just as Mr. Meister said."

"So this is the nest," Chloe said. "This is where they brought my dad."

"Yes," Gabriel said. "We should find him below."

But Neptune was gazing at the brick building, her face worried. "Gabriel," she said, keeping her voice light. "The Mordin. They led us straight here. That's not what they do."

"They did not know we were following."

But Horace hardly heard that. Neptune's words were ringing in his head. *"That's not what they do."*

And yet they would.

Horace said, "They're going to come straight here because by then, they'll know we already found the nest. There won't be any reason to pretend." Three faces turned toward him, but his thoughts were far away, working the lines of influence between today and tomorrow. Everything that was about to happen, here and now, would lead back to the ashes of Chloe's home in twenty-four hours.

"Horace," Chloe said, quiet and clear. "Why will I let them bring me back here?"

Horace focused, letting his mind work into the problem. Although he could not piece all the events together, not yet, one thing shone clearly to him. He thought maybe he'd known it right away, back at Chloe's house, but just hadn't let the connections form. Chloe and Gabriel were about to enter the nest. Chloe would come out again, and Neptune would be free too—Horace had seen them both through the box. And yet there was this troubling fact—*no one would stop Chloe from being caught tomorrow night.* Not he himself, nor Neptune nor Gabriel, nor Mr. Meister, who by then would know what the Fel'Daera had revealed. And most of all, not Chloe. Everyone would know what was coming and would *choose to let it happen.* Tomorrow—there was no other conclusion to draw—some great need would be met when Dr. Jericho came to get Chloe in the ashes of her home. Someone would set those deeds into motion for a reason. Someone would have grounds for believing in that particular path.

And Horace knew who that someone was.

"What does it mean, Horace?" Chloe asked.

"It means," he said slowly, holding on to the box, "something is about to go wrong. But it also means you believe you can fix it."

Chloe's dark eyes held his for a long moment. "So do I go in? Now?"

"You do," Horace said. He took a deep breath and let it out. "And so do I."

CHAPTER THIRTY-ONE

The Nest

HORACE WAITED FOR THEM TO TELL HIM HE COULD NOT GO in. He prepared himself to do battle with any reasons they could come up with. But no one said a word. No one even looked doubtful. Instead, Gabriel nodded firmly and said, "Come then. But take care. Stay close to me. Our instruments will keep Chloe and me safe, but yours will not. Neptune, you must go back and—"

"I'm not leaving," Neptune said. "I'll be out here, overhead. You might need me."

Gabriel's face gave nothing away. "May yours be light, then."

"And yours," Neptune sang, and then she was gone into the air.

Gabriel cocked his head as if he could hear her go, and then he said to Horace, "Walk with me. Show me the way."

Head pounding with all his new convictions, and with the speed at which everything was happening, Horace guided Gabriel across the street. Chloe followed. Gabriel spoke to them in low tones, his words swift.

"We should have little to fear until we are underground. Like us, the Riven bury their safeguards deep. Once below, however, we must be wary. The crucible dog will be prowling."

Horace wasn't sure he heard right. "Crucible dog?"

"The Keeper of the crucible. It's not actually a dog, of course, but . . ." Gabriel shrugged. "It moves on all fours. It has teeth." Horace and Chloe exchanged a glance. "Remember, stay close. With the staff, I can provide some protection from almost anything we might encounter in the nest."

Chloe tugged on the strings of her hoodie. "You just remember your promise. You don't use that thing unless I say."

"I remember the terms of our agreement," Gabriel replied coolly. "But we must all use our Tan'ji only when there is no alternative. And remember, you are as valuable to them as your instruments. They will take your instruments, yes, but they will seek to turn you, too—to bring you to their side. Without us, after all, our instruments are useless. Of course, if they can't turn you, they will kill you." Horace shuddered at the easy way the word *kill* rolled off Gabriel's tongue.

At the front of the building, two sets of double doors along the front were crooked in their frames, boarded over. Above the doors, the broad, square canopy jutted out.

"It's a theater," Chloe said, and now Horace saw—not a

canopy, but a marquee. Above the marquee, the three arched windows stood, two of them painted over and the center one a motley patchwork of panes. Through the panes, Horace could just make out a huge slab of something—the ceiling?—that had collapsed. He tried to let go of the sensation that someone, or *something*, might be watching them from the broken window above. He reminded himself that if they were, Neptune, hovering higher still, would know about it.

They trekked around the side of the theater. Horace pointed out the side door he'd seen the Mordin take Chloe into, and they gave it a wide berth. "We must find another way in," said Gabriel. "Not the way the Mordin took—this door will be guarded." A little farther on, they found what they needed. A thick, dark column rose along the brickwork: an old spiral fire escape, snaking up to a door high above.

Horace tested the bottom step. It seemed solid. He went up a few steps and shook the railing hard, but the structure held fast. "Here," he said, for Gabriel's benefit. "Stairs going up." Gabriel followed, very cautiously—clearly the staff, without the humour fully expanded, was not much help climbing stairs. He eased onto each new step, one strong hand gripping the rail. Chloe brought up the rear, staying well back.

At the top, the stairs ended at a cramped landing that couldn't hold them all. The door—battered and graffiti scarred—was locked fast. "Me," said Chloe. She slid through, and a few tense moments later, a bolt was thrown back. The door creaked open.

Inside, the theater was utterly black. The smell of mold and decay filled Horace's nose. They moved forward cautiously by the combined light of Chloe's and Horace's jithandras, a dull violet glow. Horace wondered if Gabriel had a jithandra, and if so, whether it gave off any light.

They were in the balcony. Beyond the low wall in front of them, a sea of shadow hung. High overhead, a jagged hole in the roof opened onto a patch of night sky. They moved along the aisle between rows of dusty and moth-eaten seats, Chloe leading the way slowly up the shallow steps. Debris lay all around, big chunks of plaster from above and ragged strips of fabric and splintered woodwork. As they walked, they kicked up clouds of dust that glowed lavender in the ghostly light of their jithandras. At the back of the balcony they found a staircase, broad and curving, that led down to the first-floor lobby. Here a series of gaping doors opened into the main part of the theater.

"There will be a basement," Gabriel whispered. "A level below the stage. We need to get backstage and find it."

They entered the theater and made their way down the aisle to the front of the stage. After testing its height with his staff, Gabriel leapt lightly onto the stage, leaving Horace and Chloe to clamber after him. Behind them, the auditorium was a huge and shadowed space, the balcony barely visible.

"Careful." Gabriel pointed the tip of his staff at a square black hole cut into the stage floor. An open trapdoor. Gabriel passed it on the right and Horace and Chloe went left, keeping their distance.

A few seconds later, Gabriel stopped. He tapped the tip of the staff softly against the floor, catching their attention. "Wait," he whispered sharply. "Wait." He turned back toward the yawning hole in the stage behind them.

The golem exploded from the trapdoor like a black geyser, splintering the floorboards and surging high into the air. Horace staggered as the floor shook beneath his feet. The golem towered overhead for a moment, serpentine, and then fell toward them with a mountainous roar.

Chloe darted forward, grabbing Horace's shirt and yanking hard. "Run!" she shouted. He stumbled after her. Across the stage, Gabriel charged in the opposite direction, staff out in front. Gabriel winked out of sight just as the golem's monstrous form dropped between them, barely missing them all. The golem began to gather itself again with a speed no amount of muscle could ever have managed, searching for them with its eyeless gaze, a swaying river of stone.

Horace tried to stay on Chloe's heels, following the bouncing red glow of her jithandra as she ran. The stage was littered with crates and equipment and leaning stacks of scenery and half-torn-down stage sets. They wove through the clutter, feet pounding, Horace's heart nearly punching through his chest. Behind them, the golem crushed its own path, as wide as a bus.

When the back wall of the stage loomed before them, Chloe veered left, and they found themselves entangled in a tower of metal scaffolding. They began to duck and swing their way through it, Chloe as nimble as a squirrel, not risking the dragonfly even now—or maybe, Horace thought, she just wasn't willing to leave him behind. With his bigger frame, Horace had a harder time, unable to find a rhythm through the narrow triangular gaps—banging his shins more than once, cracking his head, skinning his palms on the rough pipes. He heard the brutal clatter of the golem behind and felt the whole structure tremble. He didn't look back, but by the sound of it, the golem was breaking into pieces to trickle through the maze of heavy pipes. A piercing clamor arose, hammering Horace's ears—like a dense and endless down-pour of hail.

A dozen feet ahead of him, Chloe was through, her face again glowing red in the darkness, her lips moving but her words inaudible. The structure rocked, caught in the grip of an earthquake. A couple of boards, shaken loose from high above, came slicing down through the gaps, crashing to the floor to Horace's left and right like spears. He dared a look back. The golem was nearly upon him, all around and overhead too. The scaffolding was slowing it down, but not enough—it was going to catch him. In some places, it simply tore through the pipes, ripping them free. He saw, or he imag-ined he saw, the cruel red heart of the golem, flashing through the mass.

Chloe reached in for him, her thin fingers straining. "Here!" she shouted. Horace reached out too, but just as he did, a cold, strong grip enveloped his foot, as if it had been encased in concrete. The golem pulled on him with irresistible power. The stones crept up his leg toward the Fel'Daera. Horace rolled, and the bar beneath his chest gave way, broken loose by his weight and the golem's. Horace fell to the ground as the scaffolding began coming apart all around, snapping and screeching and clattering with a roar to rival the golem's. He threw his hands over his face. Overhead, the entire structure buckled, beginning to collapse back into the body of the golem.

Suddenly Horace was free. He kicked out hard, scattering a bucketful of the golem's stones. He scrambled forward, crawling under and then over the last few bars of the scaffold. He fell at Chloe's feet just as the near end gave way with a cascade of snaps and cracks and clangs. The scaffold plunged, a shower of swords and hammers, pushing the golem back, beating it down into the dust that bloomed all around.

"Get up!" Chloe yelled. Her jithandra glowed like a beacon. "That won't stop it for long."

They ran. Behind them the golem thrashed, trying to gather itself out of the wreckage of the scaffold. They pushed aside a heavy, musty curtain and found themselves running along a wide hallway backstage. Halfway down, Chloe slid to a stop in front of a broad, square opening in the wall, Horace at her side.

It was an elevator shaft. Cables stretched upward into the shadows above. At their feet, Horace could see the top of an elevator car, apparently caught between this floor and the one below.

Chloe stepped out onto the elevator car. She knelt and quickly found the handle of a hatch in the top of the car. "In here."

"Are you crazy?" Horace said.

Chloe twisted the handle. The hatch fell open with a *squawk*, and she bent into the darkness. "The doors are partway open. We can climb out into the next level down. Come on." Without waiting for an answer, she swung her legs into the hatch and dropped out of sight. Horace hesitated. Where was Gabriel? How would they find him again? But just then, from back behind, a crash and a truck-sized rumble announced that the golem was free. Immediately, Horace stepped out onto the elevator car. It was sturdy underfoot. He climbed down through the hatch, scraping his belly in the process. He dropped and landed heavily inside the car, hoping Chloe knew what she was doing.

And she did, of course. The elevator was trapped between floors, but the doors were halfway open; they could see a thick cross section of concrete and metal that was the floor of the theater itself—a bizarre sight. Beneath that, the doors looked out onto a new corridor below. The basement. Dusty cobwebs hung across the opening like seaweed. Lips pursed tight, Chloe swept away a palmful. The opening was small, no bigger than an open window, and the drop to the floor below looked to be four or five feet, but they could make it.

Chloe slithered through gracefully. Horace clambered out after her, hitting the floor with a grunt, stumbling. He heard the golem come roaring down the hallway above them and then stop, directly overhead.

"We'll use the dumin," Chloe said, looking up at the ceiling. "We can block off the whole elevator shaft. The golem won't be able to get through—just like back at the warehouse."

Horace shook his head, unwilling to use the dumin so early, when they hadn't so much as glimpsed any Riven, much less Chloe's dad. "No. Not yet. We've got to find Gab—"

Suddenly, a voice down the hall. But not a human voice. This was sharp and slashing, speaking a language full of hisses and cracks. And then a lean figure appeared in the gloom, far ahead. Not nearly so tall as a Mordin, but it wasn't a man, either. Lanky, with long, swinging arms, and skin so pale it seemed to almost glow in the dark. Now another figure joined the first.

The Riven. Horace and Chloe hadn't been spotted yet, but they were trapped. Horace looked back—the dangling elevator car was too high to climb back into easily, and anyway the golem still lurked above. But beneath the car, the elevator shaft ended in a dingy pit, waist-deep. Not stopping to think, Horace dropped into the pit. A moment later, in the red glow of her jithandra, Chloe landed beside him on all fours like a cat.

They pressed themselves back against the front wall, beneath the lip of the opening. Chloe's jithandra was clenched in her fist, turning her fingers pink. Horace doused his own light. He tried not to think about the tiny space they were in, or the elevator suspended overhead.

Metal screeched brutally, directly above. The golem was on the move again, following their trail. It sounded like it was tearing the roof of the elevator car open. And then the shaft shook with the deafening noise of the golem pouring into the elevator, making Horace slap his hands over his ears. But after a moment there came another sound, new and deep and alarming—a great groaning creak from somewhere overhead. Horace looked up, horrified. He hadn't considered how heavy the golem must be. The elevator car jolted and shivered, and then something cracked.

The elevator fell.

Horace twisted onto his side, throwing up his arm as if he could keep the elevator from crushing him. In the same moment, Chloe's light winked out completely as she went to the ground too. Horace clutched the box, waiting to be crushed.

But they weren't crushed. The groan came to an abrupt halt, somewhere overhead in the utter dark. Now a series of pops, and another heart-stopping creak. Horace felt a push of air against his raised palm. And then from just outside the pit came the familiar tumble of an ocean of rocks—the golem pouring itself into the corridor. It seemed to go on forever.

Horace tried to listen past the sound of his blood thudding in his ears. He began counting. After ten interminable seconds, the elevator car emptied, and outside in the hallway—unmistakably—the golem's avalanche began moving away, headed deeper into the basement. Still Horace lay there, paralyzed and hurting. A massive metal spring dug into his ribs. He itched to uncover his jithandra but was terrified of what he might see—had the elevator fallen so far that they were now trapped in this dark and dusty pit?

The roar of the golem grew more and more faint. *Fourteen, fifteen, sixteen* . . . At last Horace could stand it no more. He fumbled into his shirt and pulled out his jithandra, letting it spring to life. His chest heaved as he saw the bottom of the elevator just overhead, inches from where his outstretched hand had been. It had stopped just in time, leaving a foot-high gap through which they would be able to escape the pit—barely.

Beside him, Chloe straightened out of a fetal position, also eyeing the elevator warily. "That was close," she said. "I almost went thin."

Horace swallowed, trying to stay calm. "I think we both almost went thin, if you know what I mean."

"We need to get you out of here," Chloe said. "But first let me see if the coast is clear." Horace nodded. They would have to squeeze through while the elevator's weight hung above them—not a pleasant thought, but almost anything was better than staying here.

Chloe peeked out over the lip of the pit. Horace couldn't hear anything, not even the golem now. But suddenly Chloe gestured for him to extinguish his light.

They sank into darkness again. After a moment, though, Horace realized he could see Chloe in the gloom—a faint green light filtered through the crack and lit her face. "Don't move," she whispered, scarcely audible. Chloe lifted her nose and mouth into the light and sniffed—once, twice.

Horace did the same. Cutting through thick odors of damp and dust and mold, a piercing scent stung his nose, a sharp smell like a lit match.

Brimstone.

The crucible.

The green light grew, becoming deep and brilliant and glimmering, like the sun through water. It swayed thickly into the shaft. Chloe's eyes grew wide. "I see it," she said, her voice full of wonder, and then Horace was on his knees too, in the light dazzling and warm. It pulled at him, cradling him. There was the source, down the shadowed corridor—a rippling sliver of green light cracking the darkness open, as though they were inside an immense, slitted eye, looking out into an ocean sparkling under an emerald sun. Chloe said something, but Horace couldn't understand it. The scent of the light bit at his brain, the heat wrapping him in its hand, drawing him like a current. He could hear it now, crackling and sighing like water over rocks. There were other figures in that light, shifting and waiting. One of them was a great beast on all fours. But far from being afraid, Horace wanted to come closer. He wanted to be beside the beast, basking near the source. What if it did not wait for him? What if it did not see him? Despair filled him at the thought. He began to squeeze out of the pit, scratching at the floor, trying to pull himself toward the light. Dimly he was aware of Chloe at his side, doing the same.

And then the light was swallowed. Everything went gray. Horace cried out, but his words were buried in this new fog. The light was torn from him—the brilliance, the warmth, the low hissing song, the sting of its scent. A faint buzz in the back of his mind wouldn't leave him; he couldn't name it, couldn't shake it. There were voices, angry and confused and distant.

A new voice rang out, deep and near, everywhere at once. It spoke their names.

"Horace," it said. "Chloe." The voice filled the world like a mighty wave, like the tremble of the earth itself. Horace tried to answer the voice, full of rage that the light had been taken from him. He tried to push the name he knew to his lips, but he could not speak. He mouthed it instead, seething, knowing he would be heard.

Gabriel!

CHAPTER THIRTY-TWO

Not Yet Lost but Found

"Keeper of the Fel'Daera," said Gabriel. "Keeper of the Alvalaithen. Remember yourselves, Wardens. Get back. Hide from the crucible."

The crucible. The word summoned up the image of a cruel and grasping hand of steel. The crucible, yes, still somewhere out in that cloud, and Horace had been crawling toward it. But now Gabriel was keeping them all hidden, blinding the Keeper of the crucible and dousing that terrible, wonderful light—sound and sight and smell.

Horace pushed himself back into the elevator shaft, squeezing beneath the elevator. He thought he heard Chloe moving too, faint and distant. Sagging into the elevator shaft, Horace kept his eyes open, letting the vast blankness of the humour wash away the memory of the green light. He breathed in through his mouth and out through his nose, trying to rid himself of the stench.

"Stay low," said Gabriel. "The dog is searching for you. It searches for me as best it can." A long pause; Horace had the sense Gabriel was on the move within the humour. When Gabriel's voice returned, it was still everywhere: "There are men with the crucible dog, three of them. How will I recognize your father, Chloe?"

Chloe's voice spilled out of the ether. "The pinkie on his right hand. The tip is missing."

Almost immediately Gabriel responded: "He is here. Is this the moment, then?"

When Chloe didn't answer, Horace knew these words were meant for him. He stared into the humour, thinking hard, remembering why he was here. The plan surfaced in his mind like a sunken ship being raised: find Chloe's father; get him out. But the Fel'Daera could derail even the simplest plan, and on this night the box had revealed the unthinkable—Chloe, allowing herself to be captured, returning to the nest.

Horace was sure of what he'd seen, but he couldn't be sure he was interpreting it correctly. He had already come into the nest believing that he himself, armed with the knowledge that the box gave him, would set into motion the events that would lead to Chloe's recapture. But was that right? For a moment he felt dizzy with doubt. There would be many turnings along this path, many choices that would be his and his alone—and this was only one of them.

"We must act," Gabriel said, his voice insistent and

strained. "One way or another. I must move. The golem will return. Is this the moment?"

"Answer him, Horace," Chloe's voice urged. "You're the Keeper of the Fel'Daera."

Horace shoved his doubts aside. They needed his help. They trusted him, Chloe and Gabriel both. Chloe, in fact, was trusting him with her father's life. "No," Horace said resolutely. "No, this isn't the time." He would believe in himself, believe in the Fel'Daera. "I'm sorry," he added—not for Gabriel, but for Chloe.

Gabriel's voice came back flat and somber. "Do we stay in the nest, or try to escape?"

Horace's eyes roved through the emptiness around him, searching uselessly for Chloe. What must she be thinking? "We stay. If we leave now, we'll never get back in."

"And if we stay, we will be able to destroy the crucible?"

Horace started to frown, but realized Gabriel would see it. "I don't know yet, but I have to find Chloe—tomorrow's Chloe, I mean. She'll be brought back here, and I need to know where she'll be taken."

"If you use the Fel'Daera, they'll sense it. How will you protect yourself?"

"I don't know, but . . ." Horace searched for the right words. "Finding Chloe . . . it's what *has* to happen."

"Understood. Let's go, then."

"No. You lead the crucible dog away. We can get out of here ourselves."

415

If Gabriel hesitated, it was for the briefest blink. "Very well. Once I move away, you'll find yourself outside the humour. Get free and get to the next level down. I came across a boiler room, almost directly below us. There were little cells there with barred doors—like jail cells. They're empty now, but tomorrow . . . who knows?"

"We'll try it."

"Meanwhile, I'll lead the Riven up into the theater, keep them distracted. If I keep using the staff, perhaps they'll have a harder time sensing the Fel'Daera below. I'll come find you there when I can."

"Thank you, Gabriel."

"I must go. Wait for my signal. May yours be light."

"And yours," Horace said.

Silence. Horace could do nothing now but wait, made deaf and blind and mute by the humour. No way to tell what was happening. Chloe still didn't speak. At last Gabriel's voice rang out like the deep peal of a bell. "Now!"

A mighty tearing sound ripped the air, and Horace's sight returned. He was beneath the elevator, bathed in red light. The tiny size of the space shocked him all over again. Across from him, Chloe's eyes found his.

"I'm sorry," Horace said.

"You said that already," Chloe replied, already rising.

"I know what I'm doing."

"That makes one of us. But even if you don't know what you're doing, just do it right, okay?"

"Okay." Horace got to his knees, peeking out of the pit with Chloe. Shadows swallowed the corridor's far end. Gabriel, or darkness? Horace began squeezing out of the shaft. Chloe slid out easily and rolled nimbly to her feet. She watched him clamber clumsily to his own, and they crept down the corridor.

No sign of the crucible or Riven or Gabriel—not that Horace knew what the humour looked like from the outside. They took a right, then a left, then eased down a wide ramp into a huge, echoing room with a forest of narrow pillars. Horace realized they were beneath the stage. More theater equipment here: leaning stacks of wall-sized canvas-covered frames, lots of furniture, racks of costumes, all of it in ragged disarray. They wove through lumpy, looming shapes draped in cloth and piles of wooden crates, risking only the light from the jithandra wrapped in Chloe's fingers. They heard a heavy crash and a low, round rumble. The golem, but it was far off and overhead—chasing Gabriel, perhaps?

They reached the far wall and decided to follow it to the left, hoping to stumble across a way down to the level below. Soon they found themselves in a cramped, cluttered hallway lined with a row of doors—dressing rooms, Horace guessed. As they picked their way through a field of paint buckets and bricks, Horace thought he heard music, distant and sweet. He turned his head toward it and lost his balance, sending a stack of long metal rods tumbling. A painful fist of sound split the air.

Shouts from behind them. A moment later a lilting voice

replied, smooth and commanding and unmistakable. Dr. Jericho. Footsteps pounded.

"Go, go," Horace whispered. They dodged through the clutter, racing. Soon the hallway widened and cleared, and they began running in earnest. Almost immediately, though, Chloe skittered to a halt.

"Ladder." Metal rungs jutting from the wall led downward through a round hole in the floor. On the opposite side of the hall, another dark corridor yawned. Three short steps there led up to a landing and a brown metal door.

"Wait, I think I know where we are," said Horace. "That door leads outside—it's the door Dr. Jericho is going to bring you in tomorrow night, I'm almost sure." He dropped his voice, suddenly wary. "But Gabriel said it might be guarded."

"It won't be now, with all that's been going on inside. Wait here—I have an idea." Chloe scurried down the hall and threw the door open, revealing a concrete stairwell. A draft of fresh air billowed over Horace. Back the way they'd come, a flicker of light and bobbing shadows appeared.

Chloe dashed back. "That'll give them something to wonder about." She grabbed the ladder and started down. Horace followed, easing himself as quickly as he dared down the iron rungs.

They sank into cold and damp, and a dim light. At the bottom of the ladder, the passageway split off in three directions. Two of the tunnels were lit by glowing lights not unlike the amber lights the Wardens used, but these were dimmer and redder, kicking off faint crimson sparks. Chloe ducked instead into the third tunnel—the smallest and darkest, not much more than a slit in the wall—and Horace had no choice but to follow. He was puffing hard now. They were in some sort of utility tunnel, with broad pipes and conduits just over Horace's head. He thanked the slight breeze that told him the passageway was open at the far end. Their feet slapped noisily against the damp floor as they ran. Halfway along it, they ducked into a small alcove and crouched down.

"Do you think that worked?" Chloe whispered. "Opening the door like that?"

"I don't know. I don't hear anyone."

"Maybe they think we left."

"Maybe."

"But we didn't, did we?" She stared at him hard, eyes dark and steady.

"No. We need to find you first."

"Find me here tomorrow, you mean. I heard what you said, back in the molester soup." She picked a tiny pebble out of the sole of her shoes and tossed it away. "But Horace, so much has happened since you saw me taken. Will that future still come to pass?"

"It will. We're still on that path, even with the golem and everything. I said something would go wrong, didn't I? And it did. I know you're here—you *will be* here. Everything's been so clear. We just have to find you. We have to find that boiler room Gabriel mentioned."

Chloe gave him another long, hard silence. Even here—even now—nothing could stop Chloe from being Chloe. "You don't really know where it is, though."

"Not exactly," Horace admitted. He gestured off to the left. "Somewhere over there."

"And you think they'll take me there tomorrow night."

"I think you can make sure they do."

Chloe barked a laugh. "I am good at pissing people off." She glanced up at the pipes overhead. "Well, if it's a boiler room, we should be able to find it if we follow these pipes."

Now it was Horace's turn to laugh, relieved, as he examined the pipes. Brilliant. "Sometimes I love you, Chloe." The moment the words popped out, Horace almost slapped his hand over his mouth. Instead he scratched his forehead, hiding his face, and looked up again at the pipes as though they fascinated him.

"Well, sometimes, Horace," Chloe said, standing and stretching, "I'm awesome."

Following the pipes, however, turned out to be more difficult than they hoped. At the far end of the tunnel, the pipes branched off. They chose a likely path, but again the pipes branched. The place was a labyrinth of low, stony corridors, cavelike and damp—and rooms beyond rooms beyond rooms. There was just enough light that they could do without their jithandra. Some areas were clearly in more use than others—some lit by red crystals, others dark and cobwebby. Twice they passed crumbling walls that revealed rough-hewn passages leading farther underground, one of which smelled strongly of brimstone. They gave them both a wide berth.

They saw no one. The nest's inhabitants must have been on the floors above now, searching for them. Or chasing after Gabriel, maybe. As for the golem, they heard it overhead once and turned into panicked statues, but the slithering rumble passed by. After several minutes, when they still hadn't found the boiler room, Chloe began making very brief, cautious excursions through some of the walls, hoping to find the boiler room more quickly. They were at an intersection they'd already been to twice before . . . they thought. Chloe eased through a wall up ahead to scout, and just then Horace thought he heard music again, a strange sweet melody. Chloe burst through the wall almost at once, wide-eyed and breathless.

"What happened?" said Horace.

"There's someone here. A girl—the one I told you about, that first night at your house. I was right, she *is* Tan'ji. It's a flute. I heard it upstairs, and now she's down here."

"I heard it too."

"She was with two of those Riven, not a prisoner or any-thing—*with* them. She was playing the flute. There was no way she could've seen me—I was in the wall—but the music was . . . touching me, and then all of a sudden she stopped, and she looked right at me. But there was no way, I'm telling you. My face was barely through." Chloe turned and looked over her shoulder, as though she could see back through that wall. "She's with them, but she didn't say anything or give an alarm when she saw me. What do you think that means?"

"I think we better move."

Two minutes later, they found themselves following a likely looking cluster of pipes into a round hallway, wider than any they had yet encountered this deep. Their footsteps echoed wetly against the damp floor. Up ahead, the curved walls seemed to dead-end, but red light spilled from an opening on the right-hand side. An interstate of pipes ran out of the opening too, spreading in all directions. They slid toward it. Chloe crept to the corner and peeked in.

"Oh, thank god," she said.

The boiler room was narrow and deep. The omnipresent smell of dust was acrid here. Above the doorway, a single red light glowed. The high walls were busy with pipework and utility boxes and covered grates. Pieces of old furniture and some other junk were pushed up against the right-hand wall: a table, a busted-out chair, a shovel, large chunks of machinery. Most prominent of all, though, was the round face of a massive old furnace, protruding from the left-hand wall, as if it were the front of a locomotive buried in stone—the front of the furnace was black and hulking, eight feet high. Soot stains fanned out across the brickwork above.

Horace approached and laid his hand on the surface; it was cold and gritty. He'd seen this kind of furnace before, an old coal-burning boiler. There was one in the basement of his school that, like this one, hadn't been used in years. Mr. Ludwig had taken the class down to see it during a unit on steam power. And this one also had two heavy hatches in the front, both sealed tight—a large one in the center through which coal could be shoveled, and a smaller hatch down low.

Past the boiler, deep in the room, Chloe was checking out three shadowy doorways. She called Horace over. Crude stone bays, black and dank—coal cellars. The cellars were dark and cramped, three feet wide by five feet deep. A heavy wooden door with a small barred window had been added to each bay, turning them into grim prison cells, just as Gabriel had described. The doors were open, the cells empty. They were tall enough for Horace to stand in at the front, but barely big enough for a dog at the rear, where the arched ceiling curved down to the floor.

"This is where they'll bring me?" Chloe asked.

"Let's find out." Horace unholstered the box and took a deep breath. He gathered together all his awareness of where they were and how they had gotten here. He traced all the steps that had taken them to just this place at just this moment. The thoughts formed like a map in his head, a shifting chart of place and purpose and change, and Horace breathed it in and out until he thought he could feel the stars overhead and the dirt underfoot. And then he opened the box.

The first two cells, still open and empty—but the third cell, closed. Horace's heart skipped. He kept his focus and stepped just inside the opening of the third cell, through what would be tomorrow's closed door, and there—*Chloe, sitting cross-legged on the black dirt floor, her head bent down; now looking up toward him, just for a moment; her face sharp but now bending again; her hands blurred and fuzzy along the ground in front of her, all the rest of her solid as stone.*

"You're here. I see you." And with the sight of her, another piece of the puzzle fell together for him. It clicked into place as if it had been there all the time, like the perfect chess move.

He turned to Chloe, wondering how he would begin to explain. She examined the tiny cell she'd be occupying in a day's time. "You found me," she said. She jiggled the handle of the open door. "Am I clear?"

"Yes."

"And what about the other two cells?"

Horace shook his head. "No one's here but you."

"You sound surprised."

"Just thinking it through."

"Okay, so . . ." She faced him and put her hands on her hips. "Why am I not escaping?"

Horace had to proceed cautiously. "Well, obviously you don't have the dragonfly with you, otherwise you'd have walked out of the cell."

"Because Dr. Jericho took it. He'll take it from me tomorrow night." She spoke calmly, but her hands became fists.

"I don't think so."

Chloe ran her tongue across her teeth. "So why let myself be caught? You're going to tell me why, aren't you?"

"Dr. Jericho wouldn't bring you back to the nest with the dragonfly still in your possession. That would be foolish."

Horace held the box in front of him, as if he were presenting evidence. "The only logical conclusion is that tomorrow night, when you go with Dr. Jericho, the dragonfly won't be with you."

Chloe took the dragonfly in hand, rubbing her thumb along its back. It looked like a thoughtless gesture, but of course she was feeling its power, tapping into that connection. Watching her, and feeling now for the box in just the same way, Horace knew how much Chloe was going to hate his answer to the question she was about to ask. He waited in silence. Chloe looked down at the dragonfly and raised her eyebrows. "And so where will the dragonfly be?" she asked, light but wary, like a sword being loosened in the scabbard.

Horace took a deep breath. "Traveling," he said.

—◦◦◦—

CHAPTER THIRTY—THREE

Promises Made

CHLOE STALKED AWAY, THROWING UP HER ARMS. "OH, I KNEW it. No. No, no, no." She kicked viciously at a clump of coal, sending it skittering.

"Chloe, wait. Listen."

Chloe spun back, her face dark, her hands in fists again. "You want to put my dragonfly in that box? Send it traveling through who knows where? No. No way." She stalked into the wall and out again.

"Chloe, be careful." Horace glanced out toward the hallway. How long would it be before one of the Riven—or worse—came in? "Let me explain."

Chloe stopped and swung her arm through one of the walls between the cells. She spun and did it again, but this time let her hand smack against the stone. "Fine. Explain," she spat.

"Okay . . . you will be caught. You will *let* yourself be caught. You won't have the dragonfly with you, but because Dr. Jericho knows you're its Keeper, he'll bring you here and hold you prisoner in this cell. And that's what you want, because a little after three o'clock tomorrow morning, in this cell, the dragonfly will fall out of thin air and land in your lap."

"And you're sure I'll be here."

"You know how it works. You have to trust me."

"Like I did with the message in the toolshed?"

Her words hit him like a jab to the gut. He tried not to show it. "That was different."

Chloe rocked her head back. "I know. I'm sorry. But you're asking a lot. You're asking . . . everything. Remember my dad? When we sent the malkund? Remember the Nevren?"

Dread crept slowly over Horace. The way Chloe's father had collapsed when the malkund was sent through the box— the connection had been broken. For Chloe, sending the dragonfly would be like passing into the Nevren. A Nevren that would last a whole day.

She read the look on his face. "I'll be a zombie. How will I be able to do anything?"

"I don't know," Horace said, refusing to let his thoughts cloud over. This was the path, he was sure of it. "But you do."

"Maybe I just leave the dragonfly here. Hide it someplace safe."

"Seriously?" Horace asked, incredulous. "Is that what you want to do?"

"I don't want to do *any* of this."

"But you do."

Chloe pursed her lips and lowered her head. Her chest rose and fell. She touched the dragonfly to her mouth. "Let me get this straight. We send the dragonfly now; tomorrow I get captured, get locked up, the dragonfly appears, I escape." Horace nodded. "But before any of that happens, we escape from here tonight . . . so that tomorrow night I can return and escape *again*." Her voice dripped with doubt.

Horace rubbed his temples. So hard to keep the path in sight—so many variables. There was something in what Chloe had just said—"*we escape from here tonight.*" But did they?

Did they all?

Cautiously he said, "Look, you're the one piece I really see. All the rest depends on you doing this—if you do it, everything makes sense. What it means is we don't rescue your dad tonight. That happens tomorrow. Why else would you let yourself be brought back?" And as soon as those words came out—"*Why else?*"—he knew.

Chloe held up the dragonfly. "I would return for this. I promise you *that*. Even if my dad was free."

Horace couldn't reply. He knew exactly what kinds of things she would come back for: the dragonfly, her father.

Horace himself.

Chloe gave a deep, impatient sigh. "Check again."

Horace checked again, trying to focus his reeling mind: *Chloe, slumped motionless, waiting; slouched forward, hands on the floor—except* . . . "You're here, and . . . you've written something. There's a message in the dirt." This was it. He squinted and got closer, knowing that the next answer was here. "It's blurry, though. 'As poor'? No . . . 'Ask floor'?"

"What does that mean?"

"I have no idea. I can't make it out; it's shifty. But you're not. You're still clear."

Chloe chewed her lip thoughtfully. "If I decide to do this—and that's a big *if*—it won't be because the choice has already been made, or whatever. It'll be *my* choice, Horace. Okay?"

But Horace wasn't listening. He was looking still at the words Chloe would scratch in the packed black dirt of the third cell, trying to understand them. "Ask door"? But no—no, wait. He turned around, looking back at the massive face of the black boiler. Below the main door, where the coal was shoveled in, there was another door, smaller and square. It opened into a chamber where ashes from the coal above sifted down. And he knew this, knew what the door was called.

Ash door.

Horace hurried over to the boiler, his heart hammering. He knelt down and heaved the ash door open, revealing an opening the size of an oven that ran back into darkness. He took the box in his right hand, stretched out his arms and began to pull himself forward, into the opening, the cold stones pressing his ribs.

"What in god's name are you doing?" Chloe said.

Horace didn't answer. He wriggled forward, pushing the box into the darkness. The space inside was a coffin. It smelled of ancient ash and bitter dust, and even just here in the opening, his panic began to crush him like a giant foot. But all he needed was to get the box inside. All he needed was a glimpse.

He grounded himself again, focusing on the arc of decisions that had brought him here. With a flick of his thumb, he opened the box and looked through. His eyes adjusted to the darkness—*pitch black; black as death; nothing to see, nothing to breathe but darkness choking and crushing; a shape too big for this space, but all the same there was a shape, something there.* Horace groaned, a low, long keen pushing its way out of him.

Chloe knelt beside him. Her voice came to him, muffled by the chamber. "Is something in there?"

Not like this. Not this way. Horace strained to see.

A shoulder; a chest, barely rising; hair, shaggy and gritty—and there—a face, soot stained and staring, eyes empty empty empty—

Horace pushed himself out, tearing the box from the hole, heaving.

"What is it?" Chloe hissed. "What's in there?"

"Me." Horace dropped the word like a slab of concrete. "Me."

"Oh god. Oh god, Horace." Chloe ran a hand through her hair. "Why? Are you hiding?"

He shook his head. "Captured. *He* puts me in there. He'll

take the Fel'Daera from me, I know it. I won't be able to stop him."

Chloe looked confused. "I don't understand—how will he capture you? How do you know?"

"I think I've known it all along, I just . . ."

"But you aren't with me tomorrow night. When do you come back here?"

Horace summoned up the courage to say the words aloud. "I never leave."

Chloe fell back on her haunches, her eyes going wide. "Oh, god. Okay, so now we know. They capture you. You'll be here, and I'll come back. I'll come back and I'll rescue you. That's why I let myself get taken."

"Yes," Horace said. "I knew something was wrong when I saw you surrender and get taken here. I knew I'd come into the nest, that I'd see something that would lead back to that moment, but . . ." He shook his head. "*Knew* isn't the right word. I don't *know* anything. It's more like I was willing to let it happen. I *am* willing. When I saw you in the cell, and you mentioned how we would escape here tonight, I started wondering. And then the message . . . ash door." He looked back at the boiler and let out a sharp laugh. "From your house to here. Ashes to ashes."

"Horace, it doesn't have to happen this way."

"It does."

"No. Let's leave and try again."

"No. This is the path. But now that I see it more clearly I

just . . . I don't know how I'll survive it."

"But you do," said Chloe firmly. "If this really is the way, you will make it. You will make it and I will save you and we will escape. If this is really the way, we'll rescue my dad and maybe we'll destroy this terrible place, once and for all."

"Don't say *if*," he snapped. "This is the way." But what a way. He pressed the Fel'Daera against his chest. The thought of losing it was as unbearable as anything he could imagine, even worse than the ash door.

Chloe moved closer to him, until their faces were a foot apart. "Okay," she said gently. "This is the way." She reached out and cupped one hand around the back of his neck. Her touch was cool, her fingers thin but strong. At her touch— skin on skin, a new sensation—everything that was jangling in him went still, like a rabbit caught on a lawn. "You are the keeper of the Box of Promises, and I trust you. I'll let you send the Alvalaithen through the box. I'm your friend, and I'm here with you. I—" She stumbled here, dropping her head for a moment, but then lifted her eyes back to his. "I have a power too, and I mean to use it. You and me, Horace—together we can outdo any dark thing. We're the good guys. Okay?" She squeezed his neck.

She was ready to send her dragonfly through the box on his word alone. She was ready to walk this terrible path. He thought of how he'd seen her, waiting boldly for Dr. Jericho in the wreckage of her home, knowing she would end up in this horrible place again. "Okay," he said. "But remember where

I'll be. Don't forget me."

"Never." Chloe pulled her hand away. She closed the ash door. She brushed the ash from Horace's chest and arms. She continued to meet his gaze, unembarrassed. "When Mr. Meister told me not to be so brave that I risked not getting out again, I guess he was talking to the wrong person."

Horace laughed a shallow laugh. "Hey," he said, "we're all brave as hell, right?"

"Yes. And now's the time to show it." Chloe reached for the dragonfly. A brief flutter, and it was loose. She rose and waited for Horace to find his feet. Together they returned to the back of the room, to the third cell down.

Chloe looked up at him. "Where will you take me? After we . . . afterward."

"Back to the ladder. You can escape out the side door. I'll go by there first, and if there are any Riven there, I'll lure them away, deeper into the nest. Then you get out."

"When they capture me tomorrow, they'll ask questions. What am I supposed to say?"

"Tell them the truth whenever you can. Stick to the path. And listen: with all this stuff I've been doing with the box just now—and especially with what we're about to do—Dr. Jericho is bound to feel it, twenty-four hours from now. He may come down here tomorrow night to investigate. After the Alvalaithen comes through, sit tight for a few minutes. Play dead. Wait him out. Okay?"

Chloe nodded and glanced at the box, gleaming in

Horace's hands. "Even with what I'm about to do, I sure wouldn't trade you for that thing."

"I don't blame you," Horace said, though of course he wouldn't trade the Fel'Daera for the world, even now.

"You lie." She pushed a hand forward through her short hair. She pointed the dragonfly at him. "Promise me."

"Promise *me*."

She nodded. She laid the dragonfly carefully inside the box. It barely fit, its wingtips grazing the sides.

Horace leaned into the third cell, looking through the box to gauge his aim. The words on the floor were clear now— "ash door." So that the dragonfly wouldn't fall, he laid the box on the floor right atop them, in front of tomorrow Chloe's dark lap. She hadn't moved. "It's three thirteen," Horace said. "Remember the time."

Chloe bit her bottom lip. She gazed down at the Alvalaithen nestled in the box. "Three thirteen. Do it, then."

Horace slid the lid closed. A heavy tingle—the strongest yet, almost painful—coursed up his arms. Chloe let out a soft *unh*, as though she'd been punched. She wrapped her arms around herself and squeezed her shoulders. She sank to the floor. Horace dropped to her side, holstering the box. "It's gone," she moaned. "It's totally gone. I can't feel it. I'm so . . . heavy."

"It's not gone, Chloe. Just traveling. Traveling to you."

"No, no, it isn't anywhere. I would know if it was. It's nowhere in the world right now."

434

Horace knew there was nothing he could say to make this better, so he said the only thing he could. "We have to move. We've been here too long."

Chloe slowly rose. "I can't feel my feet," she muttered.

"You have to walk. Let's go, Chloe. This is the way back to it. But you have to walk."

"Walk," Chloe said, her voice like dirt. "Walk."

He tried to give her back some of the strength she'd given him. Slowly, agonizingly, he led her past the boiler, out into the wet hallway. He would have given almost anything to have Gabriel show up just then. If they were spotted, they were cooked; there was no way Chloe could run. And now worse thoughts came to him. Horace's first trip through the Nevren had almost cut him off permanently from his Tan'ji—dispossessed him. Were they running that risk now? Had he made a terrible mistake? Perhaps the reason no one would stop Chloe from being taken tomorrow night was because . . . there was nothing left to save.

But he'd gotten through that first Nevren, and he remembered how. "Chloe," he said. "You want it back, don't you? The dragonfly? The Alvalaithen?"

"It's gone," she mumbled.

"No, it's not. It's with me. I have the dragonfly." He released her and backed away. He held up a clenched fist. She stumbled but then moved toward him.

"That's not yours," she said. "That's mine. That's me."

"Come and get it." She came on slowly, muttering. It

could barely be called progress, but at least they were moving. They inched on, sticking to the shadows. They saw no one— no Riven, not the mysterious flute girl. They never heard the golem. Once, Chloe seemed to forget what the dragonfly even *was*, but then she remembered, calling for it, and kept after him step by aching step.

When they were nearly at the utility tunnel that led to the ladder, Chloe yanked out her jithandra, bathing them both in its red glow. Alarmed by the sudden light, Horace was faced with the embarrassing prospect of putting it back in her shirt for her. He swung it around between her shoulder blades, dropping it down along her back. But then he froze. "Oh, hell."

The dumindar was still around her neck.

The dumindar couldn't safely go with Chloe or Horace right now, and it would be a shame to lose it. If he'd been thinking more clearly, he would have sent it through the box along with the dragonfly. Now he took it off Chloe, dropping the chain over his own head. Maybe he could find a place to hide it before he was caught. So many turnings, so many things to go wrong. What else had he overlooked?

"It's gone again," Chloe said. "You're taking it again. I'll tell."

"Yes, I'm taking it. Come get it." He started moving forward again. "Here it is, Chloe. You'll have to take it back from me."

At last Horace led Chloe down to the little alcove they'd

hidden in before. She sagged into it, swaying. At the far end was the ladder that led up to the side door through which Chloe would return in less than twenty-four hours.

"Okay, Chloe. This next part, you have to do alone."

"I am alone."

"You're not alone, not yet. I'm here. Horace. Chloe, you have to listen to me. You have to remember."

"I can't remember anything. Everything."

"Remember to tell Mr. Meister, Chloe—we sent the dragonfly through the box."

"The dragonfly. It's gone."

"Not gone—traveling. Tell him that. You're traveling toward each other, you and the dragonfly. You go up the ladder and out. Get away from this place. That's the way back to the Alvalaithen."

"Up and away."

"Yes. And then one last thing." Horace bent in front of her, trying to catch her eye. "The ash door, Chloe. Remember the ash door. Don't forget me."

"The ash door, oh god," said Chloe, her voice breaking. Tears poured from her eyes. "That's so awful. It's so awful. Oh, god."

"Hey, it's okay." Horace reached out and took her hand. It was lifeless and cold, but he held it. "We're going to be okay. Together we can outdo any dark thing, remember?"

"No," said Chloe. Her tears fell from her chin, wetting Horace's arm, and suddenly he was fighting back his own.

"Well," he said. "That's okay. You just have to watch." He pointed down the tunnel, to where the ladder was. "When you see the blue light, go to it. Go up the ladder, and straight out. That's where the dragonfly is. Go to it as fast as you can, okay? But not until you see the blue light."

"Where is it? Someone had it. The blue light has it."

"Yes, good. The blue light, and then what?"

"Go to it. Up and away. That's where the dragonfly is."

"Yes. Up and away." Horace hoped beyond hope that Neptune would be there still, that she would find Chloe and take her far from this place. "Okay now. Wait here. Don't move until you see the blue light." He released her hand. It fell to her side like a dead branch. He turned to go, his throat cable-tight.

"Horace," Chloe said then. Her cheeks shone.

"Yes?" Horace replied, his heart rising. But she said no more.

CHAPTER THIRTY-FOUR

—◦◦◦—

Distractions

HORACE LEFT HER. HE MOVED DOWN THE TUNNEL TOWARD the ladder. Faint voices trickled down through the hole in the floor above. As he suspected, the side exit was being guarded now. The Riven knew someone was still in the nest. Horace removed his jithandra and held it in his fist, hiding its light. He started cautiously up the ladder.

The voices above—two, or three?—spoke the strange language of the Riven. None of them were Dr. Jericho. At the top of the ladder, Horace cautiously stuck his head out and down the hallway toward the side door. In the shadows he spied two Riven, still talking, gesturing with long limbs. They were dressed in human clothing, but their pale hands and faces shone. Their eyes were large, their heads strangely elongated. They hadn't noticed him yet. Quietly, he pulled himself up out of the hole.

Horace gathered his legs beneath himself, ready to spring. From his awkward sprinter's crouch, he held the jithandra in his fist over the hole. Straight ahead was the hallway down which he and Chloe had come earlier, the one where he'd knocked over the metal rods. It looked clear—no lights, no movement, no sound.

Horace opened his fingers, letting the jithandra fall into the hole. It flared to life, falling bright and blue and clean. *Please be looking, Chloe,* he thought. *The blue light.* It clattered to the floor far below, and after a moment it winked out. Had it been enough? Had she seen? Would she remember?

And then a shout from the side door, like a hiss and a crack. He'd been seen. Horace broke into a run, finding his feet even as the Riven tumbled from the hall, their long-fingered hands reaching for him. He tore down the cluttered corridor, his heart wrestling itself high in his chest, his pursuers' heavy footsteps close behind. He managed to yank a rack of musty clothes into their path, slowing them. He ran as though he was sure all of this was going to work.

He barreled out into the room beneath the stage. Behind him, he could hear the Riven catching up again. It was almost completely dark, and he had to grope his way through the cluttered room. He cracked his shin and banged his elbow. The Riven seemed to be having no such troubles; clearly they could see in the dark far better than he could. He knew he would be caught eventually, but he had to put off that moment for as long as possible. If they caught him now, he might be sealed in behind the ash door all day and night, waiting for a Chloe he could not be certain would return. Maybe Chloe hadn't seen the blue light. Maybe she'd been caught.

They were on his heels now, their heavy breaths hissing. And then suddenly, miraculously—gray. A gray that swallowed the world, drowning the sounds of pursuit and replacing them with far-off voices that rose in dismay and fear. Horace collided with something solid, cracking his head hard—a wall, or a column. He pressed himself against it. Gabriel's massive voice rolled into him, winded but full of surprise. "Horace!"

"Gabriel." Horace kept his voice low and clear, knowing Gabriel could hear him. He closed his eyes against the overwhelming endless gray of the humour. "Thank god."

"I was just coming down to find you. Where's Chloe?"

"Gone. You were right; we found her tomorrow night in one of those cells in the boiler room. But for now she's gone—I hope. I helped her escape."

"And what about us?" Gabriel said. "There are Riven in the humour even now."

"I can't tell you what to do." Horace tried to make himself smaller. He heard voices far out in the gray fog, searching. "But I stay. I stay until Chloe returns."

"That is a dangerous plan."

"It's not a plan. It's what happens. I stay."

"Then so will I. Come with me. I'll keep us both safe. I can't keep the humour going forever, but we can find a place to hide."

441

"No," said Horace, pushing away the power of Gabriel's voice and the temptation it offered—to be hidden and safe, to have an ally at his side. "No, I get caught. They catch me."

Horace could almost feel the questions in the air as Gabriel paused. "That's why Chloe returns tomorrow night," Gabriel said. "To rescue you."

"And her father, of course." Horace started to mention the Alvalaithen, but didn't, fearful of how Gabriel might react.

Another pause. "If they catch you, they will take the box."

"I know. And I need to get back to the boiler room first. Something important is happening there tomorrow night. I need to see."

A hand fell on Horace's shoulder, strong and unseen. Horace gasped. But instead of dragging him forward, the hand gave him a friendly squeeze. "Very well, Keeper. Follow me, quickly." Gabriel's hand steered Horace forward. Horace stumbled through the humour, keeping his eyes closed and responding to Gabriel's firm hand and words: "A little left. Now straight on. Now quick, quick." All around them, the voices of the Riven rose and fell. "You're bleeding, by the way," Gabriel said at one point. "Check your head." Horace didn't bother. "We're in the stairwell. There's a wall to your left—feel for it." Horace reached out, scraping his knuckles against a rough surface. "Straight ahead the stairs lead down. Six steps, then a bend, and six more steps. When you reach the bottom, you will be out of the humour. Do what you must. I'll continue to use the staff, to keep the Riven distracted."

"How many are around us now?"

"Six are in the humour right now," said Gabriel. "One of them a Mordin. And the crucible dog is somewhere nearby. The stairs are clear, though."

"The Mordin. It isn't Dr. Jericho, is it?"

"No. If it were, we would not be having this conversation. He is . . . keener than the rest."

"And the golem?"

"It's above, guarding the ground floor. The golem does not act entirely on its own, you know; someone must hold the reins. There is a Tanu one wields, and the golem obeys. Whoever wields that Tanu at the moment—possibly Dr. Jericho—wants to make sure we don't escape. But apparently he is wasting his time."

Again Horace's thoughts flickered back to Chloe, hoping beyond hope she'd gotten away. "If it helps," Horace said, "I didn't see you tomorrow, back at Chloe's house. Neptune and Chloe, yes. But not me or you. I should have told you sooner."

"Thank you, Keeper. I suppose it does help, in the strangest way imaginable." He squeezed Horace's shoulder again. "And . . . there's something I should have told you too. Before we left the Warren tonight, Mr. Meister told me to do what I could to ensure that Chloe would extinguish the crucible."

At first Horace didn't understand. Melding the crucible had been Horace's idea—hadn't it? "But why didn't he just come out and say that to us, if that's what he wanted?"

"I don't know. Perhaps he feared you would not listen to him."

Part of Horace recognized that the old man might have been right about that, but the rest of him flared with anger. "So this whole mission to rescue Chloe's father—it's just an excuse. We're really here to destroy the crucible."

"I did not say that. Mr. Meister wants to see Chloe's father rescued as much as anyone."

"Sure, only because he's worried the Riven will use him to get at Chloe—to get at the Alvalaithen."

"Are his motivations so important, if the end goal is the same?"

And Horace found he had no answer for that. No answer at all.

Abruptly Gabriel's hand fell away. "They are coming. Go now. Believe me when I say I am on your side. Rescuing Chloe's father comes before all else. I'll find you again before Chloe arrives tomorrow night. Go." A warm pressure enveloped Horace's hand—not a touch, but the humour itself, firm and reassuring. And then Gabriel said no more.

Cautiously, Horace began groping his way slowly down the stairs—a simple act made incredibly difficult by the loss of his senses. He took six wary steps down and found the landing. Five more steps, and then the brutal tearing sound that meant he was out of the humour. His senses returned, hitting him like a wall of water. A dim light. Silence. The smell of decay, fresh again.

Horace looked back up the stairs at the humour. He saw . . . nothing. Not a bank of fog or a cloud of smoke, but not the stairs either. There was simply nothing there, not a blackness but a *blankness*, as if his eyes could not conjure sight. Floor, walls, ceiling, yes, but the place between them just did not exist. His eyes slid from one side of the stairwell to the other. He turned away, blinking and rubbing his forehead. His hand came away sticky with blood. He wiped his hands on his pants as he lurched ahead into the gloomy basement.

So Mr. Meister wanted them to extinguish the crucible, destroy the nest. But why not just come out and say it? Why these games? He tried not to let himself get distracted. The path was all that mattered now, no matter what the Warden wanted. Fifteen minutes had passed since the sending of the dragonfly, and surely by this time tomorrow night Chloe would have escaped and rescued Horace from the boiler. But Horace wanted to be sure. He hoped Gabriel was right when he said the golem was upstairs—now if only he knew where Dr. Jericho was.

Horace wandered the tunnels cautiously, trying to find his way. Before long, something caught his ears: music, sweeping notes that rose and fell like a breeze. The flute. The sound of it seemed to somehow reach for him. He remembered what Chloe said—that the flute girl had seen her when she shouldn't have.

Horace ran. He ran from the music as best he could. Was it growing fainter, or louder? He thought he was leaving it behind, but the basement's labyrinth made everything uncertain. He took a left turn and then a right, and almost immediately he spotted the round passageway that led to the boiler room. He swung into it, his feet slapping across the damp floor. As he ran, the flute grew fainter, then faded away completely. He slowed and caught his breath, listening hard. Silence.

At the tunnel's end, Horace peeked into the boiler room. It was as empty as they'd left it. The black face of the coal boiler loomed on the left-hand wall, heavy and mute. He double-checked the time—3:32. Surely he and Chloe would be gone by this time tomorrow. Horace took out the box. He grounded himself with reminders of how he'd gotten here, focusing hard on Chloe and Gabriel and even Neptune, intersecting their lines of action with his own. So many turnings: but Horace held them all in his mind. He flicked open the lid—*a sweeping curtain of motion across everything, curling and swaying, as though he were looking through a great black flame or flood.* Horace stared, confused, trying to see through this strange new interference. Had something gone wrong? Was the box malfunctioning?

Horace spun, looking deeper into the room, trying to be quick. Relief flooded him: *the ash door, open; soot scattered across the floor.* And then, farther down the wall—*a soot-covered Horace, almost unrecognizable; crawling, legs trailing, groping along the wall toward the coal cellars.* Chloe had done it, then, she'd freed him.

446

Horace walked deeper into the room, still staring. *The cells stark and shadowy, the third door down still shut tight.* Horace looked into the third cell, stepping inside, heart pounding. *Empty; no Chloe, no dragonfly; the words on the floor scuffed and blurry, but still there.* So Chloe was free too. But why were the words blurry now? And where was she? He spun, still searching.

Another figure against the opposite wall, a great surprise—*Gabriel, both hands clasping the Staff of Obro; black flame coursing from the tip of the staff, the humour itself casting its curtain over everything; Gabriel's eyes, wide open and black, as black as ink.*

So this was the interference Horace was seeing—it was the humour! The Fel'Daera saw through it as if the humour were nothing more than smoke. But Horace's heart sank at the sight of the Warden. If Gabriel was here, perhaps he had been the one to free Horace, and Chloe was somewhere else. But where? And why was Gabriel using the staff? What danger was he protecting them from?

Full of dread, Horace moved the box along the gaze of Gabriel's black eyes, as smooth and featureless as marbles. What were they seeing?

Horace peered through the veil of the humour. His skin went cold. Ten feet up from Gabriel—*Dr. Jericho, many-headed and crouching low, like a nest of snakes, groping savagely through the humour toward Gabriel, searching half blind.* But that was not what chilled him. *Just inside the doorway, a beast like a Mordin—or not a Mordin, something far larger and far worse—crouched on all fours into the shape of a bear, a cat, a great hound, skull flat and long, eyes bulging, neck arched painfully— all beneath the cruel weight of the crucible buried in its shoulders, like an upturned grasping hand, and in the center of that shape, a sharpened oval of light burning, white-hot and almost blinding.* Horace could hardly bear to lay his eyes on that light. Even from the here and now, he felt the pull of the crucible. And this creature was its Keeper.

All around the crucible dog, a cluster of Riven, creeping closer, pale and staring blind in the humour. Horace examined them. There were three men, too, shambling mindlessly, and one of them stood out—*tall and muscular, standing on the edge of the group, eyes closed, lips curled in dismay.* Chloe's father.

Horace snapped the box closed. He'd had it open too long, and yet he still hadn't seen enough. He still hadn't seen Chloe. He shut his eyes, forcing himself to think.

Chloe would be there. She had to be. This was the moment toward which everything was rushing, wasn't it? Twenty-four hours from now, in this very room—Gabriel, Horace, Dr. Jericho, the crucible dog, Chloe's father, all together. But why? Horace felt helpless, unable to do anything but watch. If only there were something he could do—

But maybe there was. One small thing. Horace flicked open the box with a twist of his thumb. *The smoke of the humour, gone now; Horace, lying half in and half out of the first open cell, his eyes and mouth wide.* Horace stepped closer, looking down at himself—*his future self, lying half inside the first cell, looking right up at the box now, as if knowing it was there. Lips moving. Hands out.*

Counting. Waiting.

And Horace knew why. With his free hand, he took the dumindar from around his neck. He laid it in the open box. He looked through the glass at his own outstretched fingers, his own mouth counting out the seconds.

It was 3:33 . . . but that wasn't good enough. He fished in his pocket and pulled out the watch Mr. Meister had given him. The second hand was just crossing the five. He leaned into the dark cell, positioning the box over tomorrow's open hands. "Be there," Horace said aloud, as if his future self could hear him. The second hand swept across the watch face, and at precisely 3:33:33, Horace slammed the box closed. Electricity coursed up his arms, and he let out a long, staggering breath.

And then, from behind him, a silky voice spoke—high and lilting and sinister. "Oh, my dear Tinker," it said. "Now *that* was rather fascinating."

CHAPTER THIRTY—FIVE

The Willed Path

HORACE WHEELED TOWARD THE DOOR OF THE BOILER ROOM. A towering shape was peeling itself away from the wall, as if the room was coming alive. The shape began to resolve, began to color itself something other than brick and pipe and stone—white skin, black suit, leering face. "Fascinating indeed," Dr. Jericho said, striding forward and bending over Horace.

Horace resisted the urge to hide the box behind his back. Instead he stood and held it in both hands, owning it, practically daring the thin man to take it from him. "Took you long enough to find me," he said. He could be brave for this. He would be brave. No more running.

Dr. Jericho's eyes lingered first over the box, then over Horace's face. "But worth the wait, it seems. My, how you've changed. I sensed the aberration in you, that first day I saw you in the street—but the Fel'Daera! Who could have fore-seen it? And now you've cozied up to the Wardens. How quaint." He paused and reached into his pocket. "Oh! Before I forget. I found something that truly does belong to you. A key to the castle, I believe." He held out his hand, revealing Horace's jithandra.

"That won't work for you," Horace said.

"Won't it? Pity." Dr. Jericho crushed the jithandra in his massive hand. The crystal shattered with a powdery crunch. He let the dust trickle to the floor and sniffed his palm. "Smells like secret handshake. I suppose every child's play-house must have one."

"This place isn't so great either, you know."

Dr. Jericho looked around, sighing. "It is rather awful. But since my work here is nearly finished, thanks to you, I won't have to endure it much longer. I hardly imagined it would happen like this, though. This evening has been a bouquet of surprises. Gabriel here among us again, with his fabulous toy. And the girl, of course. Where has she gone?"

"I don't know what you're talking about," Horace said, trying not to be startled that the Mordin knew who Gabriel was.

"Your little friend. The girl with the dragonfly pendant. Chloe."

Horace grimaced at the sound of her name on the Mor-din's lips. "She's dead. She died in the fire you started."

"Oh, I doubt that. I doubt that very much. To whom,

then, are you sending presents through the Fel'Daera? 'Be there,' you said."

Dr. Jericho wasn't believing his lies. Horace remembered the advice he'd given to Chloe: *Tell the truth whenever possible.* "Myself. I sent it to myself."

Dr. Jericho's slitted eyes widened. He broke into a long, tinkling laugh that was like spiders on Horace's skin. "Yourself? Well, that's not going to work out, is it? I'm here now, and I'll be right here again tomorrow. You, however, will not. But tell me, what was it you hoped to send to . . . yourself?"

"A dumindar."

"A dumindar!" He shook his head and clicked his tongue. "How fascinating. Too bad you did not keep it. Perhaps you hoped that tomorrow it would buy you time. But today, sadly, there is nothing between us. Nothing to prevent me from taking the Fel'Daera from you."

"Why bother? The box is useless without me."

"Which is why I allow you to go on breathing. It's true: you are—dare I say it?—precious to me. All you need now is a little education. Perhaps then I will allow you to keep the box."

"Education?"

"To open your eyes to things the Wardens would keep hidden. To open your mind to the possibility that they do not tell you everything."

Horace had been warned that the Riven would try to turn him. "I'm already open to that possibility. But at least they don't tell me lies." Even as the words came out of him, his conversation with Gabriel bubbled into his thoughts.

"Omitting the truth is its own kind of lie. I can do for you what I did for the last Keeper of the Fel'Daera. I can teach you the full truth, and let you make your own decisions. They will not be difficult decisions to make, once you know everything. Certainly its last Keeper did not find them hard."

"The last Keeper." That tugged at Horace, but it was just a taunt. Dr. Jericho wanted to keep him uneasy, keep him wondering about everything he didn't know. Horace swallowed his anger and his curiosity. "Well," he said steadily, "it sounds like the last Keeper was a lot more lame than me."

Dr. Jericho frowned. "How amusing," he said. "Nonetheless, it seems we have two shared concerns: the welfare of the Fel'Daera, and the welfare of yourself. In the interest of both, you will hand the instrument over to me now. No struggle. No messy resistance. No—" He rolled his eyes, searching for a word. He leaned down and bared his teeth, his mouth as wide as a wolf's. "No *savagery.*" He held out his horrible hand.

"Take it. I won't stop you, but I won't hand it over."

"An odd distinction." Dr. Jericho reached out. The moment the Mordin's grotesque fingers touched the box, Horace's stomach bucked and groaned, threatened to empty itself. He clutched at the box and thought for a moment that he would not be able to let it go. But this was the moment he'd known was coming, the moment that led back to Chloe, to her father, to the crucible and freedom for everyone. The way back to the box again. He forced his fingers to loosen. The box slipped free, gone but not gone. Taken unwillingly. He gritted his teeth.

Dr. Jericho chuckled. "Do you feel it? I do. A delicious sensation. I have taken that which wishes to belong to you. Feel how it pulls until it tears, like muscle from the bone."

Horace could sense Dr. Jericho turning the Fel'Daera over, examining it. He felt it come open, close—open, close. Like little cuts inside his chest.

"It hurts, I know," Dr. Jericho said. "Are we reconsidering? As I said, things don't have to be this way."

"Maybe they do."

"So stubborn. Peculiar, since you don't even know what you fight for."

"I know my path."

"You do not," the thin man said, running a nail across the silver sun emblem on the side of the box. "You are a Tinker, and a child, and a neophyte too. You keep the company of thieves. In short, you are a fool who does not comprehend the ruin toward which he marches."

"What ruin?" Horace asked, and immediately wished he hadn't. He shouldn't even be listening to the Mordin in the first place.

"You have pledged yourself to a misguided cause," Dr. Jericho said, his voice suddenly light and reasonable. "The Wardens will use you to achieve their own desires, not yours."

Mr. Meister. The crucible. "You don't know my desires."

"Ah, but I do. All Keepers have the same desire—to be bound to their instruments forever. But the Wardens will hide the truth from you until it is too late. They would rather see the Tanu destroyed—even the Fel'Daera!—than to have them fall into the wrong hands."

More than anything else the Mordin could have said, this made Horace listen. The Fel'Daera, destroyed. For a moment Horace doubted, wondering why he was here, risking all of this. He wondered what other secrets the Wardens still kept close.

But then the Mordin held out his gruesome hand, his four-knuckled fingers wrapped around the Fel'Daera, tiny in his poisonous grip. The sight filled Horace with rage.

"The wrong hands," Horace said. "I couldn't have said it better myself." And he swiped at the Fel'Daera, hoping to knock it free, hardly daring to think about that sick pit in his brain that imagined the Fel'Daera falling to the floor and shattering on the stone.

But the thin man snatched the box away, holding it high. He studied Horace with his piercing black eyes. "I see," he said thoughtfully. "But there is no need for that. Reconsider your allegiance, and the Fel'Daera will be yours again."

"It's still mine. It will always be mine, no matter where you take it. I can feel it even now."

"I'm counting on it. The sensation will never leave you— can you imagine what a life it would be? It will call to you, just as it calls to me. But because of the bond, your experience will be a great deal more . . . painful than mine."

But Horace was no longer listening. A sudden dizzying realization had taken hold of him when the Mordin said those words: *"just as it calls to me."* Horace struggled not to panic as he reasoned through this disastrous new thought. Everything depended upon Dr. Jericho responding to the Fel'Daera's call tomorrow night out at Chloe's house, but would the thin man even listen to that call now?

Why would Dr. Jericho go searching for what he already possessed?

Horace thought quickly. "I knew this would happen, you know."

The thin man raised an eyebrow. "Did you?"

"When I saw myself here in this room tomorrow night, the box was missing."

"You are either lying or a fool. The Fel'Daera never shows itself."

Horace tried not to look surprised—how did the Mordin know that? "I used the box earlier tonight, before we got here. You'll feel it calling to you tomorrow, twenty hours or so from now. You'll feel it the way you felt it that night at that park, when you chased me."

Dr. Jericho's lip curled briefly into a snarl—remembering that night, maybe. He straightened, sliding the box into an inner pocket of his jacket. He said exactly what Horace himself had been thinking: "Surely you don't think I would chase the Fel'Daera in the past when I have it already, right now,

456

here in my pocket?"

"You might, considering what I saw."

"Which is?"

"The dragonfly girl. Chloe."

Dr. Jericho inhaled sharply through his nose but said nothing.

As he spoke, Horace tried to hold the entire sequence of events in his head, every turn and every player. He laid this present moment against the past, against the future, hoping beyond hope that they aligned. "You were right. She's not dead. She'll be back in her burned-down house tonight." Horace swallowed and took the leap: "And you'll be there, too."

Dr. Jericho stepped back and sat on the table. He crossed his spidery legs and gazed at Horace, clearly deep in thought. His tiny black eyes shimmered. "Oh, I've missed this. Wrestling with that exquisite question: *Why would the Keeper of the Fel'Daera tell me the future?* And is that future true?" He shivered dramatically. "Such a thrill. There's nothing like it." He sat in silence for several seconds. "I confess I am a curious cat. We shall see if events play out as you claim."

Horace said nothing, and Dr. Jericho stood. "There's no point asking you what you saw transpiring here tomorrow night. I do wonder, though, what must be pouring through your head right now, as I contemplate the terms of your imprisonment." He swept to Horace's side, bending to peer into the first coal cellar. "You say you sent the . . . dumindar . . . to yourself. Here in the first cell, is that right? You claim you saw

457

yourself, but you lied about seeing the box." He shook his head at Horace, scolding. "Was it your wish to be found, and then be locked up in this cell?"

Horace would not let himself answer. No step seemed safe. So many threads, so easy to break. And how many had he left carelessly loose, despite all his efforts?

The Mordin shook his head. "But no, no, no. We can't keep you here. These cells are not for honored guests." Dr. Jericho put his long hand on Horace's shoulder, steering him along the wall toward the boiler. Horace went with him, letting it happen. This was the turning he'd been taking all night—the willed path. The box called to him, so near, struggling and imprisoned, drowning just as he was about to drown. "Ordinarily, I would hold you in the belly of the golem, but I cannot spare the golem just now, not with Gabriel still on the loose—careless of me not to have brought a second. But I believe I have other accommodations that will suit you just fine."

"Deeper in the nest?" Horace said, as if he didn't know.

"Oh no, no need for that." Dr. Jericho stopped before the boiler, turning Horace to face it. He bent low and unlatched the ash door. "I'm sure you'll be very comfortable . . . right in here," he said, and then his hideous fingers tightened across Horace's shoulder. He began to push.

Horace let his knees buckle under the pressure. *Come for me, Chloe,* he thought, bending before the dark, yawning door. *Come for us all.*

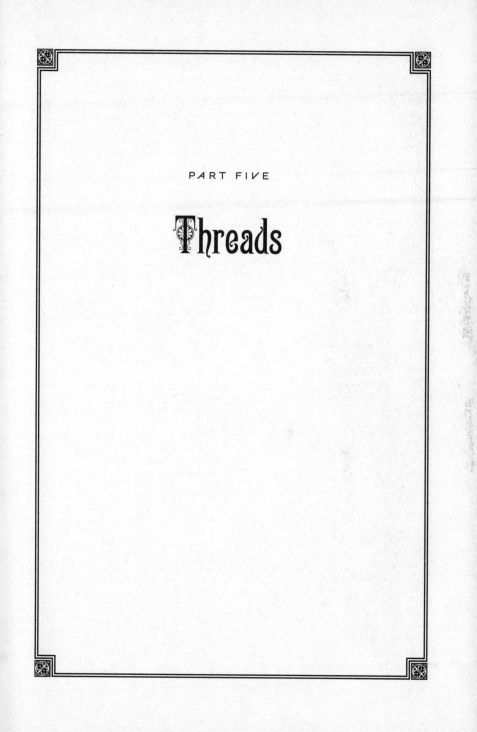

PART FIVE

Threads

——◦◦◦——

CHAPTER THIRTY–SIX

Chloe Without

The blue light. Up and away.

Chloe was cold. Everything was cold. So cold and so dark and that was all, all alone. There was something about the blue light—the blue light was the way back to herself, except there was no light here. And what was blue anyway? Little boy blue, the big blue sea, the moon but moonlight wasn't blue. Moonlight wasn't light at all, it was stolen, and everything was stolen, everything—

Movement. Light in the dark. Down the corridor—a falling star or moon, a streaking flash of yes of blue. Horace blue, the little boy. He stole the dragonfly. He took it up and away.

"Horace," said Chloe. She began to move. The falling blue light was gone already, but she saw where it came from. She went toward the spot, up and away. Hand over foot, up the ladder. A dark, empty hall beyond and then a door, right there, and the word door meant out. Out and away. She pushed through it, and then everything got big—or maybe she got small. There was fresh air, a breeze, and sky above, and somewhere out here was the dragonfly. Horace said so.

Something fell from the sky. Another falling star, or maybe the sky was falling. The sky was a girl, tall and strong. *"Chloe,"* said the sky girl. *"Where is everyone?"*

"Who are you?" Chloe asked. "Do you have it? He said it was here."

"It's me—Neptune. What's wrong with you, Chloe? What happened?"

"I had something," she said. "I lost it. Are you it? But you're not blue, you're black. Miss Mary Mack. Why can't I see you?"

"The Alvalaithen—where is it? Is it destroyed?"

"Yes. He put it in the box and now it's gone."

"The box? Horace sent it through the box?"

"Yes, yes, the promise box. He promised me."

"Come on," said the girl, and the girl grabbed her hand. She pulled her forward—Chloe swung her feet to keep from falling. So heavy. "Leave me alone. I wanted to be alone. I wanted the—" What did she want?

"The dragonfly."

"Where is the dragonfly? It flew down into the box. Down, down. I want to lie down."

"Soon, Chloe, soon."

"Sooner or later a moon elevator," Chloe sang. "Is that

how you got here? Is that where you're from?" Maybe that's where the dragonfly flew.

They stopped. They stood beneath a yellow light—not blue, not the moon—and when Chloe asked why, the sky girl said, *No more talking,* but you had to talk to say that.

Now darkness and sound. Rest and motion. The earth turned beneath her. How far would they take her? This was too far, this was not the plan. But there was no way to get back this lost thing because she was the lost thing. Light sliding over her. Now on her feet again, arms holding her up, ups and downs. More darkness. A door that wasn't a door but made her cry.

Voices spilled over her, one and then another. Or were they all one voice, all talking and no listening?

Must give her the grulna. Danger us.

We must the Alvalaithen. Dispossessed. The Box of Promises. Chloe.

So much noise. So much nonsense. She could make no sense too. She opened her mouth. "Ashes, ashes. I'm so cold. What is the grulna?"

It has never been done so young. Must be done. As far as Chloe goes so strong so wrong-headed headstrong. She must not go this route too late. Without she might die. Voices pouring over her, angry and sad.

"Die, die, die," Chloe said, and then everything was quiet black, empty and empty, and she dreamed of a walk along a gleaming floor of lace, and the holes in the lace were holes in the universe, and the white paths between grew wide and warm, and you could go anywhere along those paths if you could go at all, if you were you at all, and then the sun rose into her waiting face, and she ate fire.

Chloe opened her eyes to fluttering wings overhead. Round red walls curved above her. Her head throbbed and her throat burned. A hard nugget of heat blazed in her gut. She reached for the dragonfly in her mind, and instead of that cruel, amputated absence, she found an easy curve that caught her and steered her back. It was a prison, but a tender one, and she lay there in silence, riding her thoughts as they soared out and coasted back again, passing always back into herself. Herself and the little sun that burned inside her now.

"I'm Chloe," she said aloud.

"Indeed you are."

She turned her head toward the voice. Mr. Meister. Of course . . . this was his office. She was in the Great Burrow. Chloe sat up, surprised to discover that she could move her body. "Was I asleep?"

"Only for mere minutes. One does not sleep with the grulna inside."

Chloe laid a hand on her belly, half expecting to feel the heat from inside her radiating through her skin. "The grulna. That's what you gave me?"

"Yes," Mr. Meister said. "We saved your life, perhaps. And in time, it seems, the lives of others as well."

"I feel . . . like the tin man."

He smiled thinly. "That is an apt description of the effects of the grulna. You feel shackled, yes? Confined? But powerful too. Like a fortress."

Chloe bent all her limbs. They worked like puppet arms. "What is this thing? What did you do to me?"

"The grulna is a temporary fix for your predicament. It gives you no power, of course, but it is an artificial substitute for the connection that has been lost."

"A substitute. You've got to be kidding."

"Hardly. One might say that when you are cut off from your Tan'ji, you are a leaking vessel, doomed to fail. The grulna seals those leaks for a time, makes you self-contained. A poor substitute, yes, but your identity is intact. Your mind can function again."

Chloe felt her chest, rubbed her throat. She swallowed painfully. "It's dangerous, though. You and Mrs. Hapsteade were arguing about it."

"If you are given the grulna again, you will die," he said, and then waved off the words as if that was neither here nor there. "I know you have questions, Chloe, but please understand, I have many questions of my own. Though Neptune has told us much already, we must know everything that happened in the nest tonight."

"Must you?" Chloe lay back down. Questions of his own, he said. But all that mattered was that she get back to the nest, back to the Alvalaithen. Back to Horace, her father. Gabriel too. Everything depended upon her now, and this foreign rock of fire that fueled her. "Tell me how long this grulna thing will last. Tell me what'll happen then."

"It will last a full day, at the very best. If the effects of the grulna wear off before the Alvalaithen returns, you will be dispossessed."

"What time is it now?"

"A quarter till five in the morning."

Five o'clock. Her own words came back to her, her last sight of the dragonfly: *Three thirteen. Do it, then.* "A full day, at best—what does that mean? Do I have a full day or not?"

"I am sorry to say you have what you have. It must be enough." Mr. Meister leaned forward, his glasses glinting in the light. "Tell me what happened, Chloe. Why did Horace send the Alvalaithen through the box?"

The Alvalaithen. Chloe fiddled with the empty cord around her neck. There was an absence there, but the fire in her belly burned hotter than that now. And the sad, fragile look on Mr. Meister's face—what a nervous man he was. How funny to be worried when you sat back here in the safety of the Warren while others risked everything. "He had to send it. He saw me get captured, so he sent the dragonfly forward for me. He's waiting in the nest. I promised I would come back, and I will."

"He is safe?"

"I'll save him."

"And what of the Fel'Daera?"

"What did I just say?"

468

Mr. Meister steepled his fingers in front of his face. "I took the grulna once myself, you know. It saved my life. But an interesting side effect of the grulna is that it strips us down to those essentials of our personality most likely to pull us through. Our strongest traits are thrown into high— sometimes intolerable—relief."

"Let me guess. You were unbearably mysterious. Or no— insufferably manipulative." The old man scowled deeply, but his irritation hardly touched her. "It doesn't matter. It's Horace who's suffering now. He stayed behind so I could get away. He's probably been captured already."

"Is that so? I wish I knew more of it."

"Why? You won't do anything about it. All you can offer in return is advice, and I'm fresh out of space to keep it."

Mr. Meister stood. "Is that it, then? Nothing you can tell me? Nothing I can do to help?"

Chloe shrugged. "You can leave me alone. And when it's time for me to go back, you can call me a cab."

He left without another word. Let him be angry. What a waste—he wasn't going anywhere it would be needed.

Chloe lay there but could not sleep. Time passed—how quickly, she did not know, here underground. Eventually she got up and puttered around Mr. Meister's office for a while, then walked to the back of the Great Burrow and sat at the top of the stone steps that led into the abyss below. She dangled her feet over the edge. She leaned out as far as she dared, wondering how far she would fall. She felt no impatience, no regret, no real worry. She pulled a mint from her pocket and cracked it between her teeth. She hardly tasted it. She spit a chunk of it out into the black, watched it fall and fade.

Later she walked back toward Vithra's Eye, and on the way there she heard people talking in the little doba where she'd bathed and slept after the fire. Inside she found Mr. Meister and Mrs. Hapsteade sitting with Neptune and the boy with glasses . . . Brian. All four of them were looking at her; Neptune must have sensed her coming. Brian was wearing a black T-shirt that made his pale skin look even paler. It said PLEASE SEND HELP.

"What time is it?" Chloe asked.

"Just after noon," Neptune said.

Seven hours! It hadn't felt even a fraction as long. "Get me when it's time."

"We will find you, Keeper," said Mr. Meister.

"It feels like I should be hungry, or thirsty. But I'm not."

"That is the grulna. And it is just as well, since it is better if you neither eat nor drink while the grulna lasts."

"I had a mint. I think I might have another."

"Certainly you will do as you please, Keeper. I assume you're not asking my permission."

"No." As she turned to go, Chloe hesitated. "This was Ingrid's doba, right?"

"That's right," Mrs. Hapsteade replied, just as Mr. Meister said, "It is."

"Does she play the flute?" Every face went blank with

shock. When no one spoke, she went on. "I guess she does. I doubt she'll be coming back. She looked right at home when I saw her in the nest."

Mr. Meister shot to his feet so abruptly that his chair skittered back and toppled. Mrs. Hapsteade reached out and laid a hand on his wrist. "You saw Ingrid?" she said.

"I saw someone with a flute. She plays it, and sees me when she shouldn't. She was with the Riven last night. They looked . . . friendly."

Every eye was on her, waiting for her to say more, but Chloe was bored with this talk, bored even with the old man's dismay. She left them. She went back to the water and sat, watching the owls quietly carve the darkness. She ate mint after mint until they were gone.

She was just thinking she might walk through the center of Vithra's Eye—find out what lay at the heart of the Nevren—when they came for her. It felt like only an hour had passed. Mrs. Hapsteade and Neptune approached, looking solemn. Mrs. Hapsteade took Chloe's jithandra from her without a word of explanation.

"Why are you doing that?" Chloe asked, not really bothered but wanting to make the woman explain.

"This should not fall into the hands of the Riven. Return, and it'll be yours again."

"You don't think I can do this."

"Since you've explained nothing to us, I'm in no position to judge. I don't understand exactly what it is you're attempting to do. All I know is the Fel'Daera has asked for your trust again, and you seem willing to give it."

"Not the Fel'Daera," Chloe said. "Horace."

"Neptune will take you across the water." Mrs. Hapsteade tucked the jithandra into the pocket of her apron and stubbed her fists into her hips, glowering down at Chloe. "I will say this. If I had to choose one of us to throw into the dangerous unknown, it would be you."

Chloe studied her. "I'm going to take that as a compliment," she said.

"You'll take it with a grain of salt, if I know the grulna," Mrs. Hapsteade replied, turning to walk away.

"And *do* you?" Chloe called out. "Do you know it?"

Mrs. Hapsteade stopped and spoke back over her shoulder. "I know things I wish you never had to learn, but learn you will. Go back now. Find your father. Find your friends. Bring everyone back to us. When the stone of your fear returns to you—and I hope it does—may it be light." She swept into motion again, swift and effortless, sliding back toward the Great Burrow.

Neptune stood quietly by Vithra's Eye, waiting, looking out over the water. Something about her calmness pulled Chloe forward. "I had to leave, you know," Chloe said, not even sure why she was saying it.

"I know. And they had to stay."

"I'll get them out."

Neptune sighed, a sweet and thoughtful sound. "You'll get each other out."

Chloe looked at her. The girl really was pretty, in a way. Too bad her face only went from blank to blanker. "So tell me," Chloe said. "Who's Ingrid?"

Neptune stiffened. "It's not my place to tell you about Ingrid."

"Oh, well, god forbid you should forget your place."

The girl gave Chloe a sharp glance. So she did know how to get angry, after all. "Ingrid is—was—a Warden. She turned, about a year ago."

"She went over to the other side, you mean. But why?"

"I don't know. Gabriel might have some idea. The two of them were . . . close."

"And why did Mr. Meister get all pissy when I brought her up?"

Another sigh, this one sad. "He still believes in her."

"Why?"

She shrugged. "He always believes in us." Neptune pulled out her jithandra, richly violet, and approached the water's edge. "It's time. Let's go."

CHLOE FOLLOWED NEPTUNE across the lake. The Nevren didn't touch her at all. Before she knew it, they were in Beck's cab, and the trip back to her house happened in a flash. The streetlights passed by rhythmically, like heartbeats. No one spoke a word. In the cab, Beck's eyes kept finding Chloe in the mirror, but Chloe found she had nothing to say. Let them stare. Neither of them was going back to the nest. Neither of them could.

They arrived at the wreckage of her home, and at one thirty Chloe stepped out of the cab. Behind her, Neptune rustled into the cloudless sky without a word. The moon Chloe couldn't see the night before now sat like a sickle over the train yard. She let the heat of the grulna drive her forward, up into the ashes of her house. Ashes everywhere. Ashes for everyone. Perhaps she herself would be full of ashes soon.

She went to the ruined hallway and waited, standing perhaps in her own yesterday's footsteps. Within moments, a shadow slid along the back property line. Despite everything—despite the grulna—a brief twinge of fear darted through her as Dr. Jericho approached. He was so huge, and now she was encountering him without the dragonfly.

He began to whistle as he came near, a piercing tune that stabbed at her ears. She focused instead on the sizzle of the grulna. The Mordin grinned down at her from his great height. He bent and inhaled deeply, smelling her, his eyes sliding closed. "Oh, how lovely to find you here, my dear," he said, showing his teeth, his voice a song. "I heard a rumor you were dead."

CHAPTER THIRTY-SEVEN

Captured

HORACE CONCENTRATED ON HIS BREATHING, DEEP AND SLOW. He fought back the panic that made his heart pound and turned his skin to broken glass.

The floor of the boiler was hard and cold and gritty. Inches above his face, a heavy steel grate spanned the length of the space, separating the ash bin from the main boiler chamber. Whenever he brushed against the grate, little spills of ash trickled down through the holes in the grate and onto his clenched eyes, across his sealed lips, into his nose. He couldn't sit up, not even close. He could stretch out—the chamber was exactly as long as his body—and he could roll over, but it was so narrow that he could not turn around. Not that he wanted to—it was better that his face was next to the ash door, where at least he could sip in the occasional thin breath of fresh air.

When Dr. Jericho first swung the heavy door shut, sealing Horace inside the cold boiler, he buried Horace in a horror so crushing and so pure and so complete—obliterating every other thought and memory and sense of being—that Horace was not completely sure he had not died in that moment. He suspected that at least a part of him had. But he was breathing still. He felt his ribs expand as air filled his lungs. So he just breathed. Deep and slow.

For a while . . . how long? . . . he kept himself tuned to the box. The box had been taken, yes—violated—and it might be lost to him forever, but this was not like the Nevren. The connection was still intact. He could point to the Fel'Daera's location precisely, moving with Dr. Jericho. The movement gave Horace an outlet, a gap through which he could imagine the world outside, imagine a trickle of fresh air—even if that air was foul. He clung desperately to the connection for what felt like days. Gradually, though, the box settled and went still, somewhere below.

Nothing changed for a very long time. Or maybe there was no such thing as time. No light, no easy breath. He was so thirsty. His chest felt like a knotted fist, clutching at a struggling swarm of blades. He told himself bones don't need water, withered lungs don't need air. Eventually, lying there very still in the dark, Horace began to imagine that he was traveling, just as the dragonfly was traveling now, through some lightless space outside of time, hurtling toward the future. He let this idea take root in him, like a steady black river flowing, endless and unchanging. He tried to lose his sense of waiting, his knowledge that hours were passing. Instead he clung only to this moment suspended. When panic rose, boiling under his skin, Horace let it drown in the void. When doubts about the plan crept in—the perfection with which everything had to happen, the fact that he hadn't seen Chloe through the box—he told himself there was no plan, no expectation. When the thought came to him that he might remain trapped here forever, he let the black river flow over the very idea, drowning it. In this river, this traveling, there was no forever. Only this instant.

At last—an hour? a month?—the Fel'Daera began to move. It moved up from below, and overhead, and out. It left the nest, sliding swiftly away. Horace kept his breathing deep and slow, not letting hope bloom. Dr. Jericho was going out to meet Chloe. Of course he was. There was no need to hope because he *knew*. Horace tracked the box's movement as it was taken far out, as it came to a rest at last. He played the scene from the Fel'Daera in his head, hoping—believing—that it was coming to life even now: Dr. Jericho and Chloe in the ashes of her house.

If he was right, it must now be approaching two o'clock Sunday morning. He'd been imprisoned in the ash pit for twenty-two hours. It had felt timeless, endless, but now that he attached a number to it, a new guilt and worry struck him like ice against his heart—his mother. His father. He was missing. The note he'd written for them should have arrived, but would they have seen it? The thought that they might be at the Mazzoleni Academy even now, searching for him, made him sick and weary and rootless.

A low, booming voice broke into his concentration, startling him so badly that he banged his knees into the grate overhead. Soot showered into his face. Horace yelped—a rusty croak—and then began to cry, hearing his own name, coming from everywhere. Gabriel, calling out to him. Horace opened his eyes, not into blackness but into the endless slate gray of the humour, invisible but blindingly bright.

"Horace," said Gabriel again. "Are you all right?"

"Gabriel," he croaked, not caring that Gabriel was seeing his tears. "You made it."

Clanging at the door now, heavy and dull. "Let me get you out of here."

"No, don't do that," Horace heard himself say. "I have to stay. Chloe rescues me." He had to believe it. He did believe it.

It took just a beat for Gabriel to understand. "This is what the Fel'Daera showed you. And the Fel'Daera itself—they've taken it from you."

"Yes. I knew they would."

"What about the Alvalaithen?"

Horace's tears doubled, running down the sides of his face. "It's gone. Or not gone, but . . ."

Gabriel's voice turned grave. "You severed the bond," he said. "You sent the Alvalaithen through the box. That's the real reason Chloe comes back—for the dragonfly."

Not just the dragonfly, Horace wanted to say. *Her father, me, the crucible.* But the reasons didn't matter. He bent an arm painfully and wiped the gritty wetness from his face. "She comes back," he said firmly. "She's coming back soon—I can feel Dr. Jericho out there waiting for her. And when she returns, everything happens. We do what we came here to do."

"I'm not judging you, Keeper."

"Then help me."

"Tell me what to do."

"You'll have to distract Dr. Jericho, one last time. The dragonfly comes through at three thirteen, and he can't be anywhere near the boiler room. But by three thirty, you have to be down here. I saw you, protecting us from the crucible. We'll all be here—me and you, the crucible dog, Dr. Jericho, Chloe's father."

"And Chloe."

Horace gave a single resolute nod, willing himself to believe it. "Yes."

Gabriel sighed deeply. He sounded exhausted. And no wonder—how had he managed to survive the day unscathed? "I will distract Dr. Jericho, and then I will come to you. And then we will get Chloe's father out of here."

"Yes," Horace said. "And—" A sprinkle of soot fell into his mouth. The boiler was trembling. And not just the boiler but the room, a vast rattling roar, growing louder.

The golem.

Horace cried out. The clamor rose all around and then was sliced by the sound of the humour being ripped away. A deafening impact rocked the boiler door, shaking the floor beneath him, dumping a snowfall of soot and ash. Gabriel's muffled shout was cut off abruptly. Silence, and then another slow roll of thunder, the dragging of a titan's chain.

Gabriel was taken. Wrong—all wrong. An impossible thing. As the golem poured into the hallway, taking whatever was left of Gabriel with it, Horace scrambled for answers, for a way that this new turning could still lead to the end he'd seen. But how could it? Everything was so precariously balanced, each piece so dependent upon the other—and without Gabriel the plan could not succeed. When the crucible arrived, he and Chloe stood no chance at all.

Horace lay there in the dark, his shock chilling slowly into despair. He reached out toward the box, waiting for it to move. Waiting for Dr. Jericho to turn back toward the nest. And for the first time in that long terrible day, Horace hoped that when the thin man did return, Chloe would not be with him.

——w——

Chloe Within

"STILL ALIVE," SAID CHLOE, GAZING STEADILY UP INTO DR. Jericho's grinning face. "Sorry about that."

"No apologies necessary—you are well. And now here you are, home at last."

Chloe looked at the ruin of her house all around them. "Yes, here I am. Were you expecting me?"

"I was expecting the possibility." Dr. Jericho reached out and tugged lightly at the empty cord around Chloe's neck. She didn't flinch, even as his hideous finger grazed her skin. "You've lost a friend, I believe."

Dimly, it came to Chloe that she'd planned for none of this. She'd given no thought to what she was going to say or do. She felt no panic, though—just the burn of the grulna making her bold, making her strong, carving out a place for her and her alone in the world. A lie came to her as easily as breath. "It's not lost. It was taken from me."

"Is that so? By whom, I wonder."

"The neighborhood watch. You know."

"Ah . . . the Wardens."

"Is that what they call themselves?"

Dr. Jericho considered her for a moment longer. Abruptly he straightened and snapped his gaze across the street toward the train yard. Chloe understood. The box. Horace. Dr. Jericho was sensing the Fel'Daera from the night before. She rode her steely calm like a boat through rapids, pretending not to notice. She was beyond that fear, outside it. But maybe . . . maybe there was no reason to pretend. Abruptly she remembered Horace telling her to speak the truth as much as possible. She stayed with that thought, drifting in its current.

"Rather unfortunate about your house," Dr. Jericho said after a moment, turning back to her. "Did the Wardens do this, too?"

He was on to her, testing her. "No. You did."

The thin man spread his arms and laughed, a tinkling, grating trill. "No secrets between friends, then. Yes, a bit too much zeal on my part, perhaps. But you've been a long frustration for me. And now here we are at last, face-to-face, but without the one conversation piece that really matters. Whatever will we talk about?"

"We could talk about my father."

"And why would we do that?"

"Or we could talk about Horace instead."

"I don't believe I've had the pleasure."

"He's the Keeper of the Fel'Daera. You're holding him and my father prisoner, back at the nest."

"Horace, Keeper of the Fel'Daera. How fitting. And you say I have him?"

"You do. He was here yesterday. Watching this moment right now. You just felt him." She pointed over into the train yard. "He saw me talking to you. He watched you take me back to the nest—"

"Goodness, what a notion."

"—and he followed us there. That's how he found the nest in the first place. He's a prisoner there, right?"

Chloe spoke calmly, untroubled by the tightrope she walked. One wrong word—one step too deep into the truth— could pull everything to pieces, yet she could hardly feel the nerves that should have been jangling. As she waited, two more Mordin began moving in from the shadows. She found herself sneering at them.

Dr. Jericho spoke, his voice like wire. "What gives you the idea that we have this . . . Horace?"

The truth was no longer enough. Chloe shifted gears smoothly. "The Wardens know you captured Horace last night. They blamed me, because of what Horace saw." She gestured back and forth between herself and the thin man. "This moment that's happening right now, I mean. This conversation. They asked me why I planned to meet with you. They accused me of being a spy. A traitor. They took the . . .

dragonfly. Funny—I wouldn't be here now if they hadn't."
The other Mordin came up close and stood on either side.
They too reeked of brimstone. Chloe had the fleeting illusion that her house was on fire again, that she was in it. She
squeezed her eyes shut, brief and hard, blinking away the
memories.

Dr. Jericho hummed. "Yes, amusing. Tell me, how did
they manage to take your plaything from you, given your
power? I ask only as a matter of professional curiosity."

The real Chloe—*but I am Chloe*, part of her objected—
would never have revealed such a thing. "They found a way,"
she said. "I can't imagine why I'd share it with you."

A thin, toothy smile. "Nor can I. And you're here now,
after all, because . . . ?"

"I want to see my father. And who knows? While I'm at
it, I might try to figure out who my friends really are." She
examined her hands. Was that too much?

Dr. Jericho laughed. "And why should your friendship
matter to me now, without the dragonfly?"

"Because," Chloe said, pointing in the general direction
of the Mazzoleni Academy and the Warren, "the dragonfly is
several miles that way, three hundred feet underground. It's
with them. In their stronghold. And I know the way in."

Dr. Jericho straightened. He and the other Mordin began
speaking in their strange, slashing language. They kept glancing down at Chloe.

"Come," Dr. Jericho said to her at last. "We will go to the

484

nest now. As the Fel'Daera so wisely foretold."

Chloe followed, her feet moving of their own accord. Crunchy ash gave way to soft grass. As they slid across the lawn, Dr. Jericho reached out to her, offering her an open palm. "Will you take my hand, my dear?"

Without a word, Chloe reached up. Dr. Jericho's massive hand swallowed her arm nearly to the elbow, his flesh as smooth as plastic.

As they walked, Dr. Jericho glanced back now and again. "Your friend. I feel him watching us from the past. Very clever, I must say. Imagine—I'm leading him to the nest this very moment. He's quite resourceful."

"Wouldn't you be too, if you could see the future?"

"An excellent point. Let me rephrase: quite resourceful, for a Tinker."

They crossed the bridge over the tracks and proceeded along the exact route Chloe remembered from the night before. She tried not to look around for Neptune, even though she knew the Warden was out there somewhere, watching and following. But that didn't matter. Chloe was alone. She clung to the one thing that did matter: very likely, she had not fooled the Mordin. She'd stick to her story until it was long dead, but until then she had to assume he didn't believe a word.

They were nearing the scrap yard next to the nest when a scalding pain tore through her gut. She doubled over, stumbling. Dr. Jericho's hand tightened on her arm. "Are you quite all right?"

"Fine." But she wasn't fine, she knew.

The grulna was wearing off.

Chloe walked on. She could not feel her feet, but they seemed to be working. Her mind was going foggy, but she clung to names—*Horace, Dad, Gabriel*—letting them run grooves in her mind, holding her to the present. They descended some steps. The air grew cooler. They passed through a door. Others were here, moving figures, white skinned and lanky. Was this the nest? What was the nest? Sharp jabs of memory pricked her, like arrows out of darkness. A hole in the floor. Horace's jithandra, falling to the foot of the ladder. The room beneath the stage. Voices like wet traffic. Darkness and decay. The elevator shaft. This was the nest.

Dr. Jericho stopped. Another figure joined them: another Mordin. No, not one figure—two. But the second was much smaller. And blond.

Ingrid.

She and Chloe locked eyes, and even through her haze Chloe felt a fear that she had never felt before. The Riven were one thing—foreign, monstrous—but here was just a girl, perhaps five years older than Chloe herself. Chloe tried to imagine what could have driven her to this place, how she could have chosen these creatures as her allies. Had she lost someone too? Ingrid's gaze gave away nothing, steady and measuring and cold.

The new Mordin spoke to Dr. Jericho in their sliding,

hissing language. Dr. Jericho replied in English, apparently wanting Chloe to hear. "Really? Was he harmed? And his Tan'ji?" Chloe scraped at every word, desperate for understanding. Was he talking about Horace? After a minute or so, Dr. Jericho swung into motion again, dragging Chloe after him. Ingrid and the other Mordin followed. More corridors, more stairs, until at last they stopped in front of a door. Here at last, thank god . . . but no, this was not the boiler room.

The other Mordin passed something to Dr. Jericho, and Dr. Jericho slipped it onto his finger—a black ring with a misshapen scarlet stone. He opened the door and pushed Chloe through, telling the other two to wait outside. He stepped in beside Chloe and closed the door behind.

"Shall I show you something?" he asked politely.

"There's not much to see," Chloe said, looking around. The room was high and narrow—tall walls of brick on either side, a knobby stone wall at the back. It was empty but for a table beside the door. And on that table was a long stick, gray with silver ends—

The Staff of Obro.

Chloe cringed as Dr. Jericho picked up the staff. "Have you seen this instrument before?" the Mordin said.

The truth. The truth unless you mustn't. "It belongs to one of the Wardens. He blinds people with it."

"So I understand. A blind Warden who blinds others. A lovely irony, don't you think?"

"What did you do with him? Did you kill him?"

"Kill? What would be the use of that? No, he is here with us." Dr. Jericho laid the staff down. He lifted the hand with the scarlet ring and spoke a word. At once the rear wall—stubbled and pitted, cobblestoned and gray—began to move. It shifted and rippled. Not a wall after all, no, but a living ocean of stone. The golem rumbled, spreading wide, opening a pit deep into itself. Where it opened up, a form began to emerge: a dark head, and now broad shoulders, a sagging torso. Gabriel, buried to the waist, both arms drawn painfully back, hands and hips and legs held thick in that crushing grip.

"The golem found him while I was away," Dr. Jericho said. "We interrupt his first lesson now, a bit of conditioning. Imagine, to be so close to your instrument but to know that it is not yours unless we allow it. To know that you may hold it again—feel its *power* again—but only under our terms. Gabriel learns even now. Don't you, Gabriel?"

Gabriel lifted his head, his sightless eyes drifting over them both. Did Gabriel know she was here? Did she want him to know? And how did Dr. Jericho know Gabriel's name? Her throat and gut were a twisting ribbon of fire, but at last she found her voice. Gabriel's head cocked sharply as she spoke. "Is this your plan for Horace, too? And for me?"

"That depends upon you," Dr. Jericho told her. "Like you say, you are considering your allegiances already, yes?" Gabriel's head lifted high with these words. Chloe could practically see the intensity of his attention. "As you know, we do not take these measures where they are not needed. But of course, there is the matter of the dragonfly. We cannot . . . motivate you with what we do not yet possess."

"I don't need motivation. And I told you, I can get it back."

Gabriel spoke, his voice like brambles. "You won't get the dragonfly back, traitor," he said. "We knew you would turn on us. I never trusted you."

Chloe dodged the words like thrown knives. Surely Gabriel had caught the gist of her story and was feeding into it, helping her. Surely he didn't believe she was a traitor.

"You just keep telling yourself that," she said, knowing she had to follow her plan through, no matter what Gabriel thought.

"Fascinating," Dr. Jericho said, looking from one to the other. "But there's no need for this. Everything that needs to be said has been heard. Gabriel, you and I will speak more later." Again he raised his hand, and the golem began to draw Gabriel's limp body back into itself—arms and belly first, then shoulders, swallowing him like quicksand. At the last moment Gabriel opened his lips as if to speak, but the golem poured into his mouth. The golem became a wall once more, a tomb with Gabriel inside, alive—his Tan'ji just feet from him. Chloe felt a distant fury raging, but she could do nothing. And she was fading fast.

Dr. Jericho removed the scarlet ring, leaving it on the table. He ushered her from the room, speaking briefly to Ingrid and the Mordin outside, this time in his own language. Chloe wondered if Ingrid could possibly understand that foul tongue. And then Ingrid looked up at Dr. Jericho and said four quiet words: "Thank you. Good luck." Dr. Jericho nodded and pushed Chloe onward. Chloe looked back at Ingrid and opened her mouth to speak, not even sure why she was doing it.

"I heard a rumor," she said. "Apparently the old man still believes in you."

Ingrid blinked at her, her face slack with surprise. Dr. Jericho grabbed Chloe roughly by the shoulder and dragged her away.

They walked through shadows and light, down a flight of stairs. Dr. Jericho chattered as they went—the Wardens, the ignorance of intruders, the obedience of the golem, the disarray of these upper levels, the patrol of the crucible. He said nothing about Ingrid. Chloe could hardly follow his long train of talk. She needed to stop, needed to sit, needed to nurse her cramping belly. She needed to forget, but she couldn't forget, because forgetting was . . . something. Gabriel. Horace. Dad. The dragonfly.

Water under her feet now, slapping and thin. Echoes and a tunnel, curving walls. "Here we are," said Dr. Jericho. Pipes and grates. Coal and soot and iron. Ashes to ashes. The boiler room. Yes . . . Horace. They were here, almost here. What time was it?

Chloe let her eyes sweep around the room, let them drift across the boiler without stopping. "What are we doing here?" Could Horace hear her? Was he there, was he safe, was he real?

"This is our destination." Dr. Jericho bowed and gestured toward the three coal cellars. "Shall I let you choose?"

This was the place. This was where she had to be. She mustn't let her relief or her hopes shine through even for a second. She moved toward the cells, stopping in front of the first one.

Dr. Jericho followed. "It seems you've chosen already."

Chloe clung to a thin thread of memory. He was testing her—why? "I don't understand." She let her confusion speak for the doubt he seemed to want to see in her. She swallowed hard, letting the dying fire of the grulna paint her scared, nervous, desperate. She stepped away from the first cell. The third cell—that's where she needed to be.

Dr. Jericho pulled a glinting brown oval from his jacket. For a moment Chloe could not place it. But of course—just what she should have expected: the Fel'Daera.

"Aren't you quite the collector?" she said, trying to keep her voice steady. "So where is he?"

"He is not here, as you can see. But perhaps you knew that already. One can learn much from the Fel'Daera, yes? One can watch, and learn, and—if one is of a mind to—*change* the future the box promises. Just as I am changing it now."

"I don't understand."

"Shall I share with you your mistakes?"

Mistakes? "There's nothing to mistake. I'm not trying anything."

"Come now. Did you imagine I would not recognize the

scent of the grulna? Even now I smell it, fading away inside you."

The grulna, eating its own fire. Leaving her hollow. "What's a grulna?" she managed. Her panic was a distant, jeering crowd, but growing louder.

"And your dragonfly—taken from you, yes. Taken from you and sent *back* to you, through the Fel'Daera."

Taken, yes. It was oh so gone, its absence rising in her, filling the space the grulna was leaving behind, pulling her down into despair. Dr. Jericho knew everything. He had Horace. He had her father. The box and the staff and Gabriel. He would have the dragonfly too.

"No. No, they stole it," she insisted, but her words sounded weak. "Kept it for themselves. I can show you where."

Dr. Jericho shook his head. "No, I think not. I saw dear Horace send the dragonfly with my own eyes last night, right here." He pointed a long finger at the first dark cell. "Right where he expects you to be waiting for it, just over an hour from now."

"No, he—" Something hitched inside Chloe, kicked her to life. *Right here. The first cell.* But that wasn't right—was this another trick? "Horace betrayed me," she said, choking back a giddy hope and sticking instead to her lie. Was it a lie? But everyone lied—that was a promise. "He called me a liar and a spy and made them turn on me. He took my dragonfly to keep for himself. And that's . . . that's why I want to turn on *them.*"

"Such sweet words. But they fool no one. When your Tan'ji arrives, you will not be here. *I* will." He stepped down to the third cell, pushing the door open wide. "You will be in here. You will feel the dragonfly's arrival, two doors down. So close. You will feel me take hold of it, just as Gabriel felt me a moment ago. Just as Horace feels me now." He held the box in the air. "And afterward, perhaps, we shall talk. We all four shall have a nice talk, you and Horace and Gabriel and I."

Chloe rubbed her burning throat. She could hardly dare to hope. He was so clever, so slick, a step ahead of her all night long. But not this time. He thought he knew where and when the dragonfly would arrive, but he was wrong. Somehow he'd gotten it wrong. *"Shall I share with you your mistakes?"*

She dared not pretend to surrender. She stepped forward, pulling at his long sleeves. "You have to believe me. Horace is no friend of mine. And not Gabriel, either. You heard him. The dragonfly is with the Wardens."

His eyes narrowed to slits. "Why do you persist?"

"Because it's true." *True, true, true. True blue.* There was only one true thing, and it was coming to her here. You had to lie to get to the truth. "Don't lock me up, please," she croaked.

Dr. Jericho laid one long forefinger sideways across her aching throat, almost casually, and shoved her back hard into the third cell. She fell, skinning the heel of her hand against the wall. She clutched at her throat, gagging. Ashes. Behind this door, this promise. She would turn to ashes and burn back to life.

"Perhaps you will believe me, Tinker, when I say I hope you will survive the next hour," Dr. Jericho said. "There is much we might do for each other." He swung the door closed. The heavy *snick* of a lock rang out.

She heard him leave. She dragged herself to her knees. She combed though the gritty dust on the floor. Ashes. She couldn't forget. What were the words? Ashes to ashes, behind this door. She scratched at the floor, her fingers trembling, digging so hard into the packed dirt and coal dust that she heard, but did not feel, her nails tearing like splintered wood. She wrote but could not read. Dark behind this door.

She couldn't find any air. Something was caught in her throat, something on fire and alive and wriggling, a bristling ball. She choked, retching, and the spines digging into the sides of her throat tore their way out, spilling out onto the ground. She was empty now, empty and beyond cold. She felt nothing but the dying motion of her own atoms, spinning down into stillness, and she was a falling star growing dim, collapsing on itself, shrinking into the smallest thing imaginable, and after that there was nothing.

CHAPTER THIRTY—NINE

Convergences

HORACE WAS DEEP IN THE DARK OF SOME HORRID COUSIN OF sleep. He was so deep that when he felt Dr. Jericho enter the room, the Fel'Daera with him, he barely stirred. He clung to a thin thread of hope. Too many things had gone wrong, too many threads had been torn from his hands. He thought he could hear the Mordin talking. He heard another voice, too, but could not make out words. He wondered briefly who it was but banished the thought. That was for the future to reveal. When the future became the present, all his uncertainties would fall away. There would be no wondering—only action.

Suddenly the Fel'Daera was close, so close. Dr. Jericho's savage whisper came to him in the dark. Horace tried not to listen, tried not to feel.

"All your fortunes," the Mordin hissed, "are mine."

Horace pressed his hands over his ears. The box moved away, and he crushed his thoughts into a single point. He tried to think of nothing, be nothing. He tried to fear nothing because there was no fear. He lay there for another minute, another hour, another lifetime. And as the box continued to move, he forgot his body, going as far from everything as it was possible to be, becoming and believing in nothing but a single endless refrain: *death, death, death, death.*

HERE. HERE THEN.

Here she was, yes, flesh and breath and blood. A heartbeat. Alive. She curled her hand, a hand that a moment ago had been empty and lifeless—but no longer. Alive and whole, yes. She curled her hand around what lay in her palm, this traveler, this orbiting bit of herself come home. She knew herself, knew her name, knew she was complete again. She knew what had come back to her after oh so long.

Chloe.

Chloe and the dragonfly.

Chloe took a deep, painful, beautiful breath. The Alvalaithen had returned. She sat in the dim cell and held it tightly in her hand, feeling nothing but its presence, letting it lift her slowly to life, back to herself. Chloe Oliver. Keeper of the Alvalaithen. Her skin, and the cold grit of stone beneath her legs. Her lungs, and the scent of damp and soot.

She was in the nest. In the boiler room, in the third cell down. Beside her lay a crumpled, ruined ball of black, like a spiny seedpod. She didn't need that anymore. The dragonfly was here now, and she pressed it between her palms. The tips of her fingers stung, tender and raw. Why were they . . . ? Of course. Nails scratching into the packed and gritty floor. She looked down. Words in the dirt before her. Her words. ASH DOOR.

Horace.

It all poured back to her, filling her with purpose. Dr. Jericho. The nest. Her father. That's what she was here for, here in the third cell down.

She heard noises outside. Stealthy footsteps. Through the little barred window up high, she saw shadow and light moving. She dropped the dragonfly onto the floor between her legs without thinking, hiding it with her hands. She hung her head. She sensed but did not see a towering shape, leaning against the other side of the door—Dr. Jericho, peering in and down at her. Chloe froze, barely breathing, letting her hands hang dead over the Alvalaithen.

Horace had warned her that Dr. Jericho might show up like this, investigating. All the work Horace had done with the Fel'Daera at this time last night had drawn the Mordin here now. *"Play dead,"* Horace had said. And so Chloe went on feigning absence and emptiness—painful because at last she was anything but empty. And then Dr. Jericho inhaled sharply and pushed away. She heard him lope across the room, no longer trying to be quiet. His footsteps receded down the hall outside.

Once they'd faded to silence, she waited for another minute or two and then got onto her knees. She sipped at the dragonfly, going just barely thin, letting its powerful song rise to a whisper, a faint whistling wind and nothing more. So hard not to pull on the Alvalaithen with everything she had, to become electric with its power. But she just needed enough to get through this wooden door—and thank god wood was easy.

She pushed her face through the door. It tugged at her, snagging her—the price she paid for not going fully thin—but it didn't hurt. The boiler room was empty. No sound. No smell of brimstone. She crept out of the cell, the earth beneath her a great sea upon which she skated like a bug. Oh, how she'd missed this, even that fear. Once free, she forced herself to unplug from the dragonfly.

The boiler doors were closed tight. She hurried over and hunkered down in front of the ash door. She yanked the thick black handle back. The latch gave way with a resonant *thunk*, and from inside, a hollow cry rang out. Chloe heaved the thick door open. A dirty hand groped out of the black, grasping at the opening. Then another. Now Horace's face, almost unrecognizable—glazed and streaked with ashes. He reached out toward her, though she wasn't even sure he was seeing her. He blinked and blinked, holding one hand in front of his eyes.

"Don't." His voice was gravelly and weak. "Don't."

"Horace, it's me. Chloe."

"Can't move."

She grabbed him by the arm and heaved. He was so big. How had he even fit in there? He slid out and fell to the floor, groaning, in a small avalanche of soot. He got painfully to his feet, but his legs gave way. He collapsed again. He sucked mouthful after mouthful of air, eyes crazed and darting.

"Horace." Chloe knelt beside him. "Horace, are you okay?" She leaned in close, trying to make him see her. At last his breathing eased. He coughed. His eyes slowly focused, the wild glaze dimming gradually from them.

"Chloe."

"Yes, Chloe."

Horace coughed and spat. "You made it."

"I almost didn't, but I did. We both did."

"He came in here just a few minutes ago. The Mordin."

"Yes, just like you said he might. But he's gone now."

"What time is it?"

Chloe stared. "You're asking *me*?"

"Sorry, I . . . had to let go of it in there. Time, I mean." Horace fished in his pocket and pulled out a watch, saying, "It must be about three twenty-five." He glanced at the watch and held it out to Chloe. It was 3:24.

Kind of amazing, really. "And that's why you're you," Chloe said, shaking her head.

Horace looked up at the ceiling as if searching. "He has the box. I can feel him."

"I know. But not for long."

"He'll be coming back soon. And when he does, the

crucible dog and the rest will be with him. I saw it." He flexed his legs, grimacing. "And I saw your dad, too, Chloe, he—he's still with the crucible."

Dad. Here with the crucible. The rage that had been kept from her these last long hours rose out of nowhere, beginning to fill her, sure and comforting. "So it's happening. This is when we do it."

Horace laughed drily, making Chloe's anger flare. He said, "Whatever it is you think we can do, we can't. Gabriel—"

"I know." She told Horace what she'd seen. Horace scrunched his eyes and pressed his cheek into his shoulder as she described the golem holding Gabriel prisoner. "But it's okay. We'll be okay."

"Are you crazy?" Horace said. "We can't resist the crucible without Gabriel. You were there last time, under the elevator."

Chloe recalled the pull of that awful green light. Part of her wanted to face it again, to fight it back, to prove she could withstand it. But she also knew that not a bone in her body had resisted last time. She realized her foot was tapping. She forced it to stop. "How clear was Gabriel when you saw him in the box?"

"Clear," Horace said firmly. "I could even see a kind of curtain because of the humour, but I could see through it."

God, the box was a freaky thing. "So he'll get here. He'll escape and he'll get here."

Horace gazed up at her, his eyes warm and shining clean in his dingy face. "You saw him, trapped—do you think that's possible?"

Chloe considered Gabriel's horrible prison and the terrible strength of the golem. "No," she said. "But our lives are full of the impossible, remember?" Horace smiled, but what she didn't say—couldn't say, not yet—was that it didn't matter if the box was right. There were things she could try, things that might save them all, even without Gabriel here. If only she could find the courage. She looked down at her feet, feeling the vast earth beneath her.

Horace's eyes went suddenly dim, far away. "He's moving fast. Dr. Jericho. I feel the Fel'Daera." He pointed up into the ceiling, his hand sliding. "God, Chloe, he knows I can feel exactly where he is because of the box, and *he doesn't even care*. Maybe he knows what we've done. Maybe he's the one who knows everything."

Chloe remembered thinking the exact same thing, but she knew that wasn't right. It couldn't be. "No, he doesn't know everything. He said something about my mistakes, and then I remember thinking *he* made a mistake, too." Chloe pressed her fingers against her forehead, trying to think. "Wait . . . the first cell. He told me he saw you send the dragonfly, but he pointed to the first cell. Not the third. Was he just messing with me?"

"The first—oh!" Horace's face glowed with understanding. He sat up. "The dumindar. He saw me sending it, but he must've thought it was the Alvalaithen."

The dumindar. Chloe looked stupidly down at her chest. "Wait, what?"

"I took the dumindar from you last night. And then I sent

501

it to myself, right down there inside the first cell. After I left you. Dr. Jericho saw me and asked me what I was sending. I told him the truth."

Chloe clenched her jaw, crushing back a laugh. "But he didn't believe you. He thinks it's the Alvalaithen."

"Yes, and it means he doesn't know the Alvalaithen already arrived. He'll come down here expecting it to show up, but he'll be too late."

"He did make a mistake. I knew it."

"Yes." But immediately Horace sagged again, the light going out of his eyes. "It doesn't matter, though. My mistakes were bigger. I saw Gabriel, but he's imprisoned. And I didn't see you, but here you are."

Chloe leaned forward. "What did you say?"

"I didn't see you in this moment that's about to happen. I saw everyone but you."

"Horace . . . ," she began, but let the words fade. What was wrong with her? All her willingness, her bravery, her anger at everything Dr. Jericho had done to her and her family, her friends—all that, and she was still afraid. Afraid to make the one promise that might help put an end to this long day and night, to make sense of what Horace had seen. She was still so afraid of showing any fear. But Horace was her friend. Her great friend. At least she could offer Horace something. "I think I know why you didn't see me," she said.

"Why?"

"I'll be under."

502

"Under what?"

"You'll have to see it. Just trust me. Trust the Fel'Daera."

Abruptly, Horace cocked his head up at the ceiling. "He just dropped onto the level above us. It's almost three thirty—everything's happening. The dumindar will come through in a few minutes, and then he'll know he's been tricked. Whatever you come up with, it'll have to be before then."

Chloe nodded, her will kindling inside her, churning and familiar. Horace's presence, even his doubt, was firm and comforting, not at all heavy. She reached out her hand to him, stretched her pointer finger toward him. Horace gave her a thin smile and stretched up toward her, pointing. "May yours be light, Chloe."

She furrowed her brow in mock confusion. "Everyone keeps saying that. Fear is the stone, et cetera. Why a stone? Why not a pillow?"

Horace grinned weakly. "Fear is the pillow. May yours be fluffy."

"Fear is the eggplant. May yours be purple." Hissing, choked-back laughter bubbled from them both, rich and welcome.

And then Horace's eyes slid past her toward the door. His laughing face went slack with shock. "Holy crap," he said.

CHAPTER FORTY

Logical Outcomes

HORACE WAS STILL LAUGHING, HIS STIFF BACK COMPLAINING at the effort, when he saw the doorway to the boiler room disappear. He understood at once what it meant, and astonishment swept down his face even as hope swelled giddily inside him. "Holy crap," he said again, and a moment later the humour buried him whole.

"Horace," came Gabriel's voice, breathless and everywhere. "Chloe. Dr. Jericho is coming. He's behind me. And the rest—the crucible dog too."

"We know," Horace said. He heard Chloe's voice, dim and rubbery. "Take the humour down."

A tearing. Light returning. Gabriel stood before them—clothes torn, his neck bruised purple and black. His chest heaved, and his body was bent with exhaustion.

"You're *here*," Horace said. Was it possible? Could it be

that everything the Fel'Daera had revealed was about to come true?

"I saw you trapped," Chloe said briskly, squaring up to Gabriel. "How did you escape?"

"I didn't. I was released."

"By whom?" Chloe insisted.

"A . . . friend. A former friend."

Horace expected Chloe to bristle at that, but instead she seemed to soften. Understanding filled her face. "Ingrid."

Gabriel nodded once.

"Who is Ingrid?" Horace asked. The name sounded familiar. "What's going on?"

"The flute girl," Chloe said, still watching Gabriel closely. "Former Warden. Traitor. But apparently she and Gabriel still have a . . . thing."

"There is no *thing*," Gabriel said. "She acted alone, and I won't guess at her reasons."

"She just called off the golem and said 'Have a nice day'?"

"Clearly not. She freed me and told me to leave the nest. But obviously I haven't done that."

"Do we trust him?" Chloe asked Horace.

"Do we have a choice?"

Chloe stepped close to Gabriel. "Listen. Don't argue. When the crucible comes, you shield Horace. But when you feel me start to emerge, you pull the humour away. Understand?"

Doubt creased Gabriel face. "Emerge?"

"Don't screw this up," she said, and spun to Horace. "Where will the crucible dog be?"

"Right there, right inside the door."

"In how long?"

Horace tried to summon times from his sightings the night before. "Two minutes? But Dr. Jericho—" He felt the box turning the corner at the end of the corridor. "He's nearly here."

Before the words were even out, Chloe began sinking.

Sinking into the ground.

Wonder and horror raced across Horace's skin. "What are you doing?"

"I'm fixing it. I'm following the future you saw, Horace. This is why you didn't see me, my part of how it happens." The stone swallowed her knees, her waist, her shoulders and slid up her throat. "Two minutes," she said, and she took a deep breath. She closed her eyes, and then she was gone.

Gabriel's milky blue gaze floated over Horace. "Did you know she could do that?"

Horace shook his head. "She always said she couldn't."

"Times are changing. Do you know what happens next?"

"I think . . . I think we're about to be brave."

Heavy footsteps in the hall, and then Dr. Jericho knifed into the boiler room. The box was with him, inside his jacket, burning like a beacon. The Mordin's sharp eyes darted here and there, taking in Horace, Gabriel, the open ash door, the third cell still locked tight. He straightened, gathering his limbs and his face, becoming elegant and professorial. "I had hoped we could settle this reasonably, but I see now I was wrong."

"That's not surprising, is it?" Horace said. The box was so close now, its presence almost overpowering.

The Mordin ignored him, turning to Gabriel. "Your escape—it's come at a curiously bad time. I wonder how you managed it."

"The golem was inattentive."

"The golem does not know inattention. It only knows obedience. Was it the girl?"

Gabriel said nothing, and after a long, considering look, the Mordin tipped his eyes down at the floor, frowning at the stone beneath his feet. Horace felt a chill, but then Dr. Jericho glanced at the door. "The crucible is coming. When it arrives, I will let it take you down. The two of you, and Chloe too." He paused and sliced the air with his hand. "*Hypnotize* you, if you like."

Now Horace heard it—footsteps and voices far down the hall. He thought he saw the faintest glimmer of green light dancing along the wall outside the door. Chloe had been under for a full minute. Horace peeked into his pocket at his watch: it was three seconds past 3:32. Ninety seconds until the dumindar would arrive. His mind began counting.

Dr. Jericho, watching, laughed. "Still thinking to collect your package when it arrives? Even with Gabriel's help, you could not stop me from taking the dragonfly now." He spread his arms wide. "Blind me, maim me, deafen me—I can feel the Fel'Daera from the other side like I can feel the ground beneath my feet. Still," he said, turning toward Gabriel, "I'm afraid I cannot allow you to rain on this particular parade." He sprang, slamming Gabriel against the wall and pinning him there.

"May I borrow this, young man?" Dr. Jericho sneered, laying his hand on the Staff of Obro. The smell of brimstone was strong now. The hallway was a shifting tunnel of green light. Horace counted: *thirty-four, thirty-five, thirty-six*. Dr. Jericho, so arrogant—so sure he was a step ahead, sure everything was a lie. What would he do with the truth?

"Chloe's already gone," Horace called out. "The dragonfly arrived and she's gone."

"Arrived? Already? Oh I doubt that very much."

"Twenty minutes ago. Didn't you feel it?"

Dr. Jericho looked sharply back at him, a trickle of doubt—finally—leaking from his face. Gabriel twisted free of the Mordin's grip. As he rolled away, the magnificent green light of the crucible swept across the walls, filling the room. It washed over Horace like a dream, promising another world, another way of being. Horace wanted to be there, in the light. He sat forward, reaching, trying to get to it. He saw a great shape deep in the light, stepping into the room on all fours. And then the humour roared to life.

Gray. Senselessness and solitude. Horace pushed himself back against the wall, his head clearing. He remembered the dumindar and began to feel his way along the wall toward the first cell. Noises all around, cries and movement. A mighty roar—Dr. Jericho, or the Keeper of the crucible?

"Gabriel!" Horace called.

"I'm here." Everywhere.

"Tell me."

"They're panicking, spreading out. The dog is coming—it's here in the room. Dr. Jericho is trying to find me."

"What about Chloe?" Horace's hands found an opening in the wall and he pulled himself inside the first cell, still counting: *fifty-eight, fifty-nine, sixty.* Just a few more seconds for Chloe. Thirty seconds until the dumindar arrived. With it, they would be safe for a moment. With it, at least Chloe would be able to escape. Where was she?

And then a moment later, Gabriel: "She's coming. It's happening."

Gabriel tore down the humour. Sound and light blared—voices rising in relief and recognition, and the stink of the crucible dog flaring up again, and above all the glittering green light. Half inside the cell, Horace threw up a hand, trying to keep its irresistible heat from his face. The beast that carried the crucible was closer now, a shadow beside the sun, three shambling men beside it. Across the room, Gabriel was reaching for the green light, his face going slack. Farther back, Dr. Jericho rose to his full height, towering over everything, hissing at what he saw.

And what he saw, what they all saw, in the dazzle of that

light: Chloe, rising perfectly out of the floor as if she were a submerged sculpture and the floor was the receding sea. She emerged just beside the crucible dog, right at the feet of her own father. Chloe looked up at him, her neck bending prettily in the light, the crucible spilling her shadow far across the floor in the shape of a flame. That light—so enticing. So warm. Horace fought it off, tried to keep himself from moving toward it.

"Dad," Chloe said, her voice clear and fragile, falling like a drop of rain. The man turned and looked down at her, confusion beginning to gather on his already wretched face. Dr. Jericho surged toward them.

The crucible dog opened its great jaws as if to snap at Chloe. She spun. She uncoiled, leaping onto the low shoulder of the beast. Her face was a miracle, stone on fire. The dragonfly whirred at her chest. Horace imagined the song that came from it now, a sweet, dark song, pure and clean, railing against the green light. Chloe rose up over the top of the crucible, lifting her fist high above the light.

"No!" Horace shouted, understanding what she meant to do. Chloe threw her fist down into the center of the blazing green spindle, burying her arm in it to the elbow. The light flared and crackled violently, and then flickered, dwindled— burning still but half extinguished in Chloe's ghostly flesh, ablaze inside the skin and muscle and bone of her arm. Her face became a canyon of pain.

Across the room, Gabriel gasped, hunkering down like a

gargoyle around the staff. He swung the staff forward, as if to call the humour forth again, but Dr. Jericho took a lunging sidestep toward him and roared in anger, swinging a mighty backhanded blow that caught Gabriel in the chest and hurled him against the wall. The staff clattered from his hand.

Chloe clung to the crucible. Her arm was creased and torn with light. The dragonfly swung, wings trembling, seeming to swoop and hang, banking and slowing like a leaf on wind. She caught Horace's eye and nodded.

And then the dragonfly's wings went still.

Chloe screamed, a jagged, throated cry. Dr. Jericho froze. The green light folded into itself, was swallowed completely—gone, consumed by Chloe's flesh. The crucible dog roared, baring a grisly ridge of gnarled teeth. It reared back and bucked, throwing Chloe across the room. She hit the ground hard, tumbling to a stop a few feet from Horace, still screaming.

The crucible dog staggered forward and slumped to the ground, robbed of the light it carried. All around it, the Riven grabbed their long heads, keening. They scurried from the room, scattering like exposed bugs beneath an overturned stone. The men, Chloe's father included, fell where they stood.

Dr. Jericho launched himself toward Horace and Chloe, Horace gazing upward with his hands open and waiting, Chloe twisting in pain a few feet away. The moment was almost here. It had to get here in time. The dumin would protect them.

Eighty-eight, eighty-nine, please—and then a soft *pop* sounded just overhead. The dumindar was falling toward him, trailing its chain like a streamer of smoke. Horace reached for it.

One of Dr. Jericho's monstrous hands slashed out and snatched the dumindar from the air. Shock slid through Horace. Beside him, Chloe watched tensely, breathing sharply between clenched teeth. The Mordin crouched over them, examining the dumindar closely. A slow smile slit his face as he saw what it was. "Oh, my dear Tinkers. Fortune still sails," he murmured, and he reached out with his other hand and grasped Horace around the neck.

The Mordin straightened, lifting Horace until his feet were dangling. Horace thought his neck would crack. He clawed at Dr. Jericho's hand, but it was wrapped around his throat like a tree root. Chloe shouted his name. Horace could feel the Fel'Daera, agonizingly close, just inside the Mordin's jacket, but he could not hope to reach it. He could barely hope to stay conscious. Dr. Jericho threw his arms wide, Horace's struggling body hanging from one hand like a rag, the dumindar glinting in the other. From the corner of his eye, Horace saw Gabriel stirring against the opposite wall, reaching for the staff.

The Mordin gazed gleefully down at Chloe, sprawled on the floor at his feet. The wings of the dragonfly were a blur once again. "I have often wondered, my dear," Dr. Jericho said to her, "how long you can keep that up. Shall we find out?" And then he pinched the dumindar between two fingers, crushing it.

A soft puff of dust flew up, and the chest-thumping toll of the dumin blasted them. The scent of flowers filled Horace's nose. Across the room, Gabriel lifted his staff, shouting, but in the same instant the shining sphere of the dumin sprang to life.

Everything outside the dumin ceased to exist. There was nothing to see, nowhere to look, just a silver illumination that fell like moonlight—Gabriel had raised the humour. It enveloped the dumin but could not penetrate it. There was nothing now but the three of them—Horace, Chloe, and the Mordin, here inside this sphere carved from the nothingness outside.

Horace tried to look down at Chloe. She was on her knees, her right arm pressed awkwardly against her body, her face boiling with anger and pain. Even now Dr. Jericho had no idea what she was capable of, what the dragonfly truly was. Horace thought he might pass out any moment now, his head awash in a raging red current. Chloe stood, eyes burning. "Remember the Vora," Horace whispered at her through closed teeth.

Without warning, Chloe leapt at the Mordin. The tip of one foot went into his thigh and caught purchase inside his flesh. Dr. Jericho cried out, buckling and dropping to one knee. The hand around Horace's neck loosened, and Horace's feet found the ground. Dr. Jericho swatted at Chloe, a mighty swipe that passed through her like the ghost she was. She stuck her own hand through the thin man's jacket, into his torso, searching for the box. "Where is it?" she cried.

Horace reached up and grabbed Dr. Jericho's arm,

hoisting himself high. He scrambled up the Mordin's front and reached unerringly into the pocket where the Fel'Daera lay. His fingers closed around it—a blessed relief, a homecoming. But before he could pull it free, Dr. Jericho planted his great hand on Horace's chest and shoved. Horace went flying, the Fel'Daera coming with him. He struck the side of the curving surface of the dumin, knocking the wind out of himself, but somehow regaining his feet, gasping. Above, Chloe still clung to the Mordin. Dr. Jericho smacked at her uselessly again, pounding his own chest instead. Chloe swung her head to look at Horace. "Are you ready?" she said.

Horace nodded. He held out the Fel'Daera toward her, ready for her to take it, to take it out of here and save it once and for all.

Chloe jumped. Dr. Jericho roared, his face carved with rage. Chloe dropped toward Horace, and as they collided—if that was even the word—she passed *into* Horace, her flesh entering his. Her chest in his, the air in her lungs mingling with his own, her heart and his heart both beating together in this same mingled body. He felt—and knew at once he would never forget—the sensation of her eye entering his own. The box was between them, buried in them both, and the dragonfly too. The box was a warm fist in his gut—their gut?—the dragonfly a buzzing flutter between their ribs.

And as Chloe fell deeper into him, she caught him somehow, grabbed him not with her hands but with all of her, making his body a part of whatever she was now, whatever she became in these moments, and oh god it hurt, a pressure and displacement, an agony he couldn't name, pulling at him cheek to cheek, bone to bone, cell to cell, an irresistible embrace. He was as big as the universe, electric and vast, and there was a song with them that he was just beginning to hear, an angel's choir of pipes and horns—the Alvalaithen.

They fell through the dumin. It blew through them both like a knife-thin wave of liquid metal, threatening to tear them apart. Horace screamed. They toppled into the sightless gray of the humour, and just before Horace went, he glimpsed Dr. Jericho, trapped inside the dumin, his face rigid with shock.

They dropped to the floor and tumbled apart. Chloe's flesh slipped out of him, leaving him cold and empty. But even as they parted, the box fell loose and clattered to a stop at Horace's feet. He rolled and reached for it, finding it easily in the humour. He cradled it against his chest.

"Come," said Gabriel. A strong hand took hold of Horace's arm, tugging at him. "The dumin will not last." Dr. Jericho, trapped inside the dumin, blind and deaf within the humour—how he must be raging. Horace slid the Fel'Daera into its pouch and reached out for Chloe. He found her hand already grasping for his. He took it, and together they got to their feet. Gabriel pulled them several steps forward and then paused. "Reach for him, Chloe. He's just beside you," he said, and Horace understood: Chloe's father.

After that they ran, Horace's left hand in Gabriel's and his right wrapped around Chloe's. Gabriel led them through the halls, unrelenting. He half dragged them up two flights of stairs. They stumbled again and again, but no one spoke. Chloe's hand in Horace's felt like a fragile, sleeping animal. He held on to it as hard as he dared. He imagined she was spending all the strength she had left holding on to her father at the end of the procession. They ran and ran, three more turns and then a hundred steps in a straight line. The golem crossed his mind once—vaguely and distantly, as if it were a memory he wasn't sure was authentic—but he knew they would not encounter it. The nest was finished. Nothing would stop them now. Two hundred steps. Three hundred. At last Gabriel slowed and released him. Chloe's hand left Horace's. The humour rustled out of existence.

Cool night air. Darkness and sky. Crisp city smells and the electric glow of the scrap-yard lights. Horace drank it all in. He turned and saw the theater far behind them, two long blocks back, dark and hulking. High overhead, the vast night sky was clear and shadowed. Dimly he spotted Lyra, the harp, and remembered seeing it through the box just the night before, crisp and sharp. How long ago it seemed now, the past as much a fantasy as any future he could foresee.

A few feet away, Gabriel was bent over, rubbing his chest with one hand and breathing hard. Neptune stood beside him, speaking low. Chloe's father had already sunk to the ground. Chloe had draped one arm around him, and the other—the arm she'd thrown into the crucible—tucked limply against her side.

"The house is burning," Chloe's father said abruptly. "Did Chloe get out? The house is burning."

Chloe looked over at Horace and pressed her lips together, all the worry she'd let show. The dragonfly gleamed in the dark. "I'm right here, Dad. I got out."

"But did Chloe get out? The house is burning."

"I'm Chloe. I'm safe. The house isn't burning anymore."

Her father fell silent. Chloe went on watching Horace, her eyes still and sure and soft. "You okay?" Horace asked after a while.

"I have no idea. You?"

"I guess. I think I'm . . ." And how was he? Relieved. Clean. Empty. Cut loose. Right now he stood beyond the farthest reaches of what the box could show him—he hadn't seen this moment or anything past it, and the sensation was a little like falling. Or shrinking. Whatever threads he'd been wrangling for the last twenty-seven hours, there was only one now: life being lived, the universe following its own reasonable rules. "I'm here now," he said.

"Well, hell, Horace," she said. "That's nothing new."

They sat and waited. No one seemed worried. No one suggested they get farther away. Horace held the Fel'Daera in his lap, watching Chloe and her father and listening to Neptune talk quietly to Gabriel. After a long time, a cab approached. They all turned their heads. The cab stopped, and a small figure got out, trim and neat, and began walking toward them. White hair shone, and a pair of glasses glinted in the yellow light from the scrap yard. Behind him, the cab idled at the curb like a waiting pet. Mr. Meister came close and stopped. He looked around at them all, nodding.

"Just so," he said. "Just so."

CHAPTER FORTY–ONE

And Last

THE CAB WAS CROWDED AND QUIET. NO ONE ASKED ANYONE about anything. Gabriel and Neptune sat in the front seat beside Beck, Gabriel sagging with exhaustion. Chloe was pressed close between Horace and her father in the back, with Mr. Meister on Horace's other side. There was water, miraculously, and Horace drank until his stomach wouldn't let him anymore.

"Horace's house," Mr. Meister had said to Beck as they first piled in, and not a word since then. Horace could practically feel the old man's mind working.

Halfway home, Chloe's father stirred. "I'm sorry, everyone," he said. "I'm sorry." He turned to Chloe and gently took her tiny hand, examining her arm closely. His face was pained and worried. "Your arm. We need to get you to the hospital."

"I don't need a hospital. It's not broken."

519

"You shouldn't have done that. You shouldn't have come for me."

"You're not thinking straight."

"You should have left me." Horace realized the man was crying.

Chloe said, "I don't leave people." The cab fell silent again.

After several blocks, Mr. Meister spoke. "This night has cast long shadows," he said. "But remember, the sun moves."

Minutes later, Beck pulled up in front of Horace's house. Without turning around, Gabriel reached his hand over the backseat. Horace took it awkwardly and tried to return Gabriel's firm squeeze. Neptune gave him a peek and a nod. They seemed thin and far away.

Mr. Meister looked across at him and cleared his throat. "I can only begin to imagine what has transpired during this long day, Keeper. I would hear the full tale, in time, but for now let me just say thank you."

Horace nodded. "I didn't do it for you," he said, "but you're welcome." He glanced at Chloe. She was looking at her father. Her father caught Horace's eye and nodded grimly, his cheeks wet. Horace opened the door and got out alone. As he stood at the foot of the drive looking up at his house—it was his house, wasn't it?—Chloe stole out behind him. She stepped close, cradling her wounded arm. They looked up at the dark windows together. "So, this is where you live, huh?" she said.

"Still hilarious."

"How's it going to go for you in there? Your parents must be freaking out by now."

"Yeah," Horace agreed, but he found he couldn't even conjure up their faces, the sounds of their voices.

"You could probably use a mint. Do you want a mint?"

"Do you have a mint?"

"No." They stood silent for a while. There was no sign of daylight yet, but birds were singing anyway.

"How's your dad doing?" Horace said. "Speaking of freaked."

"Honestly? This is about as real as he's been in a while. I'd cry too, you know?"

"Yeah."

Chloe gently kicked Horace's shoe, thinking. "So anyway, I guess I'm not stupid," she said.

Horace laughed. "No. You're about as far from stupid as anyone. You were the hero today. You were—" He shook his head. "How's your arm?"

She held it up. It looked ghastly in the streetlight, swollen and streaked. Long bolts of black skin ran down either side, from her elbow onto her hand, front and back. "It's not pretty, but it'll be okay."

Horace gazed at the black streaks, like rippling tattoos. "And you pulled me through the dumin," he said. "I hoped you would save the Fel'Daera, but you took me, too. *And* you went underground. You told me you couldn't do that."

521

Chloe took a long breath and let it out slow. "I know. I wasn't lying about that, but . . . a lot of new things have been happening lately. Since I met you, or whatever. I let the golem go through me. I took the Vora through the dumin without even thinking. And grabbing you like that, inside the dumin tonight, that was . . ."

"Amazing."

"Yes. I don't even know how I did it. I don't know if I could do it again. I was just so angry, so confident, so . . . determined. I had to make sure that the future you'd seen wasn't for nothing."

"And what about going underground?"

She shivered. "It's happened before. Twice. Once when I was little. And once in the fire."

Horace finally understood. "That's how you got out of the fire without being seen. That's what you wouldn't tell us. But why?"

"I don't like to talk about it. It's . . ." She glanced back at the cab, then thrust a finger in Horace's face. "Don't tell anyone." He nodded, and she gestured to the ground all around them. "When I go thin, this is like the sea. Can you imagine that? The earth itself—everything—is an ocean to me. An ocean as deep as the world. And I'm just a speck, floating on the surface." She held up the Alvalaithen. "But I can go under if I want, if I can stand the thought of it—a bottomless sea with nothing to cling to, no shore. It's scary as hell down there, dark and buried—what if I run out of breath, or lose my way? When I was a kid I almost—what's the word? Drowned? I don't think there is a word for what almost happened to me." Horace squeezed his eyes shut for a moment, trying not to imagine it. "But I'm learning to move under there. It's like swimming, or flying. The Earthwing, get it?" The dragonfly whirred to life, and she let herself sink into the ground up to her ankles. Then she rose back up again, her feet reemerging. The dragonfly went still. Horace looked down at his own feet, at the earth beneath them, thousands of miles deep. He felt a sudden sweep of vertigo and another hard tug of panic in his chest. "So now you know what I'm afraid of," Chloe said.

Horace shrugged as if all of this were nothing. "I don't know," he said casually. "It seems like you should get over it. Could come in handy."

"Says the claustrophobe who belongs to a secret band that lives in tunnels."

Horace laughed again, and just then the front porch light blazed to life, blinding them. Chloe threw her good arm over her eyes and backed away.

"Looks like you're up. You'll let me know what happens, right?"

"That's what I'm here for."

She smiled. "Sometimes I think you're smarter than me."

"Well, Chloe, sometimes I am."

She slid into the cab, eyes on him. She yanked the door closed, and the cab pulled away. Horace watched until the taillights were figments. He checked his feet again, picturing the earth beneath him, deep and deadly. He started up the drive.

Inside, his mother's arms, firm and warm and endless, endless. Her hands on his hair, her fingers strong. He waited for her questions, her anger, unable to imagine what he could possibly say to her, what tale he could tell her about where he'd been and why. He wasn't even sure, exactly, how to name what he'd done wrong. But his mother mentioned no wrongs. Her anger didn't come. All she asked was how he was, and only once.

"I'm okay," Horace told her. "I'm sorry."

"Okay," his mother echoed. "Okay." She took him to the kitchen. She fussed wordlessly with his hair, his clothes, wiping the ash from everywhere. She dabbed the cut on his forehead with a wet paper towel. There was a shocking moment, like plunging into a pool in September, where she reached down and slipped the Fel'Daera from its pouch, laying it on the table. She did it as easily as if she were folding socks. Horace had to kick-start his breathing after it was done, but before long even this gesture seemed natural, the thing a mother would do. And having the box away from himself, sitting there in plain sight, seemed to help settle the absence he'd been feeling, the knowledge that no known moments lay ahead of him, the painfully simple fact that no outstanding promises now stood between him and the box. This was just life, unfolding however it would.

His mother made him a salami sandwich and he plowed

through it. She made him another. He drank glass after glass of orange juice. She sat across from him, watching him silently. At last he slowed and looked her in the eye.

"I'm really sorry," he said again.

She didn't reply. Instead, she laid a piece of paper on the table, pushing it toward him. It was the note Horace had left— so long ago—one corner worried into a curl by a restless hand.

"Oh, that," Horace said stupidly. He took another bite of his sandwich, even though he was full.

"You could have left it where I'd find it sooner."

"You didn't try to look for that place, did you? Those people?"

"I did not try, no."

"Good, because I was just goofing."

"Goofing."

"Yeah. Did Dad see the note?"

"No."

"Well, what did he say when I wasn't here?"

"I told him you had a thing."

"A thing. You didn't call the police?"

"What would I have told them?"

Horace chewed his sandwich slowly. "I don't know."

"The truth?"

He chopped a laugh, bits of bread spewing out. "Sorry," he said, trying to push the absurdity of the thought aside. He swallowed what he had and put the sandwich down. "Sorry. I know what I did was bad."

"What you did."

"Yes."

His mother leaned across the table. "Horace."

"Yeah?"

She laid her hand down just beside the Fel'Daera. "Horace, I know this Tan'ji."

Everything inside him ground to a halt. "What did you say?"

"I said I know this Tan'ji." She leaned back and sighed, squeezing her eyes closed for a long, hovering moment. "I know it well, in fact. The Box of Promises. The Fel'Daera."

Horace could hardly let his ears hear the sound of the name on her lips. She opened her eyes, sad and shining, pleading with him. She . . . *knew*. And for a moment she was not his mother at all, was someone else entirely, some being he had never met, never known, someone he could not trust or recall. A rival, even. "Did you have it?" he croaked, surprised to even find his voice. He looked at the box, between them on the table. He itched to snatch it up. "Were you its Keeper?"

"Oh, god, no, not me. I was not so . . ." She hesitated for several long seconds, fishing deep for a word. And it was this moment Horace would remember later, long after, remembering the sight of her face as she struggled for a word both true and kind. Because of course—he later understood—there were other words she could have summoned that night, words kinder but less true, or truer but less kind, and watching this woman choose those words might have been the single keenest lesson he would ever learn about the course he had taken, the life that had come for him, the long path that led forward and forward into the unknowable. "I was not so *needed*," she said at last. "Not like you." With those words, there she was again, just as she always was. Just as she always would be.

"How do you know the name, then? What else do you know?"

"I know enough to recognize a leestone when one is brought into my house. Enough to know what that means. I know enough to guess the reasons for your sneaking out at night, the reasons for disappearing for a day. I know enough to recognize Chloe for what she is and imagine what the two of you might have gone through together. I know the names Meister and Hapsteade. As for the Fel'Daera, I know . . ." She hesitated. "I *knew* . . ."

Horace's heart was a struggling beast in his chest. "You knew the last Keeper."

She shook her head. "Not the Keeper." She gave him a long, open stare like a wound, full of hurt and apology and hope. "The Maker."

Glossary

Altari (all-TAR-ee)	the Makers
Alvalaithen (al-vuh-LAYTH-en)	Chloe's Tan'ji, the dragonfly, the Earthwing
cloisters	small safe havens used by the Wardens
crucible	a Tan'ji that binds the Riven to a given nest
dispossessed	term for a Keeper who is permanently severed from his or her instrument
doba	small stone buildings in the Great Burrow; living quarters
dumin (DOO-min)	a spherical shield of force through which almost nothing can pass

dumindar	a Tan'kindi that, when crushed, creates the dumin
Fel'Daera (fel-DARE-ah)	Horace's Tan'ji, the Box of Promises
Find, the	the solitary period during which a new Keeper masters his or her instrument
golem	a powerful Tan'kindi controlled by the Riven
Great Burrow	the uppermost chamber of the Warren
grulna	a small Tan'kindi that may temporarily stave off the effects of dispossession
jithandra	a small, personalized Tan'kindi used by the Wardens for illumination, identification, and entry into the Warren
Keeper	one who has bonded with an instrument, thus becoming Tan'ji
Kesh'kiri (kesh-KEER-ee)	the name the Riven use for themselves (see "Riven")
Laithe of Teneves	a mysterious Tanu, a spinning globe, in Mr. Meister's possession
leestone	a Tan'kindi that provides some protection against the Riven

malkund	a "gift" of the Riven, meant to enslave
Mazzoleni Academy	the boarding school beneath which the Warren lies
Mordin	Riven who are particularly skilled at hunting down Tan'ji
Nevren	a field of influence, source unknown, that temporarily severs the bond between a Keeper and his Tan'ji; Nevrens exist to protect the Wardens' strongholds from the Riven
oraculum	a Tan'ji belonging to Mr. Meister, a lens
passkey	a Tan'kindi that allows passage through certain walls
raven's eye	a weak and portable kind of leestone, a Tan'kindi
Riven	the secretive race of beings who hunger to claim all the Tanu for their own; they call themselves the Kesh'kiri
Staff of Obro	Gabriel's Tan'ji, a gray staff with a silver handle and tip
Tan'ji (tahn-JEE)	a special class of Tanu that will work only when bonded with a Keeper who has a specific talent; "Tan'ji" also refers to the actual Keeper as well as to

	the bond between Keeper and instrument—a kind of belonging or being
Tan'kindi (tahn-KIN-dee)	a simpler category of Tanu (raven's eye, dumindar, etc.) that will work for anyone; unlike Tan'ji, Tan'kindi do not require a special talent or a bond
Tanu (TAH-noo)	the collective term for all the mysterious devices created by the Makers; the existence and function of these instruments is all but unknown to most (two main kinds of Tanu are Tan'ji and Tan'kindi)
Tinker	a Kesh'kiri word for ordinary humans
tourminda (toor-MIN-dah)	a fairly common kind of Tan'ji; Neptune is the Keeper of one
Vithra's Eye	the name of the very powerful Nevren that guards the Warren
Vora	Mrs. Hapsteade's Tan'ji, the quill and ink
Wardens	the secret group of Keepers devoted to protecting the Tanu from the Riven
Warren	the Wardens' headquarters beneath the city, deep underground

Acknowledgments

I'm so grateful to be able to thank everyone who played even a small role in shaping the path that led to this book, beginning with my parents, for whom reading and writing was always so vital.

I also want to thank Jackie May Parkison, this book's first real reader, whose early edits slid the project into an orbit it would never have otherwise found;

Miriam Altshuler, my wonderful agent, for that first long talk and all the talks since, and for all her invaluable guidance;

Toni Markiet and Abbe Goldberg, my editors, whose brave and patient work did so very much to make this book what it is;

Laura Koritz, for being such a constant friend and honest reader;

my son, Rowan, who inspired so many of these pages, for

never being too impressed and for never being afraid to have an idea I might steal;

my stepdaughter, Bridget, for being such an excellent human being to share the world with, and for teaching me so much about being a dad;

and above all, again, my amazing wife, Jodee, for almost never telling me to shut up about it already.

Much gratitude also to Phoebe Yeh, Kate Jackson, the entire Harper crew, the Bread Loaf Writers' Conference, Matt Mulholland and his physics students at Zionsville High School, Neil Archer, Philip Graham, Michael Madonick, Alex Shakar, Richard Powers, and Matthew Minicucci—teachers, believers, and friends.